I0662759

BLOOD REDEMPTION

Nova Breedlove

Nova Breedlove

Copyright © 2020 BONE GARDEN BOOKS

Cover art by M.Y. Cover Design

All rights reserved.

The characters portrayed in this book are fictitious. Any similarity
to actual persons, living or dead, is entirely coincidental.

ISBN: 978-0-578-72389-1
Library of Congress Control Number: 2020913044

"I have heard that lost silence. You have not heard it because you have not been dead."
Tenskwatana, Shawnee

"And when I passed by thee, and saw thee polluted in thine own blood, I said unto thee when thou wast in thy blood, Live; yea, I said unto thee when thou was in thy blood, Live."
The Blood Verse, Book of Ezekiel 16:6

"The living are capable of revenge the dead cannot exact."
William Gay, *Twilight*

BEFORE

Rayburn, Georgia
1987

Sara was dead before the fire swallowed her. The evil man had choked the life from her with his bare hands, while the boy stood witness, peering through the window, helpless and full of despair.

From behind the makeshift shelter, put together with scraps of rusted tin from the rotting trailer, he watched the flames grow wide and high. The image brought back a fractured piece of time he spent sitting around a campfire roasting marshmallows with his parents and baby sister. He could no longer recall their voices; just faces and laughter that had long ago grown silent. It had been two, three years maybe, but time he learned was tricky when your only reference was the sun and the moon and the hours caught between. He'd tried many times to find his way out of the hollow but each attempt had been unsuccessful. He'd return exhausted and confused. Sometimes, it seemed he walked for hours only to end up circling back to where he started. It was a strange place, the hollow, and he'd seen many strange things in it.

He wondered still why the man had chosen him that day as he made his way home from school.

"I've been looking for you," the stranger had said, calling to the boy through the passenger-side window of the rusted green van.

Confused, the boy looked around. "For me?" He hesitated but eventually walked toward the van, trying to determine whether it was a Volkswagen or a Ford like the kind his uncle had.

"I've come to save your soul. So you can be forgiven," the man said and the boy moved closer, intrigued but still not understanding.

"Forgiven? What for?"

"Sons of harlots are sinners, boy. They go to Hell. You don't want to go to Hell, do you?"

The boy contemplated momentarily. He had no idea what a harlot was, but he knew about Hell. He'd spent many nights sneaking around down by the riverside, watching the snake handlers drink poison and dodge venom inside the big white tent. Hell was full of fire and damnation. "No, sir. I don't." His voice cracked.

"Then come with me," the man insisted. He reached over and pushed open the door, an invitation the boy didn't think to question.

Once inside, he instinctively pulled the door closed and looked over at the man. Something shiny and malicious flashed in his eyes. Like sun sparking off metal. He'd seen that same look on a snake getting ready to strike. The boy knew then his mistake. He shouldn't have gone with the man. His mother had warned him about accepting rides from strangers, but the door handle wouldn't budge, and he was trapped inside the van, a Ford, he'd decided.

"Forgiveness requires the shedding of blood," the man continued.

This guy was off his rocker, the boy thought. One of those men he'd seen wandering downtown with a pint of whiskey in their grip. Tennessee was overrun with them.

"Let me out!" the boy demanded, beating against the door. Angry at first. Then frightened. "Mom!"

He'd screamed so loud that the man handed him an old jar and told him to scream into it, which he did until nothing was left. No tears. No voice. And as they crossed over the state line into Georgia, no hope. Then the man screwed the lid on the jar and tucked it into a canvas bag beside him. He promised the boy he'd give him back his voice if he remained silent and didn't try to escape. But his words never returned, and he never saw the jar again. The memory of the van's interior would always be with him though. The shag green carpeting littered with small red Bibles and a stained mattress, his dried blood splattered on the panels, and the translucent beaded cross dangling from the rearview mirror like a fallen star. It hung from a thin strap of worn leather and twinkled in the diffused light. He'd made many silent wishes on that star, but not one of them had ever come true. Not a single fucking one. The recollection, faded and grainy, played now in his mind like one of those old movies his grandfather liked to watch. A life before that seemed so distant, so removed of sound, he couldn't be sure he hadn't imagined it.

A crack of thunder snapped him back to the moment. The man had fled the trailer, smoke billowing from all sides, and was now making his way into the heart of the hollow. He'd never had any trouble finding his way in or out, and the boy believed it was because the hollow feared the man as much as he did. As much as Sara had. They'd both been brought here against their will, and he wanted to believe that she had, without intention, finally found a way out. It might have been the only way, he considered.

Tired and broken and small, the boy lacked the courage to confront the man who'd stolen him from his family so long ago that he had to carve his name into his own arm to remember it. He looked down at his hand, at the gap where his finger should have been, and shook in fear. He'd lived when he should have died. The man said there was a reason, and the boy wondered even then what that might be.

He desperately wanted to follow him out of the hollow; find a way back to his family, but the boy was torn. The baby girl was still inside the burning trailer. He looked back and forth between the fire and his freedom for a minute, which seemed much longer than it was. A train whistled in the distance, and the man disappeared into the trees. Behind him, the wind stirred a cloud of red-clay dust so thick it made the world appear out of focus and apocalyptic through the boy's eyes.

He thought again of his baby sister, then of the infant girl still inside the trailer. Her cries, sharp and penetrating, pierced his heart. The memory of Sara rocking the child to sleep the night before instilled an ache in him that he didn't know any longer existed. His own mother came to him on rare occasion and in unexpected moments. A flash of light in the blackest part of his dreams.

The boy wished now he would have thanked Sara one more time for her kindness. He wondered why she never once tried to escape. She'd been his only friend. Now she was gone, and he was to blame. He shouldn't have taken the box. That's what the man had been yelling about. He wanted the contents of that old cardboard shoe box Sara had hidden under the bed, the one she asked the boy to burn. He had rifled through it, hoping to discover something of value inside. An explanation of why bad shit happened or a map leading him out of the hollow. Or maybe, just maybe, the jar that contained his voice. But inside there was nothing but three tattered folders the color of old butter, each labeled with a different name. He'd started the fire with the intention of tossing the files in it, but changed his mind at the last minute and hid the box instead. He wanted the man to know what it felt like to want something he couldn't have. It was wrong, but it was too late to make it right. At thirteen, the boy had already learned that revenge could be just as bitter as it was sweet.

Sara was dead because of him. Nothing could change that. He had no one now and neither did the child. There was no other way. He had to save the baby. For Sara. He'd do it for Sara.

Muted light filtered through the tall trees. The boy looked toward the sky and drew in a breath so deep it burned his insides and filled his mouth with ash. The hollow was haunted by the scent of charred wood, wet and moldy, and lingering like a lost soul. He could feel it coating his throat the way he imagined soot collecting in a chimney.

A heavy dampness pressed against him, and the boy, both young and old at the same time, felt the weight of it in his chest. Lightning danced around him, and he remembered just then that he was once afraid of storms. He welcomed that fear now because it was so simple. So innocent, that it almost seemed laughable. He closed his eyes, held out his tongue, and caught the first drops of rain on the tip of it.

Perched on a branch above him, a crow, shiny and black as oil, cawed. It shook its wings erratically then became a shadow, leaving in its departure a single black feather that floated down past the boy's face. The air was dense with pine. It caught in his lungs and hardened like sap, stilling him only once as he darted for smoke and flame. It was a decision made more of instinct than courage. He was her only chance. Or so he thought.

Just before he reached the trailer, the door burst open and the woman from the hollow, the one with all the turquoise jewelry, jumped from the burning tin box, the tiny child clutched in her arms. The infant wailed in pain, while the woman rolled with her in the grass, smothering the flames. Then she began whispering near the girl's ear, a sibilant whisper, soft and secret and full of gospel. It reminded him of wind blowing through the trees just before a storm. It quieted the infant's screams, and her bloodied and blistered skin began to heal before the boy's eyes. There was no time to question how. He had once watched this woman bring a near-dead deer back to life by healing the wound that almost severed its leg.

The woman motioned him toward her, and he dropped to his knees as if in prayer. It wasn't the first time he wondered if God only answered the prayers of those who could speak.

The burns blanketing the woman's body were so deep that some of them opened right to the bone. The smell was unbearable. Once infection set in, she was sure to die. She looked near death now.

He leaned in. She handed him the child. He noticed, on the inside of the girl's forearm, a birthmark, not much bigger than a quarter. But when he looked closer, the boy determined it wasn't a birthmark at all. The woman's scorched turquoise ring had branded a scar in the child's perfect pink skin. He stared at the burn, an elongated circle, with two small wing-like imprints on each side of it. An angel, he decided before being distracted by the woman pulling him down so that her face was seconds from his, her breath hot and fermented. Fruit that had soured in the sun. She spoke delicately, words as faint and broken as a distant horizon.

Though the two had crossed paths in the woods, the woman had never actually said a word to him. Until now, they'd shared a peaceful pact, a mutual but silent agreement grounded only in eye contact. It took him a minute to understand what she was saying. Her directions out of the hollow were as hazy as the air around them but would lead him to the doctor's secret door. The entrance to the tunnel was on a ledge that overlooked the river. She carved a circle with a cross in the middle of it into the clay.

"Look for the star. The Immortals will guide you," she told him. "Don't fear them." She spoke words he didn't understand then pointed toward the dense fog that began to glow and flicker with tiny lights.

The boy nodded and swallowed hard, trying to remember at that moment what it was like to speak. To have a voice. To say aloud a prayer that had a chance of being answered. It had been so long since he'd used his vocal cords, he doubted they even worked, though he could still taste the echo of his lost pleas for help rolling across his dry tongue like thunder over a desert. But nobody ever came. And now he was here in this place of burning sorrow with nothing but feral fear and the child.

Strapping her arms across her chest, the woman began to rock slowly back and forth, the rhythm of the raindrops becoming heavier and faster with each passing second. Her eyes disappeared behind her lids and once again she started to whisper that strange prayer, only it was louder and more haunting this time. It frightened the boy into quickness, a panic that pushed him toward the forest of trees where he hoped for but did not find quiet. Instead, the woman's fervent hissing, a riverside tent of revival snakes, chased him to the mountain, the rain pounding, the infant pulled tightly to his chest.

one

The small padded envelope, addressed to Rhonda DiCarlo, arrived by mail a few days after she'd been released from Rayburn Regional. The nurses had been real nice to her. They always were. They even brought in a cake to celebrate her 40th birthday, gathered around the bed and sang to her. Rhonda understood the cake was grounded in sympathy, but the kindness of the gesture hadn't escaped her. She'd been in and out of that same hospital so many times, she was on a first-name basis with most of the staff. They seemed to understand that her brokenness went much deeper than blood and bone. To a place where stitches and splints and casts could never reach.

Rhonda tossed the rest of the mail, overdue bills and pizza coupons, on the scarred kitchen table and examined both sides of the thick yellow envelope. There was no return address. Just a postmark with a date, and the year, 2007. She stared at it for a long minute wondering where the time had gone, finding it almost impossible that six years of being a punching bag could pass by so quickly.

The envelope, she noticed, was from Pennsylvania. She didn't know anyone in that state. Had never once been out of Crow County. Born and raised in Rayburn, though there hadn't been much *raising* other than the vodka bottle her mother lifted daily. As a general rule, the woman was wasted by ten in the morning and stayed that way all day long. Rhonda's father had never been in the picture. Well, not entirely. In the one and only art class she had in high school, she'd learned to view her daddy as a study in perspective, a distant background image that was so out of focus it was indiscernible. But this didn't make her an exception in Rayburn. It made her standard.

The cast on her arm felt as awkward and heavy as a bowling ball. Some of the nurses had signed it, wrote little inspirational sayings that ended in exclamation points and smiley faces. Rhonda fumbled with a cigarette pack, used her index finger, stained yellow from nicotine, the nail bitten to the quick, to dig out a Kool. She lit it and brought the envelope closer. Flipped it from front to back. The vision in her right eye wasn't as clear as it used to be in the days before she knew Bart Tucker. In the days where even now as she looked back through the swollen lid of a darkened eye, appeared much less out of focus, somehow. Less shadowed than the life in front of her, the one she saw in the mirror when she was brave enough to look.

A stream of menthol smoke snaked up toward the drop ceiling, taking Rhonda's thoughts with it. Her memories hovered there near the water-stained tiles so that she could almost see them take shape. That happened sometimes, her mind drifting to a place in the past, the collective moments that had come to define her as Standard Rhonda.

A high-school dropout, she'd enrolled in state-funded cosmetology classes just before her twenty-second birthday, but the business lost funding and closed before she could finish. She once dreamed of being a nurse, but women like her didn't become nurses. They became waitresses at the truck stop or counter girls at the bowling alley concession stand, or in her case, cashiers at the grocery store. When her part-time job at the Piggly Wiggly wasn't enough, she supplemented her income by bartending at night in one of which was to be many shit-heeled bars in Rayburn. One would close, another would open. Men came and went. Thirteen years of one-night stands and broken promises. Then thirty-three hit her hard. She was alone and scared and suddenly pregnant, something she might have been happier about if things had been...different. Choices were limited for the broken people of the world, but she had two, and she took the one she believed God might be able to forgive her for someday even if she could never forgive herself.

It was that same year she met Bart at *Spades*. A dive bar named after something used to dig holes for dead people. Foretelling, if nothing else. Seven years later, after multiple broken bones, a recessed eye socket, and a busted spleen, the irony hadn't escaped her. For years, she'd been digging her own grave with what felt like a teaspoon. In some demented way, she believed that he was her punishment for what she'd done. She deserved Bart Tucker. Didn't she?

Rhonda hooked her twice-broken thumb under the edge of the envelope and slid it across the flap. She emptied the contents onto the table then picked up the small white box and shook it gently. A belated birthday gift perhaps? From who, though? Her mother was long gone, and Bart had scared all her friends away years ago. Her only outside acquaintance was the old woman next door with whom she exchanged the occasional hopeless glance over the fence while the woman attended to her flowers. They'd never actually spoken. It was too dangerous. There was an undeclared safety in silence, in the quiet of it all. Sometimes, the frail old woman slipped money, a couple singles or a five, furtively through the fence, and once an address for a covert women's shelter out by the lake. Rhonda was certain it was she who called the police two weeks before when Bart had beaten her unconscious. He may have killed her otherwise.

The last time she'd received a gift of any kind from anybody was fifteen years ago when her mother gave her a tiny gold cross for Christmas just before she died. It was odd she thought how so many people sought out God in the days preceding death. As if He didn't realize He'd been a last resort.

Curious and also a little excited, Rhonda tugged at

the thin blue ribbon around the box until the small bow loosened and fell to the linoleum floor like a curl cut from a child's hair. It was then that she noticed the dark red stain at the corner seam. It looked like a red ink pen leak. Or maybe dried nail polish. But the box wasn't big enough to hold either of these things.

With the cigarette still pinched between her fingers, Rhonda lifted the edge of the box and caught the scent of something rancid. She lowered it away from her face and set the lid on the table, focusing on the sticky substance oozing from beneath the brown paper inside the box. It had to be a piece of candy. Some type of cordial that had busted open, the sugary insides congealing on the paper like a scab. But who would send a single piece of candy? Some juvenile trick from Bart probably. But candy seemed too affectionate for him. It was probably a squished insect. Something disgusting, no doubt. She considered tossing the box right in the trash, but her curiosity held her hostage.

She sucked hard and long on the cigarette, exhaled impatiently at her own anxious hesitance then mashed the cherry into the ashtray next to the box's upturned lid. That's when she saw the note tucked inside. She pulled it out, unfolded it, and read what was printed.

Your bastard son sends this reminder of your sin.
His blood is the cost of forgiveness.

The words made her heart anchor into the pit of her stomach. She didn't realize she'd become so emotional until she felt her face grow warm and wet and her breath catch in her lungs. Was this about her son? The one she gave away? How could this be happening? She'd never told a soul about what she'd done. Dr. Hixson had reassured her that nobody would find out and that the child would be better off having both a mother and a father. A permanent home with some type of stable environment. Tears crawled down her face, carving lines in the thick pancake makeup she used to hide the bruises.

Who had sent this and why? And the question right in front of her. The one she held in her shaky hand. What the hell was in the box? She had to know. Unable to keep her curiosity at bay for a minute longer, Rhonda peeled back the brown paper with inquisitive caution, and immediately wished she hadn't. A small ring finger, blackened with dried blood and blue from decay was nested inside on a bed of cotton like a piece of jewelry. *Oh God, what the*—she moaned, letting go of the box. The finger dislodged, hit the floor then slid under the stove. She capped her mouth and sprinted toward the sink. Her stomach heaved, and she tasted metal in the back of her throat. She ran cold water and drank from the cup of her palm but heard the engine and the crunch of gravel before she had time to release the vileness brewing in the pit of her stomach. Someone had pulled into the drive. She tugged the back of her hand across her wet mouth and walked over to the front window.

Peering through the side of the stained polyester curtains, Rhonda tensed at the sight of Bart getting out of the passenger side of a black F-150 with muddy rims, the voice of Hank Williams Jr., loud at first then muffled with the closing of the truck door. *Shit.*

For a millisecond, she almost felt bad for him. He looked just as beat up as she did. Even had a black eye. She wondered if that had been the sheriff's doing. Old Sheriff Towns had always tried to look out for her. He'd put her up in a motel a few times, but she always went back to Bart when he threatened her. He wasn't supposed to be released from jail until the end of the week. He must have bonded out somehow. She needed more time. He'd kill her for certain now.

Rhonda let the curtain fall back into place. Her stomach twisted with nausea from the detached finger, from Bart, from life. She began to gnaw the rough red skin around her fingernail as beads of sweat slipped down her face. For a fearful, chaotic instant, she stood motionless, trying to catch her breath then snapped like a busted rubber band. She made a dash for the hall closet and snatched the sack of clothes she had hidden behind the broken Hoover. She unzipped the vacuum bag and dug for the shelter address and the cash she'd secretly stashed, most of which came from the woman next door. The cast was bulky and prohibiting, but out of fear and desperation, her lumbering fingers found the envelope containing the money. Rhonda shoved it and the shelter address in her pocket and was out the back door and down the alley by the time Bart made it inside.

two

Angela Archer packed her mother's folders from the metal filing cabinet into a cardboard moving box, labeled MOM, AUGUST 2016. Not at all as cathartic as she'd hoped it would be. She'd never been much for tears though there were mornings she still woke with them dried on her face. Her cell buzzed and the last folder slipped from her hand. Receipts, recipes, letters, and an old grocery list or two scattered across the wooden floor like a flock of frightened birds. The sight of her mother's perfect script made her heart tighten.

She let the call go to voicemail and bent to gather the loose pages. The phone clutched in her neck, she listened to the message. The Realtor. *Be by later this week to stage furniture. The market is decent right now. Should be an easy sell.* The rest of what she said drifted in and out as Angela's eyes focused on the tombstone. She picked up the clipping, a faded newspaper photo, and studied it. The small headstone had SR-0587 engraved on it and the number 15 below that. Behind the stone and out of focus, a row of white wooden crosses grew from the ground against a backdrop of dense trees.

Angela found it rather bizarre that there was no actual name on the stone. The crosses behind it reminded her of those sad road-side altars often surrounded by plastic flowers. The kind that honored a beloved pet that had inadvertently wandered onto the highway. But even those were identified with names most of the time. Much like the tombstone, the crosses behind it were also nameless.

The image of the tombstone had been clipped so close that it was left without any identifying marks such as the name of the newspaper or even a photo credit that might explain why her mother would have it. Odd but not out of the ordinary for Linda Archer who had become somewhat of a paper hoarder as the cancerous tumor progressed. Even when it began to press on the prefrontal cortex, the cognitive thinking part of the brain, Linda's ability to solve even the toughest crosswords had not been affected. She'd completed, in ink, both a New York Times and a Nation crossword hours before her death. Without a doubt, the woman was a master at solving puzzles and always trying to get her daughter to take part.

Angela took another look at the headstone and the bizarre letter and number combination engraved across it. She'd never seen anything like it. Near the thin bottom border of the photo, in her mother's handwriting, the word *fodere* was written in red ink. Angela choked back a smile.

This she recognized. The Latin word for *dig.* Her mother had an excellent vocabulary, most of which she'd learned solving crosswords and puzzles but also from watching reruns of *Law and Order Criminal Intent,* with Vincent D'Onofrio, her not-so-secret crush. Linda had a dark sense of humor that Angela had not inherited, but this didn't mean it slipped past her. *Gravesite. Dig? I get it, Mom,* she confessed mentally then tucked the clipping in the box and secured it with tape. Maybe her mother had left one for her to try and solve as a parting gift. She'd go through the box later when she had *more time,* two words that for her were never meant to be in the same sentence. Words like *dead child. Suspended prosecutor.*

With her parents both gone now and no siblings or close family other than a distant aunt who she'd never even met or spoken to, Angela should have felt more alone, but the ghosts of the missing denied her that freedom. She was well aware of the statistics. Over 2,000 children disappeared daily in the United States. She had walls of photographs dedicated to them in her Philly brownstone where she ran with profound passion, The Lost, a missing children's organization she founded in law school with the overly idealistic hope that the children who vanished were just temporarily lost and not gone forever. Not sold into the sex trade. Not tortured and robbed of life. It was an anticipation that never seemed to materialize, however, but this didn't stop Angela from putting her entire heart and soul into each missing child case she investigated. And though, she knew them all by name, it was Liam she personally said *goodnight* to every night. Then she'd count to a hundred and three before falling asleep. No, she would never be alone.

A judge had once warned her that she should keep separate who she was from what she did so she could have a place to escape. Once the two merged, they became incapable of being divided again. But there was no going back now. Those lines had crossed long ago. Angela Archer and The Lost were now one. So much in fact that she had become lost herself, incapable, she truly believed, of ever being found. But, if this meant one more child could be brought home or one more pedophile removed from society, it had been well worth the sacrifice. Where this impetus came from, Angela had no idea. Her father had owned a hardware store. Her mother had been a homemaker who taught piano three nights a week. It was a relatively normal life for a while. Angela remembered the exact moment it changed though. The moment her crusade began.

Liam, she whispered softly, the empty hollowness of the room sucking the air from her lungs like a vacuum. No thought of him ever came without the accompaniment of two others. The psychopath who killed him and the innocent man who hadn't. An image of Denny Sherman all beaten and broken and waving a white flag with *Not Guilty* written on it in his own blood came to her then as it did every day. Angela closed her eyes for a moment, wishing she could go back to that day in the park so many years ago where Liam's smile was more than just a dark memory, but there was no use looking behind. There was only the now and what lie ahead. Everything else was distorted by perspective, but also by anger and guilt, and the enduring quest for vengeance that seemingly only belonged to her. It made what was to soon be ten years into ten minutes. An old wound, a fresh cut daily.

It took several years to even locate a suspect in Liam's murder and when they did, Angela used all that pent-up anger and guilt brewing inside her to see that justice was served. And if Denny Sherman, the man wrongfully convicted of Liam's abduction and murder, hadn't been beaten to death while serving on death row less than a month after his sentence, Angela would have taken a front-row seat to watch him die. She might have even brought celebratory hats and noisemakers. She had been the kind of prosecutor, ferocious and determined that every defense team both feared and hated. Tough as nails and willing to bend the law to a breaking point when it came to child killers.

But then two weeks after Sherman's death, the body of a nine-year-old girl from North Carolina was discovered. She'd been missing for less than five days. Her ring finger had been removed from her left hand just like Liam's. Just like the others. Children along the East Coast who had been found in the same disturbing manner. Each missing a finger. Each with a pocket Bible, the same passage highlighted inside. Angela had convicted the wrong man, and his blood could never be washed from her hands.

The missing finger factor had never been released to the media but came out during Sherman's trial with the suffocation and dismemberment findings of Liam's autopsy report. Afterword, law enforcement officials had somehow managed to keep the gruesome finger detail rather quieted in an effort to weed out false confessions and copy cats. They didn't want to incite mass panic at the idea that a deranged serial offender was still out there killing innocent children and adding to his finger collection.

Pale and petite, with ashy blonde hair and deep-set, dark eyes, Angela had the diminutive features of a doll made from hand-blown glass or expensive china, however, when it came to children being harmed in any way, she had a meanness in her that could have rivaled any cold-blooded killer. This passion scared her at times. Because of her fervent determination, an innocent man had died, and Liam's killer, a man dubbed later by the media as the Redeemer, had gone on to kill other children. Destroy other lives. Her anger and resentment fed daily off this insatiable guilt.

The whole damned thing seemed surreal to Angela. As morbid and horrifying as something concocted by Poe. She blew out a breath, one she'd been holding unknowingly. It was so heavy she could almost see it.

Before leaving her childhood home for the last time, she glanced around to make sure she hadn't overlooked anything. The rooms were free of furniture, the walls bare, and yet there was something lingering in the house. Something dense but intangible. The past, she realized—an impervious layer of coal dust that hung invisibly in the air, waiting to ignite. She wondered how something only seen in retrospect could fill a room with such weight.

The real estate agent would be listing the house later that week, a reluctant but necessary choice. Angela needed a constant flow of money to fund The Lost now that she wasn't practicing and had blown through most of what she saved over the years. The sale of the house would generate enough to keep her mission going for a while. Not forever but at least until the end of the year or middle of next. Then she'd have to figure out something else. Law was probably not an option.

After loading the boxes into the hatchback of her dusty grey Matrix, Angela turned one last time toward the house then got in the car and drove down the street. She kept her eyes off the rearview mirror and the things behind her that could not be changed.

It was after she stopped for gas that she tuned into a radio station covering the breaking story of a deputy in Crow County, Georgia who made a grisly discovery the previous morning after detaining a man for running a red light. The deputy performed a routine search and found, in the trunk of the car, tucked behind a suitcase full of pocket bibles, a small cooler, containing what he believed to be human finger bones, adolescent in nature.

"Son of a bitch!" Angela hit the brakes and fishtailed

off the side of the road. She peeled her fingers from the steering wheel then reached to adjust the volume on the radio. Two long years she'd waited for that bastard to surface. That's how long it had been since Mikey Pearson's body had been discovered just outside of Richmond, a red pocket Bible tucked in his rigid, fingerless little hand. Then the Redeemer had just disappeared. Fell off the face of the earth. Until now. It had to be him.

Authorities, she learned, were now interrogating a man named Levi Knox in connection with the recent disappearance of five children in the area, which bordered the mountains near the Tennessee line. *Sadly, the body of fifteen-year-old Kelly Marsh,* the reporter relayed...*one of the first to go missing, was discovered this morning, a day after Knox's arrest. The cause of death has yet to be determined. GBI has launched a full investigation.*

Angela caught her breath then screamed so loud her lungs filled with fire.

"I've got you, you bastard. I've got you," she said then opened the car door and heaved until her throat felt as if it was lined with shards of splintered glass.

three

Working hard on his second cup of coffee, Jack Joseph Towns was trying to digest both a chicken sausage biscuit from Harley's Gas-n-Go and the front page of the *Rayburn Star*. Neither was going down very well. A rap against the door drew his attention. He reached behind to the metal shelving unit that housed his small non-discreet boom box and adjusted the volume. The gravelly voice of Tom Waits faded behind him like a haunted past, quelled but persistent. The radio didn't work very well anymore because of the broken antenna, but the CD player was just fine. Maggie kept threatening to get him an iPod, and he kept teasing her about hiring her younger replacement. Neither of which was likely to happen.

Jack's door was normally wide open. It's something he learned from his father, Joe, whose mountain blood had instilled in him a rather quixotic nature. *An open door is an open mind,* Jack could hear the old man say even though he'd been dead and buried for almost a month now. Today, the door was half-opened. Or half-closed depending on whether you were an optimist or a pessimist. Jack was somewhere in between most of the time, but with the discovery of the Marsh girl's body yesterday morning, he was leaning toward the latter.

Rayburn had its share of crime that child abductions and unexplained deaths weren't normally part of. Meth, domestic violence—frequently involving meth, and the occasional smash-n-grab were offenses that made the news on a more regular basis.

He looked towards the door though there really was no need. He knew that knock belonged to Kitty Lynch. Three solid raps because four was overdoing it and two lacked conviction. It was all business with her. Approaching seventy-five, Kitty had always been the kind of woman who likely made the devil nervous when he heard her feet hit the floor in the morning.

"Sherriff," she acknowledged him. "I'm here to turn myself in."

Upon her entrance, which was short neither determination nor fervor, the room seemed to take on a subdued sort of light. The fluorescents flickered once or twice in admiration, or possibly fear, Jack considered. Kitty Lynch's presence might be best described as a mouthful of salted nuts and molasses. Half prison guard, half Southern Belle, people often noted. A bartender for over forty years at the Legion, she'd heard more secrets than a confessional, both a blessing and a curse in Jack's opinion. Loyalty in Crow County came with a price. Secrets were gospel and promises were sealed in blood. And much like the rest of the South, Rayburn's philosophy was fundamentally steeped in the Holy Trinity of God, guns, and grits in just that order.

A tiny thing, just over five feet, Kitty's height was all internal. Her gruff voice raked across her throat like a rusty old claw and sounded like dry leaves set afire. The Barbara Stanwyck of the South, Jack had heard her regulars say from time to time. Only tougher and much better with a gun.

She sat rigidly in one of the chairs in front of the desk, dropping her worn saddle-colored bag on the floor beside her. The purse, embellished in turquoise beading and suede fringe, looked as if it had been made from the leathery skin of a hundred-year-old cow pushed through a shredder. There was no doubt she had whiskey in there. Probably something half her age and just as peppery.

Jack folded the newspaper and set it aside, young Kelly Marsh's glare following his every move like one of those roving-eyed wolf paintings at the flea market. The front-page photo, taken at what appeared to be some kind of high-school cheerleading rally, may have shown her wide smile, but her eyes screamed, *You're too late. Give me an* A *for asshole.*

He saw Kitty glance over at the dead girl, and out of respect for both parties, he reached to turn the paper over. An intuitive move, one he felt might have made a good study in one of those crime dramas where the criminal psychologist explains that the victim was blanketed by someone who knew her. Rayburn, Georgia had less than 1,000 residents. Everyone knew Kelly. She disappeared a month ago, a few days before his niece, Skyla Jane. Three other children were also missing. Jack's mind went dark with that thought, picturing each of their faces. Simon's shiny black hair, Hailey's gap-toothed grin, and the freckles across Ben's nose. Jack envisioned just for a split second choking the life out of Levi Knox who he'd already roughed up quite a bit, even somehow gave him a nose bleed. And since he was already covered in bruises, Jack wasn't too concerned about adding a few more regretting only that his father would have been greatly disappointed in his behavior. That was the thing about Jack that only those on the rarest and most unfortunate occasion discovered. It took a lot to light his anger but once ignited, it became an uncontrollable fire that could not be easily extinguished. It wasn't a trait he was proud of, but he tried to keep in mind what he learned studying literature. Any character worth a damn wasn't credible without flaws.

Vindictive was not a word that had ever before had a place in Jack's life or law enforcement career. But as he listened to the lyrics, he felt Waits might be right. Everyone *is* looking for someone to blame. And today, Jack was no exception. He wanted answers. He wanted Skyla and the rest of the children to come home. He wanted somebody to pay. What he really wanted was to close his damn door all the way and lock it.

For as long as he could remember, he had never known Kitty Lynch to travel in a way she considered unprepared. Along with her whiskey, a sharp tongue, a Ruger revolver, and a tattered black Bible had become, over the years, part of her DNA, metaphorically inseparable from her biological backbone.

"Turn yourself in? What for this time?" Kitty surrendered at least once every two or three months for something. Jack figured it was her way of seeking penance for things in her past that she'd never worked through. It was part of her story. Everyone had one. Just a few weeks ago, she asked Jack to arrest her because she'd stuck a knife in her neighbor's tire after he tried to run over her cat. Jack found out later that she'd actually been aiming *for* the neighbor and not the tire.

Kitty reached inside her bag. Jack thought it might be for a pull of the whiskey. Instead, in a resigning manner, she took out the Bible, the gold letters ghosted from age, and set it on the desk between them. On top of it, she rested the silver revolver, the grain on the wooden handle worn smooth, the barrel as straight as her nose. The air in the room suddenly took on a somber weight. Heavy and wet like it had just sunk to the bottom of the ocean.

"I killed a man, Jack—Sheriff," Kitty corrected. "Stood close to him, looked him square in the eyes, those soulless black holes, and shot him in the heart. *I've* a pretty good aim."

Jack was aware of Kitty's precision when it came to

firearms. She was, after all, the one who taught him to shoot. He felt a nervous lump, thick and scratchy like a cotton ball coated in sand, form in his throat. He massaged his smooth chin with his thumb and forefinger, a habit he swore helped him to better grasp a situation.

"Whoa, whoa, whoa. Wait a minute. You shot whom?" Jack asked, catching the lingering scent of firecrackers that a recently fired weapon emitted. It caught him off guard, pulled his mind to Skyla Jane.

Independence Day had always been his niece's favorite holiday. A memory of her confronted him. Those bright blue eyes, that infectious giggle. The way the sky above her exploded in colored light that rained down magically on her shiny wheat-colored hair. She loved fireworks. She *loves* fireworks, he reminded himself. Loves them. Hard to believe it had been almost a month since she vanished. Simon, Hailey, and Ben gone with her. Including Kelly Marsh, a total of five, though Kelly he reminded himself painfully, was no longer missing. Each child had disappeared from the woods surrounding Blood Mountain, which further fueled the dark memories of the Truelove children, who had vanished in the mid-eighties. It reignited an air of curiosity and fear in Rayburn, both of which spread around town like wildfire in the wind.

The search and rescue volunteers had started to thin and the GBI had no solid leads yet, but Jack would never give up. He didn't care what the stats said about finding abducted children alive after twenty-four hours. Those kids were out there somewhere lost in Bone Hollow, the land of the dead. But they were *alive*. It wasn't just intuition. He knew it in his heart. This wasn't a random crime. He'd turned his mind over and over looking for some sort of connection, a clue as to why they might have been abducted and by whom, but each time he came up bone dry. He'd be lying if he said he hadn't himself considered the Cherokee curse that had plagued the mountain for over a hundred and fifty years, but the very first thought that came to his mind had been the Trueloves. Whatever happened to those children and why was it happening again?

Jack took a breath, tried to remain calm. "Let's start over, shall we? Who was it you shot? And please tell me you aren't serious."

"The Cemetery Man," Kitty said with detached affectation then reached up behind her thin wrinkled neck, under the loose red curls, the color of Georgia clay. After she'd unfastened it, she let the tiny gold locket dangle midair, the engraved initials SJB worn but still prevalent under the green glint of the fluorescent light. She set the necklace down delicately on the desk and sunk her teeth into her lower lip in an effort to bite back the pain.

"I shot the Cemetery Man, and I ain't a bit sorry," she made clear.

Jack hung his head in his palm then ran his hand over his dark hair, cropped close to the scalp to keep the waves at bay. "Dear God, you're serious. I can't believe this."

"Dead serious," she said with a face blanketed in gravity. She'd never been much for wit. "Snatched this from his hand after he hit the ground. He had it clasped between his filthy fingers like a rosary while he sat in one of the pews near the pulpit, his head bowed," she continued. "Never realized the devil had need for praying." A tight smile pulled at her lips, but she cut it abruptly the way an experienced fisherman knew when to cut the line. "It's a bit ironical that it's the first time I've been inside a church in sixty years, don't you think? It's either a sign I should go more. Or less." A drop of blood beaded on her bottom lip.

Jack stared at the locket but couldn't bring himself to reach for it. He'd never seen Skyla Jane without it. Behind his eyes, dark thoughts pulsed. He pushed them away as he'd been doing since she went missing. His stomach clutched and he couldn't hide the irritation in his voice.

"What is wrong with you? You shot a man? And while he was praying? For God sakes, Mother!" Hamlet and Claudius flashed in Jack's mind. Even Shakespeare knew not to kill a man in prayer.

"No, not while praying. That might have given him some sort of chance," Kitty relinquished. "I waited for him outside the church."

Her blue eyes had grown less intense over the years, but it was the disappearance of Skyla Jane, her only grandchild, that seemed to suck the color right from them.

They appeared a flat gray now. If grief had a color, it would be brushed aluminum anguish, Jack decided.

Kitty cast her eyes like a net toward the newspaper on the desk then back to meet the scrutinizing stare of her son.

"I don't care what anybody thinks. I haven't got a damn bit of sympathy for that halfwit —the way he is and all." She pulled a pack of Marlboro Reds from the monogrammed pocket of her Carhartt shirt, which looked like it belonged to a gas-station attendant. Without intent, she had over the years become trendy with her clothing choices.

Jack cringed. "Halfwit? Mom. Please." Subtlety had never really been her gift, but it seemed to worsen with age. "Do you have to refer to him that way?"

"You prefer retard then? Just because he can't talk doesn't make him innocent," she stressed. "We may never find our Skyla Jane, but that rotten bastard won't be taking any more of our children. For all we know, he took the Truelove children, too. Damn pervert. No surprise he works for the church. It's always the *holier than thou* types." She shook a cigarette into her mouth straight from the pack and began digging once again in her purse. "Where's that damn lighter?"

"Well, just because he can't talk doesn't make him a halfwit, a retard, or guilty for that matter," Jack retorted. "And you can't smoke in here," he added. "Besides, I thought you quit?"

"That was yesterday. I ain't quit yet today." She wrestled the cigarette back into the pack with blatant disappointment and dropped it into her purse.

Kitty rarely read the paper or listened to the news, and she obviously hadn't heard about Levi Knox's arrest the day before. Jack had attended the initial appearance earlier that morning with Deputy Wayne, but evidently, that info hadn't reached his mother yet either. Somebody was off their game. He noticed then the gray roots cresting her crown. It was clear she hadn't been to Curl-Up and Dye in a long minute. In Roman Mythology, Rumor had several tongues, a trumpet, and wings. In Rayburn, Dottie West over at the salon took on this role, but because she was having her gall bladder removed, her trumpet had evidently been silenced, her wings clipped.

Jack had planned on swinging by Kitty's later that morning to let her know they may have a suspect. Not that it would have changed her mind about the Cemetery Man who went by the name of Tomb, a nickname he earned no doubt because he dug graves and maintained the cemetery. Had for years. What the hell was his real name, anyway? Jack wasn't sure he'd ever known, and this made him feel rather bad. A quiet man, Tomb had always kept to himself but none of this mattered. Once Kitty Lynch got an idea in her head, she remained devoted to it. He wished she would have used some of that same devotion towards his father. Had she forgotten that they'd already grilled everyone in town including the Cemetery Man and didn't have a single suspect? Until now with Knox, anyway.

The siren in the distance grew louder. How long had it been whining? Maybe it had been there, a white noise, before his mother even came to the door. After his niece had vanished, most everything seemed like background noise to Jack.

As if cued, Maggie's voice, scrambled over the intercom of his phone. "Sheriff, you in there?" He picked up the phone.

"I'm here." He hated the intercom system. There were only three employees at the Crow County Sheriff's Office and he was one of them. Maggie had talked him into getting a new phone system after lightning struck the building last year and cut all lines of communication because they weren't, as she put it, "digitally comprehensive," for whatever the hell that meant. All that money for a system where the phone still rang busy when a fax was coming in.

"I just took a call from Beau Carver over at the garage. He says there's a man, covered in blood, lying on the side of the church near the cemetery. Can't be positive but thinks it might the groundskeeper. What's his name? Graves? Anyhow, said he's bleeding all over the place. I called for an ambulance. Hang on," Maggie told him.

Jack could hear her talking to someone but couldn't make out what she was saying. The other phone line started ringing and he tried to answer it but gave up after pushing a few buttons and getting nothing but beeps and shrills. Digitally comprehensive. Not only was Maggie the office manager, property tax assessor, bookkeeper, records clerk, barista, and 9-1-1 operator, she was also the only one who knew how to use the damn phones.

"Also, there's a woman from- *where did you say you're from, hon?*...the Lost Foundation, here to see you. Says you're expecting her. Name's Angela Archer."

"Shit," he muttered a little too loudly. "Tell her to go ahead and have a seat. I'll be out in a second." He'd forgotten about the appointment he made with the lawyer from the missing children's organization in Philly. She'd called yesterday inquiring about Levi Knox whose arrest had apparently made national news. She sure didn't waste any time getting here, Jack considered. It reminded him that he had yet to return any calls to the overly-tenacious journalist from the AJC who was trying to connect Rayburn's missing children to the disappearance of the Truelove siblings who vanished in 1985 during a house fire. Not a single bone fragment was ever discovered in the ashes. All five children had vanished without a trace. It was a mystery turned somewhat legend that had resurfaced when a hunter caught sight of the disfigured recluse, Wanda Drake a few years back. He posted her picture on one of those unsolved mystery websites, which had all sorts of people passing through town, trying to catch sight of Wanda who was covered in burn scars from head to toe. It was because of this that some believed she had something to do with the disappearance of the Truelove children. Many even considered that she may have started the fire.

Jack focused his attention back to his mother. What the hell was he going to do about her? If Kitty had really shot the groundskeeper, he'd have no choice but to arrest her. Eventually, anyhow. He stood, his solid frame an exact replica of his father Joe, only slightly taller with broader shoulders, a little more muscle, a little less waist. He had his father's olive complexion and the same hazel eyes as bright as a pair of gold coins. At forty-three and single, Jack had somehow managed to take fairly good care of himself regardless of his terrible eating habits, abundance of strong black coffee, and a heart that had never quite healed entirely from a girl he'd once loved. A girl who had left him and never looked back, and all these years later, he still had no idea why. He admired that in people. The ability to live life without drawing on the past for reference. It was opposite from a life in law where everything was based on precedence.

Lisa Harrison's swift departure did a number on him. One he was still trying to recover from. It had been over fifteen years since she took off. Still felt like last week. He'd dated or tried to but it never worked out. His father's words always came back. *Remember son. In law enforcement, you have no friends at the end of the day.* Jack knew just about everyone in Rayburn, and yet he couldn't think of one person outside Maggie that he'd call in an emergency. And that was partially because she was Rayburn's 9-1-1 operator.

"You can stay here if you like. Or go on home. I know

where to find you," he told Kitty. "I'm disappointed in you," he added and when doing so, he realized he'd felt this way for some time. She was a good mother, but she'd never been easy on his father or him. It was his sister, Camille his mother loved best. She'd always been the angel, the perfect daughter and mother, the successful antique store owner who'd married a doctor. Now, the grieving widow who'd lost her husband in a car accident that left her only daughter, Skyla, with a brain injury that might never heal.

Camille had always been the golden child and not just because of her honey blonde hair, but this was okay with Jack because he felt that way about his sister, too. She was golden. It was his mother he had issues with. Her rigid independence, her narrow-minded attitude, her unwillingness to adapt to anything that might lean toward being politically correct. He wondered sometimes if there was a limit on how many flaws a realistic character could have. But he knew too much about his mother to think she was, in any way, identifiably one-dimensional. There was good in her; it was just buried beneath a razor-sharp tongue and a quick-to-draw-blood approach. A defense mechanism of some sort, no doubt.

Kitty had never understood why Jack, who earned a graduate degree in literature from UGA, would want to be a small-town sheriff, risking his life for mountain meth heads and a below-average salary. He wanted to tell her that professors made even less and often dealt with worse people and situations. Tenure was being replaced with adjunct in the same way the boom box had been replaced by the iPod and the book by the Kindle. Besides, there was that promise he'd made to his father to continue to uphold the family name. The Towns had been in law enforcement so long it was almost a birthright. Jack didn't even have to campaign after his father's death. The people of Crow County had elected him because he was Joe's son, and they believed that because the same blood coursed through his veins, Jack would never let them down. And he hadn't. Until the children starting disappearing. Until Kelly Marsh's body turned up near the orchard.

"Sheriff? Sheriff, you there?" Maggie shouted over the intercom again. He picked up the phone and was met with an ear-piercing screech. He held the receiver away from his ear but still thought he heard her swear. Not like her at all. Then, suddenly Maggie was at his door, out of breath and panicked, wide-eyed.

"Sheriff, Pearl's on the phone. She needs you to go over to the diner right away. Says it's real important." There was something odd in Maggie's voice. Something agitated and unsettled. Jack considered it might be fear he detected though this was not an emotion he ever associated with Maggie Sheppard, a.k.a. The Rock of Rayburn.

"I've got to head over to the church and then the hospital to see about this groundskeeper incident," Jack said, side-eyeing his mother. "Send Deputy Wayne. He's probably in the kitchen getting something to eat. After he stopped smoking, that's all he seems to do. Plus, I know for a fact he hasn't eaten since he pulled over Knox. He even mentioned something about becoming a vegetarian, if you can believe that."

Maggie didn't laugh like she normally would have when they exchanged jokes about Deputy Wayne, who had over the last few years, become an easy target due to some of his odd proclivities. He was the younger, chubbier Barney Fife of the Crow County Sherriff's Office.

"No, Sheriff. Pearl needs *you* to go over there. Said you should hurry. It's real important."

"Yes, you said that already." Fridays weren't normally as chaotic. A sure sign of a Harvest Moon. This day was already a shit show and it wasn't even noon. He had a psycho bone collector being questioned by the GBI, a mother with a smoking gun—literally, the insistent woman from the children's organization and now an emergency at the diner. What could be so damn important over there that needed his immediate attention?

"Did somebody break into the pie safe?" he asked with more than a touch of cynicism, something else he inherited from his father.

"No." Maggie's voice cracked sullenly. She shook her head slowly from side to side, mirthlessly. Not even so much as a smirk.

He could see now the glittering in her glass green eyes. Maggie was not a woman of tears. She'd worked for his father, Joe, for over thirty-five years and only stayed on after his death because Jack had taken over as sheriff. Joe used to call her Queen Maggie, and Jack learned later during a community blood drive this wasn't because she was actual royalty. It was because she had some type of rare blood disorder. "Nothing to worry about," she'd told him. "I'm just a carrier. But I still can't donate."

Over the years, Jack had watched Maggie's hair turn from midnight black to salt and pepper to the unyielding gray of a January mountain sky, and he could count with two fingers the number of times he'd seen her cry. Including today, one.

"Maggie. What is it? What's wrong?"

"It's Sky-" She put her fingers to her mouth. "Skyla." Her voice caught so that the name came out in a frail whine, a balloon leaking air. A renegade tear escaped and ran down her cheek. She didn't bother to wipe it. It trembled at her jawbone, no doubt cautious to be the very first to ever fall.

Waits had just started singing about the temperature falling ten below when the air in the room seemed to drop twenty degrees and thicken into a somber paste, as if any minute the ceiling would open up, and the office would be filled with snow. Jack's heart pinched. He couldn't move. He felt his lungs freeze up and ice over. If he exhaled, it surely would be nothing but frost that came out.

Kitty sat tensed; her creased face drained of blood. She reached inside her purse, pulled out the silver flask, uncapped it and took a generous swig then wiped her mouth on the back of her hand like some kind of Western gunslinger preparing for a fight. A streak of blood smeared across her lips. She stood. Her eyes hardened and grayed like two pieces of sharp granite chiseled from a tombstone.

"She's," Maggie closed her eyes and inhaled deeply.

That lump was back again. Jack couldn't tell if it was moving up or down his throat, but it had definitely grown larger. He tried to swallow. Rayburn was a city of ones. One church. One hospital. One grocery store. One pawn shop. One ambulance, and unfortunately, one dead girl. And he hoped to God to keep it that way.

Jack could have sworn he heard Maggie's tear, as weighted as a dollop of butter, finally hit the floor.

"For shit's sake, woman!" Kitty barked. "Spit it out."

"...Alive," Maggie finally choked out.

Jack released a breath. It was the longest twenty seconds of his life.

"Skyla Jane's alive," she repeated. "She just showed up, Pearl said. Walked right into the diner all covered in dirt. Sat at the counter, and pointed with a finger caked in dried mud to the lemon meringue pie. It's always been my favorite, too." And with that innocent confession, Maggie burst into a discordant wail that cut the dense air like a newly-sharpened knife and made up for thirty years of abridged emotion.

As they scrambled out of the office, Jack could hear Waits pleading for them to take his hand and hold on as if he somehow knew that they might need it in the days ahead.

four

Rayburn, Georgia
1935

The Trueloves grew their generations on land won in the last of the Georgia Land Lotteries in 1833. It was no secret that the land, including the orchard and most of Blood Mountain, was rightfully owned by the Cherokees who cursed it when they were forced from it. When Abraham Truelove died in 1930, he willed the house his great grandfather had built at the end of Broken Arrow Lane and the surrounding property—everything but Bone Hollow, which had always been owned by the dead, to his only surviving relative, a son named Jeremiah. The young man was twenty-five and lame and made his living as best he could as a blacksmith. He had hopes of bringing the orchard back to life, but the Truelove land had become over the years as barren as an old woman. The once thriving apple trees at the edge of the hollow had blackened and shriveled into gnarled witches' hands that looked as if they were reaching up from the grave. *The land is cursed,*

Jeremiah was reminded time and time again. But, being a tenacious God-fearing man, he refused to leave it even when the last of his cows died.

It was about that same time that the raven-haired girl with the glowing lavender colored eyes appeared on his doorstep early one morning, when the sky was blanketed in a black so dark and starless, it looked as if a piece of velvet had been draped over the world. She was sick with fever and barely moving. Her hands were locked around a small leather-bound book she had pulled to her chest in what Jeremiah assumed was an effort to keep it dry. He could tell by the swollen pages that this had not been entirely successful. Even in her apparent incoherency, her hand tightened on the book when Jeremiah tried to remove it from her grip. Other than a change of clothes, a bottle of small, white round pills, and a couple of slices of stale bread, the traveling sack next to her was empty.

It had been raining most of the night, and the girl's long dark hair clung to her body like the black tentacles of a giant squid. An unusual little thing whose blue veins traveled beneath her fair skin, a map to an undiscovered world. It was an odd combination, the formidable light eyes, the oil-colored hair. It was as if she was pulled straight from the pages of one of the dark fairy tales his mother used to read to him as a child. He half expected the girl to have wings budding from her back or branches for arms and legs. Jeremiah couldn't help but wonder if the young lady might be part of the curse that had plagued his land.

Or maybe she was a wandering gypsy like the kind he'd heard about from the folks of Rayburn. Such sly thieves, someone had told him that they could steal your breath without you even knowing it. He considered only briefly that she might be infected with influenza, but Jeremiah was not afraid of death. He carried the girl inside and made her comfortable. As weak and confused as she appeared, there was a chance she might not even live through the night. Besides, he didn't have anything worthy of taking except for maybe his time.

After heating water and cleaning the dirt from her face, he scraped the mud and clay from under her nails where it had dried and caked. It was so thick he wondered if she'd dug her way out of a grave. There was a strange purple rash around her neck, perhaps from the fever.

With an ointment made from dried rosemary and mint, a concoction his own mother had used on him as a child, he pulled the heat from the girl. He fed her broth on a small silver spoon he'd kept from his childhood. The spoon, a family heirloom passed down for generations, looked like it might be best suited for a doll. Engraved with an ornate T at the very tip of the handle, it was the only piece of silver Jeremiah owned. He imagined at one time there might have been an entire set of this same design, but it had undoubtedly been sold long ago to keep the farm going. Curses were costly, he'd come to realize.

After many days of incoherent mumbling, the girl was sitting up in bed when Jeremiah returned one day from hunting.

"You're awake," he greeted her, surprised to find her pale skin flushed pink, her eyes alert and clear. The rash on her neck had become so faint it was barely visible. "Glad to see you're feeling better. Jeremiah Truelove," he said with his hand against his heart. "Welcome to my home, Grace." He set the emaciated limp rabbit he'd shot and three shrunken apples on the table before walking toward the iron bed next to the fireplace. He poked at the smoldering coals.

The girl remained silent, warily eyeing the rotten fruit and secretly hoping that he'd left at least one apple on the tree. Her grandmother had always told her never to pick the last apple from a tree. That one belonged to the devil. If you took it, he'd surely come calling. But in her case, he'd already been on his way for some time, she felt.

The young woman continued to look around the room as she furtively tucked the black book she held in her grasp back under the thin, moldy mattress. The journal was a gift from her grandmother, a clairvoyant woman whose untimely death catapulted the girl's life into tragedy and chaos.

The mention of the name Grace made the girl's stomach twist with nausea and fear, and she felt her fingers, still numb and tingling, clench into a knot under the blanket. More than a few minutes passed before she spoke. "Grace?" she said in a soft questioning whisper. It felt as if she was conjuring an omen.

"Yes. Grace. Grace Wood. That's the name you kept whispering during the night so I assumed it must belong to you. You've been very sick, Grace. I found you on my stoop, brought you inside. To be quite honest, and I don't mean to frighten you, Miss, I wasn't sure you'd make it."

"I...my—" She started but then smiled weakly and gave in to the lie, which burned inside her like one of the hot coals in the fireplace. "I'm not sure how I got here," she confessed instead. But this was not entirely true. She was able to travel most of the way through the mountain by using the underground tunnels her grandmother had mapped out on a piece of worn parchment she left tucked in the journal. She must have known her granddaughter would one day need it. How the old woman knew about the tunnels was a mystery but must have had something to do with her only son, the girl's father, a leased prisoner forced to mine the mountain until he discovered the tunnels and his route to freedom. They were filled with snakes and rats and flooded with water in some areas, but the girl wasn't afraid—even when her matches got soaked, and she lost her way in the pitch black of the earth. Even when something slithered across her foot. She wandered blindly until she managed to find an opening and claw her way out. She needed a place to rest, to hide for a few days. The rain was getting heavier, and she could feel the edges of an attack coming. It seemed to work in the same way a hurricane hitting the coast rapidly worked its way inland. Her inner voice told her she needed to seek shelter. The two-story white farmhouse appeared as a beacon to her in the dusty wet twilight as she made her way down the mountain, hungry, exhausted, and frightened that she would soon be found. How exactly she ended up on this man's porch wasn't clear, but she likely had the attack either during or just after burying the Mason jar deep in the red clay. They were not new to her, the attacks. She'd began having them after she'd been struck by lightning some years before. Epilepsy, Dr. Frost had diagnosed, though many feared she was possessed. She had never figured out if the rain triggered the attacks or just fed them. Either way, they were debilitating, often leaving her in a weak and disoriented state and compromising her ability to remember.

"So, where are you from?" Jeremiah studied the girl's face, her unique lavender eyes a mixture of fear and confusion.

"I don't know," she lied. "I can't remember."

"When I found you by the front door," he told her, "...you were burning with fever. It may have damaged your ability to recall. Made you a little out of sorts. Probably just temporary, I'm sure," he added with reassurance. "It'll come to you in due time."

She nodded and took a sip from the cup of water Jeremiah had left on the table next to the bed.

"Perhaps you have family in town? If so, they must be worried about you. I could ask around," he offered.

She shook her head adamantly and set the cup

down. "No. Please don't. I mean, I don't have any family, Mr. Truelove. They've all gone on. To the angels."

"Jeremiah. Please call me Jeremiah. Well," he added with sincere concern, "... someone must be missing you?"

Again, she moved her head from side to side. Unspoken lies somehow seemed less immoral. Someone was definitely missing her. No doubt about that. They would at some point come looking for her. Maybe even find her. The thought terrified her. But for now, she was safe. And so was the money she'd taken. It wasn't really stealing if it originally belonged to her, but it still felt wrong. The values her grandmother instilled in her lingered long after the old woman's death.

Jeremiah sat next to the girl, put his hand on her shoulder. "You can stay here as long as you like. In your own room, upstairs," he clarified with his solemn gray eyes. But her inner voice did not need to tell her this wouldn't last long. Grace and Jeremiah were married three months later. By then, she was already six months pregnant and just beginning to show. If Jeremiah noticed the weight of three additional months, he never said a word.

five

"Got it," Maggie said as she darted behind the desk to answer the phone, which had been ringing incessantly since she'd stepped away from it. "You go on. I'll come if I can get away," she called to Jack.

"Call Camille, would you? Let her know what's happening. Have her meet us at the diner, but don't tell anyone else just yet," Jack added, heading toward the door. "At least until I can figure out what's going on." He held the door for his mother who raced out ahead of him and into the street of vehement protestors.

Angela stood and quickly gathered her things as they passed.

"Sherriff Towns?" Angela didn't wait for a response. "It's imperative I speak to you regarding Levi Knox."

Jack turned in an attempt at politeness but kept moving. "Not now, Miss—"

"Archer."

"Archer. Right."

"Angela Archer. I'm with the Lost Foundation." With.

50

Who was she kidding? She *was* the Lost Foundation. Other than a few college interns over the years and a neighbor's daughter who occasionally helped her with filing, she was solo.

"Yes, I know. It's just—I've got a situation that needs my immediate attention. We'll have to reschedule. I'm sorry. How about tomorrow?"

"No," she said more adamant than she meant to, shouldering her purse and laptop bag and following him out the door, trying to keep up. "You don't understand," she barked at his heels like a dog challenged by size but not attitude. She wanted to tell him that she'd waited so long for this, it had nearly destroyed her.

"Look, I'm sorry. I have to go," Jack said more sternly. "It'll have to wait." His heart raced in his chest with thoughts of Skyla. He darted into the crowd, trying to catch up with his mother.

Outside, the picketing erupting from the courthouse had grown thicker and more agitated. Picketers were now spilling down the stairs, out into the street and onto the square. They held signs that screamed: GUILTY! HIXSON SELLS BABIES FOR $$$$! MURDERER! PLAYING GOD IS A SIN! HIXSON IS THE DEVIL! Angela had no idea who Hixson was, but it was clear that he had quite a few enemies.

A short round woman with a pinched face stepped in front of Angela, causing her to lose her footing. The woman carried a cross with BURN IN HELL HIXSON written on it and adorned with a baby doll, tied with rope and dripping in congealed red syrup. It reminded Angela of a Hole concert she once attended in her twenties. The edges of the wood behind the cross were painted in bright orange and yellow flames, and she flinched. Fire had intimidated her even as a Girl Scout. But for some reason, it was much more frightening in the South where hellfire and damnation seemed to be a part of everyday life.

The whole scene brought about horrible flashbacks—a time when she herself was the stone thrower, and things went so horribly wrong. Denny Sherman should not have died the way he did. He shouldn't have died at all. She could not let that happen again. She'd have to be positive this time. More positive than she was the first time she was positive. But if Knox really was the Redeemer, as she suspected, as she truly believed in her heart, she would make sure justice was served. Her justice. Dead men were no longer considered suspects after all. That's the main reason she'd brought a gun with her. She'd end this once and for all. For Liam and all the others. For herself. She just needed some kind of sign. Something to let her know she was in the right place, and that this was not all a horrible mistake.

Once she regained her footing and her focus, Angela managed to worm her way through the chanting mob, momentarily losing sight of the sheriff before spotting him entering the diner on the other side of the square and racing after him. Hard to believe it took her nearly twenty minutes to reach the door.

"Have a seat wherever you like," a voice called from—Angela didn't know which direction. "Someone will be right with you."

She took a counter seat and scrolled through the texts on her phone while she waited. A waitress on the other side of the diner gathered dirty plates between orders. She held up her index finger to signify she'd be with Angela in a minute. A minute or so later, she held it up again.

A young goth-looking girl with lilac blue hair and lots of tattoos scrambled out from the back of the diner. She hastily secured a vintage flowered apron around her tiny waist. Her hair, pulled up in a chaotic bun, was held in place with a variety of sparkling clips and what looked to be a pair of chopsticks. Two long strands of hair hung loose around her heart-shaped face like a set of parentheses. She wore dark purple lipstick and her teeth, as white as chalk, contrasted starkly against it.

"Sorry," she called to her coworker across the way then greeted Angela as she began making a fresh pot of coffee. She wiped her hands on the apron. "Shouldn't take but a minute. Would you like a cup?"

Angela, peering around the diner with a casual diligence, searched for the sheriff. "That'd be great. Thanks."

"Haven't seen you before. Thought I'd met everyone by now. You live in town?" the girl asked as she reached for a cup from under the counter. Angela noticed her eyes seemed to pick up both shades of her hair color, fluctuating between the blues, almost iridescently. She placed a menu on the red Formica counter, which had specks of silver glitter, similar to her chipped black nail polish.

"No. Just passing through." She scanned the restaurant tables and decided the sheriff must be in the kitchen or office.

"Me, too," the girl confessed. "I'm here looking for someone I lost touch with. Last I heard, she was here in Rayburn. Once I locate her, I'll be on my way. I'm Nelle." She wiped her tattooed hand on her apron and reached it toward Angela. "Actually, Harper's my first name but I've always gone by Nelle." The last call she got from her mother came from Rayburn, and Nelle wasn't leaving until she found her. There were reasons she couldn't involve the law though she had stopped by the sheriff's office right before her shift. The door was unlocked, the place deserted or so she thought. She wandered around a few minutes then stopped to stare at the photographs on the wall by the reception desk. Generations of Towns that had carried the law enforcement torch. She got so lost in thought that she jumped when a woman who seemed to come from nowhere asked if she needed any help. Nelle didn't mean to be rude when she'd turned, hurried out the door and made her way toward the diner. By the time she made it through the crowd, she was late for work.

"Well, I'm Angela. Good to meet you, Nelle." She accepted her hand. "I'm actually in the business of finding people. If I can help you in any way just let me know." She dug out a card and slid it over the counter intentionally failing to mention that most of those she found were no longer alive.

Nelle cocked her head. "Angela. It means messenger of God. Of all the signs I've seen today, that's the best. Did you bring a message with you? This place sure could use one," she said, studying the mob outside. Again, she thought of her mother and what she'd revealed to her the last time they spoke. It was a lot to process. Two days passed after that conversation with no word. Three, then four. Then all calls went straight to voicemail. On the sixth day, her mother's cell phone no longer rang when she called it. That's when Nelle got in her car and drove to Rayburn. Almost a month had passed with no word from her mother. She knew she shouldn't have let her come to this place. She should have warned her about the dark visions she'd been having. Black butterflies swarming like locusts; a bird trapped in a cage at the bottom of the ocean, and most recently, upon her arrival in Rayburn, the children whose eyes and mouths were filled with dirt and ash, their skin scarred by burns.

Angela didn't know quite how to answer Nelle's question without causing alarm, considering the message she had involved killing a man—another man, she acknowledged silently but not without great remorse. Besides, God really wasn't her thing. At least not when it came to the Lost Foundation. It wasn't so much His existence she questioned but His motive. Spoken (or rather, unspoken in this case) like a true prosecutor, she thought.

"Hmm...a message? Too early to tell," she replied. "I'll keep you posted." She noticed then that most of the tattoos covering Nelle's arms were of black and gray angels and gargoyles in different shades of light, surrounded by Scripture. The girl was a walking Bible.

Angela spotted what looked like an image of the devil, and her mind fell into that hole that had swallowed her each time she thought of Liam's killer and the biblical messages he'd left behind. She wasn't surprised. Not really. Georgia was after all the bulls-eye of the Bible Belt. But Angela had never been able to view religion and scripture the same once the Redeemer became a part of her life, and the mountains were rife with both. She'd lost count of all the hubcap crosses she'd seen once she hit the Georgia line. It was formidable even to a former Catholic schoolgirl such as herself. Not that Catholics didn't have their own crosses to bear. It was just that religion below the Mason Dixon line seemed to have a whole new level of fear as its foundation. It was an odd marriage of rattlesnakes, talking in tongues, moonshine, and Appalachian folklore—all in the name of God and enough to scare anyone. A message? How about? *You people are frightening the shit out of me,* give or take an expletive or two.

"I'm an Old Testament kind of girl," Nelle said when she saw Angela staring with intensity at her artwork. "An eye for an eye. That sort of thing." She rotated one of her sleeved arms back and forth. "Most of these are renditions from *Paradise Lost*. Stories of retribution. A few are Blake, some are Dore. And a couple are my own design," she added humbly. "This one though," she tugged the neck of her t-shirt down to reveal the head and wing of a bird, "is for my mom. She's my"—her words got caught in her throat, "best friend." *And I have to find her.*

There was a longing in her voice that made Angela think of her own mother. The grief she should have been dealing with over her passing had been placed on a shelf once the news of Levi Knox surfaced.

Above the inked bird, dangling around the girl's neck, a silver half-heart necklace caught Angela's attention. Hadn't she had one similar in high school? As she tried desperately to recall who had the other half, her thoughts were hijacked by Nelle's innocent curiosity.

"So, do you have any?"

"I'm sorry?" Angela pulled herself from the lapsed moment.

"Tattoos? Do you have any?"

Angela shook her head. Did the images that were forever tattooed in her mind or on her heart count? Memories of a single moment she could never change but one that forever changed her.

"No. I have a problem with permanence. Things I— things that can't be changed. Yours are stunning, though," she said inspecting one of the angels whose face was partly obscured in shadow and surrounded by small black stars that seemed to wink on her fair skin. "Very detailed. Is that...?" Angela pointed.

"He has many names. Satan. The Dark Angel, Lucifer. The Fallen Star. People fear him, not realizing that many share his same characteristics. He's the quintessential map of humanity and the most human of all God's angels because of his flaws. Instilled with both light and dark, he is his own antithesis, the world's adversary if you really think about it. Life can't exist without this contradiction. We have to have it. Or at least that's how I see it."

"Adversary. There's a word I can relate to," Angela acknowledged with a tight smile. The girl smiled then, too. Genuine but careful. She seemed out of place here in Rayburn. Philadelphia had thousands of people with tattoos. Some of them covered from head to toe, accompanied by facial brandings and piercings. It was the norm there. But here, in the mountains of Georgia? Religious fervor Angela expected, but the tattoos and Manic Panic hair caught her completely off guard. Even more surprising was when the young lady set the coffee in front of her and pulled a small book of crosswords then a pencil from her apron pocket.

"So, Angela. You any good at solving puzzles? My mom got me hooked on these darn things. Now I'm obsessed."

Was this the sign she needed? "Is that so?" Angela sipped her coffee, wondering if it was the hot beverage or the memory of her own mother that pushed warmth down into her chest and pulled a reticent smile across her face. It was good to be reminded sometimes that not all of the past was painful and full of regret.

A grandfatherly man in a Cubs cap sat next to her and ordered a cup of coffee and the daily breakfast special. He flipped through the *Atlanta Journal-Constitution* until he found the sports section and with a wink pushed the rest of the newspaper towards Angela when he noticed her interest in the front page. She got caught momentarily in the dark shriveled eyes of Dr. Hixson, the Rayburn Baby Seller, at least according to the headline.

"I'm usually really good at them but this one has me stumped," Nelle admitted, staring intently at the puzzle she held in one hand while topping off Angela's coffee with the other. "Do you happen to know another word for retribution? Eleven letters. Starts with a C, ends with an E."

Angela took another sip of coffee then set it back on the counter, cradling the hot cup with both hands and enjoying a moment of nostalgia, both sweet and bitter.

"I think I might," she replied, but before she could answer, the diner door flew open and a disheveled blonde woman ran in crying hysterically, calling the name Skyla Jane over and over. The tall thin woman had shadows for eyes, and her hair hung greasy and unwashed. She obviously hadn't slept or bathed for days. It reminded Angela of one of the addicts wandering around in the North

Philly Badlands, squatting in the vacant warehouses. Delirious, the woman exuded an odor of exhaustion that seemed to hang in the air like a pheromone from a wild animal.

Angela had seen that crazed look before and not just with tweakers. She started to get up to see if she could help the woman before she collapsed in a heap on the floor but then it registered. Skyla Jane was one of the missing Rayburn children Angela had read about only yesterday. Skyla Jane Brady. This woman wasn't a meth head; she was a mother in anguish, looking for her daughter. Angela's heart sank. She found it odd that a drug addiction and the grief over a lost loved one were so similar in characteristic at first glance.

Just then the sheriff appeared from behind the aluminum swing door that led into the kitchen. A long-limbed girl hung on his hip. The pint-sized fiery red-haired woman walked close behind him. An older waitress with skin the color of midnight and large kind eyes stood next to her and bathed the room in a gossamer glow. Her wiry gray hair was smoothed back away from her pore-less plump face. The two things she seemed to be missing were wings and a halo. A name tag, pinned to a white handkerchief with a scalloped edge, read, Pearl. Angela couldn't help but consider the woman's name in sharp contrast with the color of her skin. Shadows and light. What had Nelle called it? The map of humanity? Light and dark locked together because life couldn't exist without one or the other.

Pearl placed her hand on the red-headed woman's shoulder and pulled her close. "You gonna be okay, Miss Kitty," she said in a hoarse whisper. "The good Lord takes care of his people."

"Jack," the blonde woman sobbed. "Oh God, Jack. Was she—" she started but couldn't finish. "Where has she been? Did she—Did they—has she been—?"

"She seems o...kay, Camille," the sheriff reassured. "Try and calm down. I don't know much. She isn't really talking, and we still need to take her and have her examined, but she's all right. She's alive. That's what's important." The small girl clung to Jack. Her waist-length flaxen hair was tangled with clumps of dirt and leaves, her blue dress filthy and torn.

Camille, her fingers across her mouth, tried to suck back the tears. "Skyla?"

The girl slowly raised her head, obviously exhausted and turned. She stretched her arms out toward her mother and spoke in a soft calm voice. "Hi, Mommy." She reached toward her neck and fingered the emptiness. "I lost my...my lock...et but grandma found it. It's in Uncle Jack's office. Can we go get it?" Her speech was slower now, disjointed, but her eyes were dry and clear.

This child was a rare survivor. There were so few of them. Angela studied the girl carefully from head to toe, wondering where she'd been and how she managed to escape her captor – if indeed there was a captor. Maybe she'd just been lost in the woods like some had speculated.

One thing Angela knew for certain was that it wasn't the Redeemer who'd taken her. She'd find out soon enough the details. This seemed like the kind of small town where news got around rather quickly. Besides, she wasn't about to interrupt. This kind of thing didn't happen often. In fact, she couldn't remember the last time a child had been reunited with their family. At least not a living child. No, she refused to steal this moment. It belonged to them. Not her. She had waited this long. Knox wasn't going anywhere just yet. Besides, she needed to find a place to stay for a night or two. The only motel she spotted looked a little rundown and sketchy. The last thing she needed was bedbugs or whatever else the South had to offer in the way of insects and critters. She'd find the sheriff first thing tomorrow morning.

The main door of the diner opened again, and three women in a variety of ages and shapes marched in and grabbed a booth near the front. Fueled by heated chatter, they scooted into the red vinyl seats after they leaned their picket signs against the window.

"I don't care how old and sick that bastard is. He needs to pay for what he done," one of the women snipped bitterly in an undeniable southern dialect. The other two voiced their overzealous agreement with a *God Bless*, nodding in unison.

"The Hixson trial," Nelle said to Angela from across the counter when she turned back around. "It started the same day I arrived and gets crazier by the minute. From what some of the customers are saying, Dr. Hixson—he ran a women's clinic in town for many years, told women their babies were stillborn when they weren't. Then he would sell the babies. You know, to couples who thought they were getting a legitimate adoption. There are quite a few other rumors circulating too, abortions and stuff, but that's the one I hear the most. People are real angry. They don't care if he's an old man with dementia who can't remember how to pee. Rayburn is out for his blood. I suppose I can't blame them, but they should be careful carrying around the swords of retaliation."

"Why's that?" Angela asked, intrigued.

Nelle, reaching for three menus, directed the back of her hand toward Angela so that she could see PROVERBS 1:18 beautifully inked across it.

"Because a person lying in wait to for another's blood might be sealing their own fate," Nelle explained. Angela only needed to think about this for a minute before coming to the conclusion that Liam was worth that risk.

When she finished her coffee, Angela pulled a five from her wallet and tucked it under her empty cup. She grabbed a napkin and printed the word COMEUPPANCE on it then slid it near the edge of the counter where Nelle would be sure to see it. You didn't have to be an Old Testament kind of girl or even appreciate Milton to understand retribution. It was something Angela knew was dormant, a sleeping giant, in everyone's blood. In her case, it ran much deeper, down into the bone.

six

May Truelove was only a month old when the two strangers came knocking on Jeremiah's door. Before him stood a Crow County Sherriff by the name of Elijah Towns and his deputy whose name Jeremiah didn't catch due to the fact that his mind was still trying to grasp just how they'd come to know his wife, Grace. They even had a photograph of her. The hair was pulled back, the face more gaunt, but even from a distance, the eyes were unmistakable.

"So, you're looking for a woman by the name of Grace Wood?" Jeremiah asked, his stomach suddenly clutching. Grace was upstairs resting with baby May. What could they possibly want with her?

"No sir," the sheriff clarified. "We're looking for a woman *from* Gracewood, an asylum south of here. She escaped several months ago. Killed a man in the process. She's a mental defect, sir, and considered dangerous. A ward of the state. Has been since she was orphaned at thirteen. We'd just like to know if you've seen her around?"

The deputy again held up the black and white photograph. Jeremiah leaned in. His insides soured, and he tasted it in his mouth.

"May I?" he asked. He reached for the picture, pulling it closer to inspect it, but there really was no need. It was his Grace. No doubt about it. When he turned the photograph over, he saw the name, Emily Capeheart, age seventeen, written in black script across the back.

"Can't say that I have," he said, handing the photograph back, a knot forming in his stomach. "It's incredibly remote out here. Not many people passing through if you know what I mean. The mountain is difficult for even a man to navigate."

"Well, this is a determined young lady, Mr...?"

"Truelove. Jeremiah Truelove." He stretched out his hand.

"As I was saying, Mr. Truelove, she's very resolute in her actions, and—" A noise from upstairs caught Elijah's thought momentarily. He peered around Jeremiah. "You live alone, Mr. Truelove?"

"No, sir. My wife and infant daughter are upstairs resting. The baby's our first and she's been a little colicky." This was true. Grace's pregnancy had been difficult. She nearly died giving birth.

"To be expected, I suppose. How long you been married?"

Jeremiah tried not to let too much time pass in answering. He could feel beads of sweat forming on at his hairline and neck.

"Just about a year, sir." It had really only been six months but the *about* left him some room for a little soft dishonesty that the good Lord might overlook when the time came.

"Very well, then. We'll leave you to it. Good luck," Elijah said. Both men tipped their hats then turned away. Just as he reached the stairs, Elijah turned back around. "One more thing, Mr. Truelove. I should also warn you that the young woman in question might be in the hands of the devil. A witch, sir," he clarified in the event that he wasn't keen on subtlety. "Don't be fooled by her devastating beauty. I mean should she show up here."

Jeremiah nodded then watched until their horses disappeared from sight, grateful they didn't fall in one of the many mysterious holes he kept finding dug around the house. Moles or burrowing owls possibly. He couldn't say for sure.

Reaching for his handkerchief, he wiped the dampness from his forehead and neck, wondering how long Grace had been listening from the stairs.

Later that night when Jeremiah sat on the bed next to his wife, he found her eyes glossy and wide. She continued to focus intently on the ceiling. Her voice was weighted and weary.

"My real name *is* Emily Capeheart, and I did escape from the asylum, but as God is my witness, I never killed anyone," Grace confessed. "And I am by no means a witch."

Long minutes passed before she spoke again. "But I have something those men want. They'll be back," she whispered then closed her eyes but did not sleep.

seven

As far as lodging, the choices were limited. It was either, the rundown motel called the Southern Pines Angela had spotted it on her way in, or the space above the pizza place on the small downtown square. She'd noticed the *Room for Rent* sign in the window when she first arrived, and she hoped it wasn't an hourly kind of thing. Did they even have that sort of thing here? Her smartphone listed two other lodging possibilities. One, an Airbnb that didn't have any availability, and the other, a rent by the week fishing cabin on Ghost Lake, which was about five miles farther than she wanted to travel, and from the sound of it, a little too menacing. She'd overheard someone at the gas station saying the reason it was called Ghost Lake was because it was often so masked in fog, the actual lake wasn't visible. People had driven right into the water and disappeared. Regardless, she didn't need any more ghosts in her life. Besides, in order to keep an eye on what was going on with Levi Knox, she needed to stay close. Knox was not getting away this time. She'd see personally to that, but Angela couldn't help being haunted by Nelle's words about revenge. It was almost as if the girl had known—seen right through her, but that was impossible. They'd only just met. An interesting girl for sure, though. She looked a little young to be on her own even though it was clear she had an old soul. Angela wondered where she came from and who she was looking for here in Rayburn. Was it Hixson related? Not her business, but that didn't keep her from being curious. She was, after all, the daughter of a woman who had challenged any and every kind of puzzle in front of her and some that weren't.

The woman behind the counter at the pizza joint had thick salt and pepper hair cut short in a masculine style. She had the type of olive-toned skin that camouflaged aging, but her deep brown eyes told a different story.

Round but curvy, the woman was dressed in a black V-neck t-shirt and black jeans, both dusted in flour. She had a small gold cross around her neck and a name tag that read, Ronnie. Angela expected her to have an Italian accent and was only slightly disappointed when she responded in a drawl as soft and sweet as country butter.

"The owner will be back shortly," she told Angela. "Name's Joey. You can talk to him about the room," she added, sliding the gold cross back and forth across the delicate chain. Her nose was slightly crooked, and she had a chipped eye tooth, dark around the gum. When she saw Angela take notice, she pressed her lips together.

Angela thanked her, ordered a slice of pizza and a

beer and slid into one of the booths in the back of the small aromatic restaurant. The entire upstairs no doubt reeked of garlic, but it had to be better than the fishing cabin on the lake. She wouldn't have to be concerned about ghosts, and now she wouldn't have to worry about vampires either.

While she waited for the owner to return, Angela worked on the pizza. She watched the picketers outside passing in front of the door and coagulating on the courthouse steps before she remembered the section of newspaper the old man at the diner had kindly passed to her. She pulled it out of her laptop bag and dug into the dirty details of Dr. John Hixson who had over fifty plus years of experience performing illegal abortions on minors and selling babies that he claimed were stillborns. Hixson had a small office in Chattanooga before opening up his practice in Rayburn. He had one nurse for the duration of his career, but she moved to Rome, Georgia after she retired and declined to be interviewed by anyone.

The doctor retired a few years back at the age of seventy-nine after suffering a series of debilitating strokes and was now plagued by dementia. He'd been in a wheelchair for two years and Nelle was right. He probably couldn't remember how to pee. It was an ethical dilemma, similar to those her law professor had confronted the class with frequently. Should a person be charged for a crime they couldn't even remember committing? In this case, however, it appeared to be several crimes. Angela caught the faint scent of cigarettes and mint and looked up when she heard the waitress speak.

"Quite the story isn't it?" the woman noted. She laid a few napkins down on the table. Her nails were bitten back, the cuticles raw and ragged. "Especially for a little old place like Rayburn. Would you like another beer?" In the stray beam of light, Angela noticed the mist of soft hair above the woman's lip and guessed her to be between forty-five and fifty-five give or take a few years. She sensed something in the woman, a softness disguised as complacency that no doubt developed from a long, painful journey of some sort.

"That would be great."

The woman reached for the empty bottle. "You know, for all the terrible things Dr. Hixson may have done, he did help out a lot of desperate women for whatever it's worth. The media hasn't been very kind to him. I mean, I'm not sticking up for him." But she *was* in a way. Ronnie remembered how he handed out candy every year at Halloween and how he made house calls for people without cars. He even set little Jimmy Duke's arm when he broke it, knowing his mom had no money to pay for it, and besides the fact that he was a women's doctor. "But I understand why so many are angry with him. What he did was wrong. People feel lost and betrayed. They don't understand. He was the only hope for some women."

Angela felt for certain there was experience backing that statement. The woman carried a distraught desperate look like a caul over her face.

Ronnie continued. "I notice now there's even a Facebook page dedicated to finding the biological parents of Hixson babies. People from all over have come forward trying to locate the mothers they were taken from. I had a woman in here just yesterday. She spent thousands of dollars trying to find her blood mother. Had no idea she was even adopted until six or so months ago."

Ronnie wondered if her boy would ever come looking for her, but deep down inside, in the part of the soul that housed a maternal instinct, she knew there was no way he could. And she couldn't blame Hixson for this. It was her decision to give the boy up. All Hixson did was reassure her that it was the right thing to do. Ronnie had never told anyone about the finger even after hearing two women customers chatting quietly once about a judge's daughter in South Carolina who had also received a child's finger in the mail not too long after Ronnie's experience.

"The sad thing is that she was told her infant son died during birth," one of the women had said. "And because the whole thing was *hush hush*—you know, her father being a judge and all, she couldn't tell anyone about the finger she got in the mail. Can you believe that? In the mail? I think it was a ring finger. And that dreadful note about being an unwed sinner. Some religious nut, no doubt. I bet it was a Catholic. Bad enough she was raped by an unstable relative. The poor dear is still a wreck and it's been years. She has to take *psy*chiatric medication and everything." Her S's, slithered out, long and slow.

"Well bless her little heart. The finger couldn't have belonged to her child if it died, though, right?" the other woman quietly reassured her.

"That's just it. What if he lived and was adopted out? With all this Hixson mess coming to light, one has to wonder."

And Ronnie did wonder but she wasn't about to come forward now. It had been too long. What good would it do? Her guilt had just about eaten her to death. There wasn't a day she didn't think about what she'd done. And what she hadn't done. He'd be a man now if he were alive.

"Everything okay?" Angela asked when she noticed the woman's eyes drifting, focused on a boy of about six standing in one of the booths. He had pizza sauce all over his face and shirt. It looked like blood.

"Sorry. Yeah. Fine. My mind wanders sometimes. Too much going on in this world, I suppose."

"Did the woman you mentioned ever find her birth mother?"

Ronnie nodded. "She did. In the cemetery across the street. Unfortunately, it was too late. Her mother died last year. Cancer, I think. In sad irony, she's buried next to Mr. and Mrs. Truelove who spent many years searching for their missing children but passed on before ever finding them. In fact, they were never found. None of them. All five of those children gone without a trace. It's a mystery to this day as to what happened to them. Some people think it's happening again with the missing Rayburn children. Blood

Mountain is cursed, you know. From the Cherokees. People take that sort of thing seriously around here. Always have. Look at me going on," she said with derision in her tone. "Who would ever think that all this could happen in a city as small and nondescript as Rayburn?" She smiled wistfully. "It looks like Joey's back. I'll get you that beer."

A short barrel-chested man with a thick brown mustache made his way back to the booth. His Giants' baseball cap and Hawaiian button-down shirt gave Angela the impression that he might be in hiding either from the Mob or perhaps just good taste. In a thick Long Island accent, Joey explained to her that the room wasn't really suitable for the female persuasion though he'd had one there recently, and it hadn't gone well.

"The broad took off without paying me. She even left her shit behind. Clothes, toiletries, documents—you know, personal looking stuff. I think there's even a journal of some kind. Who does that? I mean, I expect it from a man but—a woman? They don't usually leave their belongings behind like that, you know what I'm saying. Anyhow, I'm holding it all hostage until she returns with what she owes me. I never would have pegged her for a skater, but now I gotta ask for payment upfront. You okay with dat, Mrs. Archer?"

Angela nodded. "Miss, but call me Angela and that's fine."

"Okay, Miss Angela, now you understand that it's nothin' fancy. Just a room with a twin bed, a dresser with four drawers, and a small bathroom. Shower. No tub. No refrigerator. No microwave or coffee pot. But it's clean and comes with bedding and towels. There's a laundry mat just up the street." He kept going. "Rents for $575 a month or $150 weekly, electric and water included. You can use the restaurant's Wi-Fi. The password's *pizzapie,* one word, all lowercase. You good with that?"

"Let's start with a week," Angela said digging cash from her wallet and sliding it across the table. "I'll need a receipt."

Joey returned with a handwritten receipt and the key for the room upstairs. "The entrance to the stairwell is just outside the front door to the right. You're in B, second door on the left, facing the square. The guy in A is okay but keep your distance from C and D. They have issues they're trying to work out and I don't need any trouble around here." He wrote his number on the receipt. "Here's my cell. Call me if you need anything, Miss Angela," he said. "Anything at all."

Angela thanked him and wondered what kinds of problems her new neighbors were trying to *work out* that warranted a word of caution. Prosecuting the sociopaths of the world was a whole lot different than rooming next to them. Too bad the garlic thing only worked on vampires.

eight

It didn't take long for the news to spread about Skyla. People were anxious to know where she'd been and how she made it back. They wanted to know the whereabouts of the other children and if she'd been with them. By the time Jack had reached Crow County Regional, a small curious crowd had already gathered in the hospital's waiting room. Security was working to calm them.

Because Camille was so distraught, Jack had called ahead to see if Skyla's primary doctor might be able to examine her discreetly. Dr. Tash had a special way with children though his were all grown. He'd been the one to save Skyla's life after the accident that took her father. Dr. Tash stayed late and prepared a room so Jack was able to whisk Skyla inside quickly, her mother and grandmother trailing close behind.

"Trust me," the doctor reassured them when he asked Jack, Camille, and Kitty to leave Skyla with him and the pediatric nurse on duty in the examining room. "Even though the law requires parents to be with minors, sometimes it's easier for children to talk to grownups who are no relation. Besides, Donna here has a way with children," he said looking over toward the nurse. "Lots of experience. She knows what she's doing."

"No," Camille whined. "I don't want to leave my baby. I just got her back."

"I know. It's difficult but necessary," Dr. Tash confirmed. "We have to discover what has happened to her so we know exactly how to help her. I promise not to take too long. We'll call you when we're ready for the physical exam part. You can hold her hand."

"Come on, Cami. Let's get some coffee," Jack said as he put his hand on his sister's shoulder. She reluctantly let loose of the grip she had on her daughter's hand and with Jack's help made her way toward the door. At the last minute, she ran back and embraced Skyla with both arms.

"Don't worry, Mommy. I'm not scared."

Camille tried to smile, her eyes pooling with tears. "I know, honey. You're my big brave girl. I've missed you. That's all. Just don't want to be away from you any longer."

"I missed...you...too, Mommy. A whole bunch. I'll be okay."

"We won't be long," the doctor reaffirmed. "She's going to be fine, Camille," he said lightly squeezing her upper arm. "I won't let her out of my sight."

"I'll make sure of that," the nurse chimed in to comfort her.

Camille took a deep breath, and Jack guided her out into the hall where she kept looking over her shoulder at her daughter. While Camille and Kitty settled into a couple of lobby chairs, Jack inquired at the nurses' station about the Cemetery Man.

"Gunshot in ICU? He's alive, but barely," one of the nurses relayed in a thick southern drawl. "Lost quite a bit of blood. I told your deputy the same thing just moments ago when he called." The woman had short curly hair and rosy round cheeks that gave her a cherub sort of appearance even though she had to be in her mid-thirties. "That's all I can tell you, honey. The doctor will be out soon. You can talk to her, but I'll warn you. She is not going to let you in to see him right now if that's your intention." She looked over her shoulder then whispered toward Jack. "Also, she has a problem with authority figures, if you know what I mean, but you didn't hear that from me." She winked and zipped her fingers across her lips.

Security had cleared most of the crowd from the waiting room. Two journalists were still hanging around. One from the AJC who took a brief statement and quickly departed after taking a phone call and the other—the only reporter the *Rayburn Star* employed who was also the managing editor and the ad sales director. Jack had gone to high school with Buddy McCay who had evolved over the years from an emaciated rail of a kid with thick black glasses and a greasy combover to a solid man with a full face, a tamed but wiry fro, and a forest of facial hair. Same type of big black oversized glasses though but at least now they were in style. Everyone loved Buddy. People always commented that he was too nice to be a reporter, and really, he was. He cared about stories, but he cared about people more, Jack felt.

In a plaid flannel shirt that exposed his doughy stomach between buttons, his faded jeans, and his signature chocolate brown Chippewa's, Buddy resembled a Seattle lumberjack. This made perfect sense, of course, because he'd graduated from U-Dub. Jack wasn't exactly sure why he hadn't sold the newspaper business he and his younger sister Tabby, inherited from their father. Tabby, who at thirty was still mapping out a route for herself by way of online courses offered through a local technical college, ran the front desk at the Star. *The Star's star receptionist*, Buddy had always said, smiling brightly either because he really meant it or because he was being completely facetious in that sibling kind of way. Jack couldn't tell which, but he'd always liked Buddy. Law enforcement and journalism weren't exactly ideal partners all the time, but there was an unspoken mutual respect between the two men and neither would say how it got there.

"Jack, I heard about Skyla. Great news!" Buddy offered genuinely as Jack fed his dollar into the vending machine.

"It is great news," Buddy. "We're happy to have her back." Jack caught the scent of licorice-flavored gum. Black

Jack was the only gum Buddy ever chewed for as long as Jack had known him.

"Is she okay? I mean..." He stumbled.

It was an uncomfortable subject for everyone. "We think so," Jack responded. The doctor's with her now." The machine dropped a cup then sputtered and spit out a black liquid that had the consistency of motor oil.

"I was here trying to get some info about the shooting by the church when Tabby called and said Skyla been found. Where'd you find her?"

"She found us, actually. Apparently, she just followed the scent of Pearl's lemon meringue pie."

"No, seriously. What happened?"

"I am being serious, Buddy. Pearl makes a damn good pie." He smiled coyly, then added. "Skyla showed up at the diner out of nowhere. Walked right in as if nothing had happened. I'm afraid that's all I have for you right now. I'll let you know more when I can." He pulled the coffee from the machine. The plastic door snapped back into place, catching the tip of the cup and sloshing hot coffee onto Jack's hand.

"So, any news about the others?"

Jack shook his head. "Nothing." He wiped his hand across his jeans.

"Well, I'm glad that she's okay. By okay, I mean, alive. Everyone's been worried."

"I appreciate that, Buddy. You want coffee?" Jack waved a single then sipped the sludge from the paper cup.

"Nah thanks. Stumptown turned me into a bit of a coffee snob, unfortunately. I had a couple Mountain Dews. Been here a minute trying to grab a lead on this shooting thing. Can you tell me anything about it? Deputy Wayne didn't know much. Rumor has it, it was the Cemetery Man—you know—the maintenance guy from the church, Tomb or Tombs. Somebody gunned him down just outside the front doors. Poor dude. I always felt kind of bad for him. He's in ICU now and they're not letting anyone in. One of the nurses my sister knows from her book club said that he may not make it. If he does, he probably won't be able to function on his own. For me, that's worse than death. Anyway, it's not looking good."

No, it certainly wasn't, Jack considered. He eyed his mother sitting in one of the lobby chairs, sipping her coffee and looking like the promotion's manager for some kind of ancient philosophical school of Stoicism. Camille sat next to her with her forehead cradled in one of her palms. She looked pale and uneasy and tired. So very tired.

"Yeah, I got the call at the same time we learned about Skyla. Haven't had a chance to look into it yet in all honesty. It's been a little hectic. I'll get on it first thing in the morning. Maybe he'll be coherent by then." If he's not dead, Jack thought, hoping to God he wouldn't be for Kitty's sake. Attempted murder was still a felony that would get her ten to twenty in Georgia. Half the time of actual murder but with Kitty's age, neither would allow her to see the light of day again. She'd die in prison. Not something he wanted to think about right now or ever, really.

"Gotcha," Buddy replied. "I'll catch up later with you then. Tomorrow?"

Jack nodded. "Yeah, tomorrow. Should know more by then."

"Good talking to you, Jack." He walked on toward the ER doors that slid open for him but then turned just before accepting their offer. "I'm really happy Skyla made it home," he said. "She's a good kid."

Jack was happy about this too, but it didn't mitigate the fact that Kelly Marsh was dead and three other children were still out there somewhere.

The doctor called Camille back, and after another cup of coffee, Jack walked outside to grab some fresh air. He checked in with Maggie, filled her in on the details. When he returned inside, he saw Dr. Tash walking with Skyla who was holding hands with her mother.

"She did just fine. In fact, I think she might be my best patient ever," the doctor said winking at Skyla. "Can I talk to the both of you, privately?"

Camille motioned Kitty over who took Skyla over to the vending machines for a drink and some chips.

Jack and Camille followed Dr. Tash down the hall in the direction of the nurses' station. He couldn't bear to think that Skyla might have been assaulted in some way. She was already so delicate from the accident, so heartbroken over the loss of her father. How much more could her frail little body take? As if Dr. Tash knew what

Jack was thinking, he spoke softly but with assurance.

"Let me just say right away because I know it's your main concern. Skyla does not appear to have been sexually assaulted in any way. In fact, she came right out and told me the only adult she had physical contact with the entire time she was a man named Tommy who appeared after the fairies."

"Yeah. She's really into fairies right now. But who's Tommy?"

The doctor shrugged. "No idea. Said he helped her get to the diner.

Jack didn't know anyone named, Tommy. At least not in Rayburn. "What about the other children? Hailey Martin, Ben Talbot, and Simon Lee? Did she mention them? Or maybe Kelly Marsh?"

"She told me that there were three other children in the place with her. Two boys, Ben and Simon and a girl Hailey, a close neighbor and *bestest*—her word, friend. No mention of Kelly."

"Did she say what place? Or how she got there?"

Dr. Tash shook his head. "She doesn't know where. She remembers only that it was a cold, damp room with strange overhead lights. The beds were narrow and on wheels. Sounds like a hospital surgery room to me, but we have to remember that her mind is still quite frail from the accident, Jack. Her memory is broken, but in my opinion, not irretrievably so. She might remember more in a few days. It's hard to say. Children are more resilient than we give them credit for. Regardless, we need to set up an appointment with the staff psychologist. She's the one Skyla saw after the accident. As you might remember, she specializes in child trauma cases and is one of the best in Georgia. Perhaps she can pull more from Skyla in a way that won't traumatize her further."

Jack cringed at this. Those children might not last that long. He had to find them and right now the way things were going with Levi Knox, Skyla was his only chance.

"She claims she and the others weren't mistreated in any way, which is more than I expected in this type of case. We should be grateful for that. They were fed and given blankets. They even had a few toys and books. And most importantly, as I mentioned, she wasn't sexually compromised, at least that we have surmised so far. This could be so much worse. Believe me, I've seen it."

"I know. I realize that. I just—I need to find the other children before it's too late. And I need Skyla's help to do that. I don't want to harm her in any way. I love her so much, but I need to ask her some questions."

"She's tough and incredibly smart as we both know," Dr. Tash clarified. "Just don't push her too hard. Even though she doesn't appear so, she is traumatized. And we both know she is still suffering in many ways from the accident. Give her a day or so. Once she has a good night's sleep, I have a feeling she'll remember more, which could be good or bad. I'm sure you understand. I'll put a rush on the lab results and let you know as soon as I hear something."

Before leaving, Jack again asked one of the nurses at the ER desk about the gunshot victim in ICU. She wasn't a nurse he recognized and neither was the doctor she motioned over. A tiny stout woman with cropped gray hair and glasses, she reminded Jack of Dr. Ruth Westheimer, who according to the biography he just read had once been a sniper for the Israeli Army.

Flipping through pages on her clipboard, she answered tersely. "No ID. Goes by the name of Tomb. Probably not going to make it and, no, you cannot see him. Law or no law, the man is in bad shape. We're still trying to locate family. Know of any?"

Jack shook his head. "Pastor Briggs might."

"We're waiting to hear back from him now. You can try again tomorrow if you like. No promises." Jack could have sworn he heard a slight German accent.

When he tried to ask another question, the doctor cut him short. "Have a nice evening, Sheriff." Her attempt at a smile was tight and drawn and looked almost painful.

nine

Angela was waiting outside Saturday morning when Jack arrived for work, a copy of the *Rayburn Star* tucked under his arm. He'd grabbed breakfast and coffee at the diner where he read the article about Skyla that Buddy had written. Not surprisingly, it was tasteful and terse and carried an empathy not usually held by journalists. Buddy was a good guy.

Jack had a full schedule today, which, without a doubt, and especially because of the front-page news about Skyla, involved returning emails and phone calls. People would have questions. Lots of them. Most he probably couldn't yet answer. His first call would be to the GBI. Because of the drug factor, they had become a part of the Knox investigation, and would no doubt be involving the FBI once the bones in the bag were identified as human. Drugs and serial killers didn't have jurisdictions or state borders when it came to the law. At least in the U.S. They might not take over the case, but they would certainly lead the investigation in an effort to secure federal charges.

Jack wasn't through with Knox. He had more questions for him. Knox was now being detained at the Fannin County Jail because Rayburn only had a small holding cell in the far back of the building, which got rare use. The questions for Knox would have to wait until Jack got proper clearance. The GBI basically had him on lockdown. Only counsel and agents could get in to see him. It'd be an interesting ride for certain, one he didn't have that much experience with. Nothing like this had ever fallen upon Rayburn before. His father would know exactly what to do if he was still alive.

The October mountain air was cool and thick. Ribbons of lavender light were breaking through the morning darkness otherwise Jack might not have noticed the woman on the bench.

"Good morning, Sheriff," Angela called as she stood and moved quickly toward him. "If it's any consolation, I never have weekends off either."

"Miss Archer. I had a feeling I'd be seeing you today. Not quite this early but..."

"Yeah. Sorry about that. Why is that by the way?"

Jack smiled coyly, fishing the keys out of his jacket pocket. "You just seem like the determined type."

"You say that like it's a bad thing."

"I believe I saw you at the diner yesterday. Did you follow me over there or just hear about Pearl's famous pies?"

"Guilty. I followed. Desperation trumps patience and

civility some times. I'm sure you understand. I'll look into the pie thing though." Without so much as a pause, she spoke again. 'It's really great news about Skyla. I didn't realize she was your niece. You and your family must be quite relieved." She tried to recall the number of times a living missing child was reunited with family.

"We are thrilled, however, and I'm sure you are already aware of this, there are three more of our children out there so we're not out of the woods yet, so to speak." He twisted the key and opened the door.

"Well, that's what I'm here to talk to you about. I don't think Levi Knox took those children. Or your niece for that matter."

"And why do you believe that?"

"If you give me just a few minutes, I'll tell you."

Jack pushed open the door and hit the lights. "Well, come on then," he said, motioning her to follow him before realizing she was right behind him. He felt the toe of her shoe tap the heel of his.

Maggie didn't normally work weekends unless necessary, but she'd probably stop by at some point to find out more details about Skyla. Any 9-1-1 calls were directed to Fannin County during her absence.

"Let me make some coffee." Jack led her down the hall to his office. The door was already open. He must have forgotten in all the commotion yesterday to lock it. "Make yourself comfortable. I'll be right in."

Angela could hear him rustling around and the water

running as she pulled out her laptop and the folders that were filled with headshots and crime scene photographs. They were the kind of images that were brand new each time you saw them. The shock never wore off. Tiny bodies, small hands missing fingers. She hoped that one day the gruesome detail that was kept from the public would help catch a child killer. No matter how much time had passed, the photographs still made her shiver, her insides churn.

"Sorry it's a bit chilly in here," Jack called down the hall. "It takes a minute for the heat to adjust in this old place. We used to be in a free-standing building just outside the square. The heat was better there but after the last tornado blew through, the building suffered too much water damage to continue to occupy. You take cream and sugar?"

"Cream, no sugar for me, please," she answered loudly.

"So, what makes you think Knox is innocent?" Jack asked as he walked into the office and set two coffee mugs on the edge of the desk. "Be careful, it's hot." He noticed his message light blinking on the phone.

Angela moved her files over out of the way. "I never said he was innocent. In fact, I believe he is guilty of many things. I just don't think he had anything to do with your niece or the other missing children. Thank you. This is good," she added, sipping the steaming coffee.

"And how is it that you came to this conclusion, Miss Archer?"

"Angela. I think I told you when we chatted briefly on

the phone a few days ago that my organization—"

"The Lost Foundation. I remember." Jack's desk phone rang. He let it go to voicemail. His cell rang shortly after and he silenced it too.

"Correct. I started the company while in law school in Philly after a neighbor's little boy, Liam Tate was abducted. And murdered."

"Penn?"

She nodded and continued, hoping he wouldn't delve any deeper into the subject. "We do our best to find missing people, mostly children and teens, though I have taken on a few adult cases in the past as well. It wasn't until I became an assistant DA that I learned of the man I now believe to be Levi Knox. A man responsible for Liam Tate's abduction, mutilation, and murder." She pushed a photograph across the desk. It was like shoving an anvil through thick sand. "Along with several other children across the eastern coastline."

"I remember. The Redeemer, right? The serial killer? Didn't they convict him years ago? I thought I remember reading that he'd died in prison."

Angela's voice hitched and nausea swirled in her stomach, making her feel like she'd swallowed curdled milk. "That was Danny Sherman. He was an innocent man, wrongly convicted. Beaten to death in prison." Her mouth tasted suddenly of rusted nails. "The Redeemer was actually never found. Then out of the blue and years later, I hear about Knox's arrest. The Bibles, the finger bones. They belong to children, don't they?"

"It appears so. Still awaiting the results. My deputy found the cooler in the trunk of the car Mr. Knox was driving. A small Igloo, it was dirty and wrapped in gray duct tape that was worn and frayed along the edges. It obviously hadn't been opened for some time. Inside was a quart-sized Ziploc bag of what the deputy believed to be human bone fragments that upon further examination appeared phalangeal and adolescent in nature. So, it's a good chance they belong to children. The Bibles I understand are how the Redeemer earned his name. He left them at the scene and the tabloid media ran with it, right? But I don't recall reading about finger bones? How are they relevant to the case?"

"The media glamorized the fact that a pocket Bible was left with the body of each child. They even reported on the passage highlighted inside. Psalm 51:5: *Behold, I was brought forth in iniquity, and in sin my mother conceived me.*" Angela still could recite it word for word as if the passage was in front of her, tattooed on the insides of her eyelids. "And yes, this is how he earned the name, the Redeemer. However, there was a detail purposely kept from the news as much as possible though it did leak. A graphic detail. Something out of a horror movie. Something law enforcement believed would eventually help them nab the psychopath killing these children and avoid copycats and attention seekers. This detail is also how I know that Knox didn't have anything to do with abducting your niece."

"And that is...?"

"Well, for one, she's alive. And, when I saw her at the diner, I noticed she had all her fingers. The ring finger of each of the Redeemer's victims was removed." Angela spread photos of dead children on the desk in front of Jack. "These are just a few. There are many more. Starting as far back as 1984 and stopping in 2014. This young man was taken in 2007." The photo of Liam made her throat tighten. She carried a smaller version of it in her wallet, an act of contrition that would have made any devout Catholic proud. "Liam's body was discovered by hikers near Lake Harmony in Pennsylvania. His ring finger was missing and a small red Bible was tucked in his jacket pocket with that same Psalm highlighted." It seemed so wrong, still. Liam's small bones and harmony in the same sentence. A cruel oxymoron. After his abduction, Angela saw Liam everywhere. In the bathroom mirror when she brushed her teeth, on the ceiling when she went to sleep, and on the merry-go-round, his freckled face a continuous loop of torment. Months after his abduction when she saw his image flash on the television screen, she had to rub her eyes. But that time, he really was there. They'd found his body, and that image would never leave her mind.

"His finger, the coroner speculated, had been removed after death. Quick and painless. Well that's a fucking relief, right?" She delicately touched Liam's photograph with the tips of her fingers. "Liam Tate's parents divorced a short time after his death. Mrs. Tate committed suicide two years ago because seven long years of suffering was enough. Does any of that sound quick and painless to you, Sheriff?"

Jack drew in a breath, held it there and blew it out slowly. This was a subject he wished never existed. Not in Rayburn. Not anywhere. "So, why the ring finger?"

"No idea. The ring finger aspect is obviously significant; we just don't know how. Likely, it has something to do with his idea of God or religion. Marriage. I don't know. Maybe it has nothing to do with anything, and he's just a psycho. The reports I've read—and believe me, I've read many of them over the years, indicate that we are dealing with someone who believes children are sinners." The note she received in the mail after Liam's death flashed in her mind and she pushed it back. "But as far as I know, most of the children came from loving homes with both parents present and relatively normal lives. No connections found. Seemingly random victims. It doesn't make sense. Sixty-three that we know of, dating back to 1984."

"Wow. Sixty-three innocent children. That's unbelievable."

"Yes, over a period of thirty years. That's a long stretch. Sometimes only one child a year, other times two or three. Some years, no children at all."

"These children, were they... Jack had a hard time even saying the words. Sexually assaulted?"

"No. Not one of them. This isn't a pedophile we're dealing with. Sexual gratification is not his motive."

Jack studied the photos spread before him. He didn't see any ligature marks or wounds other than the obvious. But he did notice the contorted shapes of the bodies. "What about cause of death?"

She opened a file folder. "Technically, suffocation. You see how the bodies are arched, locked in a rigid position? It's called opisthotonus and is caused by poison, mainly strychnine, which isn't hard to obtain really. Hair analysis determined trace levels of it in each case, and there's a slim chance you may find levels of it in the finger bones, but after a certain amount of time, this becomes almost impossible to detect. I mean, it's odorless and tasteless so it could have been easily administered orally without notice. A laced milkshake or cookie." Angela slid the folder with copies of the coroner's report across the desk to Jack. "You're welcome to have a look."

Jack opened the folder but just couldn't get his mind around the idea. "So you're saying that because my niece is alive, that Knox didn't take her? What about the other children?"

"I'm saying that because I counted five fingers on each of your niece's hands and that the others haven't already been discovered, dead and dismembered, their bones laced with poison, Levi Knox is not your man. He's mine. He didn't abduct your niece or the other children. You have to trust me on this. The girl recently found dead. Marsh, right? How'd she die? I'm telling you, it's not him. Besides his MO has always been children not teenagers.

Most likely because children are easier to manipulate. They make better victims. Besides, you ever try to make a teenager do something? It's impossible. Whatever it is, he feels he's saving them, I guess. I don't know."

"Saving them from what?"

"That's what we need to find out."

Jack understood that sometimes it was easier to catch a perpetrator by first identifying motive, but if Knox didn't take the children, why was he here in Rayburn? Criminal psychology was not Jack's specialty. A handful of classes in college did not make him any kind of expert on the subject. Until now, it had never been necessary when it came to Rayburn's small-town crimes. He preferred it that way.

"So, next question: Did you find strychnine in the trunk of that car, Sherriff?"

"You know I can't legally tell you that even if I knew. But off the record, the suitcase with the Bibles contained several old prescription bottles, all empty, with traces of a white powdery substance. Could be strychnine. He was also carrying on his person some type of capsules in his pocket. It all went to forensics."

"What about the last few years?" she interjected. "Where's he been? What's he been doing?"

"Other than a few unpaid parking tickets and a drunk and disorderly in college, his record is spotless before this arrest. Can't find a damn thing. I've got Maggie, my assistant, working on finding out more, but I'll be honest with you, I'm still not convinced that Levi Knox isn't responsible for the disappearance of Hailey, Ben, and Simon, who are at this time, still missing. It just seems too much of a coincidence."

Angela was shaking her head. "Never a fan of coincidences myself, but he didn't take those children. They would have been discovered by now. And not alive. Look, I know this is difficult to digest, but I've been searching for this evil prick for a long time. An innocent man was sentenced to death because of him." *And because of me,* she thought. Sherman, the loner who'd been arrested several different times on charges ranging from petty theft to peeping Tom, had always maintained his innocence even though Liam's blue windbreaker had been found in his basement. He'd been telling the truth and no one, including her, had believed him.

"These murdered children deserve justice and so do their parents," Angela continued. "If Levi Knox is the Redeemer, which I believe he is, I'd like to see him extradited to Pennsylvania and tried for murder there. Law enforcement and or the FBI will have to be involved, so I'll need your help to make that happen." She had no real intention of letting the bastard live long enough to make it to Pennsylvania, but Jack didn't need to know that. No one needed to know that.

"Why Pennsylvania? You know, Georgia is a death penalty state, too, if that's what you're aiming at." Sounded personal to Jack.

She had amends to make. Denny Sherman's parents were still alive. She owed them. Liam's father was still alive. She owed him, too. She had made a promise to the Tates after Liam disappeared that she would find out who killed him. They despised her regardless. Had she been paying attention, they said, he wouldn't have been snatched in the first place. They were right. It was only Mr. Tate left now, and he'd moved out of state. At one time she had visions of a front-row seat to Knox's execution, of gaining her dignity and reputation back. Making people believe in her again. Even maybe believe in herself. But these idealistic scenarios were no longer her goal. She'd lost faith in the justice system. There was no denying it. She hadn't come to Rayburn to ensure Knox faced charges in Philly. She'd come to kill him. And that's what she was going to do no matter how many strings she had to pull. "Because that's where I feel the most justice would be served," she lied.

Jack stroked his fingers over his chin then sipped his coffee. He never had been one to detect deceit in people's eyes, but he could feel it in other ways. A slight vibration lifted the hairs on the back of his neck almost canine-like. He ran his hand there along the underside of his shirt collar, tucked his tag back inside. Where he got this sixth sense, he had no idea. If he had to guess, he'd say his father. It certainly wasn't Kitty. Regardless, this woman was not being totally truthful. She was up to something. Through the small window in his office, he watched the dark clouds spill across the sky like bleeding ink. A storm was brewing, and the eye of it was sitting right in front of him. Joe would have called it an omen had he been there. *Watch out son,* he would have said. *It's coming. Moving fast and hard. Be ready.*"

"Well, because of the human remains found with Knox, I had to inform the GBI. And the FBI can't be too far behind especially if they've made the same connection you have, which means my access to Knox is becoming more and more limited. Though I plan on being fully involved in the proceedings, once it goes from state to federal, I'll be completely out of the picture. A mere bystander."

"Look. I'll do whatever I can to help you find the other children," Angela pleaded. "I have lots of experience with this. I can offer a great deal. I just need to confirm that Knox is the Redeemer, and we can go from there." How she was going to go about this, she had no idea, but the first step was making sure this was the man who killed Liam. Once that was established, she'd figure out how to take him out.

Jack knew that the longer an abducted child stayed missing, the slimmer the chances were of finding that child alive. But Skyla had given him hope. Maybe the others were alive, too. They just had to be. "What do you want from me?"

"I need to see him."

"Absolutely not. Besides, I don't have that kind of pull, lady. There is no way that's going to fly. I'm still waiting for my turn to have another go at him." Jack cringed remembering the bruises on the man's body. He had tried to explain to the lead investigator with the GBI that not all of them were from him. Deputy Wayne noticed quite a few bloody tissues in the car. Knox had obviously got into some kind of scuffle before he was arrested. "Only counsel is allowed visitation right now. And as far as I know, he has none at the moment."

"I just need thirty minutes, maybe even less."

Jack kept shaking his head from side to side. "Out of the question."

"Okay, what about Skype? Plenty of states do this now. I could sit in."

"What you're asking is impossible. This is Crow County, Georgia. We are light years behind the technology required to do that." As he said this, he was sure Maggie had mentioned something about Skype when she got the new computer set up in the digitally comprehensive office. "Besides you know how it works. Prisoners, even the worst of serial killers, have rights. Georgia nabbed him so they get him first. He'll be tried and sentenced here if they find reason. Philly may not even get a chance until he's old and gray—and that's if he even makes it out of the system. Child killers don't fare well on the inside. As I'm sure you already know. If indeed he is a child killer."

Angela did know, but she didn't want to know. Not a day passed that she didn't hate herself for the mistake she'd made. Denny Sherman was an innocent man in the wrong place at the wrong time. Just like Liam and the other children, he'd been a victim. She'd seen to that.

"Of course, if they don't charge him, you may have a window of opportunity," Jack offered. "But unless the State of Pennsylvania came for him or claimed him, he'd be a free man. It's out of our control."

"A window of opportunity? I don't particularly care for that phrase. It implies some sort of light. This is not a situation I feel that should be bestowed opportunity and hope. Because hope is not a word I think of when I think of all those dead, dismembered children. And how the hell would this animal not be charged anyway? He's a psycho carrying around a suitcase full of Bibles and a pack of children's finger bones like Christmas ornaments for fuck's sake. I assure you. He's guilty."

"Well, we don't know the entire story yet." The desk phone rang again. Jack pressed the volume button until no bars showed on the screen but not before seeing Camille's number populate.

"Sheriff, you don't understand. This man is a ruthless, conniving child killer, for the love of Jesus. That's a phrase, ya'll understand down here in the South, right?" The bitterness in her tone had not been planned. She wanted to apologize but couldn't. The horrific images of those children would be forever ingrained in her mind. In her soul. Tattooed beneath the skin and only visible to her. The memory of the note came back then. And this time she couldn't push it away. It arrived a week after Sherman's death.

I promise you, counselor, I really do exist. The road to salvation is paved with the blood of sinners. Maybe one day, you will come to understand as I have that forgiveness is the best revenge.

It wasn't signed, but the accompanying photograph of her and Liam in the park the day he disappeared let Angela know just who'd sent it. The same man she convinced the jury only existed in the mind of Denny Sherman. She wished she would have kept the note, but she was so torn up about it, so riddled with guilt, and burning with anger that she ripped it into tiny pieces.

"Strychnine isn't illegal and whether or not the Bibles and or...bones," Jack added with latent care, "belong to Mr. Knox, must be proven. That's the law, Miss Arch- Angela. He could say that he stole the vehicle not realizing its contents. You already know this."

"Don't you dare play that devil's advocate bullshit with me. The man is deranged. A sociopath, a psychopath, and a litany of other *paths*."

"The man you are looking for may be, yes, but we can't even be sure they are the same person. Knox might not be this Redeemer. Are you going to be able to tell just by seeing him that he's your guy? Appearances change. How long has it been?"

Angela sipped her coffee and set the cup back down on the desk. "Until the AJC newspaper headline, I'd never actually seen him so what he looks like now is irrelevant."

Jack felt his jaw go slack. "Let me get this straight.

You are ready to convict a man of these horrendous charges and you can't even positively ID him? No composite drawing? No witness testimony? No DNA or fingerprints. Strictly intuition then? Unbelievable."

Clearly, this woman had the same blind faith his mother was cursed with. "Though I will admit, I've relied on my own from time to time, intuition doesn't hold up in court. But you already know that. The law doesn't allow us to condemn a man because you know intuitively, he's guilty. I'm sorry but that's just how it is. I shouldn't have to explain this to you. I admire your passion. I really do. But we both know what a double-edged sword it is in regards to the legal system. We need it to perform our jobs, but it can be a handicap when it comes to reasonable doubt. We can't let our own feelings get in the way of the law." An image of him slamming Knox against the wall with his hands around his neck tumbled in his mind and made him feel hypocritical in the worst way, but this woman had fire in her eyes. She was trouble and no matter how attractive he found her, he wasn't about to share his embarrassing unethical tactics with her.

Angela crossed her arms and sat back in the chair. "I've waited a long time for this man, and as I said, I'm not leaving here without him."

"You don't think I want to catch the bastard just as much? Until yesterday, I thought I might never see my niece again. And there are still three missing children I can't find." He eyed Skyla's locket resting on the desk next to his mother's Bible, noticing only then that Kitty's gun was gone. Had she grabbed it and put it back in her purse? He ran out of the office so quickly yesterday, he hadn't even locked his door. Now that he thought about it, he wasn't even sure he closed it. Jack started casually opening the desk drawers in hopes that he had involuntarily slid the gun in one of them on the way out. Things look disheveled in the drawer directly under his keyboard but no sign of the gun. What the hell had happened to it? Maybe Maggie grabbed it. Locked it up. She must have.

"I understand that, but the person who took your niece and the other children is still out there. You're wasting your time if you think Knox is going to be able to tell you where they are. He doesn't know. Because he didn't take them."

Jack's cell started vibrating, and he could see Camille's number again. "Look, I have to grab this. Give me a call later. I'll do what I can but understand that my hands are tied."

"I bet theirs were, too," Angela said in a tone sharp enough to cut paper. She began collecting the photos, shoving them in her bag. "Thanks for your time, Sherriff Towns," she added curtly as she picked up her purse and dug through it. She set her card on the desk. "I'm staying in one of the rooms over the pizza joint for now. Should your conscious start to bother you."

"Camille," Jack answered, pulling the card toward him. "Sorry about that." He watched Angela sling her bag over her shoulder and head out of the office. "What's going on? Okay. Try and calm down. Just take a deep breath. I'll be right there."

Jack swiped the locket off the desk and followed Angela out.

"Hey," he called as he ran to catch up with her.

She stopped and turned, and Jack could swear he felt the heat from her anger fill the hall. It was the warmest the building had been in some time.

"There is one way you can guarantee you'll be granted a visit with Knox."

"I'm listening," she said.

"You can represent him. You know, with the help of a Georgia attorney—what's it called?"

She turned quickly on her heel. "Pro hac vice," she snapped then turned without looking back. "It's Latin for *no way in hell*," she called. This man was out of his mind. Even if she was in good standing with the Pennsylvania Bar, there was no way she'd even consider representing the man responsible for Liam's abduction and murder and all that guilt that accompanied it. She'd rather die first. And the way things were looking as far as time was concerned, she just might.

"The first appearance was Friday. A public defender has been appointed, but I heard the poor dude was in a car accident yesterday and is going to be laid up in the hospital with a broken pelvis for six months. You still have time before the preliminary," he beckoned, as she continued on ahead of him. "He'll need representation."

Angela increased her pace and threw a middle finger up over her shoulder without bothering to turn around.

Just as he thought. Full of fire. Even if he didn't want to admit it, she reminded him of Lisa in some odd way. Probably the fire part. Jack was still chuckling over her reaction as he tucked the locket in his jeans and headed over to the cemetery, a block off the square. Above him, the sky was black glass.

ten

"I'm not sure," Camille said to Jack as he stood next to her over a freshly dug grave with a mound of dirt on one side. "It's more than a little disconcerting though, don't you think?"

As far as Jack could tell when he hesitantly peered down into the hole, it was still unoccupied. He was grateful for this. He thought of Kelly Marsh's perfectly preserved body the day he found it. Her clothing dirty and torn, her eyes and mouth caked in mud as if she'd once been buried. And dug up.

"We were on our way to see you. Skyla wanted her locket, and out of nowhere, she shouted for me to stop when we passed by the cemetery. She said she remembered something. She wants so desperately to help find the other children. It's all she talked about last night."

He walked over to his niece and squatted down so that their eyes were level. "Skyla, honey. What's going on?"

"Hi, Uncle Jack. The doctor said that if I...If I remember anything, I should let you know," she took a breath, "right away."

"And you think you remember the cemetery? This grave?" Jack asked.

"No, not the cemetery or the grave. Not really. The dirt. I remember the dirt. It fell on me. Got in my hair and eyes and mouth. It tasted yucky."

Jack cringed at the thought that someone might have been trying to bury her alive. Is that what happened to Kelly? He couldn't help of think of the Cemetery Man. Maybe his mother had been right. "Honey, do you remember how you got to the diner yesterday?"

Skyla shook her head, confused. "No, Uncle Jack. I sort of just walked by the church and then crossed the street. I saw Miss Pearl through the glass windows of the diner. She's a real nice lady. She was the first person I recognized, which is why I went inside. She makes good pie. I remembered that."

"Yes, she does. Did you see any other people along the way?"

Skyla's brows knitted. She remained quiet, biting at her bottom lip as she tried desperately to recall. "I'm not sure. Maybe. You mean after Tommy?"

"Tommy? Skyla, who's Tommy?" Jack asked.

"I don't know who he is, Uncle Jack. I've never seen him before. He's real nice though."

"Well, where's he from?"

Skyla shrugged looking helpless. "I don't know. He came after the fairies disappeared."

"I see. Skyla honey, where were you? Please try to remember. It's important."

"I don't know, Uncle Jack." Her voice cracked.

Camille mouthed the word, *enough.* Jack nodded, feeling like a heel pressing his niece so hard.

"It's okay, Skyla," Camille comforted her. You remembered something. That's what's important. The rest will come when it's ready," she assured her as she slid a hand down the child's silky pale hair. "You're doing very well."

Camille zipped up her daughter's jacket, pulled the hood from behind and secured it over her head. The heavy air was moist and peaty, the sky full with the promise of rain.

"Why didn't you come save us, Uncle Jack? I made paper bird notes for you and slid them under the door, but you never came."

"The origami birds I showed you how to make?"

She nodded proudly. "Yes, just like you showed me. I thought they would fly to you and tell you where we were. And that you'd come. But you never did."

"Well, maybe they got lost or flew in another direction, honey. We'll make more, one day soon, okay?"

"Will they lead you to my friends? They're scared. And Simon has a bad cough. He threw up a couple of times in the bathroom. He's always sick at school."

"There was a bathroom in the room where you were kept?" Jack asked, a little surprised. He immediately thought of the Old Mountain Arts Hotel. It had once been a place for lodgers, and some of the rooms were still intact, but he'd checked the whole place himself.

Skyla nodded. "Yeah, but it was real dirty. Stinky too. The toilet flushed at first but then stopped. It was filled with poo and gunk. You have to get them out, Uncle Jack. You have to find them so they don't die."

"I'm going to find them, Skyla. I promise. No one is going to die." As soon as Jack said it, he regretted it. Somebody already had died, but Skyla didn't need to know that. Jack wasn't a quitter by any means, but even if he did find Simon, Ben, and Hailey, he couldn't guarantee they'd be alive. "Now what else can you tell me about *the place?* Do you remember how you got there?"

"I went outside to play before dinner. Mommy told me to stay close because we'd be eating soon. But I didn't listen. I'm a bad girl for not listening. I went into the woods—you know, to the orchard—to see if I could see the Fire Bride. The kids at school think she's a real live witch. We play there all the time, but I promise we never go into the hollow. That day, when everyone headed home for dinner, I should have, too, but then I got distracted."

"Distracted? By someone? A person you recognized from school or the neighborhood?"

"No. Not a person. An apple, Uncle Jack. The only one hanging on the tree. Most of the others were on the ground, rot...ten and gross with worms. But this one... was so beautiful. I'd never seen an apple that red before. When I reached for it, someone lifted me up...from...behind." She took a breath. "I thought they were trying to help me get the apple. Instead, they put a stinky rag over my nose and mouth. When I woke up, I was in the place. All by myself with a basket of apples next to me. I was so hungry I ate three. They made me tired and I went back to sleep. That's mostly what we did there. Eat the apples and sleep. Just like Snow White."

Just like Snow White. This was no Disney fairytale Jack knew. "Honey, are you sure you were all alone? There was no one else with you? Kelly Marsh wasn't there?"

"I don't know who that is, Uncle Jack."

"Sure, you do. She used to babysit you. Before the accident."

Skyla's face contorted in pain. "The one where daddy went to Heaven?"

"That's right, sweetheart."

"I don't remember. I think I was the only one there until Ben came. And then Hailey and later Simon. There were a few toys and some books, but it was hard to read because there wasn't much light. Sometimes we got peanut butter and jelly sandwiches but mostly we ate apples. I never saw the Kelly girl."

Once again, the memory of Kelly's body lying on the ground at the edge of the orchard, punched Jack hard in the face. Those milky eyes locked open in a death stare and packed with dirt. He recalled the dark bruising around her neck, and Jack's first thought was that someone had strangled her. Then buried her. Or maybe she'd been buried alive. Then for some reason dug up. The rain had likely washed away any trace evidence, but Jack took that route regularly and knew she wasn't there the day before. Someone had stolen her life, and Jack wanted to know who and most importantly, why. Her death had triggered other tragic events, one of which included the girl's mother losing her job at the gas station because she was so full of grief that she could not pull herself out of bed. Then she was evicted from the duplex she'd rented for years and now had a room at the Pines, Rayburn's only motel. Jack was almost positive that she'd started using again. He'd seen the marks on her arm, the hollowness in her eyes. Kelly had been her only child. The one thing that kept her fighting. The toxicology report was taking too damn long. The closest coroner was in Fannin County, and she had to be three years older than God.

Skyla took in a breath then blew it out. It was much too heavy for one belonging to a child. Her eyes were glossed, but she fought back the tears. She was brave, and he wanted to tell her it was okay to cry, but instead, Jack reached in his pocket and pulled out her locket. "I bet this will make you feel better," he said, dangling the necklace in front of her before securing it around her neck.

"My locket," she squealed then immediately opened it to check for her father's photograph inside. "Thank you, Uncle Jack. I thought it was gone forever."

A drumbeat of thunder hit the sky, followed by a few

faint but cold drops of rain. "Come on, let's go get a chocolate milkshake," Jack said grabbing Skyla's hand and quickly walking in the direction of the diner as the sky continued to darken. Camille grabbed Skyla's other hand though it was clear from her expression that she didn't think ice cream was any way appropriate for her daughter or anyone else this early in the morning.

As the trio walked in the direction of the diner, the sky became even more distended, the rain heavier and faster. It was then that Jack noticed someone standing in front of one of the markers on Strangers' Row. It caught him off guard because those graves were unmarked and never had visitors. The decedents in this area of the cemetery had never been identified. Some of the markers dated back to the early 1900s.

The woman remained motionless in front of the tombstone marked with the year, 1987. It was the last of these types of deaths in Rayburn. No one had been buried in Strangers' Row since, thankfully. Jack recalled seeing flowers on it last May around Mother's Day. Found it rather odd but not alarming. He remembered something else strange just then. While moving the office to the new location, he'd come across the victim's records. Young Jane Doe. Died in an explosion of some sort. She was so badly burned, she couldn't be identified. Enclosed in the file was also an order form for a coffin and a tombstone. According to the accompanying receipt, both had been paid for by his father, Joe. He was always doing nice things like that for people so it wasn't that out of the ordinary.

In front of the headstone, the woman stood immobilized. She had a jacket draped over her arm, but Jack didn't see an umbrella. He wanted to warn her that she should seek shelter because she was about to be soaked, but more than that he was curious.

"Take Skyla on over to the diner. I'll be there in a minute," he told Camille. "Hurry, it's going to pour."

He was about to call out to the woman when he realized it was Angela Archer. "Everything all right over there, Miss Archer?"

Angela didn't answer. She just kept staring at the tombstone, so distracted she didn't seem to hear him or even acknowledge that she wasn't alone. A bolt of lightning as sharp as an ax split open the sky, and rain poured down upon them. Jack grabbed Angela's arm and pulled her toward the church for cover. They were dripping wet by the time they managed to open the door and dart inside to the vestibule.

"Why does that gravestone not have a name on it? In fact, none of the white crosses behind it have names either," Angela said as they both wiped the rain off their faces with their sleeves. The cold water must have snapped her out of the trance she'd been in. She wiped at her eyes and came away with black smears on her fingers, making a side note to invest in better mascara. Something waterproof.

"It's called, Strangers' Row. Many cemeteries,

especially the more historical ones, have a row devoted to the unidentified."

"So, no family ever came forward for these people?"

"I guess not. This is why the grave markers only list the month and year of their death. They are the nameless dead."

"Well, how'd these people die? You know?"

"Different ways. Some naturally. Some in accidents. At least one unexplained death and maybe a few by the hands of others."

"You mean murdered?"

"Possibly. Likely, really."

"So, it's basically a row of buried cold cases."

"You could say that."

"The stone with SR-0587 on it...that would be May of 1987?" It was the year of her birth, and she'd already mentioned she didn't like coincidences. Angela didn't wait for an answer. "Do you know anything about the person buried there?" Fodere. Dig, she recalled. Her mother was trying to tell her something. But what?

"No. I was just a boy, but I think she was a young woman who died in a fire of some sort. I remember that from the records. We may still have them. Most were moved to an offsite storage facility due to lack of room at the new place. Some of them were destroyed completely. My father, the sheriff before me, was working on getting the records digitally transferred but it didn't happen...in time," Jack added latently, his words trailing off. "His death was rather unexpected. I can tell you that I've seen flowers on that particular grave before. I guess there are still some nice people left in the world." Or maybe just a person with a secret Jack considered. He knew at least one person who harbored more than a few in this town. "Can I ask why you're so interested?"

Before she could answer, Pastor Briggs made a mad dash through the vestibule toward the double wooden doors. His faded blue Lynyrd Skynyrd t-shirt was shrouded in a gray cardigan with elbow patches and pockets. He wore black dress pants and cracked leather cowboy boots as red as the blood of a martyr. The pink umbrella at his side glittered in the church's golden light. A paperback book was wedged under his arm.

An interesting man, the pastor. Mid-fifties. Straight. Divorced but dating. Two children, both married with kids of their own. He swore to Jack that his calling came while he was smack dab in the middle of a line dance one night at the Blue Stallion, a notoriously famous country gay bar that closed down some years ago after the bikers moved in and took over the jukebox.

"Hey," Jack called. "Where's the fire?" Not the best choice of words in a church, he acknowledged a little too late.

"Sheriff," the pastor reached to hug Jack. "More like the deluge. So grateful to hear about Skyla. Regardless of what people think, prayer circles work even if they're conducted in the middle of a line dance. You just afraid of melting or did you come by to tell me the good news about my caretaker?"

"He pulled through then? They said last night that he might not make it." Jack momentarily envisioned his mother flipping off the judge after hearing the guilty verdict and her sentencing.

"He did pull through. The hospital called a few minutes ago. He's out of the coma. The hand of God, I tell you. First Skyla and now Tomb. Both miracles. I didn't even know he'd been shot until I got back from my sister's late last night and got the message to call the ER after one of the nurses recognized him. Can't figure out who would want to harm such a gentle soul. There sure are a lot of unexplained things happening in Rayburn right now. Poor Janet Marsh," he said shaking his head. "I'm Pastor Ross" he extended his hand to Angela and she took it.

"Angela Archer."

The pastor raised a brow towards Jack and did his best to hide his smile.

"I was up at the hospital most of last night," Jack spoke up. "But he was still unresponsive. They were actually trying to figure out Tomb's legal name. He does have one, right?" Jack felt bad having to ask this. Rayburn was too small not to know the first and last names of each and every resident. There weren't that many and none quite as eccentric as the caretaker.

"Well, I wouldn't know, Sheriff. He doesn't talk. Never has to my knowledge. Let's just say communication isn't his best skill. I leave him detailed notes all the time though and the work gets done so I know he can read. He can write, too. Prints like a 5th grader but it's legible." He reached for the copy of *Frankenstein* he'd tucked under his arm. "This is his favorite book. Thought I'd bring it by for him. You know Tomb just showed up here as a boy out of the blue years ago. Pastor Nelson took him under his wing, and when I started, I sorted of inherited Tomb. The pastor asked me as a personal favor to look after him on account of his *condition* for lack of a more PC word. He's been with me ever since, but he has never spoken a single word. I do know that he's not deaf and has no problem understanding. And that he can read and write. I call him Tomb for the same reason everyone else does. It's on his arm. Shoddy work. Looks like a prison tattoo that might have once been infected, but I guess we'll never know for sure. I'm just glad he pulled through. I may be all he has besides," he motioned up with his umbrella, pink and glittery, "you know." A few specks of glitter twinkled in the air. Jack eyed the white unicorn peeking through the folds. The pastor noticed his curiosity. "It's my granddaughter's. A real man embraces his feminine side," he said securely.

"Of course," Jack conceded. He realized then that he had never been close enough to the Cemetery Man to take detailed notice of the tattoo on his arm. He had seen him mainly from a distance, and he was always wearing work gloves. Jack had been too preoccupied at his father Joe's service last month to pay much attention when Tomb used a shovel to cover the coffin with dirt. Joe had fallen from one of the rocky cliffs on Blood Mountain, landing on Devil's Backbone below. Hit his head on a rock and died instantly. He had recently stopped drinking so alcohol wasn't a factor. Hard to believe it had only been thirty days since his death. That's how life was sometimes, which is why Jack didn't worry too much about his daily gas station fare and coffee consumption. You couldn't plan for death any more than you could plan for a lover deserting you, a child being abducted, or a bag of fingers being discovered in the trunk of a car.

"So, he has never showed you an ID of any kind? Who do you make his paycheck out to?"

"There is no check, Sheriff. Tomb and I have an unspoken agreement. He works for room and board, which means he always has food and shelter and free line dancing lessons if he wants them. I've never given him one dime and don't even think about reporting me to the IRS or DOL or whatever. I won't hesitate to recommend the good Lord put a plague on your ass," the pastor said, winking at Jack before opening the door and hurrying out into the rain.

"Gotta run. Headed over to see Tomb. Nice meeting you, Angela," he called over his shoulder while launching his tiny pink umbrella, an action that sent a spray of glitter catapulting through the wet air and onto the pavement behind him.

eleven

Pastor Briggs was helping the caretaker sip water from a small clear cup when Jack found the room. He'd been given strict instructions from the nurse that the patient, though strong enough to be moved from ICU, was still not out of danger and was not to be harassed, questioned or upset in any way.

"Straight from the doctor's mouth," the nurse continued.

"Understood," he reassured her.

Jack couldn't tell if the man's eyes grew momentarily large at the sight of him because he knew that it was Jack's mother who'd shot him or if he was just in fear of the star-shaped patch on his shirt, which often had that effect on folks. Either way, he looked small and terrified. Jack nodded in his direction to try and comfort him then moved next to the pastor, who was seated by the bed and now replacing the clear plastic oxygen cup back over the man's mouth. There were several machines scattered about, each with their own noise, a choir of distinctive beeps and sighs.

"How's he doing?" One of the machines picked up speed at the sound of Jack's voice.

"As well as can be expected, I guess. The bullet would have hit his heart had it been where it's supposed to be. Whoever shot him knew what they were doing. What they didn't know, and what I just found out myself, is that Tomb's heart is on the other side of his chest. Which is why he's still with us. Isn't that right, Tomb?"

"Well, I'll be damned," Jack said. "Never heard of such a thing."

"According to the doctor—she was checking his bandage when I arrived, Tomb suffers from a congenital condition called *situs* something or other. Means your organs are reversed. She said it affects about one in ten thousand people and often goes undetected unless...well, I guess unless you get blasted in the chest." He held up his palms toward Tomb but turned away when an amorphous red stain soaked through the bandage on his chest.

"I'm surprised she gave you so much info. HIPAA and all."

"Dr. Kohl? We sort of have a past."

"Pastor, I'm not even sure I want to know what you're talking about."

"Don't be ridiculous. I'm not her type if you know what I mean. A line-dancing past, silly. She took lessons from me for two years when we were both regulars at the Stallion. You know she owns a motorcycle, right? A big one. And a shit ton of cats. Do I need to add anything else for clarity?"

Jack pulled a chair next to the pastor. "You know entirely too much about this town, Briggs. What else can you tell me about him?" He nodded in the direction of the caretaker who stirred at the sound of Jack's question. He opened his eyes and slowly closed them again. They looked small and distant in their effort to focus.

"Not much more than I've already told you. What else do you want to know?"

"For starters, I'd like to find out where your caretaker was yesterday morning. Just before noon."

"You mean before he was shot? Why?"

Because Jack wanted to know why he had Skyla's locket and where he got it from. "I have my reasons."

"Well, I assume he was using the backhoe to prepare Mrs. Birch's grave. She passed you know. Bless her heart. Ninety-six years old and worked at the library up until last month."

"What about the day and night before?"

"That I can't help you with. I was in Dalton at my sister's for dinner. No cell service. Had too much wine and stayed the night. Didn't hear what happened until Tomb was already here at the hospital. Do you think this was some random shooting or was he a target, and if so why? Who would want to hurt him? I mean he's...a lonely, broken soul with no family or friends," the pastor whispered. "He can't possibly have any enemies."

Definitely not random, Jack wanted to say but didn't.

Might be easier in this case if it had been. It would have to come out eventually though. He knew this. Just not yet. "One thing I've learned in my forty some years is that everyone has enemies, Pastor. Even you and I."

The pastor's cell phone vibrated, and when he stepped out to take a call, Jack stood and moved closer to the bed, eyeing the worn copy of *Frankenstein* on the table next to it. He placed his hands on the rail, gently but with determination. He spoke softly in the same manner. "I know you can hear me. You might not be able to respond, but you can hear me."

The man's eyes remained tight, his breathing labored. The machine monitoring his heart grew more agitated as Jack spoke. He could see the numbers on the screen increasing, the beep becoming more rapid.

His tone was patient but spoken with genuine conviction. Non-threatening but promising. "I'm not here to frighten you," Jack said, "...but if you know anything about my niece's abduction or the whereabouts of the other missing children, you better come clean. Figure out a way to tell me. Morse code, telepathy, spell it out in graveyard dust. Whatever works."

The heart machine continued to pick up speed. The numbers bounced higher then lower then high again. The beeping intensified. "If I find out you had anything to do with their disappearance...well, let's just say, that's when you should be afraid, Mr. Tomb. Now, I'm sorry I disturbed you. And most of all, I'm sorry for what happened to you.

The proper channels will be taken toward justice, I assure you. I just want to make sure we are on the same page."

The door of the room flung opened and a pack of wild nurses ran toward the bed like wolves ascending on prey. They shoved Jack out of the way, and frantically began adjusting knobs and buttons, flipping switches and swearing.

"Out!" Jack heard the voice behind him demand. "Right now," Dr. Kohl commanded. "I warned you, Sheriff. Now out!" She threw her thumb over her shoulder.

'Sorry," Jack said scurrying towards the door. "I didn't mean to upset him."

"Right," the doctor snipped. "Just so you know, Sheriff, I'm the authority here in this hospital. And *don't* you forget it. I'll have HIPAA on your ass in a heartbeat."

"Yes, ma'am," Jack responded, politely. He wondered if he should address her as Fraulein but refrained for fear of his safety.

"Well, if you didn't have one before, you certainly do now," Pastor Briggs said, smirking from just outside the room where he stood waiting.

"Have one what?"

"An enemy."

twelve

Kitty had just turned seventy when she made the decision to divorce Joe. It wasn't like she'd spent months considering it. She just woke up one day and knew it was time then went down and filed the papers. It was the talk of the town and brought about a great deal of erroneous over-speculation as to why. Was it his drinking? Had she met someone else at the Legion? Were their finances in arrears? Maybe Joe was having an affair. He and Maggie did spend a lot of time together.

The truth, which Kitty never felt the need to reveal, was that time didn't heal all wounds unseen. That was a bunch of bullshit. Some wounds were irreparable. Dug deep, right into the bone. She would always love Joe, but she was a broken woman. The birth of her first child had made her that way. It wasn't Joe's fault that what life had handed her rendered her incapable of showing much emotion. But just because she didn't show it didn't mean she didn't feel it. People had condemned her for not crying at Joe's funeral, but she'd locked her tears inside long ago when she learned how worthless they really were. How folks judged you when they saw them. How weak they made you appear. As soon as a moment passed, it became fixed and unchangeable. Forever ingrained in the past and made permanent by the moments that followed. No tears could change that. Only death would take it all away. That's when it would end. The pain, the guilt, the sorrow. She wondered if it was wrong to be looking so forward to it.

By the time the divorce was finalized, she'd already learned of the cancer. There was no need to tell anyone. It was too late for that. She took what little savings she had and paid six months' rent on a mobile home that sat a few hundred feet from Shadow River, which ran behind Rayburn's only cemetery, in the shadow of death. It was, Kitty believed, a place she had lived in her heart long before she moved there. The whole goddamned town was in the shadow of death in her opinion. Had been since they ran off the Indians. Not that she felt they were so wrong it doing it, but she wondered now if it was worth all the floods, fires, curses, and missing children. And though she wanted to hate the doctor who ruined her life by stealing her child, she couldn't, because he saved it years later by giving her another. Jack always said that Rayburn was the living breathing pages of a Faulkner novel. She'd never been much of a reader, but if this was true, it was no wonder the man was a drunk.

Kitty poured a fat four-fingered glass of Jim Beam and took it outside to the plastic Adirondack chair she'd set out back of the trailer near the bank of the river. She found comfort in the sound of the running water where nothing ever lingered. Where the past was constantly washed away.

She didn't feel bad about what she'd done. She couldn't. The Cemetery Man was guilty. Why else would he have Skyla's locket? It was worth going to prison for, and the only thing she hated was that Jack had to be involved. He would arrest her without a doubt, and she was proud of his ethics. It didn't matter though. Her doctor said she most likely wouldn't finish out the year. Not exactly in those words, of course. Diplomacy was so goddamn condescending sometimes. She'd be dead before they even selected a jury. At least she could go to her grave knowing her granddaughter was safe. It had occurred to her that she killed the only man who might have known the location of the other children, but she still refused to regret what she'd done. She'd made a promise to herself when she left Joe. No more regrets. No more secrets. The two seemed to go hand in hand. She'd been harboring a deep and tortuous secret for so many years, she was sure it had brought on the cancer. Disease feeds on that sort of shit.

When she went back inside for another drink, Kitty noticed the light blinking on her cell, a crappy burner phone she picked up from Walmart. It was easy being non-committal when you'd set a deadline of six months on your life. She wasn't going to bother listening to the message until realizing she'd missed three calls from Dottie. Nobody in their right mind blows off their hairdresser even on their deathbed.

Hi Kitty. Dottie, here. Heard the news about Skyla. Nothing short of a damn miracle. So glad she's safe, honey. I'll be back to work in a few days so hope to see you soon. Frankly, I could use the money. Oh, by the way, a nurse at the hospital told me that the maintenance man from the cemetery was shot. I can't believe it. That poor man. He's expected to make a full recovery, praise Jesus, but still. What the hell has happened to this town? Rayburn used to be a nice place to live. Now it's full of child abductions and random shootings. I'm scared to death to leave my house these days. Anyway, call me soon, sugar. I know your roots have missed me even if you haven't.

A storm was brewing. Had been coming for some time, and it had nothing to do with the drops of rain Kitty heard tapping against the roof of the aluminum trailer. She placed the phone back on the counter and added three more fat fingers of whiskey to her glass. Standing there, she could feel her own shadow growing larger and darker behind her. It had every intention of consuming her. She capped the bottle, her mind a cyclone of irrational thoughts. "Well, shit," she spat out then picked up the drink and slammed it.

thirteen

After hoisting the cardboard storage box onto the bed, Angela began to rip the packing tape from the lid. She'd almost forgotten that the box was still in her car, the very last load from her mother's that had not made it to storage. She was still trying to catch her breath from the stairs, the whole time trying to shake the eerie feeling she had of being watched as she made her way down the hall. Her clothes were still damp, and she was in desperate need of a hot shower. Also, there was the matter of unpacking which she had yet to do.

Angela had spent the greater part of the morning researching Knox from her laptop downstairs at the pizza joint. She'd managed to locate an old girlfriend from Clemson, where Knox attended college. Angela left a message on her voicemail asking about Knox then began googling local attorneys. She blamed Jack for planting the seed. What she had in mind was ludicrous not to mention beyond unethical and illegal, but she didn't have much time. Or choice for that matter. Besides Liam was worth it.

Elliot Boone practiced criminal defense (and the art of public intoxication according to his most recent arrest record), in a city the size of a speck of dirt, twenty miles north of Rayburn. Population 150. Mr. Boone's office, a one-room structure with a window AC unit located, according to Google Maps, in the heart of downtown Porter, a single lane road on which sat two other lucrative businesses: a wing shack and a gas station with only one pump. It didn't take much investigative research to discover that he drove a beater and was a regular at Tiny's, a dive bar and obscure oxymoron in relativity to his size. If she had a chance in hell of pulling this off, Boone was her man.

As Angela devised a plan, she rifled through her mother's personal folders, searching for the newspaper clipping with the image of the headstone she'd discovered earlier at the cemetery on Strangers' Row. It was, she decided, the resting place for those whose bodies may have been found but whose souls were trapped in limbo while they waited for a name. Her victims at least had an identity.

It was in the second folder that she found what she was looking for. Once again, she scanned the image for any kind of credits identifying the newspaper or photographer but there were none. The ink on the back of the photo was smudged and faded, but she could make out certain words and partial sentences about a missing Atlanta woman named Julie Love.

Angela pulled out her laptop, set it on the nightstand next to her cell phone and plugged it in. She typed *pizzapie* when prompted for the password just as Joey had instructed her then logged into the Philadelphia Library. She went straight to the databases of archived newspapers. Starting with the *Atlanta Journal-Constitution,* she worked her way down three or four Georgia publications before remembering that Sheriff Towns had been reading a copy of the *Rayburn Star* earlier that morning. Hard to believe a place as small as Rayburn even had a newspaper. Even harder to believe it might be a *Star.*

The online search for 1987 rendered several pages of results that she limited with the name Julie Love. This pulled up the full article about the woman's disappearance which happened in July when her car ran out of gas and several follow-up articles in which authorities were still searching for her. One article, from August, appeared to match what was written on the back of the clipping her mother had saved. Angela hit the *page previous* arrow and there it was. The same photo her mother had kept for whatever reason. Only this one had a story accompanying it.

Remains of Unidentified Woman
Interred at Rayburn Cemetery

The charred remains of an unidentified woman whose body was found in an abandoned, burned-out trailer in the woods near Blood Mountain last May, was laid to rest today in Rayburn Cemetery. The eulogy was given by Pastor Nelson and the attendees included Sheriff Joe Towns, Maggie Sheppard and a young man seen placing a handful of wilted wildflowers on the fresh grave near the fourteen other white wooden crosses that comprise Strangers' Row and date back to the early 1900s. Officials estimate that Jane Doe, Number 15, the last on the row, was between 16 and 19 years of age, and likely dead before the fire started. The only other detail released was that the young woman had recently given birth. This is an ongoing investigation. Those with any information about the identity of the decedent or how she may have died should speak in strict confidence to the Crow County Sheriff's office.

Angela did a quick Google search for Doug McCay, the journalist who wrote the clip and discovered he covered mainly crime, and that some of his articles were syndicated in major papers throughout the U.S. She'd recognized the name. Many of his articles were about the missing children along the East Coast and the serial killer he referenced as the Redeemer. From what she could find, Doug McCay hadn't published anything after 2012, but Buddy McCay had. Maybe they were related. A few more links and she found Buddy's contact info, which directed her to the *Rayburn Star*. Was it convenience or coincidence that she could see the office from her window, partially blocked by a rusty air conditioner that looked as if it was going to detach itself from the frame at any minute and drop onto the sidewalk below.

The air in the room was thick and stagnant. Angela had cranked the unit down when she first arrived but it wasn't doing much good. She yawned and stretched back on the bed, stared up at the ceiling. The place seemed so empty, so quiet without all her photos taped to the walls. The missing, the lost, the dead. Though Liam had been found, Angela still kept his picture tacked up on her wall with the others because he'd always be lost to her, and she'd always be haunted by him. They had that understanding. She'd built a life on hope and despair. On guilt and revenge. On one hundred and three steps. The moment came to her as it always did at dusk for it was this time that her life changed forever. The moment her destiny was altered. Liam on the swing. Liam on the monkey bars. Liam climbing the ladder to the slide but never sliding down. She'd looked away, been distracted for only a second or was it longer? A few minutes? How long did it take to snatch a child? Had they walked home together that day, she'd probably be an accountant right now. She might even be married with children of her own instead of living on the memories of those that belonged to others. A noise in the next room pulled her into an upright position. It sounded like someone dragging a heavy piece of furniture across the wood floor. Angela got up and checked the lock on the door. She turned and leaned against it, focusing her tired eyes on the box. There had to be something in there that would provide a clue as to why her mother was so interested in a woman who died under mysterious circumstances almost forty years before and five states away. *What are you trying to tell me, Mom?*

Two hours later, Angela had made her way through the contents of the last folder. She felt defeated and exhausted and a little irritated. Her stomach lurched and she reached for the foil containing the leftover pizza slices from lunch. She opened the bottle of red wine she brought with her and poured as much as she could into her plastic travel mug, which still tasted like stale gas-station coffee. Then she dug out a nightshirt and started the shower. The cold water after ten minutes forced her out before she had a chance to shave her legs. She didn't think to ask if hot water was included in the weekly rent.

Still feeling traces of conditioner in her hair, Angela dried off and began placing some of her clothes in the small shaky bureau. The rest she hung in the even smaller closet. Above the wire hangers scattered across the rod was a narrow piece of wood. Her empty suitcase met with resistance when she tried to shove it onto the shelf. She set the case down then stood on her toes and patted around before grabbing a hanger and dislodging a black spiral-bound notebook that smacked her in the face. She bent, picked it up and flipped through it. Research of some kind. Pages of handwritten notes overlaid with random yellow Post-its. The notebook must have belonged to the woman who stayed in the room before her. The one who ran off without paying. Joey would have to add it to his ransom collection. Angela sat it on the dresser and crawled into bed. She whispered, *Goodnight Liam. I'm so sorry,* but sleep never came easy for her even after this. In her mind, weighted thoughts tumbled around like wet clothes in a dryer. Lying on the pillow, her eyes wide and wet, she began to count to one hundred and three just like she did every night before drifting off. But she wasn't counting sheep; she was counting steps.

Morning arrived too soon and without the scent of brewing coffee, which made it all the more difficult to actually get out of bed. No caffeine was cruel and unusual punishment. She would have to pick up a cheap coffee pot somewhere or she wasn't going to be able to function.

Angela propped herself up with pillows then checked her emails from her phone. She'd received a text during the night from an unrecognizable number. SONS OF PERDITION

That was the entire text. It took a minute for her to realize this must have been Knox's old flame responding to her message. What the hell were the Sons of Perdition? She called the number back, but it was no longer in service. That meant one thing to Angela. The woman was terrified and didn't want to be found. Angela typed Sons of Perdition into her phone's search bar and found very little. What she did find scared her too. A fundamentalist sector known to be violent. The only thing they seemed to hold sacred was marriage and something called blood atonement in which forgiveness could only be attained with bloodshed. Could this be why Knox was killing children and cutting off their ring fingers? It was a lot to digest before coffee and breakfast. Tossing the sheet aside, she crawled out of bed and made her way to the bathroom.

If it was there before, Angela hadn't noticed the yellow sticky on the floor in front of the dresser. It must have slipped out of the notebook she found in the closet. Something unsettling twisted in her stomach when she bent down to retrieve the note and read what was written.

Meet Joe Towns about the Truelove girl. He knows. September 8th, Old Mountain Arts Hotel, 10 a.m.

She recalled the story of the Truelove children the waitress downstairs had told her. How they disappeared and were never found. She walked past the Truelove headstone yesterday before being distracted by the white crosses on Strangers' Row. But Joe—was this the same Joe Towns mentioned in the article about the burial of the unidentified woman? The sheriff? Jack's father? Too small of a town not to be. Now the woman was missing and Jack's father was dead. What did he *know* and had it gotten them both in trouble somehow? Angela wondered if she should mention any of this to Jack, but at the last minute decided against it. This was distracting her from what she came here to accomplish. With this in mind, she slipped the note back in the notebook on her way out the door.

fourteen

Jack got an early start on his Monday morning walk. He had a lot on his mind, and the sharp air helped him cut through some of the shit so he could focus. Instead of heading toward the cemetery on the worn trail that led him behind the library and past the high school, he turned at Broken Arrow Lane, which had once been a wide red clay road that ended at the Truelove house. Now it was so overgrown with wood phlox, ferns, and wiregrass, it was much more of a gravel path than a lane but wide enough to navigate. Or at least that's the story the empty beer cans told. The entire area had become a dumping ground for old bed springs, broken refrigerators—cocked open like caskets, and skeletons of unwanted furniture left to the elements. It was also a late-night party hangout for teenagers. Jack had been called out here several times this past year but not since Kelly Marsh's death. People were scared. He didn't blame them. Someone had been out here recently though. Someone with a motorbike. The misty morning rain hadn't washed away entirely the tire imprint in the clay. The deep tread made him think it was probably some type of off-road bike. The toe of his boot hit a PBR can and sent it flying. Stale beer sprayed the air but was soon replaced by a tart, sweet scent that pressed into his lungs as Jack moved forward.

September through October was apple season, and the Rayburn Apple Festival was less than a week away. Downtown would soon be flooded with city folk who drove a hundred miles for a basket of apples, a jar of apple butter or one of Pearl's legendary pies.

The apple orchard was nestled behind the burned-out two-story structure that had at one time been home to Will and Lorraine Truelove and their five children. Bone white with scorched black holes where the windows and front door used to be, the house reminded Jack of a skull, and this seemed appropriate for what it represented. It had been uninhabitable after the fire in 1985 when he was just ten years old. He'd been inside before though plenty of times as a teen and a few as an adult. The walls were covered in graffiti and as he passed by today, he studied the red words, BURN THE WITCH, spray-painted on the side of the house above a black pentagram. Both had been there for a while, but the eye in the center of the pentagram was new. Maybe that's why he felt like he was being watched. His most recent trip out here had been to recover his father's body, which was found by a couple of hikers making their way from Neels Gap toward the Appalachian Trail. They were heading across the patch of sharp rocks known as the Devil's Backbone, just below the old Mountain Arts Hotel property when they noticed the old man's twisted shape. They walked until their cell phones had enough bars to call it in.

Scheduled for demolition years ago and not safe by any means, the abandoned hotel had a word-of-mouth reputation among hikers and served as a shelter during extreme weather conditions. Though it was considered a state park, due to budget cuts, rangers no longer patrolled the area. For the life of him, Jack could not understand what his father had been doing up there that day. An old knee injury prevented him from walking long distances especially the rocky, steep and rough terrain of Blood Mountain.

The Cherokees believed the mountain to be sacred, home to the Nunnehi or Immortals as they sometimes called them. According to their legend, these fairy-like people guarded the land vigilantly, but they were also known to guide the lost, especially children. Jack wanted this to be true more than ever right now. Hell, he'd put his faith in elves and unicorns if they could bring Hailey, Ben, and Simon home.

To honor the Immortals, the Cherokee had planted the Tree of Lost Souls on the summit of the mountain hundreds of years ago. Over time, the two- hundred-year-old cedar had been adorned with personal items in the way of photos, jewelry, letters, journals, and even shoes, hung on the branches by those who had felt spiritually or physically lost. The tree, which hadn't yet made it to the popular culture of guide books or tourist attractions, had a clandestine sort of following. It had become a pilgrimage people sought when they needed to be found. But it was also a place where people went to die. People who must have felt they had no other choice. Those who believed they would be eventually found probably never counted on all the coyotes being the first to get there. Sometimes all that was left were gnawed bones draped in tattered clothing. Scavengers liked to search the base of the tree for jewelry that had slipped off the decaying bones. Some of it ended up in Rayburn's pawn shop while other pieces found their way to eBay and to customers who appreciated morbid keepsakes and the lore that accompanied them. Jack wasn't judging as he himself had found and kept a few of these souvenirs as a boy. His father had warned him never to remove anything, not even a leaf from the Tree of Lost Souls.

"Doing so," he'd told him, "would incite a chain of unfortunate events in a person's life. You see, son, we Towns have a dark history. One better left buried. Stay away from the tree if you know what's good for you."

But Jack being a somewhat rebellious child never heeded his father's warning. He thought now of the small wooden box of items he'd collected from under the tree when he was a boy. Arrowheads, coins, bird feathers, bullet casings, and once, a tarnished silver spoon ring engraved with the letter T in ornate cursive. These were his own morbid curiosities, and though he knew it was ridiculous to consider, he couldn't help but wonder if his disrespect for the tree might have helped in some way set the curse, once again, into motion. He pushed this irrational thought away as fast as it had come.

For certain, everyone knew about the Blood Mountain curse. During the Indian Removal Act, the Cherokees were forced west and their land was taken from them. They cursed the entire mountain and the area surrounding it. This curse was still whispered about in the pews at church, questioned over coffee in the booths at the diner, and met with a lifted brow in the line at the grocery store. People passing through may have considered it Appalachian folklore: stories quilted together by generations of Rayburn families, but there wasn't a soul from Crow County who didn't believe that the curse was responsible for the blight of the apple orchard and both cases of missing children. There were even rumors circulating that Sheriff Joe Towns had fallen victim to it with his untimely demise. But what Jack understood was that the people of Rayburn believed they would be forever cursed for taking what didn't belong to them. As much as he hated to admit it, it seemed justifiable in some screwed up Hammurabian way.

Jack sucked in a deep breath and continued behind the decaying farmhouse where the scent of apples grew stronger with each step. If he weaved his way back through the dense cluster of pines, covered in velvety green moss and entwined with overgrown wisteria, he'd reach the orchard. Wanda Drake's place sat just beyond that, nestled at the base of the mountain in a place known as Bone Hollow. It was an area that no one dared venture because it was believed to be the most haunted place in North Georgia. Even curious teenagers trying to dispel the paranormal theories or prove their bravery to peers after ingesting liquid courage were terrified to go any farther than the sign nailed to an apple tree near the back of the orchard where a thick layer of mist shrouded everything beyond it. Though Jack never had any trouble finding his way in or out, there was a ubiquitous understanding in Rayburn that finding the entrance to the hollow was difficult; finding the exit, impossible. It was best to avoid the area at all costs. Jack who'd never put much stock in urban legends wouldn't want to admit to anyone that even he felt the weight of the air change as he passed by the old wooden board with the words, YOU ARE NOW ENTERING BONE HOLLOW, seared into it. More of a warning than a welcome, most believed, but he had never once felt threatened by it.

Jack was on the fence about most of the legend and lore of Rayburn. It wasn't that he didn't believe in ghosts; it was just that he felt most people were likely haunted more by things that were still alive. At least he was. This wasn't to say that he hadn't seen a ghost or two in all his years living in Crow County. In fact, he had a special sense about them that he had never shared with anyone else. He saw things, heard things, and sometimes knew things that others didn't, but he kept this to himself, and relied instead on the laws of nature and logic, in which all things could be explained with rational thought, to keep grounded. This meant he pushed his intuition away, forcibly at times, whenever it tried to lead him in any other direction, especially where the law was concerned.

Though few outsiders knew of this part of the mountain, the residents of Rayburn, especially the older folks who'd grown up with the stories of people entering this area and disappearing or returning with no memory of who they were, considered it to be a fearful ungodly place. They believed the clay soil it contained was much darker than the rest of the mountain because it was mixed with blood. And partly this was true Jack had learned from a history professor at UGA. The area had been a bloody and savage war zone between the Creeks and Cherokees then later a makeshift cemetery for the dead during both the Indian Removal Act and years later, the Civil War. Indians couldn't be buried in the city cemetery and women weren't strong enough to bury what was left of their sons and husbands who had lost their lives in battle. So, the bodies were often left in the hollow to decay. Some were burned to keep the animals from carrying them off. Jack found it rather ironic that after all the damn bloody battles over the land the rivals were forced to share it in death regardless.

Wanda had always lived in Bone Hollow. She'd been there so long that some believed she'd grown up out of the ground from a seed of one of the cursed apple trees. Or that she was formed from a bolt of lightning that struck the clay and hardened into an overly-textured shape of a woman the same way fulgurites were created. At least one or two believed she was the offspring of an Immortal left behind and to care for the land after the Indians were forced from it. But most people when asked where they thought Wanda might have come from offered the same theory. They didn't know. She was just there and always had been.

Jack pressed on through the weighted air, which he noticed had taken on a musty charred scent like the pages of an old book rescued from a fire or the memories of thousands of souls burned into the soil. All those decaying bodies certainly would have altered the chemical composition of the dark clay earth in some way or another. He walked forward through the dense mist that hovered high above the ground. Jack couldn't tell where it began or where it ended. The hollow was a place of mystery and strange things. The fog seemed to warm as he passed through it then grew cold again. It was an odd feeling. Like drifting through someone else's dream. The taste of ash filled his mouth and Jack brushed delicate black cinders from his sleeve. When he looked over his shoulder, the orchard and everything beyond it had disappeared behind the wall of mist, which began morphing into odd shapes that dissolved as quickly as they'd manifested. Just a trick of light Jack thought to himself then heard what sounded like whispering near his ear. Hundreds of lingering souls spilling their secrets. Maybe, Jack considered, it was the secrets that kept them tied to this area. An image of his mother came to mind. He swatted at the side of his face, irritated at his over-active imagination then moved ahead until he saw Wanda's place come in to focus in the distance. It wasn't much more than four walls and a splintered wood floor and made living off the grid seem like a resort though apparently it at least had running water and a hearth.

He disliked disrespecting the old woman's privacy, but Wanda was the only one he could think of who might be able to answer the question that kept him up many nights after his father's death, but with Skyla's abduction and the other missing children, he had no time to try and process it. And to be truthful, Jack was a little nervous about what he might discover, but he'd let it go as long as he could. He wanted answers. He wanted to know where the children were and what happened to Kelly Marsh, but right now, he wanted to know about the photograph.

Wanda, who looked like she was made of crumpled paper because of the severity of her burns, had always lived a reclusive life. She could have been forty or a hundred and forty. Nobody knew for sure. She rarely ventured into town, and when she did, she shrouded herself in white lace tablecloths to conceal her appearance, which did little to keep from frightening people. This had earned her the title, the Fire Bride, but those old enough to remember the Truelove family believed that Wanda had something to do with the disappearance of the five children when a fire destroyed their home. Many of the older residents believed that she had taken them to the hollow where they vanished forever in the land of the spirit people. Jack was just a boy then. He only knew the stories because he'd been warned so many times during boyhood that the Truelove land, including most of Blood Mountain, was haunted, cursed by the Cherokees long ago when they were forced from it during the Removal. There were two rules Jack's parents had instilled in him as a boy. He was never to take anything from the Tree of Lost Souls, and he was never, ever, ever to enter Bone Hollow for any reason. He'd broken both rules by the time he was nine. And the truth was, some unseen force always seemed to pull him to the hollow. He felt safe there. As an only child, he'd come to think of it as a friend. And though he'd never told a soul, he'd often seen tiny lights dancing in the mist. Moths or fire flies that seemed to follow him around but disappear when he took notice. One of many mysteries the hollow held.

Whatever Wanda's real story was, she must have had reason for keeping it to herself, and Jack felt that she should be entitled to that, though he had stopped by her place a few days ago to ask if she might have any idea what happened to the missing Rayburn children, who much like the Truelove siblings had seemingly up and vanished without a trace. He'd spoken to Wanda only a handful of times before when she brought apples and jams by the diner while he was having breakfast and she'd been pleasant. Reserved with few words and hard to look at, no doubt, but polite, often going out of her way to acknowledge him. Once, he was surprised to find her staring at him through the diner window while he was eating breakfast. Something in her eye told him she was hungry, but by the time he went outside to ask her to join him, she was gone. Wanda Drake had been around forever and never once caused anybody any kind of trouble as long as Jack could remember. When he was a kid, he'd heard the rumors, some of which still circulated, of how she could heal people, talk the fire right out of them, and he'd always wondered why she hadn't been able to talk it out of herself.

Jack took in the land around him. The hollow wasn't a vast area. A person could probably walk the entire perimeter in less than a couple hours and yet it seemed like an entirely different world. One that didn't show up on any map, which was likely the reason it was and always had been, ownerless. *No one living owns Bone Hollow, son,* his father had told him. *It belongs to the dead and always will.*

The Trueloves had at one time owned the surrounding land, the orchard, and a good chunk of the mountain but never the hollow. That a portion of the mountain could be owned felt odd to Jack. It was like owning a piece of the sky or part of the ocean. But, by the time Will and Lorraine Truelove died, childless, heartbroken, and destitute, their house was a pile of ash, and their land had already been sold or auctioned or reclaimed by the bank. Jack couldn't remember which. The fire that destroyed their home had started in the middle of the night. The Trueloves thought at first their children had all perished but the fire department found no bones or bodies inside. All five had simply vanished and were never seen again. Well, all but one of them if the date on the photograph in his pocket was accurate. He'd heard that Wanda had been close to the family, watched over the children and helped with chores around the house. This was the reason Jack believed she might be able to help him understand the picture he had to pry from his father's stiff grip, the same way he pried the old man's rigid body from the mouth of Devil's Backbone.

The photo was creased around the ages, the colors muted but the subjects undeniably identifiable. The oldest Truelove girl and his father, Joe, sharing a private moment. The girl couldn't have been more than sixteen or seventeen. She'd thrown a hand up to try and shield her face, but she hadn't been quick enough. The outstretched palm, slightly out of focus, instead extended over her stomach. Joe was wearing his favorite sunglasses, a pair of mirrored Ray-Ban Aviators that had once again gained popularity with the hip who had little time to develop their own trends. The image had an unsettling air of infatuation and apprehension attached to it. Innocent and disturbing at the same time. Jack wondered who had taken the photo. But it was the date marked on the back of it that gave Jack the most difficulty.

Though he had never met the Truelove children, he

felt like he knew them. He'd seen their faces hundreds of times over the years. They had pretty much reached urban legend status and could be found on coffee mugs, t-shirts, and even shot glasses at any of the surrounding gas stations. The milk carton thing had subsided, but on occasion, they'd still be mentioned by the media or highlighted on an episode of *Unsolved Mysteries*. And lingering like the memories of the children, there was a decaying billboard on the interstate near the Rayburn exit. Most of the words and faces had long ago peeled off like some sort of diseased skin. All that remained was HAVE YOU SEEN and five pairs of glowing pale eyes that never seemed to fade. But nobody had ever seen them or if they had, they never bothered to come forward, and so the ghosts of the Truelove siblings did the only thing they could do on their quest for justice. They haunted. Not so much in the ghost sense but in the way that made people always wonder just what had happened to them. Uncertainty, Jack had learned from personal experience, was relentless and much more haunting than any apparition.

Wanda was sitting under the rickety tin awning of a place that should have been condemned long ago, peeling apples when Jack approached. Her hair, long and white and thick was pulled back away from her disfigured face, the bad eye seared with white scar tissue.

The orchard had never flourished. Some folks believed it either still carried the curse from the Cherokees, or that hollow had claimed it and because of this, the trees would never thrive, but they produced enough apples to keep Wanda going. This could have been, Jack felt, because she was at least in part Cherokee, and maybe the mountain somehow knew that she was the rightful owner even if the land purveyors and banks disagreed. The scars from the burns may have concealed Wanda's coloring but the Indian features buried in the depths were still prevalent. Deep wide sockets and putty-like skin that stretched over bones as sharp and shiny as a new blade.

Since Wanda had no real means of properly maintaining the trees, disease seemed to manifest in them more and more with each passing season. Every year, another row of trees succumbed, but Wanda refused to leave the land. And even if she could have, Jack knew in his heart that she would never leave Bone Hollow. Most likely because of her heritage, but he felt there was another reason. Something she kept close to her heart. What that was, only she knew. Last week there'd been a gas and oil man having breakfast at the diner, and he was very interested in the Truelove property and Wanda. According to Pearl, he was one of those untrusting fellows who had a single brow instead of two. She was convinced he was a werewolf because his index fingers were substantially longer than the others. Also, he didn't care for pie, a sure sign of some kind of disorder in Pearl's eyes.

"Morning, Wanda."

Wanda's one good eye locked on Jack like a target as he made his way toward her. She was peeling an apple.

"Sheriff," she nodded, holding his gaze as long as her heart would allow. A long curly red S fell into the basket between her legs. She dropped the peeled apple into a large pot next to her then reached, without looking, for another piece of the fruit. Her bad eye, as milky as a glass marble, seemed to focus on something behind Jack that only she could detect. Jack looked over his shoulder to err on the side of caution but saw nothing except for the fog.

"Sorry for the intrusion. I just need a minute of your time if you can spare it."

"I've told you already what I know about the missing children. I have not seen them nor do I know what may have happened to them. They are not in the hollow, I assure you. I would know. I know every tree, every path, and every shadow that lingers here. It is my duty to watch over those who cannot move on to the Darkening."

"The Darkening?" Jack asked, confused but interested.

"The Cherokee resting place for the dead. It is where Cherokees must go before returning to the Great Life in animal form. But in order to do this, their death must not have been caused by another. Those that are trapped here linger because of the violent manner in which they died. Restless souls cannot enter the Darkening. They cannot leave Bone Hollow. It will always be their home. And mine. At least until the screech owl flies away with my breath."

It was the most Wanda Drake had ever said to him, and Jack let her go on out of politeness but also curiosity.

He did wonder though, why exactly she was telling him all this.

"May I?" Jack asked motioning to a stack of upturned crates next to the woman.

Wanda continued to look straight ahead, peeling off another red S that dangled like a snake before falling into the basket. She nodded and Jack sat.

"This was all Cherokee land, once" she continued. The lotteries forced my people out. Those who weren't slaughtered were pushed westward, and as you already know, they forever cursed this land even though two of their clans refused to leave it. The Anitsiskwa, the Bird Clan, and the Aniwaya, the Wolf Clan, both stayed behind and lived quietly here for many years, raising their families and avoiding white men. Then the Civil War came and once again destroyed our land and nearly wiped out both clans entirely. Years passed and the few remaining survivors did their best to repopulate their tribes; it was forbidden to marry anyone from the same tribe, you see. My mother was Aniwaya as am I. Descendants of wolves. Another member of the Wolf Clan became enamored with her but she shunned him. Partly because of our laws but also because she had fallen in love with"...she hesitated. "...a white man. A holy man of French heritage with a Christian Bible and magic prayers. My father. He was on a healing mission and wandered into the hollow by accident, but he couldn't find his way out. It's common for those not born here to become lost and confused."

"I've heard this before," Jack said. "But I've never personally had any trouble."

Wanda looked over at him strangely then and smiled. "You wouldn't," she said so softly he almost didn't hear it.

For the first time, Jack noticed that her functional eye was the color of a tarnished nickel. This piqued his curiosity even more about her heritage. "So, I take it you were born in the hollow?" he asked.

She nodded. "Born to it, really. My mother was pregnant with me when she was killed. Not too far from where we are right now. My father was out hunting. Upon his return, he discovered a fresh mound of earth, and his dead wife beneath it. Killed by her own clan because they felt she had betrayed them for a white man. He dug her out of the shallow grave then cut me from her womb. My hair was as white as the moon and it remained that way. I was a half breed in heritage but also in existence. Half alive, half dead. My father later told me—when I was old enough to understand, that being born from death would make me forever connected to it. I'd always be a part of this place where souls are trapped." She wiped the blade of the paring knife against the stained flour sack apron secured around her thick waist. "My apologies. I didn't mean to go on. You've come here for a reason, and I'm keeping you from it. But as I told you, I know nothing of the children or their whereabouts. They are not in the hollow. I wish I could help you."

A dark moment passed between them before Jack

reached into his shirt pocket and pulled out the small square photograph. "I'm not here about the children."

Wanda kept peeling, her eyes nailed to the trees before her where blackbirds skittered in and out of the branches, and the strange patch of thick fog shifted. She offered Jack a piece of apple without ever looking his way. It was difficult for her to accept at times, the past. She wondered if Jack remembered her. He was just a boy playing in the woods. It wasn't the first time they'd met. But that day, he'd wandered into the hollow. She'd only wanted to speak with him but instead frightened him with her appearance. He ran off and a part of her would stay in that moment forever. She wondered now if he was still scared of her. The first time she was burned was during the Truelove fire when she went searching the house for the children, but it was rescuing Sarafina's infant daughter that made her unrecognizable even to herself.

With a wave of his hand, Jack politely refused her offer. "I thought maybe you might be able to..." he pinched at his chin searching for the right words. "To help me understand this." He held out the photo of his father and the girl not mentioning what bothered him most was the date on the back of it. Wanda reached for it, brought the picture close to her good eye. She held it there for a time but said nothing.

The sound of chattering birds punctuated the silence, their wings snapping like sheets on a clothesline. Wanda remained quiet. So much time passed that Jack considered rephrasing his plea for help but then she spoke.

"Sarafina," she said softly turning towards him. A look of pleasure placated her face but morphed into a painful grimace. She handed back the picture then looked away as if the moment never happened. This time it was a letter J that dropped in the basket. "I was sorry to learn of your father's death."

Jack found himself nodding without realizing he was doing so. "Me, too."

She wiped the back of her hand, knife still clutched in it, across her forehead. The silver blade sparked in the stray stream of sunlight. She started peeling again. "You are here with doubts?"

"I am. You see, this photograph was in his hand when I reached him that day. I don't understand why. I thought maybe you could shed some light in my direction."

"Light is just a perception, boy. Without darkness, it is impossible to differentiate between the two. It's the same indistinguishable line that separates the present from the past. Do you understand?"

"I'm not sure," Jack said. Was she trying to tell him—

"My father referred to it as *entre chien et loup*. When light and dark are equal, it is difficult to distinguish between dog and wolf."

Jack was doing his best to understand.

Wanda continued without further explanation. "Your father and Sarafina were friends. He was fond of all the

Truelove children but especially Sarafina."

"Wait. Are you saying—"

"I'm saying that your father and Sarafina had a special relationship."

Jack watched another red S drop, a scarlet letter in a basket of many. His father carrying on with an underage teenager while being married? It just wasn't possible, was it? This was Joe Towns, a man of relentless integrity and blatant honesty. Jack's mind was a mixture of repulsion and doubt but also full of sudden anger and...sadness.

"Is that why she's trying to hide her face in the photograph? To protect their *special* relationship?" He hadn't meant to sound that bitter. He stared at the picture then tucked it in his shirt pocket. Wanda's attention was still focused on the orchard.

"It's not her identity she was concerned about." Wanda remembered how the girl had begged her not to reveal her whereabouts. Staying in that old rusted trailer that had dropped from the sky one year when a tornado hit. She didn't want to be found. She believed the doctor had already killed her siblings. He had to be the one that set the house fire, she'd told Wanda. She couldn't risk her parents' lives, too.

"You've lost me," Jack admitted.

"She was protecting the soul of her unborn child from the camera. People around these parts once believed it captured the soul. Some still do. Sarafina was pregnant. I'd say about five months in the photograph." Wanda stopped

155

peeling for a moment then picked up where she left off. She'd delivered that baby but there was no need for anyone to know that. She'd later rescued it and had the mute boy take it to Dr. Hixson's after Sarafina had perished in the fire. Wanda was not fond of the doctor, but he once saved her own child, and for this she was grateful. She'd seen Sarafina's girl in town recently, a woman now. Seeking answers of her own. The hollow rarely let anyone go entirely. Wanda knew this first hand. She was wrong to think that she could fool it.

Before Jack could ask if she thought Sarafina's child belonged to his father, a question that was burning a hole in his tongue, a cloud of blackbirds exploded from one of the apple trees.

"Shhh...," Wanda whispered. "Someone is here." She stared straight ahead with her one silver eye like a Cyclops detecting an approaching enemy. A dark shape darted in the distance barely visible in the shroud of thick fog. Jack wondered who would be brave enough to enter the hollow. Whoever it was changed their mind, turned, and fled.

He stood. "Hey," he yelled then took off running, cutting a path through the eerie fog toward the orchard, and when the air suddenly became clear again, Jack knew he'd left the hollow. Barreling between the trees, he kicked rotten apples along the way and did his best to avoid the branches that seemed to be reaching out for him. When he reached the end of the orchard, he caught the blur of a black hoodie shooting through the pines on the other side as if fired from a gun.

"Wait," Jack called stumbling through the woody wisteria vines and pushing pine needles from his face. "I just want to talk to you," but he was shouting to empty air. He kept moving, the bottom of his jeans now wet and splattered with mud and clay as red as blood. His boot slipped, and he slid down an embankment, catching himself on a knuckled tree root just before busting his ass. This set him back a few seconds, but he plowed on remembering what his father always said about the difference between tenacity and stubbornness. One involves a strong will, the other involves a strong won't.

It's when he rounded the bend in the trees near the Truelove house that Jack heard the crank of a motorbike. By the time he reached the clearing and got a direct view of the dilapidated structure, the sound of the cycle had already grown faint. Half of Rayburn owned dirt bikes, and though he'd had one himself as a teenager, deciphering what kind by sound alone would be impossible for him. He stopped to catch his breath, bending slightly and placing his hands on his thighs. The morning sun was a spotlight through the trees. He wouldn't have seen it otherwise. The charm glinted like a piece of glass on the red velvet earth beneath it. Jack brushed off the silver jagged half- moon and read what looked like, BE FREE, engraved on it. Lost by one of the high-school girls no doubt. Up here doing something they shouldn't be in an attempt at being unfettered. He shoved it in the front pocket of his jeans then choked down the scent of burning wood that suddenly snagged in his throat.

It was odd that after forty years, the smell of fire still ghosted the house, trapped forever in the decomposing frame and the area surrounding it. It was almost as if it was haunted by the memory of what happened here. An eternal smoldering of tragedy. Jack wiped at a scratch on his face, his fingers smeared the blood and ash across his forehead.

Sitting on a downed tree, he pulled the photograph from his shirt pocket. He studied it for a long minute before turning it over and trying to register once more that written on the back in pencil, nearly faded from sight, was the year 1986. A year after the Truelove children had disappeared. If there was ever a time that he needed to hear his father's voice, it was now. Something about *things not always being what they appeared to be* or *how assumptions were for the weak-minded.* He listened hard but none of this came. The only sound he heard was the guttural growling of his stomach.

Jack tucked the photograph back in his shirt pocket and headed toward his truck, a black Tacoma he bought three years before and had always used in place of a cruiser. He added the lights and had the Crow County Sheriff logo put on after his father died, but only because it was necessary.

Jack was desperate for a cup of coffee and one of Pearl's breakfast specials. All that running had him famished. It had also jarred loose a crazy notion in his head about his father. One fueled by what Wanda had told him about Sarafina being pregnant. One that he wished would go the fuck away.

His cell phone vibrated and he stood. He'd missed a call from Dr. Tash. Jack accessed his voicemail and listened to the message about the results of Skyla's labs.

"I'm concerned about the substantial levels of lorazepam in her panels," Dr. Tash said. "Now, I know she was prescribed anti-depressants after her father died, but I just spoke with Camille who confirmed that Skyla hasn't taken them in months. Many months. They would have been out of her system by now. I'm going to run the labs again just to be sure. I'll get back to you with the results."

fifteen

The diner was jam-packed or as Pearl said to Jack when he sat, "Apple-jelly packed. I'll get you *da* special." she offered, filling up a cup with coffee and setting it in front of him. "What da hell happened to you?" she asked after getting a good look at him.

Pearl's big, bright smile took up most of her round dark face. So much that one rarely noticed the white scar that ran along her hairline near her temple. A gift from her ex-husband. She once told Jack that even though she temporarily lost sight in that eye, it helped her to see things more clearly than she ever had before. But Jack had decided long ago that Pearl Jenkins was more than a little clairvoyant. Though she'd been at the diner since Jack began high school, Pearl was an enigma. Originally from St. Helena Island in South Carolina, she'd come to Rayburn for love, "*somethin,*" she always added as a disclaimer, "a teenage girl knew *nottin bout.*"

Though Jack never saw it first hand, he'd heard the chatter throughout the high school walls and around town.

People talking about the poor colored girl at the diner who always had a swollen eye and a busted lip. Pearl had put up with Freddy Jenkins' drinking and beatings until she lost the baby. Then Freddy just up and disappeared one day. Nobody ever saw him again. Now when people inquire about what might have happened to her husband, Pearl, in a melodic blend of Gullah and Appalachian asks, "Have you ever seen *da* movie, *Fried Green Tomatoes*?" and leaves it at that. Behind that wide mysterious smile is a secret or two.

"Just a little early morning run," Jack answered latently. "And yes, on the special." He took a big gulp of coffee trying to get some caffeine in his system as fast as possible. His ass was sore and his mind a whir of unhealthy thoughts. "How do you always know exactly what I want, Pearl? I've told you before, the Psychic Hotline is calling...you could be the next *Long Island Medium*, you know."

"Mmhmm. Well, they *gonna hafta* wait. I got a diner to run. The only medium I'm doing is *over* medium. You see this place in here, today? It's all Hixson trial folks. Reporters, witnesses, people looking for their biological parents. Part of me wants to choke that evil little man, the other part wants to thank him for all this business. Besides, you get the same damn thing every day unless you sneak over to Harley's for a sausage biscuit thinking I won't find out. But old Pearl always knows." She smiled again, her eyes pinched small by the plump of her cheeks. "How you doing today, anyway? And how's my Skyla, that poor child? I've been praying for her and the others."

"Both better than we were two days ago."

"I know that's right." Pearl turned and snapped a ticket into the holder that faced the kitchen. "Order in," she called through the arched window where Jack could see at least twenty other tickets.

"You shorthanded this morning? Thought you hired a new girl."

"I did. Real nice young lady by the name of Nelle. Hope I can get her to stay. This is *s'pose* to be her day off, but I had to call her in. She's on her way. Surprised you haven't met her. Speaking of surprises," Pearl said out of the side of her mouth, her eyes on the front door. "Here comes the werewolf. That damn gas man. He's headed this way. Look at his fingers when he sits down," she whispered, wiggling her two forefingers out of view from everyone but Jack.

He bit back a smile and sipped his coffee as the man approached. He wore a cheap-looking grey suit and a blue tie that screamed clip on. The man set his briefcase on the counter and took a seat next to Jack. The air became misted with a combination of gin and inexpensive cologne. Pearl squished up her nose in distaste while he got settled then placed a menu before him.

"Coffee?"

"With cream." The man dug in his jacket pocket and pulled out a pair of round glasses and shook them open.

"Mmhmm, I remember." Pearl reached under the

counter and pulled out a chipped saucer containing the half-and-half creamers and placed it next to his coffee cup. While he looked over the menu, she nonchalantly tapped at her index finger under Jack's individual surveillance.

"That gonna do it for ya then?" Pearl asked after taking the man's order and adding the ticket to the rest of the collection. She didn't bother telling him to save room for pie, Jack noticed.

The man emptied seven creamers into his cup then stirred it with his finger. This did not go unnoticed by Pearl. Between sips of coffee, he pulled from his briefcase a large gold envelope. He pinched the clasp open and began removing the contents. He spread out a map marked with red circles and crawling lines that reminded Jack of capillaries. They led up and around Blood Mountain, the heart of Rayburn and the only thing Jack could identify on the map. The man began sorting through official-looking documents with signature blocks until he came across a page of printed names and addresses that he set aside. All of the names had been crossed through except for five near the top, the first of which belonged to his sister, Camille. The Carsons, the Lees, the Martins, and the Talbots followed. Wanda Drake's name was off to the side with a question mark next to it. Hers was the only one without an address. Jack didn't try to hide his curiosity. It was his job. Besides, he'd always had an innate desire to know what the story was all about, to understand the underlying piece, which almost always involved some sort of degenerating human condition. At least in the South.

Seeing his sister's name unnerved him, but what was even more disturbing was that other than Wanda, the four families at the top of the page whose names had not been crossed out were those missing a child. His niece had escaped somehow but Simon Lee, Hailey Martin, and Ben Talbot were still out there, locked up somewhere in a cold dark room according to Skyla. Jack didn't see the Marsh's name on the list at all.

The man noted Jack's interest and tapped Wanda's name with a pen he'd pulled from the inner pocket of the briefcase. "Are you familiar with this woman? She's the only one I can't find an address for." He turned toward Jack. Pearl wasn't lying. Mr. Gas and Oil had one long eyebrow that stretched across his dark deep-set eyes like a furry black caterpillar.

"Who's asking?"

He reached inside his jacket and slid a card with a gold star logo across the counter. The metallic lettering blinked under the fluorescent lights of the diner. Jack had to force himself not to laugh aloud when he read the name.

"Randolph Wolfe." The man offered his hand. "Starpoint Explorations. Gas and Oil. We're out of Texas."

You've got to be kidding. Wolfe? Pearl was going to lose her shit over this. "Jack Towns. Sheriff," he added as an afterthought. He couldn't get used to that part. Never had that problem with the deputy title. Now, he was trying to fill a man's shoes that in his mind had always been too big, but after what he learned today, just might be too small, and he hated himself for thinking that.

"Thought I recognized you from the *Rayburn Star* piece a few weeks after your election. Sorry to hear about your father."

The new girl had arrived now. She studied Jack with a curiosity that bordered on scrutiny while refilling both of their cups with coffee. Jack nodded in gratitude.

"You knew my father?" he asked the man.

"Our paths crossed once or twice."

"I don't recall him ever mentioning you."

"Well, under the circumstances, he probably wouldn't have."

"I don't follow, Mr. Wolfe."

"In my business, you don't make many friends without the promise of money. Your father didn't care much for me because of the Truelove transaction."

"Again, you've lost me."

"Ah, you are unaware of the matter at hand, here, then. Will and Lorraine Truelove may have owned the surface of their land but Starpoint Explorations owned the mineral rights, the land beneath the surface. We own the mineral rights to much of Blood Mountain. Everything under the surface up until where the orchard ends is ours. Has been since the early 1800s."

"I thought the Cherokees owned Blood Mountain and the land surrounding it?" Jack asked.

"Well, they owned the skin, we own the blood and

bones so to speak." He rifled through a few papers and continued. "In 1985, we also bought the surface level of the land where the Trueloves resided but allowed them to rent a portion of it.

"Let me get this straight. You *allowed* them to live on their own land for a fee?"

"That's one way to look at it. The bank had already foreclosed on that property. John Hixson bought it, and the Trueloves paid rent to him initially. Then he sold it to us."

Jack could feel his blood start to boil. "In '85 you say. Curious. Was that before or after the fire?"

"Just before. We were just beginning to set up test sites. But the house was inhabitable anyhow. We did them a favor."

Jack felt like punching this narcissistic bastard in the throat. "I bet you got it for a real steal, too, didn't you?"

"Like I said, the house was destroyed by the fire and so was some of the land. All uninsured. The Trueloves had nowhere to go once we bought the land from Hixson so we made them an offer. They could rent a portion of the land until their expiration. I tried to explain this same thing to your father but he wouldn't listen. He claimed we preyed on innocent people who were rich in love but poor in cash."

"Here you are, gentlemen," Pearl said, setting a plate of hot food before each of them in a moment of awkward silence. "Enjoy." She tucked a receipt under each plate and threw Jack a discreet *what-in-the-hell-is-wrong-with-that-man* glance.

"Well, I don't feel he was too far off in his assessment. Expiration? You make them sound like old milk. They were people. People who couldn't even be buried on their own land with the rest of their ancestors because they no longer owned it. Damn shame. And what exactly is it that you want with Wanda Drake?" Jack motioned with his eyes toward the document on the counter.

"As I mentioned, I'm having trouble finding Ms. Drake's residence. By law, when there's a drilling planned, I'm required to directly speak with people being affected or if that's not possible, hand deliver a letter of intent regarding our plan of action. It's only by word of mouth that I know of Ms. Drake. From what I understand, she lives somewhere on or near Blood Mountain, which means she has been living on Starpoint's land far too long and far too free. She will have to vacate. But that's a future matter. Right now, I'm just trying to do my due diligence and tell her in person about the drilling. Along with these other folks." He tapped the list with his two fingers. To Pearl's credit, his index finger was about an inch longer than the middle one. Jack didn't believe in werewolves. He did take into consideration however that Georgia had its fair share of snakes.

"Drilling? As in fracking the Conasauga for natural gas? I don't recall Georgia being a state that allows that sort of thing." Jack shoved a fork full of omelet into his mouth and swallowed hard. But it was too late. His appetite was gone. "I wish I were sorry to tell you this, but any wildcatters I've known to pass through here left disappointed."

"I'm not a wildcatter, Sheriff Towns. Used to be. In another lifetime. That's a young man's game. I'm a legitimate employee of Starpoint. And yes, that's exactly what I'm referring to. Natural gas. We know it's there, and we have streamlined the process of locating and extracting it. As soon as the law allows, we'll make our move. We're setting up test wells in preparation. And I hate to be the one to break it to you, but we've been mining that mountain for over 150 hundred and fifty years. We even helped the state out by leasing prisoners as laborers."

"How philanthropic of you. So, let me get this straight. All the people on that list have given you permission to drill on their land? I find that hard to believe." He knew damn well his sister, Camille, would never agree to something like that when and if she was approached about it. She was a hardcore hippie at heart, a true nature lover.

A slimy smile tightened across Wolfe's face. "I'm not here to petition for permission, Sheriff. I'm just here to make people aware that we will begin setting up a test well on the Truelove property on Thursday morning. There will be lots of trucks and noise and bright lights at midnight. The people on the list are the ones that will be impacted the most. I just want to alert them personally about the possibility of this disruption. It's just a polite gesture, you see."

Jack pushed his plate back, dropped his napkin on top of it. "Thursday, as in three days from today?" he asked louder than he meant to. The new waitress eyed Jack as she rolled silverware near the end of the counter. He was thinking it was a look of contempt but decided she was of one of those very serious contemplative youths. What did they call them? Emo? Eno? Something like that. Pensive and reticent.

"That's right. Seven in the morning. We like to get an early start."

Seven creamers. Seven in the morning. Maybe Pearl was on to something with this werewolf nonsense. Jack had a good mind to ask him if he was the seventh son of a seventh son. "You can't just go drilling on people's land."

"We won't be. We'll be drilling on *our* land. As I said, Starpoint already owns the mineral rights of the mountain, and we bought the surface level of the Truelove property years ago. It'll be the origin of our operation. That's where the rig and rest of equipment will be stationed for the vertical test drills. Once we establish the gas beneath the shale, we'll be well prepared for fracking it out. All of this will be done from below surface level so technically, we won't be drilling on people's land. We'll be drilling under it. I'm sure you are already aware that ownership only extends so far below and above a plot of land. Otherwise, airplanes would need an owner's permission to fly over a house. And just to be up front, we're looking into getting the Hixson property for the same purposes, once it's in foreclosure, which I'm assuming won't be much longer with him being so frail. From what I understand, he has no living relatives. Who was it that said, 'Buy land, they don't make it anymore?'"

"Twain." Jack muffled a sarcastic snort. "The same man who found it curious that physical courage was so common and moral courage so rare. Certainly, there must be some kind of regulations or laws, environmental or other to protect people, prevent this kind of predatory land bullying...bullshit."

"The last time Georgia regulated fracking was in 1975. However, since you brought it up, there's a new bill going before the Senate, and it will likely push through the capitol next year in 2017, which is why you can understand our sense of urgency."

"I understand just fine your *sense of urgency*. You want to exploit natural resources, destroy wildlife, and contaminate our waters before you get taxed on it. An early start."

"People will be compensated for the noise and inconvenience, I assure you."

"This isn't about noise or money. There are lives at stake. I have three missing children out there somewhere on that mountain. What if these test drills cause land shifting or explosions or whatever and those kids are trapped? This can't happen. I won't let this happen."

"Well that is unfortunate, but there isn't anything you can do to stop it. We own the land, we've paid our fees, we have a DP Number issued by the State of Georgia, and we're pressed for time. Besides, there is no real danger of an explosion unless the natural gas comes in contact with an ignition source. And I don't hire smokers." He began gathering his documents and sliding them in his briefcase. "I apologize. I truly do. This is just business, Sheriff. The test drill will go in Thursday morning as planned. Hopefully, the children will have been located by then. You know how kids are. I'm sure they're fine. Probably exploring one of the tunnels or something. The mountain has plenty of them I've heard. They'll turn up." He tossed two fives on the counter and stood. "I'll find Ms. Drake on my own. It was good meeting you. And I am sorry about your father."

"Bye now," Pearl called then fingered the empty creamers on the counter. "Seven," she whispered to Jack. "Who the hell uses seven creamers? A werewolf that's who. Old Pearl knows a werewolf in a cheap suit when she sees one."

Wait until she found out his last name was Wolfe, Jack thought as he gripped the counter with both hands until his knuckles whitened and his fingers lost feeling. Werewolf or not, she was right about the cheap suit.

When Jack felt the blood flow again into his fingers, he paid his tab and marched over to the office in a quiet fury, unable to escape the feeling that he was still being watched.

sixteen

"Maggie, see if you can get Governor Deal on the line," Jack spewed walking by the front desk. "Or his aide, assistant, his mother. Somebody."

"Well, good morning to you, too," she replied, reaching for the phone and punching in a number on the speed dial. "Who pissed in your Wheaties?"

"Sorry. I'll fill you in. It's been a tough one. Also, will you see if you can round up an old cold case file for me? From 1987. The unidentified girl buried in Strangers' Row. The records might still be in the storage facility."

"It's ringing busy. I have his office on redial. Some of the older records were digitally transferred. I couldn't get to them all. I'll dig around, find them for you. I've been meaning to finish that project...I just...with your father and Skyla... What's with the sudden interest in that old case, anyhow?"

Jack knew there was some kind of connection right in front of his face. He just couldn't see it. Maybe he didn't want to see it. "Not sure yet. The woman from the Lost

Organization asked about that particular plot. You were here when it happened, right? Perhaps you might have even been working that day. Do you remember anything about that girl's death or her burial? Where she was found or...I don't know...?"

"Hard not to remember. Biggest news since Freddy Jenkins. And yes, I was around for that too. I'm that old."

Maggie blew out a breath. "Well, one thing I recall was the rain. Buckets of it. Enough that people started thinking about building an ark. May is our wettest month as you already know. But that May was particularly wet. We had all kinds of storms. A few tornadoes touched down, one right next door in Blairsville." Maggie reached for her coffee, laced her fingers through the handle of the oversized mug and took a sip. "Damn. It's cold." She set the cup down. "The young woman's remains were found burned beyond recognition in a mobile home in the hollow somewhere. No one ever knew the trailer was there. I mean, how would they? Nobody steps foot in *that* place. Not even your father who knew the mountain like it was his own backyard. The trailer had no running water, no electricity. It's called living off the grid these days. But then it was just considered being dirt poor. Anyhow, Joe believed the remains belonged to Sarafina Truelove. That was never made public, of course. And DNA analysis wasn't as advanced so the body was never identified."

"Did he say why he thought she was Sarafina?"

Maggie shook her head. "Instinct, I guess. He had

known that family for a very long time. Sarafina grew into a young woman right under his nose. Anyway, all the rain extinguished the fire..." she trailed off for a second, her mind going back to that day. "...otherwise her body would have never been discovered. It was tragic. I didn't go, you understand. You couldn't pay me to enter the hollow." Maggie had never told anyone she had been to Bone Hollow only one time and that was enough.

"I saw the crime scene photos though. They were...difficult to say the least. Pieces of shag carpeting had fused with the poor girl's skin. Most of her limbs had blackened to nubs and crumbled like burnt crackers upon contact. Her body looked like an old piece of charred wood. I don't know how they figured out she had been strangled. There were other things. Ungodly things. Scorched baby furniture and melted toys scattered all over. A rattle covered in soot in the yard. Horrible images. The kind you don't— can't forget."

"Wait, I didn't realize there was a child involved. Is he buried with his mother in Number 15?

Maggie cast her eyes toward the floor then looked up and straight through Jack as if she could see the internal workings of his mind. Know that the things he was thinking, had been thinking about his father weren't good. In fact, they were bordering on disgust. He felt his face flush.

"She," Maggie corrected, shaking her head. "And no. The child was never found. No body. No bones," she added softly. "It's like she never existed."

"She?"

"The rattle was pink under all that soot. A perfect pink rattle. I cleaned it off myself. Not something easily forgettable." Maggie didn't bother mentioning that she'd kept the rattle. That if she reached all the way back in the right-side middle drawer of her desk, it'd be there.

Maggie had never married or had children, and Jack had never known her to date or have a serious boyfriend. He didn't even know if she liked men, really, but this case had stayed with her. He could tell. A maternal pull, maybe. A longing for something she had never experienced. Something at her age that she would likely never experience.

"It's ringing now," Maggie confirmed.

Jack made a dash for his office hoping he could get some answers about Starpoint Explorations. He had to figure out a way to stop them. Or at least postpone the test drill. Maybe he needed to get the EPA involved.

It took a few minutes. He was transferred three or four times and passed back and forth between Planning and Zoning and the Board of Natural Resources in the Environmental Protection Division before he got an answer. One he didn't like when an assistant to the lead geologist explained the lengthy process of placing a moratorium on a test drill operation in the state of Georgia. Test drilling sites had been in effect from the early 1900s on, but because the process had not been regulated since the 1975 Georgia Oil and Gas Deep Drilling Act, which superseded the Oil and Gas Act of 1945, the entire area was gray, Jack learned. Dark gray, from the sound of it.

"Things related to gas drilling will be better defined if and when House Bill 205 passes in early 2017," the man clarified. "When a company owns the land as you mentioned, the only legal way to halt the operation would be if the test drill came in contact with a water source. Then by law, they would be forced to discontinue the test operation or risk severe penalties. It becomes a federal issue at that point. That's when the EPA would most likely get involved. I can email you the state law on exploration if you like."

"That'd be great," Jack said, retracing over and over the 1985 he'd doodled on the back of an envelope next to the word, FIRE. An idea started taking shape in his mind. He didn't want to credit intuition as the source; he'd have to go with a random hunch. Jack would be the last to admit he was instilled with any kind of sixth sense but while trying to escape the fire, had the Truelove children become victims of an old drill hole? How far down did those things go, anyway? Maybe Simon, Hailey, and Ben had met the same fate? It didn't seem possible though since they all disappeared at separate times. And then there was Kelly. Had she'd fallen into one of the drill holes, pulled herself out, crawled to the place he'd found her then died? None of this was making any sense. It was too outrageous to even be considered.

Jack's father had taught him never to overlook even the smallest detail or notion no matter how unlikely or absurd. It was a long shot but the only one he had at the moment. "One last thing," he asked. "Where would I find a record of test drill sites in Crow County for the year 1975 to 1985 if such a creature exists?"

When he got off the phone, he plucked the photograph of his father and Sarafina from his pocket. He smoothed out the thin creased edges. What was he missing? The fire happened in 1985, the same year the Truelove children disappeared. Starpoint bought the land right after, though they could have been drilling on it before because they owned the mineral rights to it. In 1986, the oldest sibling is captured on film, alive and pregnant. In the company of his father no less. Almost a year later, an unidentified woman is found allegedly murdered, her child missing. Joe paid for the coffin and burial. The pieces were coming together but not fast enough. If he could just make the connection, it might lead him to Hailey, Ben, and Simon.

Jack opened the center drawer of his desk and grabbed the antique magnifying glass, a Christmas gift Maggie had given to his father one year. It had a white bone handle that was long and smooth, and Jack put his hand where his father's had been many times. He didn't know what he was looking for, but Jack waved the heavy glass over the faded photograph like a witch dowsing for water in hopes that something would jump out at him. He was just about to give up when he caught it. The dark stain reflected in one of the mirrored lenses of his father's sunglasses. Could have been nothing more than a smudge. He held the photo up toward the light and moved the magnifier back and forth until he was certain. Had he not stood in that same spot many times as a boy and more than once as an adult, Jack might not have recognized the blackbird on the Crow County water tower. There was only one place in Rayburn that offered such an unobstructed view. Just why Joe and Sarafina were at the Mountain Arts Hotel only added to Jack's bludgeoning curiosity about their relationship. The place had been condemned for years. Started out as a lodge in the Sixties, exchanged hands a few times before becoming a bohemian sort of art commune and resting spot for travelers on the trail. It was abandoned in the Eighties and remained unoccupied though hikers still took shelter there not caring about the *condemned* signs trying to dissuade them. The GBI had searched that entire area over and over again, and Jack had been up there a few times solo looking for clues that might lead him to the missing children. He found nothing but cobwebs, discarded liquor and beer bottles, and random hiking gear. He even searched the adjoining restaurant. And though he knew about the tunnels in an old legend kind of way, he'd never actually seen them first hand.

What the hell were you doing with that girl, Dad? And what happened to her siblings? That his father had known that Sarafina Truelove wasn't actually missing made Jack question everything about him and he hated it. How and why would he keep that from her parents? Did it have something to do with her pregnancy? That's the only thing that made any kind of sense. Maybe he was protecting her. Or himself.

Jack slid the magnifying glass back in the drawer then took out his wallet and tucked the photograph inside the compartment across from his ID and badge. There was only one other thing in that spot. He hadn't taken it out in a long time, and he wasn't even sure why he'd kept it, but it was there. It had been over fifteen years since Lisa Harrison left that note for him. He remembered exactly where he'd found it that day he came home. On the counter next to the coffee pot on her way out the door. On her way out of his life. Powdered with age and as delicate as a moth wing, the note was folded, its creases worn and fuzzy. He swore he could still smell her as he carefully unfolded it. Inhaling deeply, he read the words in which the ink had faded but the sting had not.

I'm sorry, Jack. I can't do this. Don't look for me. I have my reasons. Please respect them.

And he had for the most part. Sure, he'd poked around for a while but felt insolent in doing so and quit. He couldn't decide if by respecting her wishes, being honorable was more or less admirable than being a quitter. It was Maggie who'd found her. Just last year. She said it was by complete serendipity that she came across the AJC online article covering the Decatur Book Festival, but Jack had his doubts about such a coincidence. Maggie was as tenacious as they come. She was also fiercely loyal.

She'd always been a book lover, and it didn't surprise Jack that Lisa was manning a table covered in *Go Set a Watchman* books by her favorite author. He still had a first edition of *To Kill a Mockingbird*, she'd given him as a birthday present. To be expected, her appearance had changed some. Her hair, lighter in color and shorter in length. Her face a little rounder but the eyes, like the glowing blue of a gas flame, gave it all away. On the inside of her forearm, Jack spotted the small black butterfly tattoo that fluttered above her wrist and just below her birthmark. He had gone with her to the tattoo shop in Blue Ridge on her birthday one year with the intent of covering the birthmark, but the skin was too scarred to take the ink, so the artist tattooed the butterfly beneath it.

After doing some more digging, Maggie had discovered Lisa had a husband and a daughter. This made Jack happy and also sad in ways he had no idea how to express. Sometimes it came out as anger, which he tried his best to hide. Other times he wanted to contact her just to congratulate her, tell her how excited he was for her, meet her daughter. But he never did. He just couldn't bring himself to do it. His father always told him that pride was the stepsister of stupidity, and Jack never bothered to tell him that it wasn't either of these things that kept him from reaching out. It was just plain fear. The fear of rejection, the fear of her being in love with someone else, and mostly, the fear of revisiting that heartbreak. But there was one thing he knew for certain. Lisa Harrison was the only woman he'd ever truly loved. And though he felt pitiful for not moving on, there was a piece of him that understood that how preserving even the most painful of moments was better than letting the last memory go. He tucked the letter back into his wallet.

Maggie had never really cared much for Lisa. "Women's intuition," she always claimed. "I don't know. Mysterious isn't the right word. Surreptitious is a better one. She's hiding something. In her defense, it might be buried so deep she doesn't know it even exists. But it's there," she told Jack. "She sure is pretty, though," Maggie had added with a curt smile. As if she thought for one second beauty was enough for the son of Joe Towns.

Jack's direct line rang, jerking him from the intrusive past. He answered as soon as he saw the call was coming from the Fannin County Coroner. Belladonna Flowers was a name that implied she might have been a florist instead of a woman who dissected bodies on a regular basis. Undersized and round, her hair was dyed the color of cabernet and bobbed just above the ears. She wore cat-eye rhinestone glasses that further accented her arched brows, which looked to be drawn on with a fine-point brown sharpie. She'd been the coroner for the Blue Ridge area for over fifty years and a two-pack-a-day smoker longer than that. There was no one older or better. Belle had recently quit smoking she told Jack. He could hear her rifling through drawers no doubt looking for nicotine gum as she gave him the news about Kelly Marsh.

"Preliminary findings include hyperinflated lungs, small bronchi occluded with mucus, fluid beneath the retina, altered extracellular matrix composition in the large and small airways, and prominent bronchial inflammation in the adventitial layer of the small airways."

"And all this means...?"

"It means that, *off the record*, my belief is that our young Miss Marsh suffered asphyxia."

"From being buried alive?"

"No, though there were traces of mud and clay in her throat and paranasal sinus cavities, her lungs were clear. If she was buried, which is a very likely possibility, she was already dead. The asphyxiation was brought on by an asthma attack."

"Okay. Why off the record?" Jack asked. He could hear the snap of gum against the click of her dentures.

"Well, number one, I'm not ready to officially release the cause of death yet, which is directly related to reason number two: I believe the asthma attack was caused by a myocardial infarction.

"English, please," Jack insisted over the metallic static, amplified by the speakerphone as she extricated another piece of gum from the foil. Or that was his guess from the sound of it.

"A heart attack. Without having a congenital condition, a fifteen-year-old girl's heart should not give out that easy." He could hear her chewing, hard and determined.

"So, she wasn't strangled? What about those purple marks on her neck?"

"Maybe an allergic reaction from the formaldehyde."

"Formaldehyde? You mean like embalming fluid? Is that what kept her from decomposing?"

"Well, yes, but what's interesting is that her preservation started on the outside and worked its way in. Embalming works the other way. From the inside out."

"So, how would that happen?"

"I have no idea. Not yet, anyhow. Never seen anything like it in all my years as a coroner. But there's something else not quite right. I don't know. I need more time. I'll call you as soon as I find what I'm looking for."

When he got off the phone, Jack got in his Tacoma and headed over to Camille's to talk with Sklya. He wanted to hug her again, hard. Tell her how much he loved her. He also wanted to see if she'd remembered anything else since he last saw her. If Hailey, Ben, and Simon were alive—and he hoped to God they were, they were in more danger now than ever. In two days, Starpoint would start drilling, and who knew what would happen once they did. Those kids, if on the mountain somewhere, might be buried alive.

He was passing Harley's Gas-n-Go when he noticed one of the Thrasher brothers pulling into the lot on a dirt bike. They weren't twins but the boys looked so much alike, Jack had a hard time telling them apart.

"Hey there, Bobby," he called from his open window as the teen started to head inside.

The young man turned, indignant until he saw who'd made the mistake. Then nervous. "Billy, sir," he responded politely.

Jack got out of the truck and walked towards him. "Sorry. Billy. That's a nice bike you got there."

"Thanks. Got it for Christmas a couple years ago."

The boy seemed distant. Uncomfortable, might have been a better description. Jack eyed the bike. It had a flat black finish and had been deconstructed. There was a silver alien skateboard sticker on the tank and red clay wedged in the deep tread of the tires.

"How's your old man doing these days?"

"He's all right, I guess. Still laid up from knee surgery."

"Well, you tell him I said I hope he feels better soon."

"Yessir. Will do."

"Hey, let me ask you something. You been out to the old Truelove place recently?"

Billy hesitated. He had a difficult time meeting Jack's eye with his response. "No, sir."

"You sure?"

"Yessir." Again, no eye contact.

"You ever been out there?"

The young man hung his head. "Yessir." He looked up. "But not after, you know, with Kelly and all."

"Understandable. Well listen, you be careful on this

thing," Jack said, gently slapping the seat of what he believed to be a Suzuki or maybe Kawasaki. "And stay away from the Truelove place. It's dangerous. I don't want to catch you out there drinking. Okay, son? You got plenty of time for that."

"Okay. I mean, yessir."

Jack got in the car and started to pull away but stopped next to the boy when he got a random thought. "Your brother have an off-road cycle?"

"Yeah. More of a tricked-out street bike. He's had that crappy thing forever; it's always broken though. Hasn't worked in months. He borrows mine sometimes."

"Did he borrow it today?"

"If he did, he didn't ask me. He better not have. Am I in some kind of trouble?" he asked nervously.

"You do something to be in trouble?"

"No. Sir," he added.

"Well then, you have nothing to worry about. Just stay away from the Truelove property and tell your brother to do the same."

The boy nodded, straddled the bike, and after a few determined cranks, pulled carefully out of the lot, making sure to use a hand signal when turning.

Jack had no doubt that he was hiding something. But what?

seventeen

Tiny's was one of those bars that opened at 8 a.m. and closed when the last person left, which from the looks of a few of the patrons, had yet to happen the night before. Angela took a seat at the bar and ordered, not without concern, a Bloody Mary. She had just finished breakfast a half-hour before and couldn't stomach the idea of a Jack and ginger at ten in the morning. Though clearly, this wasn't the consensus. A bowlegged woman in acid-wash jeans was feeding a dollar into the jukebox and taking long pulls from a bottle of Coors Light. She was stick thin and swayed back and forth as she and Tammy Wynette spelled out *d-i-v-o-r-c-e*, between drags of the woman's cigarette. The entire room reeked of smoke, which seemingly had become part of the paint and paneling after so many years.

Angela sat and the bartender greeted her. She reminded her a little of an older, shorter, more sun-damaged Anna Nicole Smith. "You want salt, Sugar?" she asked. The two words ran together like warm butter and syrup so that Angela, trying to figure out what *saltsugar* was, took a minute to respond.

"Salt. Yes. That'd be great. Absolut Peppar if you have it, please."

"We have Smirnoff and Tabasco sauce, but I promise you won't be able to tell the difference, Sweetie. I'll even add extra olives." She placed a napkin on the bar top and a few minutes later returned with the drink. As promised, there were five olives floating in the tomato juice although one of them was shriveled and tarnished.

"Thanks, this is great," she lied kindly.

Well, you're not a regular, and this isn't really a vacation destination, if you know what I mean. So, you're either a narc or lost."

"Neither, thankfully. I was actually hoping you might be able to help me."

"You're not selling anything, are you, honey? There's a sign on the door that says, No Solicitors. Salespeople eat their young, you know. They're worse than narcs in my opinion."

"No, not selling anything either, but I am looking for someone. A man by the name of Elliot Boone. You know him?"

"Eli? Oh, I know him. He's a fixture in here. In fact, he does most of his work from that corner stool over there...that is when he's sober enough to get work. He's had a rough go of it after his wife ran off. With his brother," she whispered across the backside of her hand. "And his health isn't the best either. He has dialysis twice a week now because of his kidney trouble and then there's the diabetes. But it doesn't stop him from drinking. I had to have him hauled off the hospital a few weeks ago when he forgot to take his insulin. Fell right off the barstool and bashed his head. How do you two know each other, anyhow?"

"We don't, really. At least not yet. We're in the same line of work."

"You talking about *drinkin'* or *lawyer-in'*?"

"For the moment, *lawyer-in'*, but after a couple of these, I might change my mind. I'll let you know." This got a huge bellow from the woman.

"You must be from Atlanta. We don't have many women who look like you around here. At least none with so many teeth."

Angela wasn't sure if she was supposed to smile at this. "No, actually, I'm from out of state. Pennsylvania."

"Pennsylvania? Well, aren't you a long way from home. What in the world do you want with Eli Boone, for Heaven sakes anyway? He in some kind of trouble?"

Before Angela could figure out how to answer this question, the front door of the bar opened, and most of the light coming through was blocked by a large round silhouette.

"There he is now. Well, look what the cat dragged in," the bartender called across the room then reflexively grabbed the Southern Comfort bottle, scooped some ice in a glass, and filled it to the top with the amber-colored liquid.

Once inside, the man ambled toward the corner of

the room. Disheveled was the kindest word Angela could think of to describe him. He had out-of- control sideburns, a beard that needed serious landscaping, and long, thick wiry hair that rebelled in his efforts to secure it behind his head. He sat at a stool at the end of the bar, where the bartender had placed the drink she'd made for him. He guzzled it down and another appeared almost magically on the napkin in front of him.

What Angela was about to do was not only a violation of ethics but against the law as well. But it would take time for the courts to discover her unethical, illegal behavior, and by then she'd be well on her way to fulfilling her promise to Liam. He deserved justice. The Tates couldn't have children of their own, but they loved Liam. There was no doubt about that. And Angela knew they blamed her. It was, after all, her fault, but somehow, she also knew they blamed themselves. If only they had done this or that. Liam never even knew he was adopted. They planned on telling him when he was older, but he never made it to older. *Adopted*, she heard herself whisper. The word seemed to manifest on its own without any volition and linger for a few seconds in the air like an unsettled spirit. It was an angle she hadn't considered previously. Maybe his death had something to do with a biological parent?

Angela waited until Eli had nearly finished off another drink before she took the stool next to him and introduced herself. She laid the envelope containing a check for ten grand between them on the bar top then ordered another drink for herself. Money, the greatest motivator, second only to revenge and possibly lust. Once she handed it over, she'd have less than five grand in savings and maybe two in checking until her parents' house sold. This wasn't including her mortgage or paying her assistant. Not that Eli Boone didn't look like he could use the money. She didn't know if it was the cheap vodka or the gut feeling that this was a very bad idea that made her stomach twist and turn. Never one to walk away from a challenge or a promise, Angela did something that probably wasn't exactly foreign in this bar but completely new to her. She propositioned him.

eighteen

Grace Truelove didn't recall the exact day she stopped digging for the jar she buried upon her arrival. When she tried to remember the rainy evening she came upon the Truelove place, the memory was as blurred and out of focus as if she was viewing it from beneath deep water. The last thing she remembered doing that night was writing a clue in her journal as to where she had dug the hole. Something only she would understand. But when she came out of the fever and studied the words written on the yellowed page, they didn't mean anything to her. She must have been in the midst of an epileptic attack when she wrote them, and any memory of it was further destroyed by the fever she developed. It was the only explanation. Now that she had May and Jeremiah, the contents of the jar had become less important, the attacks seldom. Sure, they could have used the money, but it was just money. Not nearly as essential in life as what she already had and the risks that she took to get it. What she really wanted was to find the jar and give the money to the men looking for her so they'd leave her and her family alone. In an effort to remember where it was, she wrote the words over and over on the blank pages, but they never once sparked her memory.

She thought about destroying the journal, but it was the only proof that Emily Capeheart had once existed. She'd let that name go—she had to for Jeremiah and May, but she refused to let go of the injustice she suffered at the hands of Dr. Frost. He had promised her grandmother that he'd keep her safe, but as soon as the old woman was dead, he imprisoned her and took the money that had been left for her care. Epilepsy made it easy to convince anyone who may have been concerned that she had fallen into the hands of the devil. Possessed by darkness, the good doctor had said. She'd even been subjected to an exorcism to try and rid the *demons*, which had been epilepsy all along, something the doctor was fully aware of. No, she couldn't destroy the journal because by doing such, the truth would be lost. Her truth. Even if she couldn't remember much of it after her brief illness, the written words would serve as her memory. She wouldn't let them go.

It took her five years at the asylum to gain the doctor's trust. Meanwhile, she lost herself in books of astronomy, mythology, alchemy, and history. But as she grew into a young woman, she began to understand that women with knowledge were feared as much as those possessed, so she used her extraordinary beauty for gain instead. Manipulation had never been a flaw of hers, but she became skilled at it anyway because there was no other way she could escape the asylum. She even shared Dr. Frost's bed not once considering the repercussion, only concentrating on the idea of freedom. This went on for some time before the perfect opportunity came into view as bright as a Southern star on the night she fled Gracewood.

The doctor, who drank regularly before turning in, had one too many scotches and didn't notice the bitter taste of Luminal in his peaty nightcap. Grace had saved two of the epileptic tablets in the hem of her skirt and crushed them into his drink, praying that she would not need them herself. He went to sleep and she removed the money from the safe. She took only what her grandmother had left her.

One of the janitors, an older man she'd developed a friendship with over the years, led her down the least used hallways and out through the back delivery door, showing her a gap in the fence where she could squeeze through. When she was out of sight in the midst of pines surrounding the asylum, she watched in horror as the man was attacked and beaten by Dr. Frost and a group of security personnel. She had no doubt that she would be blamed for his death. And though she felt so much guilt over it, she would not let his loss of life be in vain. He paid with his life for her freedom, and she would die herself before ever going back to the asylum, to Dr. Frost. He would never know he had a daughter, and May would never know about him.

May was nearly seven years old when the men came

again as Grace knew they would. She and Jeremiah had produced two other children by then—a boy and a girl. The children were playing outside when through the kitchen window, Grace saw a Crow County Sherriff, accompanied by three other men approach. It was Jeremiah's birthday, and she was busy making a cake. He was fishing at Ghost Lake and not expected back until later that evening. Her children were her first concern. She could hear the youngest counting near the back porch. Hide and seek.

"Gil," she whispered through the back screen. "I'll be the seeker. You, Evie, and May all run and hide in the hollow."

"The hollow? Gil asked wearily. But we're not supposed—"

"It's okay." Grace knew that what she'd protected her children from for years, may just keep them safe now. It was her only hope.

"I give you permission," she comforted Gil. "Don't be afraid. You'll be fine. Just pick the best spots and don't come out until I find you no matter what happens or what you hear. Whichever one of you is the quietest will get to lick the bowl. Tell your sister and brother, okay? Shh...go on now. Hurry. Run. I love you," she screamed, but it came out in a whisper.

Grace blew out a sigh of relief as she watched her children flit into the apple trees like small perfect birds and disappear before her eyes, the faint sound of innocent laughter and crunching leaves lingering in the air behind them. She said a small prayer and began to nervously twist the spoon ring Jeremiah had made for her once their last child was too grown to use it. They couldn't afford a wedding ring the day they were married, but Grace wore the spoon ring with the ornate T on her ring finger. It fit perfectly. She'd always heard that this custom was established because the ring finger led to the heart, and she wanted desperately to believe this.

Please keep my babies safe, dear Lord, she whispered then ran upstairs to document the arrival of the men and the end of her own hiding in her journal, which she kept secreted under one of the wide pine planks in the closet. It was after she closed the door that she turned and found May standing behind her.

When Jeremiah returned from fishing that night, he was met by a very hungry and scared Gil and Evie, but May and Grace were gone. Months later, some travelers found the badly decomposed remains of a woman hanging from the Tree of Lost Souls. The news eventually reached Jeremiah who knew in his heart that it was his Grace. Sheriff Elijah Towns and those men from the asylum had killed her and taken May.

nineteen

On the way back from Tiny's, Angela discovered in a vacant stretch of strip mall, a random and very lonely Kmart where she bought a bag of coffee (did every place carry Starbucks now?) and a large coffee pot. She'd rather be out of toilet paper than coffee.

Before heading upstairs, a spontaneous pull drew her to the cemetery and to Strangers' Row. She just couldn't understand why her mother had saved the image of Number 15 so many years ago. And what had kept her from "digging" into it herself? Maybe she forgot about it and something triggered her memory. Did she have some kind of connection to the dead girl? Considering these questions and many more, Angela sat in front of the grave and ate an apple she'd bought at the gas station earlier when she filled up. Then for reasons she couldn't explain, she walked around looking for the Truelove grave, but before she could locate it, her eyes caught sight of another grave. Joseph Macon Towns. His headstone was not ridiculously ornate or overdone. Just a simple memory stone, honoring a father, a grandfather, and according to the epitaph, the best sheriff Crow County had ever had. However, it was his date of death that most interested Angela. She couldn't be sure, but her memory rarely failed her. This was unfortunate most of the time. Maybe not today, though. Maybe today, it served a purpose other than torment.

She pulled out her cell and captured an image of the marker then hurried across the street and up the stairs to her room. Angela set her bags down then tossed her purse and laptop on the bed. She snatched the former occupant's notebook from the bureau where she left it, sat down and opened it. The yellow sticky note was still attached to the first page where she'd stuck it. She pulled up the image on her phone and compared the date on Joe's gravestone to the one on the note. Both September 8th. Jack's father had evidently died on the same day he was to meet the woman who rented the room before her. The woman who never returned. It was too much of a coincidence to think they weren't somehow linked.

Angela didn't want to be distracted by this. Not now when she was so close to getting justice for Liam, but she wasn't sure there was a way to ignore it. Something was very wrong in Rayburn. Something other than the psycho Redeemer and the three missing children. It was, she felt, in all four chambers of her heart, somehow, in some way, connected to her mother and the unidentified dead girl on Strangers' Row. But how?

After brewing a pot of coffee, Angela started going

through the notebook, page by page, word by word, determined to discover exactly what the hell was going on in this town. In order to accomplish this, she first needed to find out the identity of the woman who previously stayed in the room and more importantly, what had happened to her. She also had to discover just who was buried in plot Number 15 on Strangers' Row.

twenty

On Tuesday morning, the Fannin County Magistrate Court sat on West Main Street, nestled between the churches of Blue Ridge like a malediction. But just to be fair, Jack thought to himself as he got out of his truck, it sat the same way every other day of the week. He wasn't entirely sure what made today feel different. It might have been the warmer weather or quite possibly the stray reporters circling the courthouse—vultures waiting for some dead thing to bleed out.

Because of the limited jurisdiction of the Magistrate, Knox might be extradited to Cherokee County for arraignment and further prosecution after the preliminary. Unless, of course, he was only charged with car theft and was able to bond out. What a crime that would be. Then the lines of criminal and civil would be as astigmatic as Judge Dawson's eyesight. On a Friday night. Two hours into happy hour.

Jack slammed the rest of his coffee and got in the security line. Once he was through the checkpoint, his gun secured in a locker, he took the stairs, two at a time, to the second floor. By the time he reached the courtroom, the proceedings had already started. Scanning the room, he recognized a few local news people, but most of the others appeared to be law students, vigorously taking notes. Jack nodded toward Deputy Wayne seated in the witness area and slid into the first seat available near the front of the courtroom. Wayne was the only witness up there. The DA must not have been able to yet locate the man who owned the stolen car.

Jack found it hard to believe that the GBI hadn't come to the same conclusion Angela had—that Levi Knox was the Redeemer, otherwise the courtroom would have been flooded with chaos and the venue redirected to another jurisdiction. What were they waiting on? He had to admit, it was a bit odd that Angela herself hadn't called every news source possible with her speculation. Why was that? The more attention she garnered, the more likely Knox would face extradition if he really was the serial killer known as the Redeemer. That's what she wanted, right? He figured she'd be here, today, but he scoured the room several times and hadn't seen her. A woman like that didn't seem like she was capable of waiting in the shadows.

"My function and responsibility as Magistrate," Judge Dawson continued, "is to handle what are called preliminary hearings. These are hearings to determine whether there is probable cause if you committed the offense with which you are charged. We are not here today to have a trial to determine whether you are guilty or innocent. Probable cause means the likelihood that you committed an offense based on the facts presented and not legal technicalities. To explain even further. It is my duty, today, to hear if the evidence presented has enough weight for you to be bound over to Superior Court for further prosecution. Do you understand this?"

"Yes, your Honor, I do," Knox responded.

"For the record, and I know there was an issue with the assigned public defender, the attorney now representing Mr. Knox, pro bono..." the judge eyed his paperwork...is Elliot Boone. Is that correct?"

"Correct, your Honor," a tall large man whose tiny head looked like it belonged on someone else's body spoke up. He was pale and sweaty and sickly looking. His wiry auburn hair was pulled back, and he wore glasses that looked like they belonged to a seventies high-school gym coach. His beige suit jacket may have once fit him but it was too small now, a tear at the seam visible from all the way across the room. The pits were stained with perspiration. "I am awaiting approval for a pro hac vice admission. The application went in yesterday after learning the unfortunate fate of the assigned public defender, the only one available to my knowledge. My pro hac vice is paying the required fees now and should be here directly after if you'll make an exception."

"Just to clarify, your pro hac vice is also pro bono?"

"Yes, your Honor."

"Interesting. Let the records show that because we are currently limited in the public representation factor, I'll pre-approve the application as long as the out-of-state attorney has paid the mandatory fees and meets the requirements for the Northern District of Georgia Local Rule 83.1B admission to pro hac vice. As local counsel, these responsibilities will ultimately fall on you, Mr. Boone. Do you understand your role and accountability in this?"

"Yes, your Honor, I do."

"Prosecution, are you ready to proceed?"

A thin man with a beak nose and salt and pepper hair replied. "Yes, your Honor."

The man's pale grey suit fit him like a second skin, something Jack felt might come in handy in such a position. With his ashy tone, Jack had a difficult time deciding where the suit ended and the skin began. Across the room, his peripheral caught Buddy McCay sliding into a seat.

"Very well, then. Shall we begin?"

After a moment of rustling papers, whispers, and a few muffled coughs, the judge took a sip of water and addressed Knox.

"Now, the charge against you, Mr. Knox, states that on or about Thursday, October sixth of this year, you violated Georgia Code, Title 40, Chapter 6, Article 2, constituting an initial charge of failure to obey a traffic-control device. Basic traffic violations of this caliber would normally be considered civil. However, as I understand, the vehicle..." he glanced at the paperwork before him, "...a 2014 Toyota Camry, silver in color, used in the aforementioned offense had been reported stolen and because you could not provide proof of insurance or registration for the vehicle in question..." The judge scanned the paperwork again, "...Deputy Charles Wayne conducted a routine search, in which, he discovered inside the trunk of the vehicle what he suspected to be," the judge took a breath, "human remains of a phalangeal nature." He poured fresh water from a clear pitcher into his glass, took another drink then continued. "These allegations constitute a criminal charge should your connection to them be proven beyond a reasonable doubt and considered a matter for a higher court. Do you understand what I'm saying, Mr. Knox?"

"Yes, your Honor."

"Very well, let's proceed. Prosecution."

Deputy Wayne was sworn in and seated. He gave a detailed description of the events that prefaced Levi Knox's arrest, including the search of the stolen vehicle, which led to the discovery of the Igloo cooler containing human remains. He also described the suitcase that was packed with plastic prescription bottles and pocket Bibles. According to the report, which the prosecutor had him read in part, he also found some type of medication in Knox's jean pocket. Capsules containing a white powder. Deputy Wayne spelled out the name written on the label after making several unsuccessful attempts at trying to pronounce it.

"Sorry, it's Oriental," he relented. "I mean, Asian," he quickly corrected. "Japanese, Korean, Chinese, something. I'm not certain."

Jack took a look around to try and gauge any reactions concerning the distinctive contents of the suitcase. He didn't see anyone making a connection until Buddy McCay's eyes caught him in the crosshairs of his horned-rimmed progressive lenses. Jack could almost see the wheels spinning. Only then did Jack recall that Buddy's father had taken a deep interest in the Redeemer story for years. Even wrote an award-winning feature that was picked up by some of the major newspapers. Buddy always said that was the piece that broke the old man. Sent him over the edge into early dementia. In journalism, Buddy once told Jack, there's one story that makes you, and it's usually the same one that breaks you.

If Buddy ran a story on this, it would become a media circus, and Jack would likely be removed from the picture entirely. He wouldn't have another shot at Knox, and Hailey, Ben, and Simon might be gone forever. He was running out of time. They were running out of time. He received daily calls from the parents of the children, and it killed him not to be able to tell them he had some kind of lead. A clue that they were still alive and that he would be bringing them home. Where in the hell were they? Who took them and why? The truth was, he had no idea.

Just then the courtroom door opened, and a figure

that moved toward the front like a drill sergeant on roller skates blazed passed the spectators. She wore a fitted black suit, the jacket tailored, the skirt tapered tightly just above her knees. Her shiny blonde hair was pulled into a neat bun at the nape of her neck, and as she marched toward the defense, she adjusted her expensive-looking tortoise-shell eyeglasses. Jack only caught a side view but he could tell. Emory all day. Their graduates carried a certain ambiance about them: a perfect blend of beauty, brains, and an overt confidence bordering on entitlement. This combination rarely went unnoticed especially in a field dominated by men. All eyes were upon her as she took a seat next to the defense attorney who quickly leaned and spoke near her ear. The woman pulled a notepad from a distressed brown leather messenger bag. Jack still couldn't get a proper look at her from where he sat.

The judge acknowledged the woman and she stood and introduced herself. The voice was familiar but before Jack had a chance to place it, the woman said her name. He craned his neck to get a better look then choked trying to swallow.

"Well, I'll be damned," he said softly. He'd been joking when he suggested Angela Archer should represent Knox. What the hell was she up to? Whatever it was, Jack wasn't sure he liked it, but regardless he was impressed with her fierce determination. He didn't want to condemn her until he understood exactly what was going on, but it didn't look good morally in his opinion. Definitely not the type of woman who lingered in the shadows.

"You're just in time. Cross."

"Thank you, your Honor."

"Deputy Wayne," she addressed austerely. Angela had enough experience to know the importance of defense leading the questions during preliminary proceedings where the stage belonged to prosecution. "You pulled Mr. Knox over because he ran a red light?"

"That's correct."

"Curious. Is there a camera at that particular light or did you just happen to *catch* him running the light?"

"No, Ma'am. No camera. I was at Harley's Gas-N-Go. On the corner. That intersection has quite a bit of speeding activity. We monitor it regularly."

"So, a speed trap?"

"Now, I didn't say that. However, I do catch speeders there from time to time."

"And you normally search the vehicles of these types of offenders? Speeders, red-light runners?"

"Objection your Honor," the prosecutor called. "Deputy Wayne had probable cause to search the vehicle because it had been reported stolen."

"Stolen?" Angela pressed. It's my understanding that the owner of the vehicle cannot be located. Who reported it stolen?"

The prosecutor stuttered and the judge interjected. "I'm going to allow this. Please answer the question, Mr. Wayne. How did you know the vehicle was stolen?"

The deputy looked toward Jack with a face that was full of either regret or embarrassment or a combination of both. "I searched the vehicle because I recognized it. I see it around town all the time, but I didn't recognize the man driving it that day. I knew something was wrong. The guy who owns that car works at the pawn shop. His name's Mark Garrett. His mother confirmed that he hadn't been home for days when she called to report him missing."

Jack hung his head slightly. Why hadn't Wayne told him that? Christ. This wasn't good. And was that a grease stain on his shirt? Thank God for fluorescent lighting.

"I see," Angela said. "So, did you know this Mark Garrett person was missing before pulling over Mr. Knox?"

"No Ma'am."

"So the car hadn't actually been reported stolen?"

"That's correct."

Just one more thing. At any point did you see Mr. Knox load anything into the car he was driving? The car that you *assumed* belonged to Mark Garrett, the *guy* from the pawn shop?"

"No Ma'am."

"Thank you. No further questions."

Prosecution swore in two more witnesses, both experts. One an osteologist from Atlanta, the other a forensic pharmacologist from Jacksonville, Florida. The osteologist confirmed that the five digitus quartus or fourth finger bones found in the car Knox was driving were human, and that they belonged to children in the age range of seven to eleven. "But without a DNA match for comparison, it would be close to impossible to determine who they once belonged to. However, without a doubt, I can verify that they were cut cleanly from the hand they were detached from. In other words, they were not sawed nor broken off, but cut in a single swift motion be that an ax or garden shears or meat cleaver, post mortem. Additional investigation might help pinpoint or at least narrow down the instrument in question. This, of course, will take some time."

The pharmacologist ascertained that the old prescription bottles, ten in total, though empty and labelless, all contained traces of strychnine residue. Either the contents evaporated over time or were emptied before being stored. It's difficult to determine which at this point."

"And where would one obtain strychnine, Doctor?" the prosecutor asked.

"Well, rodent poison used to be the best source but nowadays it's mixed with LSD or heroin or cocaine and sold on the street. It is also easily attainable through the Dark Web and is, believe it or not, the drug choice of weightlifters and athletes. Goes by the street name of White Devil. Distributed in modest amounts, it can produce a feeling of euphoria."

"But," the prosecutor interrupted. "Just to confirm. It can be deadly?"

"Oh, most definitely. And the danger is that each person has a different reaction to it. Where one person might get high, the same dose given to another might stop the heart or restrict the lungs. Respiratory failure is not a pleasant way to go."

"Can you tell us about the other findings?"

"Yes. The capsules Deputy Wayne described are Qu Huanzhang Panacea or Yunnan Baiyao as it's sometimes called. It's a powdered styptic agent used during the Vietnam War by soldiers who had been wounded and needed to cease bleeding. It helps the blood coagulate. It's not a controlled substance. And though still available and sold mainly as an over-the-counter herbal remedy, it's not widely used or respected in the medical field."

"Thank you. That'll be all for now," the prosecutor said pulling a large white envelope from his briefcase. "Exhibits," he identified, handing over a set of documents to the bailiff to pass to the judge. "In light of the issues involved with securing a public defender for Mr. Knox, I went ahead and made copies of the photographs for defense. There's also an accompanying list of what we are presenting here today, including a list of names we've pulled from the boxes of medical records discovered in the vehicle Mr. Knox was driving at the time of his arrest. The records date back to 1966 and belong to women who were patients of Dr. John Hixson from the Hixson Women's Clinic." The bailiff placed an envelope on the table in front of Angela.

"Hixson's practice," the prosecutor continued, "has been closed for some time now. Dr. Hixson—"

"I'm aware of Dr. Hixson and the unfortunate circumstance surrounding his demise, counselor. You'd have to be living under a rock not to be."

"Of course. Sorry, your Honor," the prosecutor said like a child who'd just been reprimanded by his father. "We're not exactly sure how the defendant obtained the files or why, but we feel they are significant in some way to the empty drug bottles found in the car and the missing person, Mark Garrett. I also have a written statement from the GBI agent leading the investigation into Mr. Knox's arrest. The agent is in trial in Atlanta and could not be here today, but he feels strongly that this case should be bound over and not dismissed for reasons he cannot discuss openly at this time. May I approach?"

"You may," Judge Dawson said then fished out a pair of glasses from the inside of his robe and adjusted them on his face before reading over the agent's statement. When he finished, he cleared his throat, took off the glasses, and used his fingers to massage his eyes and bridge of his nose.

"Because I feel there is sufficient cause to believe Mr. Knox is involved in some type of unspecified drug activity not to mention a morbid disrespect for human remains, I'm going to bind this over to Superior Court in which I also reside. In other words, I'll be seeing you again in the near future, Mr. Knox." He put his glasses back on and shifted some paperwork on the podium. "Monday, January 23rd, 2017. And because defense brought up some valid concerns about probable cause, I'm going to set bail at $250,000. A little higher than normal but considering the factors, a responsible decision in my opinion. Court adjourned." The judge smacked the gavel and called the next defendant's name among the hushed chaos of shuffling papers and loud whispers.

Jack waded his way through the stream of people exiting the courtroom and slid into one of the pews as Knox was being guided from the table where he'd been sitting by an officer. Jack knew Knox had to be at least fifty, but he certainly didn't look it. He appeared to be in good shape outside of some minor bruising and the dark circles under his intense green eyes.

When Knox was ushered past Angela, he spoke directly to her.

"Good to see you again, counselor," he said, smiling devilishly at his newly-acquired attorney. "I thought you might come."

His voice was deeper than Jack remembered. It had an educated southern inflection that he hadn't caught the first time. Slow and charismatic, drawn out in that meticulous way that keeps Charlestonians from letting go of their vowels. A compact, older, and not quite as handsome Matthew McConaughey. Something else to knock the profilers for a loop.

"Hope you liked my gift," Knox said. His eyes glowed with some sort of pernicious triumph.

Angela stared intently at him or maybe through him, Jack thought as he stood across from her, watching this uncomfortable scenario unfold. Her eyes were like daggers, sharp and penetrating, and Jack knew then that Angela Archer was seeking her own justice. A very dangerous and often unsuccessful quest. Her demeanor changed suddenly when she noticed she was being studied. She gathered her belongings then turned toward Knox and spoke in a professional tone that bordered on curt.

"I'll be in touch, Mr. Knox."

Jack thought he saw her hands shaking, but when he took a closer look, either he was mistaken or she had somehow gained composure.

"Just what do you think you're doing?" he whispered near her ear as they walked out of the courtroom with him on her heels. Before she could answer, Jack continued his inquisition. "I thought you said you never met Knox. What was that little comment he said about seeing you again? And the gift? What gift? What the hell is he talking about? You better start leveling with me if you want my help."

In the cavernous hallway, Angela stopped and faced him being careful not to speak too loudly. "So now, you're willing to help? Your hands were tied before if my memory serves me. Who or what untied them?"

She turned and marched down the stairs before Jack could respond. He followed close behind.

"I'm saying what you're doing is wrong on many levels. You cannot, in good faith, represent a man..." People passed and Jack lowered his voice. "...you want more than anything to be convicted. A man you feel in every beat of your heart is guilty. A man you'd like to see get the death penalty."

They reached the atrium now. Jack moved ahead of her and stopped, blocking her way. Her dark eyes shined with what Jack thought was anger but recognized after a few seconds as apprehension. He'd go as far as to say, fear, even.

"Your pretense is unethical," Jack admonished. "The man deserves proper representation even if he is guilty. It's not right what you're doing. You aren't going to fight for him; you're going to hand him over to prosecution on a silver platter."

"No, I'm not," Angela spoke calmly. "I'm going to get him acquitted."

"What? Not if he makes bail, you're not."

"Unlikely." She moved around him as if she'd once played professional football and headed toward the main doors.

"Maybe so but not impossible. I've got Maggie working on a warrant to search his bank records. If they show what I suspect, Levi Knox will be out and gone before you have a chance to put a defense together even if it is a false one. I've got missing children out there, Angela. Three of them. Three beautiful children who are loved and cherished, and the only suspect we have bails out and disappears. What am I going to tell their parents? Sorry. He left town."

Angela wanted to tell him that she knew from

experience that *sorry* didn't help but she refrained. Instead, she said, "Why don't you tell them what I already know? What I've already told you. Levi Knox did not take their children. You are wasting valuable time."

"You are an infuriating woman. You do know that, right?"

"I have to go," she said.

"Sherriff," Deputy Wayne called as he scurried down the stairs. The stain on his shirt was even more prevalent in natural light. It was definitely a grease stain. A big one.

"This conversation isn't over," Jack said in a quiet firmness, but Angela had already started walking away again. She turned only slightly when she reached the front door, and Jack thought he saw it again, the fear. He watched her through the tinted glass walk down the stairs and onto Main Street wondering what was keeping him from disliking her.

"You know her?" Deputy Wayne asked when he caught up to Jack.

"We've just recently met."

"Well, it looks like you either want to arrest her or kiss her."

Jack shot his deputy a look spiked with irritation. "What we really need to be discussing here, Wayne, is why you led me to believe that you pulled over Levi Knox because the car he was driving had been reported stolen. You never even ran the tag, did you?"

Deputy Wayne answered by hanging his head, and

the two walked outside to their cars, but were separated when Jack was approached by local journalists inquiring about Levi Knox and his possible connection to Rayburn's missing children. He was grateful they hadn't yet made the same association Buddy had. That Knox could be the Redeemer. But that was coming soon. It was only a matter of time. Jack suspected Buddy would be waiting for him when he got back to the office with a litany of questions. Others would not be far behind.

twenty-one

As soon as Angela got back to her room, she ran hot water through the coffee pot and made a cup of herbal tea. She wasn't a tea drinker but her nerves were shot. Other than Lipton, Jasmine was the only tea they carried at the drugstore she stopped by on the way home from the courthouse. To get to the section where it was kept, she had to pass by an entire row of shelves dedicated to Civil War memorabilia. Mostly t-shirts, shot glasses, and coffee mugs adorned in rebel flags or plastered with sayings like, *The South Will Rise Again*. For some reason, Jasmine tea wasn't a big seller. The boxes were covered in a thin layer of dust and Angela wondered momentarily if they would sell more if they labeled it Confederate Jasmine. Regardless, the tea did nothing to calm her nerves even after two cups. She'd been shaking so badly when she left the courthouse; she hoped Jack hadn't noticed though it was ridiculous to think he hadn't. Not much got by him, she'd come to realize. If he wasn't so damn unbearable, she might have found him attractive, likable even. She couldn't remember the last time she was on a date. No time, no desire, and that one thing that kept her from ever wanting to even think about love and relationships. Guilt. Besides, she didn't even like herself. How could anyone else?

It was the photograph, the *gift* as Knox had called it that was giving her the most grief. She couldn't erase it from her mind. Her encounter with Knox had been more unsettling than she ever imagined it would be. All those talks she had with herself had been futile. There was no way she could have prepared for seeing him face-to-face, and she hated herself for not being stronger. She'd been terrified just sitting near him in the courtroom. Fearful and angry. It took everything in her power not to reach over and choke him to death with her bare hands. But this wasn't the plan she had devised. She needed him freed first. Then she'd take care of him her own way. Leave him somewhere he'd never be found. But in order to do this, she'd have to keep her composure, maintain her focus. Get him out of there.

With this in mind, Angela powered up her laptop and began drafting a discovery motion for document production. She had the photographs and a list of what was presented as discovery. The medical records were of particular interest to her, and this was because she already knew why Knox had the bones in his possession. The records though, that was a real mystery. How did he get them and why did he have them? She didn't know how long the DA would take to provide her with copies of each record once he got her request to produce, but at least he'd been kind of enough to provide her the list of names on the records. Maybe kind wasn't the right word. Over-confident. She'd been that way once. He was so sure he was going to get a conviction. Not that it mattered much. The women on that list were probably all dead by now, and those still living would neither remember their experience nor want to talk about it if they did. But at least it was something. She took a closer look at the list and sighed as she quickly scanned over the names. Hundreds of names, many of which had last names that had faded or been scratched out. These names were followed by a date. Angela guessed this might be either the patient's birthday, or day of her last appointment, or...What else could it be? After a minute or so, she put the list aside, feeling overwhelmed.

She tried to recall the year that HIPAA came into play. Mid-nineties? The prosecutor claimed the records dated back to—she looked down at her notes—1966. She began searching her computer files until she found what she was looking for. The Redeemer's first victim was killed in 1987, though Angela remembered that there had been a young boy who disappeared three years before this, but because his body was never found, authorities couldn't be sure he'd actually been a victim. She searched her files again until she saw the folder with his name. She opened it and stared at the grainy newsprint image. Thomas Blake, age ten. Disappeared from Shelby County, Tennessee in 1984. His family refused to believe he was dead, so they never claimed him as such. Angela typed his name into the search bar, and Google returned hundreds of results. After scrolling through pages of them, one grabbed her attention. "A Mother's Dying Wish" from the *Wolf River Times*. The article began with a letter written by a woman named Diane Blake, who was sick with terminal cancer and longing for her only son, Tommy. She begged for his safe return or any information that would let her know what may have happened to him, and wrote that she only wanted to see him one last time before she died, which Angela assumed must have already happened because of the age of the article. It was near the end of the story that Angela's eyes caught on the word, *adopted.* Like Liam, Thomas Blake had been adopted. She opened another window on her computer and searched the death records in Ancestry.com for Shelby County, Tennessee and Diane Blake's obituary. She'd died in 2003, survived only by her daughter, Carolyn, who Angela discovered with more research still resided in the same town, a Memphis suburb along the Wolf River. She'd worked for the same bank for fifteen years, and because she was a notary, her information populated on the first page of searches. Unable to reach her, Angela left a voicemail message. She wanted to confirm that Thomas Blake had been adopted and if so, from where. A theory was taking shape in her mind. She was beginning to feel that whatever reason Knox had for killing innocent children and taking their fingers, had to do with Hixson and his adoptions.

She needed help, and the one person she could think

of that might be able to offer it to her was miles away so an email would have to suffice. She logged into her email account.

Chad Stein had worked for NCMEC, the National Center for Missing and Exploited Children, for over twenty years. He started off as a volunteer when his younger sister disappeared. His father, an FBI agent, now retired, still had connections in many different states. Between the two of them, there wasn't much Angela couldn't find out. They'd help her with just about anything. This was mainly because years ago, she prosecuted the man who'd held Chad's fifteen-year-old sister captive and raped her repeatedly for weeks, inviting his friends, for a small cost, to join it. Then he choked her until he thought she was dead and dumped her on the side of the road. A man who worked for the train station discovered her early one morning as he made his rounds. She was still breathing and vocalized later when she finally was able to speak that she wished she would have died.

Her captor came from a prominent family who hired the best defense team available, but none of this mattered to Angela. That fucker was going down. And he did. It just took a very long time. Not that it wasn't worth it knowing that he'd never hurt another innocent victim. His friends had gone down, too. Not in the legal justice kind of way but vindicated, nonetheless. One of them was knifed in a bar fight. Another a suicide. The last, killed in a hit and run. In the middle of the night. On a secluded road. After he'd left a bar so intoxicated the bartender had taken his keys. The unidentified woman buying him drinks all night—a woman who looked suspiciously like Angela, left shortly before he did and was never even considered a suspect. She wasn't exactly proud of some of the things she'd done, but Liam's death changed everything about her. Her moral compass had been irretrievably broken, or at best, the needle stuck in the remorse and vindication position. Both had manifested so deeply in her bones she feared they had become part of the marrow.

It's been a long time. Sorry I haven't been in touch sooner. I'm working on a new lead with the Redeemer case, she'd written in the email to Chad. *If possible, can you find out how many of the his victims were adopted? It's important.*

As she waited for his reply, she picked up the list and once again started scanning the names the prosecutor had supplied. She didn't know any of these people. It wasn't like she was going to recognize one of them by name. However, three-quarters of the way through the list, when she was seconds from considering her efforts futile, something grabbed Angela's attention. Not a name but a date. Not just any date. Liam's birthday. Right next to the name Rhonda whose surname had faded so badly she couldn't read it. Only the first letter, D, was legible. Rhonda D.

Once she caught her breath, Angela reached for her phone and scrolled through her contacts until she found the last known number she had for Glen Tate, Liam's father. She hadn't seen or spoke to him in years but not because she hadn't tried. He'd made it clear at his ex-wife's funeral. He never wanted to see or hear from Angela again and she understood this. There were still days she couldn't even look at herself in the mirror. She'd been solely responsible for the horrific death of his only child, and the only thing she could do about it now was find the son-of-a-bitch who killed him. Not just find him. Kill him. And even this wouldn't make it okay. It would never be okay.

When she got the recording that Glen's number was no longer in service, Angela decided to try his email. She'd heard from an old neighbor who had managed to keep in touch with him for a while that Glen had moved to a remote part of Arizona, and that he was doing his best to drink himself to death among the cacti and desert sand. It made sense to Angela. She'd thought many times about moving to such a place. No grass, no trees, no flowers. Only miles of desiccated forever. A place where the horizon was nothing more than an illusion, an imaginary line that blurred what was real from what wasn't.

It took over an hour to compose the email, which consisted of five lines and a single question that might make a world of difference. If Liam had been adopted from Hixson's Women's Clinic, she'd have a place to start. Could he have been Knox's biological son? Maybe Liam had been stolen from him and this Rhonda person. Had they been told he was dead by Hixson who then sold the child illegally to the Tates? And did the Tates know they were buying a baby stolen from his parents? They couldn't have known. Could they have? Desperation made people do things they wouldn't normally do. Angela knew this first hand. It was in the news all the time, too. Women pretending to be pregnant so they could befriend actual pregnant women, kill them and cut their babies out. But even if Liam belonged to Knox, why would he want to maim and kill his own child? None of this shit made any kind of sense. In the middle of all this confusion was the clipping of the tombstone her mother had saved. Could the unidentified woman buried in on Stranger's Row be Rhonda D, Liam's biological mother? And if so, Angela wondered, why had her mother felt the need to solve whatever mystery lay beyond this woman's grave?

Angela kept deleting and recomposing her email to Glen. There were times that words just weren't enough. This was one of them. But she gave it her best heartfelt shot. Unlike all the other letters and emails to him, this one was less of an apology and more of a plea for help. Her finger hovered over the mouse a long minute before she gathered enough courage to hit SEND.

She spent some time researching Knox and was anxious to compare notes with Jack if he was willing to share. She hadn't expected Knox's parents to be wealthy and successful. It would have made more sense to her if they were dragging him around the South as part of a traveling carnival. Because he was an only child whose parents were now dead, Angela was going to have to dig deep to obtain any kind of personal information about him.

Her eyes burned and she closed them briefly then did the same with her laptop, stood to stretch and walked over to the window. The library might have old phonebooks and maybe even cross-reference. How many Rhonda D's could there be in Rayburn? If she had ever even lived in Rayburn. She might have been from out of town or passing through. Angela had spotted the tiny library nearby, just off the square. She could probably walk to it, but she'd have to work her way through the crowd of picketers and pro-lifers who had taken over downtown Rayburn. Their shouts, muffled only slightly by the window pane, reverberated against the glass. Angela placed her hand on it and felt the vibration. It was like a savage drum circle where there was about to be some type of sacrifice on an altar or something. She saw it then, a purple blur making its way slowly through the crowd. The girl from the diner. For a minute, it looked as if she might be taking part in the protest, but after watching her a few minutes, Angela noticed she was showing every person she passed, a flyer with a photograph on it or at least that's what it appeared like from a distance. Evidently, she had not found her friend yet. Angela originally thought it was a Facebook acquaintance or an old high-school friend the girl lost track of, but now she wondered maybe if this might be a more serious missing person's case.

Angela watched for a few more minutes but became

distracted by a noise in the hallway behind her. Something being dragged across the wood floor. She turned and listened. The sound grew louder the closer she moved toward the door. What was that? Being as quiet as possible, she latched the chain—something she kept forgetting to do, then pressed her ear gingerly against the wood. An unexpected knock made her jolt.

"Hey Miss Angie, you in there?" she heard from the other side of the door. "It's Joey. I got *dat* stuff you asked about from the lady that bolted."

twenty-two

It was hard not to notice the new waitress Pearl had hired. The lavender blue hair was a dead giveaway, but it was also the way she carried herself through the crowd that gained Jack's attention. Confident, determined, and curious. He hadn't plugged her for a protester though. What was she doing out there? He pulled into his designated spot in front of the office and studied her as he read over Buddy's article on the front page of the Star. "Caretaker Survives Gunshot Because of Heart Being in the Wrong Place." It was lunchtime and Jack had picked up a BBQ chicken sandwich and sweet tea from the Pink Pig drive-thru on his way back from Blue Ridge. Curious, he sat in the car and monitored the young girl while he ate his lunch. When he finished, he got out and made his way over to the trash can close to where she was standing. The person she was speaking to was apologizing and shaking their head, but Jack couldn't hear what was being said.

"Hey there," he called to her as he dropped his empty lunch bag in the garbage can.

The girl turned and tucked whatever she had in her hand into the tapestry tote bag hitched over her shoulder.

She had quite a bit of ink. Gothic sort of stuff. Jack saw that in Athens and Atlanta, but it was definitely out of the norm in Rayburn. The delicate silver chain around her neck was an odd contrast to all the angels and demons waging war around it. There was a pale heart-shaped spot just below the hollow of her neck.

"You're the new hire at Pearl's, aren't you? I didn't catch your name the other day."

"Name's Harper but I prefer Nelle."

"All right. Good to meet you, Nelle. I'm—"

"I know who you are," she interrupted, studying him intently. Her eyes, a vibrant violet blue, glowed in the sharp sunlight.

"Right. I guess the star kind of gives it away." He gestured toward his shirt.

She said nothing. Just kept searching him with her eyes.

More than a moment of uncomfortable silence passed between them before Jack broke it. "You from Georgia?"

She nodded. "Born in Summerville. It's—"

"Near Rome. I'm familiar with it. I'm a huge Howard Finster fan."

Her demeanor changed slightly then. "Really? Me, too." She'd become a fan of the prophet's art before she discovered that he also had visions. "Do you know about

Paradise Garden? It's really cool. One of my favorite places." She couldn't wait to get back there. And she was missing school though she had no real friends there. Most of the students at Rome High thought she was a freak, but this was her last year. Then college. Maybe. Everything was in a holding pattern right now.

"I do. Been there many times. You're right. It's an incredible place." He'd first learned about Finster from REM, but doubted she would even know who they were, so he didn't bother mentioning it, or the fact that he and his college friends liked to hang out at Paradise Gardens and get high.

The Finster connection brought out emotion in the girl that Jack had not expected. Enthusiasm accompanied by something resembling a smile. But this quickly faded with his next question.

"You here in Rayburn visiting family?"

She hesitated. "Sort of. I guess. It's complicated. I'm renting a room from Pearl right now. Until...things get, you know, worked out." Deep down inside she knew this was impossible. Her mother would have been in touch with her by now if she could have.

Jack nodded. "I see." He knew everybody in town and wondered who she was here to see. Or maybe she was here to *avoid* seeing someone. He wanted to ask her why she wasn't in school. She couldn't have been more than sixteen or seventeen. But a lot of young people dropped out of school these days. Some of them even had their parent's permission. Or maybe she was just one of those who graduated early. He studied her casually trying to figure out why she seemed so familiar but decided against prying for the moment.

The girl looked over her shoulder in the direction of the diner then back at Jack. "I have to get going," she explained. Pearl's expecting me."

"Okay then. It was nice talking to you, Nelle. You know where to find me if you ever need anything." He hooked a thumb over his shoulder in the direction of the sheriff's office. "Welcome to Rayburn."

Jack was halfway across the street when he heard the girl call him.

"Sheriff?"

He turned. Even from a distance, her eyes sparkled like iridescent blue glass, and that sense of familiarity caught him again. It was a color he associated with fire. The glowing blue in a flame.

"I'm glad your niece is okay," she said. She wanted to tell him that other children would also be okay. But she couldn't because she wasn't sure they would be. Each time they came to her, their eyes and mouths were packed with dirt, their skin charred. Her visions had always been dark even as a young girl, but here in Rayburn, they were almost apocalyptic. She was afraid for those children, for her mother. She was beginning to think she'd never see her again alive. And the black butterflies swarming all around weren't helping any. Lately, every time she closed her eyes, they were there fighting for space behind them.

"Me, too," he nodded then continued on across the street.

Jack's cell buzzed, but he ignored it when he saw that Buddy McCay was waiting for him when he got inside the building.

"You got a minute, Sheriff?" he asked following him to his office. "I've got two things on my radar. I'll make it quick and be out of your way. I know you got a lot going on right now." He took out a pack of Black Jack from the pocket of his plaid shirt, removed the foil wrapper and folded the gum into his mouth. He held the pack out toward Jack like he was offering him a cigarette. Jack waved it away.

He wondered momentarily if Buddy had been born with gum in his mouth since he never seemed to be without it. That would give Freud something to chew on in regards to his oral fixation theory.

Buddy took a seat, leaning forward in it uncomfortably and locking his hands onto his knees. "Number one: I saw you in court today for Knox's hearing. Give me one reason that might convince me that Levi Knox is not the child killer known as the Redeemer because I'm thinking he is."

Jack remained silent. What could he say? The spicy scent of licorice filled the air around him. It reminded him of Good & Plenty candy and this made him think of his childhood, which immediately brought Hailey, Ben, and

Simon into his mind. He saw their faces, their gapped tooth smiles. Felt that sickness in his stomach and that ache in his heart that accompanied it. Were they buried out there somewhere like Kelly. Like Skyla.

"Look, Buddy…"

"I know. You probably can't talk about it," Buddy relinquished. "There's confirmation in your silence. I'm going to have to look into this you realize. I mean, there's no way, I can't. My father…this story nearly killed him. He was obsessed with it until the dementia took over. I often wondered if that damn disease was a gift from God. Some sick blessing in disguise."

"I suppose that's one way to look at it. About the story. Can you do me a solid and give me a couple of days, Buddy?" I'm asking as a friend."

Buddy sat for minute digesting it all then nodded. "Okay. But I want this story. For my father. I owe it to him."

"I understand. Just give me a little more time, and I'll tell you everything I know." Jack hoped it would be more than he knew right now, which was nothing. All speculation at this point. His phone buzzed again. He'd missed several calls from his sister. This time she texted. *Call me, please.*

Buddy began patting his pockets. "Number two: I was at the hospital earlier trying to find out what happened to the caretaker from the cemetery. They've moved him to a room, and he's getting around so well they may release him to the pastor's care soon. He's not talking though. And I'm still waiting for him or *you* to fill me in on the details."

Jack knew that the Cemetery Man was well on his way to recovery. He'd been calling daily to check on him for many reasons but one in particular. "Yeah, well, Tomb doesn't talk much from what I understand. And I don't have any solid details at the moment."

"Well, talk or no talk. He can write." Buddy pulled out a crumpled slip of paper from the zippered pocket of his gray canvas messenger bag. He unfolded it and slid it across the desk so Jack could read it. DON'T KNOW was printed across it in what looked like a child's uneven block handwriting. "This is what he wrote when I asked who he thought shot him."

Jack stared at the note, wondering why this man felt the need to protect the woman who did her best to kill him. "And your point is..."

"My point is," Buddy clarified, "that the man is lying. Plain and simple. I think he knows who shot him. And you know what else? I think you do, too."

"Now, why would you say that?"

"Gut instinct." Buddy took the gum from his mouth, wrapped it in the foil he'd saved and tossed it in the trash can next to the desk. "Also, there's a witness."

"A witness? To the shooting?" Jack wondered momentarily if his mother had confessed to Buddy but then realized how ridiculous this sounded. That woman could burst into flames and deny ever smelling smoke. He reached up and massaged his chin, curious and nervous. "And who might that be?"

"A little lady by the name of Skyla Jane Brady. Saw her yesterday at the diner. She was wearing fairy wings in the booth next to me when she leaned over and asked if I wanted to know a secret. When I said yes, thinking she was going to tell me about fairies or princesses, she whispered in my ear that her nana had a gun and that she saw her with it by the church a few days before. I'm sure your sister registered the look of shock on my face because she practically grew fairy wings of her own and flew out of there."

"Well, Kitty does have a gun—probably has had one ever since she could walk, but she also has a permit." As soon as Jack said this, he remembered that his mother had forfeited her gun and said gun had disappeared. "Okay, let me get this straight. Skyla told you that she saw her grandmother shoot the Cemetery Man?" Jack was fishing at this point. Trying to figure out how he was going to handle this.

"Not exactly. According to her, on the same day she returned from that dark damp place—her words—she saw her grandmother through the diner window, pointing the gun at *someone* near the church—someone she couldn't see. Said she didn't remember any of this until this morning when she woke. Rather coincidental don't you think?"

Jack stared long and hard at Buddy. He didn't want to lie to him. Kitty had shot the Cemetery Man, and he was going to have to arrest her, witness or no witness. He rubbed his hand across his forehead then over the rest of his face, exhaling slowly.

As if Buddy knew what Jack was thinking, he stood and grabbed his bag, slung it over his shoulder. "Look, I understand. She's your mother. I didn't come here with that news to threaten you with a front-page story. I came here as a friend to let you know you have a major situation on your hands. I want to do the right thing, and I don't know what that is right now, but I have faith that you do. You're the son of Joe Towns. You don't know anything but right. We'll talk later, okay?"

Buddy's words lingered long after he left the room. Words that would have, any other time, comforted Jack. But now everything he believed about his father had become questionable. Sarafina Truelove's secret pregnancy. Her disappearance and possible death. That damn photograph of Joe and her together. The missing baby. And to make matters worse, he was going to have to arrest his own mother at some point.

Jack was leaving a message with his sister when Maggie brought by a box that she hoisted upon Jack's desk.

"Here are the files you wanted from the young woman buried on Strangers' Row. Last person ever to be added to that lonely row of old bones. Just a warning. The pictures are horribly graphic. Of course, you studied Shakespeare so you should be fine." She smiled coyly.

"You're the best, Maggie."

"Also, I've been making headway with Knox. So far,

this is what I got. Christopher Levi Knox got a football scholarship to Clemson but dropped out after an injury. He also legally removed the Christopher from his name. His father was in real estate in the Raleigh-Durham area. His mother, a former beauty queen and heir to some banking fortune that makes the Carnegies appear impoverished. Blue bloods. Good people, it seems. Wealthy and god-fearing. More money than you and I will see in a lifetime. Both died in a plane crash some years back. I've never liked small planes. One good gust of wind and it's all over. Anyhow, they left a trust for Levi. He was their only child. Quite a bit of money from what I understand. Not sure there's any left. Still working on that piece, but I can tell you that Levi Knox has been in and out of hospitals over the years. The last time must have been quite serious because he was in for two years, most of which was spent in ICU."

"Two years? That's a long time to be hospitalized. What for, you know?"

"Not sure. That will be a little more difficult to uncover with HIPAA. I can do it, but it will take some time. He was admitted in 2014. I know that much."

"Shit. That's when they stopped."

"What stopped?"

"The Redeemer killings."

Maggie's face grayed. She plopped in the chair almost involuntarily. "Sweet Jesus, I remember those horrible murders. Is that what this is all about? Knox. You think he's the Redeemer? You mean with the Bibles and...?"

"I'm not entirely sure yet. But yes. No. I don't know."

"So that's why that lawyer lady from the missing children's organization came here, isn't it?"

"Angela. Afraid so. But none of this leaves the room, Maggie, okay? Not a word of it."

"Do you think he's the one who took Skyla? What about Ben and Hailey and Simon? Oh dear God."

"I did think that. I'm not so sure now."

"And Kelly? Did he kill her? That poor sweet girl."

"No. That's one of the reasons I'm uncertain. Kelly Marsh died from a heart attack. But that hasn't been officially released yet."

"Natural causes?"

"Well, the coroner doesn't believe it was so *natural* for a fifteen-year-old girl. I'm waiting for her to get back to me with a full autopsy report."

"What is happening in this town, Jack? I don't understand. Your father must be twisting in his grave."

"I wish I could answer that. Lots of questions, very few answers at the moment. Which reminds me, did you take a gun off my desk? Lock it up, maybe? It belonged to my mother. She surrendered it the day Skyla returned, but I can't seem to find it."

"Kitty Lynch handed over her gun? Were the four horsemen of the apocalypse rapidly approaching behind her? I can't see her handing it over for any other reason. I'm not even going to ask. But to answer your question, no.

Never even saw it. Wayne might have grabbed it."

"Maybe, but I don't think so." Jack knew without a weapon, it would be more difficult for his mother to be convicted. Not impossible. Just more difficult. But this was his mother. It couldn't get any more difficult—any worse really. Then Jack heard his father's voice. *Things can always get worse.*

twenty-three

"You think you might be able to find this woman?" Joey asked Angela as he handed her the plastic storage bin. "I mean, I'm not looking for her to go to jail or anything like that. I just want what she owes me for the room."

"Of course," Angela said. "I understand. I'll do my best to locate her. I'm sure there must be a valid reason for her disappearance. Maybe she was involved in an accident. Did you check the hospital?"

"Nah. Rayburn's so small I think I would have heard about something like that. Besides, she only gave me her first name. No credit card or anything like that. She paid cash daily for the room. Nice lookin' lady. Tall, skinny. These real wild eyes. Not my type you know. Too thin. Said she was working on a research project, but I got the feeling she was hiding out."

"Why's that?"

"You know, always wearing baseball caps and dark sunglasses. Once, I saw her in a short black wig and on the same day, a long red one. The next day, bleach blonde. I know a thing or two about being on the lam if you know what I mean, and that woman was doing her best not to be recognized. But she was quiet and never bothered anyone so I figured it was none of my business. These days, I try to stay in my own lane. Anyhow, I should have known when I didn't see her car out front for a few days that she bolted. After a week, I figured she wasn't coming back so I chalked it up as a loss and packed up her room."

"Do you recall what kind of car she drove?"

"Some type of sedan. White. Kia, I think."

"And you remember her name?"

"Yeah. Same as my sister. Lisa. Her name's Lisa. If you find her, and she pays up, I owe you a pizza and a beer."

Joey handed over the bin, and Angela used her hip to bump the door closed behind him. Her motive for finding this woman didn't have anything to do with her outstanding debts, but Joey didn't need to know this.

Angela set the plastic container on the bed, unsnapped the lid, and started rummaging through the contents. There were some clothes and toiletries inside, sunglasses, a handful of baseball caps, wigs in a variety of colors and lengths, and three or four spiral notebooks similar to the one she discovered in the closet. She picked up one and leafed through it. Pages and pages of research on the Trueloves dating back to the early 1900s. On the inside cover, circled in red was the name Anna Cave. Beneath it, Guardian Angels Assisted Living Facility, Rome,

Georgia. Her mother had an older half-sister named Anna but they had some type of falling out and never spoke again. Angela had never met her though she knew she lived—if she was even still alive—in Georgia somewhere. It bothered her that she had no way to let this woman know her only sister had died. She would find a way, eventually. When this was all done. *If* it ever was done.

Angela picked up another notebook. This one was dedicated entirely to the Hixson Women's Clinic. Again, she saw the name Anna Cave sprinkled throughout and discovered by reading through the notes, she'd been Dr. Hixson's only nurse until she retired the same year the clinic closed down.

It's when she reached for yet another notebook in the bottom of the bin that Angela became distracted by the worn leather-bound journal beneath it. Intrigued, she picked it up. The stitching and binding were so loose it almost fell apart in her hands. She tightened her grip and carefully opened the cover, the spine snapping and cracking as she did. The inscription on the first page had bled a little onto the paper, but it was still decipherable.

The Journal of Emily Louise Capeheart
Gracewood Asylum, 1930

The book's pages, warped from time, were thick and musty and resembled the folds of an old accordion. Near the center, an edge of a photograph peeked out and Angela tugged on it gently. A wedding picture. The man was tall, thin, and austere looking. The woman was mesmerizing with long dark hair and pale eyes that even a black and white photograph could not conceal. The names, Jeremiah and Grace Truelove were written on the bottom edge. The writing so faded it was nearly illegible. On the pages the photo bookmarked, the same set of words was written over and over again.

Where the devil watches the dead forget where the devil watches the dead forget where the devil watches the dead forget where the devil watches the dead forget where the devil watches the dead forget where the devil watches the dead forget where the devil watches the dead forget where the devil watches the dead forget where the devil watches the dead forget...

Three pages of the same words over and over again. Mesmerized and also a little disturbed, Angela sat on the edge of the bed, flipped back to the beginning of the journal and began to read. The library would have to wait.

Two-and-a-half hours later, in the time it took her to finish, she had without realizing it, slid down onto the floor where the bed braced her back. She'd been so engrossed in reading that she had somehow missed a call from Jack. After listening to his message, she noticed a new email had arrived and was shocked to find that Glen Tate had actually gotten back to her. She didn't expect to hear from him, especially in such a short amount of time. Her finger hovered over the email for what seemed like forever. Then she tapped it open.

There was no salutation. Just three sentences.

We adopted Liam from the Hixson Women's Clinic in Rayburn, Georgia on the day of his birth. Please don't contact me again. It's too painful

The last sentence was left without punctuation. Whether intentional or not, it reestablished what Angela already knew. That certain types of pain had no end. There was an unreachable hurt inside of people that could go on forever like a desert horizon or a sentence without a period.

Angela returned Jack's call. He was headed over to the diner and wanted her to join him. He had learned something about Knox he wanted to discuss with her. She still had reservations about involving him in whatever this Lisa person had going on, but she had a sinking feeling that something tragic had happened to this woman. She hadn't just run off. The fact that she had met with Jack's father just before she vanished and on the same day of his death was just too coincidental. And hadn't Jack mentioned that his father had died suddenly? One unexpected death, another person missing. The two instances were somehow related. They had to be.

In the journal, Angela discovered that Grace Truelove had actually been a woman by the name of Emily Capeheart who had escaped from an asylum south of Rayburn in 1935. She'd taken quite a bit of money from a doctor there, and from what Angela could decipher from the blurred penmanship, a man had been killed in the process. Grace hid the money on the Truelove property somewhere according to her entry but fell ill and couldn't find it when she pulled out of the fever. The clue she'd written in the journal in regards to where this money had been buried did not ignite her memory no matter how many times she'd written it across the ivory pages. This explained the repetition of the words, *where the devil watches, the dead forget.* She was trying to recall where she hid the money. Angela wondered if it was still there somewhere on the Truelove property. It couldn't be worth anything if it was, but maybe Lisa thought differently and maybe that's why she'd come to Rayburn. Lisa's notes didn't mention anything about the money though. She seemed more interested in finding out what happened to the Truelove children, and she obviously felt Joe Towns knew something about it.

The very last entry in Grace's journal was likely the last thing she'd ever written. Sheriff Elijah Towns and two other men were knocking on her door. Angela wondered what had happened to her and what all this had to do with Lisa, Jack's father, and the girl buried on Strangers' Row. If she wanted answers sooner than later, she was going to have to get Jack involved.

Angela tucked the journal in her bag and walked across the square, through the dispersing crowd toward the diner, wondering with each step if involving the sheriff was the right thing to do. She learned something valuable over her years as a prosecutor. The law and what was right were often two entirely different things.

twenty-four

In all his years of eating at Pearl's, Jack had never once waited for a seat. He wasn't complaining. He was happy for her. She deserved to be successful even at the hands of such tragic chaos. But he had to admit, the staff looked disheveled and exhausted. Pearl was sitting over in the corner at the only booth available, rolling silverware. She had a colorful scarf wrapped around her head.

"I'm waiting for counter space. You want some company?" he asked.

"Well if it ain't the sheriff of Crow County," Pearl said, motioning him to sit. She divided the napkins and pushed the silverware tray in his direction. "Just in time. I could use some help."

Jack watched her remove a knife, a fork, and a spoon and place them in the corner of the folded napkin, which she rolled up tight and neat. He did his best to emulate her technique, but his attempt looked loose and sloppy at best.

"I met your new girl today," he confessed. "She seems

like a nice young lady."

Pearl looked over at the counter where Nelle was busy with customers. "Yeah, she's a good girl, I think. Having a bit of a hard time right now, but she'll get through. I do worry about her though. Awfully young to be on her own."

"Where are her parents, you know?"

"Not sure about her mother, but her step-father lives in Rome. They aren't close from what I understand. Parents divorced a few years back. That's about all I know other than she's here to find a friend she lost touch with. Must be somebody important because I saw her passing out flyers today on the square. She doesn't divulge much, but she's definitely determined and headstrong. Kinda reminds me of somebody I used to know."

"And who's that?"

"Me."

"Is that right?"

"Mmhmm. You know who my very first friend was when I came to this little ol' town? Your father. A white man of law befriending a fourteen-year-old runaway in a mountain town full of hate for black folk. I remember the day I met him. Freddy was beatin' the shit out of me in the parking lot of the Piggly Wiggly when your father came out da store, carrying a bag of groceries. He wasn't even in uniform. He dropped that bag then he dropped Freddy and helped me to my feet. I was a child carrying a child. Your father told him then not to touch me again or he'd end him.

Freddy should have listened. He looked out for people, your father. Especially lost young ladies trying to find their way in this big ol' scary world. Joe was a good man, and I miss him every day."

Jack missed him, too. Until recently, he'd always thought of his father as a hero. Pearl must have known he was suffering with this. She always seemed to know things. The woman was clairvoyant, no doubt about it. Maybe not intentionally so, but she had an innate gift of some sort.

"Can I ask you something, Pearl?"

"Anything you want, darlin'. I'm always here for you. You know that. You like a son to me."

Jack felt his face flush. "Did you know the Truelove children?"

"I knew the oldest girl, Sara. She was a sweet thing, pretty too. Always kind to me. We were about the same age. She'd come in here hungry sometimes without a cent to her name, and I'd sneak her a slice of pie or half a grilled cheese. That's *befo* I owned the place you see, so I had to be careful. I think I may have been her only friend besides your father. Right before she and her siblings disappeared, she told me she was gonna have a baby, and that she had to get away for a while."

"So, she *was* pregnant when she disappeared?"

"That's right. Your father knew, too. She told him. He cared for that girl so much. Even met her up at the old Mountain Arts place once to give her money. He suspected she was hiding out up there somewhere because she didn't want her parents to find out she was pregnant. Your father was trying to find her a safe place to stay when that strange man came into town and stole her away somewhere."

"What man was that?"

"I don't know. Some drifter. Good-looking fellow but he had the devil in his eyes. Drove one of those old Ford vans, you know the kind they show now on some of those serial killer shows. I didn't like him the first time I ever saw him. Knew he was trouble. Kept quoting from the Bible like he was some kind of preacher man. But he was no man of God. Pearl knew that for sure."

"I'm going to ask you something very important now, and I want you to be completely honest with me, Pearl."

"I'm always honest. Ain't no other way to be. Now, tell me: what's on your mind? And why all this seriousness all a sudden?"

"My father...was he, did he..." Jack didn't even know how to ask such a question. "Who was the father of Sara's child? Was it my father?"

"Boy, are you out of your mind?" Pearl tossed a crumpled napkin at Jack. "Your father was a good man. He saved my life and would have saved Sara's too if he could have. You ought to be '*shamed* of *yo'self*." She shook her head and kept rolling both her eyes and the silverware.

"I'm going to tell you somethin' I ain't never told a single soul," she whispered across the table. "And you better listen closely cause I ain't never gonna repeat it or ever admit I said it. I know you already know that I lost a baby. Freddie done beat me so bad that poor little thing couldn't take it. Made it so I couldn't have any more children. After I lost the baby, when I finally got my senses about me, I made me a plan, and God gave me the strength to follow through with it. You see ol' Freddie went to sleep one night, after eating one of my delicious homemade pies, and I made *sho* he never woke up. Why you think I call them Pearl's Heavenly Pies? Not that I think he ever saw Heaven. Anyhow, I called your father in the middle of the night because I knew what I'd done was wrong, and I was ready to pay the price. When he got there instead of arresting me, he asked if I had a shovel. Then he dug a hole in the woods behind my house. Took all night and his hands were covered in blisters, but that hole was so deep, Freddie Jenkins would never be able to claw his way out," she said in a voice free from contrition and barely audible from across the table.

"And then you know what your father did? He helped me get a tombstone, and I buried my sweet angel, her bones so small like a bird's on top of that devil so that if he ever opens his eyes, he'll be forever reminded of what he done. If anyone says anything bad about your father to me, they better be prepared *fo* a fight. You included." She pointed a butter knife in his direction.

Jack tried to take this all in. It was a lot even with someone whose shoulders were as broad as his. "So, who *was* responsible for getting Sarafina pregnant?"

"Well, Sara worked part-time for Dr. Hixson, cleaning

the clinic. Running errands and whatever. Stuff like that. One day, she came in here with that drifter and a young boy who never spoke a word, and I overheard the conversation between them. He said he'd help her so that Hixson wouldn't take the baby and adopt it out but that he needed a favor in return. You see, Hixson told her if she told anybody about the baby, he'd take her parents' land from them, house and everything. Right then and there, that's when I knew that Hixson was a no-good *sombitch*, and I also believed he was the father of her unborn child. I could have put money on it. I've often thought that maybe he was the one to set the fire. Anyhow, a few days later, *afta* I thought it over, I told your daddy what I'd heard, and that's when he tried to find Sara a safe place to hide, but then their house caught fire, and she disappeared and so did her brothers and sisters. And I never saw dat man again. But the boy..." She hesitated. Trying to pull the memory of his face into the present.

"What about the boy?"

Pearl looked down, her brows furrowed in contemplation. "Ah, it's nothing," she waved her hand."

"Tell me," Jack insisted.

"Well, I think I saw the boy at the church a year or so later, but I can't be sure. In all honesty, I never got a good look at him while he was in here. I was more focused on that stranger and Sara. That man gave me a real bad feeling."

The bells on the front door jingled. The diner was

starting to clear out, and when Jack looked around, he noticed Angela taking a seat at the counter.

"Is *dat* your plus one?" Pearl asked. "Too late. I done seen the light in your eyes, boy. She was in here the other day. Pretty little thing. Full of secrets and heartache though, so you best be careful."

Jack shook his head, trying not to smile. "Just an acquaintance," he reassured. "It's business."

"Mmhmm. What you think? Pearl was born yesterday? Pearl always knows, *suga.* Go on. You just as bad at lying as you is at rolling silverware. But I still loves ya, boy."

He stood and headed toward the counter but turned. "Thanks, Pearl. For everything."

She tapped her closed fist against her heart then pointed toward Jack. "I got you."

Jack saddled up to Angela who was already looking over the menu and pondering whether or not she should give the house wine a try. The alcohol selection included one red, one white—brands she'd never heard of and two domestic beer choices. She opted for coffee and Jack ordered the same.

"I appreciate you meeting me over here, last minute. I wanted to let you in on some things Maggie discovered about Knox."

"Well, you know, I had wild plans for this evening but they fell through," she joked. "Heard there was a line-dancing scene here somewhere. Besides, there's something

I need to show you." She pulled the Capeheart journal from her bag and set it on the counter.

"What's that?"

"The short answer is that it's Grace Truelove's diary."

"Truelove? As in *the* Trueloves? Rayburn's Trueloves?"

"I'm guessing so."

"How...Where'd you get it?"

"That's what I want to talk to you about."

"You all ready to order?" Nelle interrupted, filling their mugs with coffee and paying close attention to the worn journal the sheriff now held in his hand.

"Turkey club for me," Angela replied. "Hold the bacon."

"Same," Jack added opening the journal. "I'll take her bacon and extra mayo, too."

"Well, as you know I'm renting a room above the pizza place, right? Apparently, the woman who stayed in the room before me left it along with a bunch of other stuff."

"Who's Emily Capeheart?" Jack asked as he read the inscription.

"She was a young woman who escaped from an asylum known as Gracewood in the early 1900s—with quite a bit of money that she took from her doctor. Money that may have belonged to her. Anyhow, during the escape, a man was killed, and she was held responsible, though I don't really think she should have been. Somehow, she ended up at the Truelove property where she hid the money but then got sick and couldn't remember where when she recovered. Later, she and Jeremiah Truelove were married, and she became Grace Truelove—here's a photograph of the two of them. I think it's a wedding photo."

"I think you're right," Jack agreed.

"The whole story is all there. She recorded everything."

Jack flipped carefully through the crisp pages of the journal, stopping when he came across the repetitive words, *where the devil watches, the dead forget.* He spoke the words aloud, and Nelle turned suddenly towards him, her eyes narrowed in scrutiny. She looked like she wanted to say something.

"Are you okay?" Jack asked.

"Yeah, I need to run out to the car and grab something. Your food should be up shortly."

"Couldn't come soon enough," Jack said. "I'm starving."

"What do you think it means?" Angela asked, motioning toward the strange words.

"I have no idea."

"Well, there's more."

"More words?"

"More to the story. It has to do with the Truelove children. One of them, anyhow." Angela hesitated. "And your father," she added cautiously.

"*My* father?"

"I believe so. You see, I discovered a spiral notebook

in the closet of my room my first night in town. I didn't think much of it, and I was going to hand it over to Joey to put with the rest of the stuff the woman left behind. But a sticky note with your father's name on it slipped out. And I...I don't know. I just thought you might want to know. I should have given it to you earlier." She dug in her bag and pulled out the note she tucked there earlier. She handed it to Jack and watched his face grow pale as he read the note aloud.

"Meet Joe Towns about the Truelove girl. He knows something. September 8th, Old Mountain Arts Hotel, 10 a.m. September 8th," Jack said softly. "That's—"

"I know. The day your father died. I saw it on his tombstone when I was in the cemetery."

"Who is this woman? I need to talk to her immediately. I..." He stood, no longer hungry and rather speechless.

"Well, that's a problem. Joey doesn't know who she is or why she never returned for her belongings. She's MIA."

They both looked toward Nelle, who now stood in front of them with two plates of food. She was swaying, her eyes rolling back in her head. The plates trembled in her hands.

"Nelle? Nelle?" Jack called louder, but she was in some kind of trance and didn't seem to hear him.

"The fire," she cried. "Oh God. Save them. The fire. It's coming. You have to save them."

"Save who?" Jack asked frantically. "Nelle?"

The room was spinning now and Nelle became sick with nausea. She could see three children, a girl and two boys, huddled in a room that was swimming in flames. The girl reached out but her skin began to melt and fall away from the bone. Then all three children burst into flames. Nelle watched their floating ashes morph into black butterflies that swarmed around her face until she lost her breath. "The children. You have to save the children. They're all going to die down there. They'll burn to death. The fire's coming." She started to shake violently, and Jack reached across the counter to steady her, but she slipped through his hands and fell backward. The plates she held crashed on the floor around her like a glass puzzle that was missing pieces.

twenty-five

"I still think you should let me run you over to the hospital to be checked out," Jack tried to persuade Nelle who now sat in a chair in the office. Pearl had been the first one to her when she fell, and after applying cold rags dipped in vinegar and marjoram to her face, the girl opened her eyes and was able to sit up and eventually stand. Jack, Pearl, and Angela were gathered around her, concerned in many ways about what had just happened.

"No hospital. I just need some rest that's all," she assured them." I've had these attacks as long as I can remember. I'll be fine."

"Could be a seizure, Nelle," Pearl said. "The marjoram will help, but you need to be checked out by a doctor."

"It wasn't a seizure." Though her mother had told her recently that she'd discovered epilepsy ran in the family bloodline. "I promise. It's just something that happens. I'll feel better once I get some sleep."

"Do you remember what you said?" Angela asked.

"About the children. And the fire?"

"Not really," but this was a lie. She did remember, and it made her sick.

Jack helped her up from the chair. "You said a fire was coming, and the children were going to die. Down there. What fire and where is down there, Nelle?"

"I don't know. I swear I don't. If I did, I'd tell you." She rubbed her temple.

"Okay, let's get you home."

"I can drive myself. I'm okay. I'm fine. Really."

"If you wait just a minute, I'll close up and follow you home," Pearl offered. "Or I could call someone to come get you, if you prefer." But she knew the girl had no one. It was a foolish offer.

"Not necessary. I appreciate you all being so concerned, but I can take care of myself. My mom raised me to be independent." She grabbed her purse and her jacket and headed for the back door. "I'll be here tomorrow for my shift. See you then," she said then pushed the door open and walked out into the darkness. Jack watched her get into her car and drive off.

"That was something else," Angela said blowing out a breath. "She might need to be evaluated. I've never seen anything quite like that before. Did you see her eyes? The poor girl."

"Can't say that I have, either," Jack admitted. "It was a little disconcerting for sure." He understood now the girl's intense connection with Finster.

"Well, it's clear da girl's a seer," Pearl announced. "On the island, we call them Sibyls. We have many. My great aunt was a Sibyl, God rest her sweet soul."

"So that's where you get it," Jack said.

"Being blessed with good intuition and *seeing* are two completely different things, boy."

"Well the whole thing freaked me out," Angela confessed. "What did she mean by the children dying in a fire? Do you think she's talking about the children from Rayburn?"

"I don't know," Jack said. "I'll try and talk to her tomorrow."

"You all want me to make you something else to eat? You could take it with you."

"No thanks, Pearl. Not for me," Jack said.

"Me neither," Angela chimed in. "I'm exhausted. "And," she turned to Jack, "I have my first meeting with Knox tomorrow."

"Come on, I'll walk you across the street. I'd like to have a look at what that woman left behind. I need to figure out who she was and how she knew my father."

Before they could reach the door, Pearl caught up to them. Handed them a white paper bag with grease stains on it and another smaller brown bag. "Here. The last of the fries, and two bottles of beer. Nothing fancy. Domestic. On the house. You tell anyone that I let alcohol out the door, it ain't gonna go well for you. I'm good friends with the sheriff." She winked. "Now, God Bless, and get on outta here so I can clean up this mess."

The night was cool and for once, the square empty and quiet. They snacked on the fries Pearl had given them as they walked slowly across the street. In the distance, Angela could see a silhouette in the shadow of the awning at the pizza place. Ronnie, smoking a cigarette, the embers glowing like fireflies in the twilight. It reminded Angela of what Nelle had said about the fire during her seizure or whatever the hell it was.

As they walked, Jack shared information that Maggie had discovered about Knox.

"Why do you think he was hospitalized? Any idea?" Angela asked.

"Not a clue. Obviously, something serious to be in for that long. And according to you, the killings stopped in 2014. More than a coincidence, I feel. Maggie said she has reached out to a few neighbors of the family. They were loaded by the way. Ton's of money. Lived in some gated community, one of many properties they owned. Someone must know something."

"Well, I managed to locate Knox's former girlfriend from college. I didn't speak with her but she alerted me to a group known as the Sons of Perdition."

"Is that a biker gang?"

"No, it's a fundamentalist splinter group whose members were once a part of the Church of Jesus Christ of Latter-Day Saints. Apostates who espouse marriage above all and are believers in the concept of blood atonement."

"Blood what?" Jack asked.

"I had to look it up, too. It's a Mormon-based doctrine that supports that no amount of prayer or repentance can wash away certain sins. Sins like adultery and murder, and I imagine, abortion. In these cases the sinner's blood has to be shed or there can be no forgiveness, according to the laws of Heaven. In my opinion, it's basically a sacrifice but considered better than suffering eternal damnation in the afterlife in the eyes of the Church. It's an archaic belief no longer supported by the LDS. Too controversial. But the extremists still honor it."

"Sounds similar to the Old Testament eye-for-an-eye principle."

"I guess, but interestingly enough, there are three states that offer a firing squad method of execution based on the blood atonement doctrine. Utah, no surprise there. Mississippi and Oklahoma. Tennessee and South Carolina are also considering it as an option."

"Well, who forgives the firing squad for spilling the sinner's blood? I mean, that's murder too, right?"

"Good question. I don't know. While researching, I found an article about a man whose life is continually threatened because he left the Church. Apostasy merits blood atonement as well. It's quite the commitment, apparently."

"Like marriage, right?"

"Maybe."

"Do you think that Knox may not be working alone

then?"

'I'm not sure. It's hard to believe there is one person out there wanting to poison and dismember children. But a whole group of them? Of course, there are some who would argue most religions poison their followers in some way or another."

Once inside the building, Jack followed Angela to the top of the stairs and to the left, hoping his boots weren't leaving mud on what looked like freshly-polished wood floors.

"Joey keeps a clean place."

"Clean, yes, but he's not exactly picky with his renters. You know anything about the other occupants here?" Angela asked quietly.

"Nothing first hand. Haven't had any trouble with them, but I've heard a few things in passing, and I'd have to agree with you."

"Great. That's comfort—" She stopped short when she saw the door to her room slightly ajar. Had she left it that way because she was in such a hurry?

Jack saw it then, too, and quickly moved ahead of her, passing the take-out bags to her. He used his hand to guide her behind him, put a finger to his lips, and unholstered his gun. He pushed her even further against the wall, held the gun up and bumped the door open with his boot. "Stay here," he mouthed over his shoulder. It was the first time he had pulled his gun in years, and it felt strange. He'd always believed that words were a person's best defense even though his father warned him that there would come a time when he was going to have to use his weapon. He hoped today wasn't that day.

After checking the closet and the bathroom, he lifted the edge of the white blanket to look under the bed then gave Angela the okay. "It's all clear. They're gone." He slipped his gun back in its holster with an ineffable relief.

"Look at this place," she whined when she saw the room. "What a mess." The small bureau drawers were pulled out, her clothes disheveled. Her toiletries were scattered, the sheets were pulled out from the mattress, some of her clothes in the closet were on the floor and something else was off. But what?

"Did you lock the door when you left?"

"I think so. Yes. Maybe. I don't know. I can't remember. I thought I did. I was anxious to talk to you. Who would do this, anyway?" Her first thought was of her creepy neighbor next door. She nonchalantly tucked her pink lace underwear back in the top drawer, trying to push away thoughts that a complete stranger had his hands on her panties. She felt a sense of relief when her fingers brushed the gun she had hidden in the far back.

"Well, if it was a robbery, they overlooked your laptop."

Angela scanned the room. Other than the laptop and her messenger bag both still on the bed, there was nothing to take. "Shit," she said when she noticed that the storage bin was not anywhere in the room. "It's gone. The notebooks with the research on the Trueloves and Hixson. All of it. Gone. The entire container. I wonder if she came back for it?"

"If who came back for it?"

"Lisa. The woman who stayed here before me."

Surely it was just a coincidence. It was a popular name. Still stung like a son of a bitch though. Just hearing it took Jack to another place and time. He could almost smell her almond lotion, the conditioner in her hair. He was never going to be able to forget her, and sadly, he was okay with that. His face lost just enough blood for Angela to notice.

"Are you okay?" she asked. "You look pale."

"Yeah, I'm okay." What could he say? No, I'm a grown man suffering from unrequited love after being dumped years ago. "I'm not so sure you should stay here tonight though, Angela. I have an extra room at my place. No strings. No weirdness. You're welcome to it. Or you could try the Pines but..."

Picturing the Glock 27 tucked in one of the cups of her Victoria's Secret bra that cost nearly as much, she replied with confidence. "I'll be fine. Thank you for the offer, though."

Jack removed a card from his pocket and wrote his cell number down on it. "Just in case. I never turn it off."

Early the next morning as Angela prepared for her visit with Knox, she glanced out the window and saw Jack sleeping in his Tacoma parked just outside the stairwell door. This may have been the reason she allowed him to accompany her to the jail and sit in on her meeting with Knox. Or maybe she just didn't want to admit that Knox frightened the shit out of her and being alone with him might push her over an edge, one of which she was already dangling precariously.

The room dedicated for attorneys and their clients at the Fannin County Jail was small and smelled of pine cleaner shadowed by bleach and dashed hope. It was a smell that Angela recognized but not without nostalgia. Sometimes she missed her career. Other times, she wished she would have studied accounting as her mother wanted her to do.

Knox was waiting at the table, his hands cuffed and folded in front of him and Angela wondered if a man like him ever prayed. Of course, he did, she reminded herself. He preyed on children. The guard who opened the door for them stood outside the room, leaning against the wall directly in front of the window. His arms, entwined like two oily black pythons, were crossed on his chest. He had eyes that were both intense and vacant at the same time. They focused straight ahead and didn't seem to blink.

She and Jack pulled out chairs and sat across from Knox.

"Counselor. You brought a friend. How nice. One with a temper if my memory serves me."

Angela glanced at Jack who didn't make eye contact. "This is Sherriff Jack Towns. He'll be sitting in with us today."

"Sherriff Towns. You find those children yet?"

Jack started to stand and Angela pulled him back down into the chair.

"So, now tell me: How have you been?" Knox continued, his eyes pinned on Angela. He laughed through the back of his teeth. His perfect smile glinted in the overhead light; his green eyes flashed.

"I'll ask the questions, Mr. Knox," Angela said, adjusting her chair.

She seemed to be in control, but Jack saw a slight tremble in her hand as she spoke. She picked up a pen, clutched it tightly in her palm, and the shaking stabilized.

She pulled a legal pad from her bag and set it on the table. "You are facing some serious charges, here."

"Well, being accused with something is different from being convicted for it," Knox retorted. "Though you know all about conviction, don't you? Seeing how you used to be a prosecutor and all. And I must say, I'm surprised after how things went down that you weren't disbarred. Or were you?" He laughed again with that same maniacal chortle caught in the back of his throat like water gurgling over rocks.

"What is he talking about, Angela?" Jack interjected. "What are you talking about?" he redirected toward Knox.

"Oh, she hasn't filled you in on our history, I see."

"What history?" Jack was growing more agitated. "What is going on here?"

"Ignore him," Angela said sternly.

"The counselor and I met in 2007," Knox confided. "Well, we didn't actually meet per se. She was too busy with her boyfriend when she should have been watching little Liam Tate. Ain't that right, counselor?"

"Shut up," Angela demanded. "Just shut. Up." She closed her eyes and took in a breath. She blew it out slowly.

"Now don't be that way. I sent you the picture. Didn't you like it? I bet you carry it with you wherever you go, don't you? You shouldn't beat yourself up. I would have got to him one way or another, regardless. He was a necessary part of the process. You just made it easier that's all. Believe it or not, he was chosen randomly. They all were."

Jack stared on in disbelief. What the hell was going on here? He wanted to choke this bastard right here on the spot in front of God and everybody.

"If you continue confessing, I won't be able to represent you," Angela reprimanded.

"Oh, come on now, counselor. This is a silent room and we have client-attorney privilege. Nobody but us three can hear this conversation anyhow. They can see it; they just can't hear it. Even I know that. Besides, you're not here to defend me—that's illegal by the way what you're doing, I'm sure you know. You're here for answers. You want to know why and you're playing the side of defense to find out. Clever, I'll give you that. A tad bit unethical, though, don't you think? But don't worry. I understand desperation."

"Well, you're wrong. I have every intention of getting you out of here. And I will."

"Is that right? Even when you know who I am and what I've done? I did them all a favor, you know. Blood. It's the secret to salvation. Theirs and mine. Mormon scripture believes that spilled blood cries out for retribution. Besides, those children could have grown up to be like me." He chortled maliciously, his eyes shiny and poisonous. "That's worse than facing eternal damnation."

"Like you?" Jack asked. "I don't know. You seemed to have had a pretty good life. Better than most. Prominent family, excellent education, all the money you could ever ask for."

"Nice to see you're doing your homework, but that's just it, Jackie boy. It all sounds so damn good, doesn't it? Education, wealth, and anything I ever wanted in life. And yet it wasn't enough. You want to know why? Because I'm fucked up. It's in my blood. All that shit doesn't mean a good God damn if you were poisoned with bad blood. You think I don't know what I am? Who I am? It could have been different for me. One person made me who I am today, and she isn't even aware of it. But she will be."

"What are you talking about?" Angela asked.

She startled when the guard tapped on the glass. He held up five fingers.

Jack acknowledged him with an over-the-shoulder-wave. He didn't like at all how Angela was handling this. It wasn't his place, but he didn't care. Lives were at stake, and she was tap dancing around this psycho. He stepped in aggressively.

"What are you doing in Rayburn, Knox? Who are the Sons of Perdition, and what's their involvement with my missing children? Why are you here?"

He laughed loud and hard. "Do you even know what a son of perdition is? It's someone who will never be exalted into Heaven no matter what they do. According to Mormon scripture, I've got nothing to lose in this world. But, I kind of threw a little kink in their ideology. Who knew that what destroys a person might one day grant them eternal life. Now that's irony, don't you think? Why I'm here is none of your business, but I suppose in the end it will become your business, you being the law man and all."

"What the hell do you mean by that?" Jack could feel his anger bubbling up inside of him. "You better tell me why you came to Rayburn. What do you want? You took those children, didn't you? Why?"

The guard tapped again on the glass and held up two fingers this time.

Knox remained silent for a long minute as he started without blinking into Jack's eyes. Then he smiled coyly. "I didn't take those children."

"Liar," Jack shouted and stood, jarring the table into Knox's chest. "You're a lying son of a bitch."

"I'm not lying, Sheriff. I didn't take them, but you're right about the son of a bitch part."

Jack could hear the key in the door behind him. Time was up and he still didn't have the answers he wanted.

Just as the guard made it inside, Knox smiled serenely and said in a low breath. "But just because I didn't take them doesn't mean I don't know where they are. Then he started to sing. *I've been redeemed by the blood of the lamb, filled with the Holy Ghost I am. All my sins are washed away, I've been redeemed.*"

Jack lunged for him then, his fist connecting directly with Knox's nose. A spray of blood freckled his face, but he didn't lose his cocky smile.

"Jack, no!" Angela jumped up, reaching for his arm and pulling him back. "You can't."

The guard moved like lightning to reach Knox, yanking his chair back out of the way. Fast and skillful, he pulled Knox to a standing position then moved his cuffs from the front and secured them behind his back. The front of Knox's orange jumpsuit was splattered in blood. The officer guided him swiftly toward the open door, eyeing Jack along the way. "Not cool, brother," he said. "Not cool."

"Well that is not how I pictured this going down," Angela said, shaking her head. "I expected more of you."

"You've got some nerve. You froze up. What was I supposed to do? We are running out of time. You're not here to catch a child killer. You're here to placate your guilt. You're here for revenge. This is your last chance to be straight with me. Either you tell me everything or you're on your own. I mean it, Angela."

"Okay," she said. "Is there some place around here to grab a drink?"

"Not at nine-thirty in the morning. Logan's is just around the corner. We can get some coffee and breakfast."

She was on her second cup of coffee and wishing for something stronger when she removed the photograph of Liam from her wallet. "This is Liam Tate," she told Jack. "I killed him. More or less."

Jack recognized the boy from the photos of dead children Angela had shown him in his office upon her arrival. "I don't believe that for a min—"

"Just listen. I need to say this. The Tates were my neighbors. I watched Liam for them to earn extra money while in college. I was going to be an accountant, you know. But..." Her breath caught. "I changed my major after he was abducted. More than just my major. My entire life."

Jack started to say something but she held up her hand. "Please. I need to get this out. You see, I was supposed to be watching him. We'd gone to the park around the corner. It's crazy to think that one block could make such a difference in a person's life. I walked that block so many times in the days following that I must have worn out two or three pairs of shoes. One hundred and three steps from my front door to the slide. People still refer to that slide as the Tate slide. Even children call it that though most probably have no idea why. It's become an urban legend. My mother used to find me out there in the middle of the night just sitting on the slide wishing the chaos theory could somehow be reversed. Had I not been flirting with some guy from one of my classes—I can't even recall his name by the way— I might have noticed sooner that Liam was gone. He went up the slide, and I looked away for just one minute. Or maybe it was a few minutes. One too many. I don't know, but he never came down. It was the very beginning of my search for justice. For him. For me. What I didn't realize then—hell, I'm not sure I realize it now, was that the justice I was seeking had nothing to do with the law. But I pursued it anyway."

"Oh Angela," Jack sighed. "I—"

"No, wait. It gets even better. If anyone would have told me that a handful of years later, after I'd graduated magna cum laude from Penn, that I'd be prosecuting the man suspected of Liam's death, I wouldn't have believed them. But there I was, and I nailed that mother fucker. And the crowd roared," she said bitterly, cupping her coffee mug with both hands, trying to calm her shaking hands. "The only thing is..." Angela fought back the tears. "I got the wrong fucking guy. This man, Denny Sherman, was innocent. They beat him to death, you know. In prison. Child killers and all. And the thing is, he'd been telling the truth the entire time. He'd never even met Liam Tate."

The waitress cleared the plates and Jack moved to the other side of the booth to sit next to Angela in an effort to comfort her. He placed his hand over hers and she pulled it away.

"No," she said firmly. I don't need your pity. The only true justice I can offer now is to see that Knox pays for what he's done. It's my personal promise to Liam. To

Denny. It's the only way I can make it right. It's the only way I can make me right."

"Listen. I'm all about keeping promises, but we have to rely on the justice system to make it right. There's no need for you to carry around that burden. I get where you're coming from. I wanted to rip Knox's face off when I thought he might be connected to Skyla's disappearance. I understand how painful this must be for you to be hauling around so much guilt for so long, but it's time to let it go. Have faith in the system."

"I can't. The system doesn't always work. I'm living proof of this. I want Knox dead, Jack. I'm sorry, but it's true."

"And that's a totally normal feeling. Just don't do anything you might later regret. You have enough remorse in your life. Besides, you may be full of piss and vinegar, but you are not a killer."

"Really? Because I've killed two people already." And I plan on killing a third, she thought.

"Will you stop it?" Jack pleaded. His phone buzzed then. "I have to take this. We're going to resume this conversation though."

The man's voice on the other end of the line was excited and he spoke fast but Angela could hear a few words loud and clear. *Ghost Lake. Submerged car. Two bodies.*

"I'll be there in ten minutes," Jack said into the receiver while digging money out of his wallet and tossing it on the table. He drained the contents of his coffee cup. "I gotta go."

"I'm coming with," Angela said.

"No, you're not. Finish your coffee. This is my job. Not yours. I'll catch up with you later," he called over his shoulder as he darted for the door.

Angela emptied her coffee, grabbed her bag, and headed outside where Jack was still frantically scanning the parking lot. She held up her keys, gently shaking them. He'd obviously forgotten that she drove.

He took the keys from her hand. "Christ."

"Hey. Wait a minute," Angela said.

"No time. Come on. We have to hurry," Jack motioned. "I know a short cut. It'll be quicker if I drive."

twenty-six

Deputy Wayne was on his cell when Jack pulled up. Beau Carver, the only man in town with a tow truck, was unhooking the chain from a muddy sedan. In rubber waders that were chest high and a John Deere baseball cap, he gave Jack a wave then walked over toward Wayne, handing him a clipboard and a pen. With the phone pressed between his ear and shoulder, Wayne signed, handed back the clipboard then slipped his phone in his shirt pocket.

"Once the bodies are removed, the vehicle goes to the Fannin County impound lot. We'll take care of any extra fuel charges," he told Beau.

"You got it." The man wiggled out of the waders. "I've had these things forever and never had a chance to use them. Too bad it had to be for something like this. Not exactly the fishing I was hoping for."

"Thanks, Beau," Deputy Wayne said, motioning Jack over.

"Whose car you driving?" he asked.

"Mine," Angela called as she opened the passenger door. "Well, technically the bank's but..."

"You stay put," Jack told her, which he knew was useless. "I mean it." He walked in the direction of his deputy. "What do we got, Wayne?"

"Once the fog lifted this morning, a fisherman spotted the taillight from his boat," he explained. "The car got snagged up on a log wedged in the sand otherwise we may have never found it." He walked with Jack over to the sedan, which may have once been white but because of all the muck appeared gray now.

Jack didn't know where they came from so suddenly but they were there. Chills on the back of his neck. The immense feeling of loss. It was dark and haunting and made him feel broken. But his intuition had no place here. No place in law at all. He shook it off then approached the driver-side door where water drained from under it. He placed his face close to the window and peered inside. Two stiff contorted bodies were inside, partial skeletons. One of them Jack noticed had small features and patches of dark shoulder-length hair attached to chunks of scalp. A woman. Her fleshy chest bones crawled out from a blouse missing buttons, and Jack could see her organs where the skin had eroded.

There must have been an air pocket on her side of the cab because she appeared to have more skin on her than the other body. The skin that was intact had started to deteriorate from being immersed in water. The sight made

Jack's insides twist. He'd seen more stomach-churning things in the last month in Rayburn than he had ever read in Shakespeare his entire time at UGA.

A flash of light caught Jack's eye. Across the seat, a man's silver watch, struck by a stray sunbeam, dangled on the wrist of the other skeleton. There was just enough skin left to keep it from slipping off the bones of his hand. The man's head was turned toward Jack, and he could see that one of his eyes was completely gone. The other eye stared straight ahead, clinging to the socket and covered in a gelatinous looking film, which gave it a reptilious appearance. The remnants of a Judas Priest t-shirt pressed against his rib cage while his jeans, ragged and torn, floated loosely around the bones of his hips and legs.

"I just got off the phone with Maggie," Wayne said. "She's sending the coroner but it may be a minute. A rig overturned on the highway and there was a fatality." He looked toward what was left of the two bodies in the front seat. His stomach lurched. "I shouldn't have eaten breakfast this morning. Do you think they just misjudged the curve?"

"Not sure, but I didn't see any swerve marks coming in. Also, there's no tag on the car. Not a good sign."

Never a good sign when you find two dead people before ten-thirty in the morning. "How long you think they've been in there?"

"Not long enough for the tag to rust off if there was one. Guessing by the decomp and fatty deposits though, I'd say maybe three or four weeks. When did Mark from the pawn shop go missing?"

"He stopped returning calls to his mother about a month ago." Deputy Wayne handed him some latex gloves then walked to the other side of the car and slid on a pair himself. "I asked Maggie to run a missing persons' report."

"Good work," Jack said as he engaged the door handle. It took a minute to get the door open, and when he did, stagnant lake water poured out of the car. A gray saturated New Balance followed. It was clear right away that both inside door handles had been removed. From what he could tell, these people had been trapped in the car. Had they gone in alive?

Jack unsnapped the seatbelt then patted the clothes on the female skeleton looking for an ID or wallet but didn't find either. Around her neck, clinging to skin and bone, hung a tarnished chain, the charm attached to it sunk deep into the cavity of her sternum. Jack tried to unhook the necklace from behind her neck, but the clasp was rusted, and his fingers were useless in the gloves. He looked the other way when he noticed that something had been eating on her eyes. Crabs, maybe. This was somebody's daughter, sister, mother, friend. Somebody's somebody.

"Any luck?" he called to Wayne on the other side of the car.

"Nada. Nothing in the glove box either."

Jack popped the trunk. It was empty except for a spare tire, an empty canvas bag, and a bunch of beer cans.

"What happened?" he heard Angela ask over his shoulder.

"Didn't I tell you to stay put?"

"I'm not that kind of girl," Angela said. "Besides, you think I got where I am by following rules?" This got a big chuckle from Deputy Wayne who was busy tugging at a corner of the soggy carpet. Jack threw him a side eye.

"Who are they?" Angela asked, her face shifting in disgust. The smell was fetid and moldy like wet decaying leaves. She covered her mouth.

"No idea," Jack answered. We're going to have to rely on dental records to tell us that. They've been in the water too long."

"Wayne, will you see if you can grab the VIN while I walk Ms. Archer back to her car?"

Behind them, Buddy's wood-paneled Grand Wagoneer stopped short. He threw it into gear and turned it off. The engine was ticking, and Jack knew he must have raced to get there. Buddy jumped out of the vehicle, his camera slung over his shoulder, his mouth full of gum.

"Heard over the radio. Got here as quick as I could. Just an FYI, WSB-TV is headed this way. What's going on?"

"Hey, Buddy. Two cadavers, possibly drowning victims, not sure. All we can confirm at this point is that earlier this morning, a fisherman noticed the car submerged in the water. When Deputy Wayne arrived, he found two bodies inside. Both unidentifiable at this point. One female and one male. Been in the water for roughly three weeks, maybe longer. This is Angela Archer by the way. Angela, Buddy McCay from the *Rayburn Star*. Angela was just leaving." Jack nudged his head in the direction of her car.

"Archer? Knox's attorney? Levi Knox?"

"That's right." Angela stuck her hand out and Buddy took it cautiously. "You any relation to Doug McCay?"

"He was my father. He passed on last year. After a long illness. Why do you ask?"

"I just recognize the name. Nice to meet you, Buddy."

Buddy nodded but didn't respond. He couldn't get a feel on this woman or what made her want to represent someone his father had deemed the devil incarnate. In Buddy's mind, if Knox was the Redeemer, he was responsible, at least in part, for his father's death. It wasn't that Buddy didn't have faith in the justice system. He did. It was just that this was different. He wanted to hate the man, but he couldn't because Buddy McCay didn't know how to hate. It wasn't part of his makeup. And this pissed him off greatly because he so badly wanted it to be.

"I didn't realize you were close with Knox's attorney."

"I wouldn't say that we're close," Jack said as he watched Angela's car disappear down the narrow clay road, flanked on both sides by the overgrown pines and thick sagebrush that surrounded the lake. "I'm not sure she's close with anyone. Even herself."

A half a second later, they were both distracted by the white Fannin County Coroner van that zipped into the space beside the tow truck. At first glance, it looked like the van was driverless. Then Jack saw the sprout of hair the color of dried blood peeking over the steering wheel. Belle. She opened the door and dismounted from the front seat, all fifty-three inches of her, sticking her landing and firmly planting her Doc Marten six eyes on the ground. It was a move that would have made any skilled gymnast proud. She adjusted her lab coat and secured her glasses.

"Jack," she called. "Sorry for the delay. It's been a busy day at the bone house." Belle turned quickly and headed toward the back of the van. She yanked the doors open and snapped on a pair of gloves she pulled from the box on the inside pocket of one of the doors. Then with the dexterity of a band roadie, she unloaded two gurneys, draped in black zip bags.

"Maggie said there were two?"

"That's right. A male and a female. No ID on either."

"Accident?"

"I don't think so. The missing door handles and absent license plate say otherwise."

Belle didn't flinch. "All right. Let's get 'em in the chariot."

After the bodies were transported to the van, the tow truck driver winched up the waterlogged car and made his way slowly from the area, Deputy Wayne following. Water continued to seep out from the vehicle, filling the air with a foul smell that even Buddy's gum couldn't mask.

"I'm on a deadline so I'm out of here, too," he said

hopping into his Jeep. He rolled his window down as he backed out. "Let me know what you find out."

If we find out, Jack considered. Dental records are great if people actually ever visit a dentist. "Will do, Buddy. Take care."

Belle closed the back doors of the van and leaned against them, bracing her heel on the bumper, and retying the lace of her boot. She reached in her pocket and pulled out the foil packet containing nicotine gum and popped a tiny square piece in her mouth.

"I was going to reach out to you today about the Marsh girl, but then I got the call about the overturned rig. And then this. Anyhow, I got to thinking last night about the Belle Elmore case from 1910. You familiar with it?"

"Can't say that I am. Were you named after her or is it just a random coincidence?"

"Random coincidence. Besides, hers was a stage name. Mine is the real deal. Anyhow, and there has been some dispute about this over the years, Belle's husband, Dr. Crippen, poisoned her with hyoscine—enough to kill three people."

"I'm trying to understand the connection here, Belle. Can you help me out?"

"Well, I found trace levels of hyoscine throughout Kelly Marsh's organs. Maybe not enough to kill three people, but enough to kill one, especially one with breathing problems."

"So, she was poisoned and this is what led to her

heart giving out?"

"It would appear that way, however, it might not have been intentional. Hyoscine can be found in over- the-counter remedies for motion sickness and nausea. It produces a euphoric feeling, which is why it's popular among today's youth. They crush it up. Snort it. Shoot it. Whatever it takes. That being said, a person would have to ingest an entire bottle or package to cause death but it is possible. These types of drugs are becoming increasingly popular with date- rape cases as well, which is what I originally suspected once I discovered concentrated levels of hyoscine in Kelly's liver. *However,*" she stressed. "Ms. Marsh, I discovered, was a virgin."

"Maybe the last one in Georgia," Jack said, dryly. "Where does this hyoscine come from anyway?"

"From a plant in the nightshade family—something like belladonna, which, by the way, is where I get my name from. My mother was a horticulturist. And a pot smoker so my name could have been Mary Jane. Just a little trivia there for you." Belle spit her gum into tissue she'd pulled from her pocket and headed toward the front of the van. She opened the door.

"So, what you're telling me is that Kelly's death might have been accidental?" Jack asked.

"In my professional opinion, yes, more or less. Ninety-eight percent positive. The poison triggered the asthma attack, which caused her heart to fail." She hoisted herself up into the driver seat, which Jack noticed was drawn way too close to the windshield. So close, he looked for traces of Belle's dark red lipstick on the glass but didn't see any.

"What about the other two percent?"

"Well..." Belle said with more than a hint of optimism in her tone. "That's where you come in. I'll let you know what I find with these two," she motioned towards the back of the van with her head. Then she yanked the door closed, started the engine, and pushed another piece of gum in her mouth.

Jack could hear some type of death metal music blaring from inside as she pulled away. Not his thing but under the circumstances, it couldn't have been more appropriate. The news crew pulled in just as Belle was leaving, and Jack filled them in on what he knew, which wasn't much.

twenty-seven

The Thrashers owned acreage on the outskirts of Rayburn not too far from the lake. Jack had gone to school with Clint Thrasher until the eleventh grade when Clint dropped out to start a landscaping business and marry his pregnant girlfriend. He'd done well for his family, and from what Jack had heard, raised his boys the same way Kitty poured drinks. With a heavy hand. Jack and he were never really friends, but they weren't *not* friends either. Clint was recovering from knee surgery so he'd likely be home. His boys were both in high school and shared classes with Kelly Marsh. Jack felt this is where he needed to focus his two percent. What happened to Kelly wasn't random. He had a feeling that one if not both of the Thrasher boys knew something about her death whether directly or indirectly. Getting them to talk about it was another story.

"Clint," Jack called as he knocked on the door of the two-tone double wide. "You home? It's Jack Towns."

"Door's open."

Jack wiped his feet on the WELCOME rug on the

front deck then went inside.

Clint was sitting in a recliner, his leg incapacitated, propped on stacked pillows. He was a compact guy but broad-shouldered and thick. He picked up the remote and adjusted the volume on the TV but still kept one eye on the cars racing around the track. "Well, shit fire. It if isn't Sheriff Towns. How ya doing, buddy? Haven't seen you in a minute. Everything okay?"

"Sorry for the intrusion, Clint. I'm good considering all that's going on right now."

"I heard that. We're turning into Atlanta around here with all this crime. You want something to drink? I got to stay off my leg but help yourself to coffee or whatever. I think there's some Mountain Dew in the fridge. Maybe a beer." He winked and chuckled.

"I appreciate the offer. I can't stay."

"My boys in some kind of trouble?" Clint asked in a more serious tone.

"No. I just have some questions for them about the Marsh girl. Thought maybe they could help me out."

"That's a real tragedy right there. Cute little thing. Smart, too. My wife does housekeeping for the Pines. Said her mom ain't doing so hot. Thinks she's back on the shit. They figure out what happened yet? People been saying it was a serial killer."

Jack shook his head. "No, her death was related to asthma possibly brought on by some over-the-counter drugs. They're still trying to determine, which is why I wanted to speak to Billy and Bobby. See if they might have heard something around school or..."

"My boys don't do drugs, Sheriff. They're good boys. Mischievous but good."

"I'm not here to make accusations, Clint. I just thought maybe they would know if Kelly had been hanging with the wrong crowd or if she'd gotten herself involved with the drug scene. We do have one here in Rayburn, unfortunately. Wish we didn't."

"Sign of the times, I suppose. Well, you're in luck. There's no school today. Service day or some bullshit. Billy's here, outside somewhere. Bobby should be back in a little while. Not sure what good it will do, but you're welcome to talk to them."

"I appreciate that."

"I think that's Billy coming now."

Just then Jack caught the sound of a motorbike outside. Minutes later he heard footsteps running up the stairs and across the wooden deck.

"Dad, you all right?" Billy said pushing the door open and hurrying inside. He glanced toward Jack uncomfortably.

"Fine, son. I'm fine. The Sheriff here just wants to ask you a few questions, that's all."

"Bout what?"

"The Marsh girl. And mind your manners, son. Tell him everything you know. And get him a cup of coffee, would ya? He looks like he needs it."

"Yessir."

"Sheriff, he's all yours. When Bobby comes, I'll send him your way. Always good seeing you, Jack. I mean, Sheriff." Clint chuckled again, shifted his leg and turned up the volume on the TV.

Jack followed the boy into the kitchen where he grabbed a mug and filled it with coffee from a glass carafe. He stuck the cup in the microwave and waited for it to beep. "You want cream and sugar?"

Jack shook his head. "Black is fine, thank you."

Billy grabbed the mug of coffee and snatched a can of Dr. Pepper from the fridge. He sat next to Jack at the small round kitchen table. It wobbled and the coffee sloshed over the rim of the mug as he pushed it towards Jack.

"What is it you want to know, Sheriff?"

"You had classes with Kelly, right?"

"Yessir. Math and Comp. She was smart. Helped me out a lot."

"You mean she tutored you?"

"Sort of." He looked away, focusing his eyes on the floor then over towards his father. "She let me copy her homework. I'm not good with numbers or English."

"I see. So, you two were friends then?" Jack drank some of the coffee. It was lukewarm and bitter.

"Yeah, I guess so. I mean, we weren't going out or anything like that, but we hung out sometimes." Billy popped the top on the can and took a long pull from it. He set it back down and began to chew the skin around the dirty nail of his index finger.

"Hung out where?"

"Man, I knew you were going to ask that. I ain't no snitch."

"Billy, no one is in trouble here. I'm just trying to find out what happened to Kelly. That's all."

He blew out a deep breath then glanced over his shoulder at his father then motioned Jack to follow him. The boy walked back behind the kitchen and down a narrow carpeted hall to a small room on the right. Once inside, he pushed the door so that it nearly closed. "I don't want my dad to hear. He'll be real mad."

"Okay, fair enough. Hung out where?" Jack pressed.

"The Truelove property. Everybody goes there. But we haven't been back there since Kelly died. That's the God's honest truth."

"When *was* the last time you were there?"

"Billy?"

"The night Kelly died."

Jack tried not to react, but he'd caught Billy's mistake. "And how did you know it was the night Kelly died? Her body wasn't found until a few days ago."

"I don't know."

"Yes, you do. Because you moved it, didn't you, son? You moved her body from the Truelove place, right? That's where Kelly died, isn't it?"

"No. I don't know. We were just partying, and it got

late. We didn't kill anyone, Sheriff. I swear. We just got really fucked up, which is why we didn't notice her convulsing until it was too late. The next morning, I thought I'd dreamed the whole thing. We didn't know what to do with the body so we rolled it into some old charred insulation we found at the Truelove house and buried her in the orchard. But then I started feeling real bad about it so we dug her up and moved her closer to the trail so someone would find her."

"Who else was with you?"

"Just my brother."

"Who else was there the night she died?"

"Just a few of us from school. But no one but Bobby and I knew what had happened."

"Okay, well I'm going to need names,"

"Derrick, Gavin, the older Thompson boy—you know the one on the football team, and some girls. Alexa, Deb, and a couple of new girls I'd never met. Freshman. Becca and...I don't remember. Carrie? Carol? I don't know. They were kind of bitchy. They didn't do much partying."

"What kind of partying?"

Billy remained silent. He started to chew on the edge of his lip.

"Billy. WHAT. KIND. Of partying?"

"Drinking and stuff," he whispered. "Just the usual crap. Beer. Am I going to get arrested?"

"That's not my intention. I just need answers. What else?"

"Well, one of the guys—I think it was Gavin, had some pot."

"So just beer and pot? Nothing else?"

Jack casually scanned the room. It was relatively tidy other than a few items of clothing tossed around and some shoes scattered across the floor. The furniture was sparse and consisted of a twin bed with a blue flannel blanket, a ripped club chair, and a wooden dresser with a tarnished mirror that made everything in the room seem old and marred like a vintage photograph. A skateboard was propped up against the wood paneling. The board was covered in stickers of all shapes and sizes.

"Fuck. I'm going to be grounded for life, and my brother is going to kill me if he finds out I ratted."

Jack walked over to the small window and peered through the blinds to the woods that lay beyond then turned and stopped in front of the dresser. On top of it, he eyed a pocket knife, a rusty looking jar with old papers stuffed in it, some coins scattered about, and a few graphic novels. The jar was partially covered by a gray t-shirt. Jack cocked his head in an effort to read the black and red logo printed on it.

"Thrasher," Billy said. "It's a skateboard magazine that has my last name. But that's not the only reason I like it." He was rambling.

Jack could see beads of sweat forming near the boy's temple. "Listen, Billy, I have a feeling you aren't being totally honest with me here. But let me be straight with you. Drugs were found in Kelly's system. A lot of drugs, and I'm not talking about beer and pot. These drugs may have been the cause of her death. Do you know if she took anything that may have had a bad reaction to her asthma? Maybe somebody laced her drink or slipped her something without her knowing it that night?"

Billy stood without saying a word but Jack could see he was terrified.

"Think back. Was there anyone trying to, you know, get with her? This is serious, Billy. I'm not blaming you, but if someone gave Kelly drugs, I want to know who, son. Look, I'm going to find out with or without your help, but it will be better for you if you tell me what you know."

"I don't know anything," Billy said. "She ate them on her own. No one forced her. We all ate them. We've been doing it for months."

"Ate what?"

"I can't—" he jolted when the phone in his plaid shirt pocket started vibrating. He made no attempt to answer it.

"You going to get that?" Jack asked after the vibrating continued.

Billy fumbled in his pocket for the phone. It slipped from his grip and landed face up on the carpet near Jack's feet. He scooped it up.

"Hello. Oh hey. No, I'm good. I can't talk right now. When? I guess so. It has an oil leak though so it's smoking. Yeah, I should be here then."

"Everything all right?"

"Yeah. Just someone wanting to borrow my bike."

Jack didn't need to ask who. He'd already seen the name Nelle on the phone screen. It was interesting, he thought. Odd really, but he was too busy to devote any time to speculation right now, so he placed it on the back burner of his mind.

"Are you going to tell me what Kelly ingested the night she died? What were you kids eating? Pills? Acid? What? Tell me."

The bedroom door flung open then. It slapped against the paneling. "What the hell are you doing, Billy?" his brother yelled. "Are you crazy? You told him, didn't you, you fucking punk ass." He pushed Billy backward onto the bed.

"I didn't say anything, Bobby! I swear to God."

"Liar! Yes, you did. You told him about the flowers. Now we're both going to go to prison, you idiot. Hope you like getting fucked up the ass, bro."

"What the hell is going on in there, boys?" Clint screamed over the racing engines on TV, which suddenly went dead silent. "Both of you get your asses out here. RIGHT damn now."

twenty-eight

When she left the lake, Angela mapquested the Crow County Library just off the square. It was a small Carnegie library that from the looks of it had recently been renovated. The smell of new carpet permeated the air, and the furniture was modern and patterned with geometric shapes incongruous to the 1915 brick structure. The woman behind the circulation desk explained to her that they had gotten rid of all the Criss Cross directories a while back due to lack of space, but she gave her a password to log in to one of the computers where she was certain she'd be able to find the information she was seeking. But Angela had no idea just how many Rhonda D's she'd find in and around Rayburn. Virtual pages and pages of them in the online directory. There was no way she could contact them all. Besides, she hadn't decided exactly what she was going to say should she locate this woman. *Hey, saw your name on a list of patients who visited the Hixson Clinic. What were you doing there? Did you happen to have a son that you gave away? A child that was murdered because of me?*

"Liam," she whispered more loudly than she meant to and while searching for a breath, she felt her phone vibrate. She reached in her purse, blindly feeling around to silence it, and wondered if the clerk had heard it because she was now was heading her way.

"Ma'am, are you doing okay over here? Maybe there's something I can help you find?" she asked politely.

"No, I don't think so," Angela said. "Sorry about the phone. I'm just...I'm searching for someone. One of those needle-in-a-haystack situations."

"Well, I've lived here my entire life and know just about everyone. Who are you looking for?"

"A woman by the name of Rhonda?"

"Do you have a last name?"

Angela shook her head. "No, just an initial. D."

"Rhonda D. She from Rayburn?"

"That's just it. I don't know. She may have lived here at one time but I can't be certain. It would have been about in or around the year 2000."

"Wait a minute. Does this have to do with the Hixson trial?'

"In some way, yes."

"Let me think about it for a minute," she said. The woman excused herself to help a patron waiting at the front desk.

Angela tried to find more on the Sons of Perdition but came up short. She gathered her things and was already out the door when the clerk called to her.

"Miss," she said. What about Ronnie over at the pizza place? Rhonda DiCarlo. She's lived in Rayburn her entire life. She's the only one I can think of."

Angela thanked the woman then listened to the message Chad Stein from the National Center for Missing and Exploited Children had left on her voicemail. He apologized for not getting back sooner, but it took him some time to confirm that she'd been right. Most, if not all, of the Redeemer's victims had been adopted. "Been working night and day on this. Still waiting on complete results but... Are you sitting?" he asked. "Of the adopted parents still alive and of those willing to talk, it looks like the adoptions were all orchestrated from the Hixson Women's Clinic in Rayburn, Georgia," he revealed. "The adoptions were actually listed in quite a few of the files but never thoroughly investigated because they weren't considered leads. No one ever connected them. Not sure how but I think you might be on to something, Angie. Keep me posted. I'm curious to know where this is headed."

Angela walked across the street to Joey's. She'd remembered speaking with a waitress there on her first day in Rayburn when she was looking for a place to stay, but she hadn't recalled the woman's name. What she did remember though was the way she spoke so forgivingly of Dr. Hixson and the trial. She said he had helped many women out of bad situations or something like that. Had she been one of these women? Could she be Liam's biological mother?

"She'll be in soon," a teenage boy behind the counter told Angela when she asked for Ronnie. He had unusually clear skin for a kid his age and a hook nose that looked like it belonged on the face of an aging Italian diplomat. "She closes on Wednesdays."

Angela ordered a beer then took a seat in a booth in the back to wait. She sent a few texts and listened to messages she'd ignored over the last two days then once again tried Thomas Blake's sister, Carolyn, at the bank where she worked in Tennessee. Though the boy's body was never found, Angela still felt it was significant to know if he'd also been adopted from Hixson's. Carolyn's assistant informed her that she was out of town on a family emergency, but that she'd make sure that Carolyn got the message when she returned.

Angela placed an order of parmesan breadsticks and nursed her beer while she ate them. Forty-five minutes later, Ronnie slid in the booth across from her.

"Hi. Nick said you were looking for me?"

"Ronnie. Hi. Yes. Do you remember me?"

She nodded. You're renting the room upstairs, right?"

"That's right. You told me a little about the Hixson trial, and well, I was hoping you could answer some questions for me. They're important questions but they may also be uncomfortable and very personal. Do you have a minute to talk?"

Ronnie looked over her shoulder to her coworker who

gave her a nod. "Nick will watch the floor for me, but he has to leave in twenty minutes. What's this about?"

"It's about Dr. Hixson, Ronnie, and I'm so sorry, but I don't have time to be diplomatic." She could see the concern on her face but no sign of fear. "And the thing is, I can't even promise you anonymity."

But Ronnie didn't care anymore about hiding her past from people. The fact of the matter was that it wouldn't change what she'd done all those years ago. It had taken her a long time to come to terms that she was her own judge; her own worst enemy. People didn't hate her. She hated her. And all this hatred had made her so very tired. Ignoring her past was not in any way helping her to heal like she hoped it would. "Let's go outside so I can smoke," she told Angela. "Do you mind?"

twenty-nine

Jack took his time driving over to the Southern Pines Motel to try and locate Janet Marsh. His heart was heavy and his mind overworked. He wanted to let her know in person the reasons behind her daughter's unfortunate death. He wanted to be the one to tell her that Kelly had died days before she was discovered because she had taken an overdose of poisonous flowers. Not because someone had killed her. It was the right thing to do no matter how difficult. No matter how fucked up Janet was these days. She needed to know what happened to Kelly.

He hadn't taken the Thrasher boys in, and Clint was grateful for this. It gave him a little time to secure a lawyer before bringing the boys by to fill out a statement. Jack didn't know exactly what was going to happen to them other than a substantial ass whipping, but because they were minors, they had a better chance with the law. They did conceal a dead body, which wasn't a boy-scout move, but according to both brothers, Kelly ingested the flowers on her own. Billy said she was the one who first discovered them at the Truelove property. She'd read somewhere that they were hallucinogenic, and you could trip hard on them. Bobby said, they called them "witch bells" and before they started eating the petals, they burned the leaves. This gave them a sense of euphoria. "It was like flying," he told Jack. "When we ate them though, it was even better."

Jack recalled seeing BURN THE WITCH spray painted on the side of the Truelove house. It hadn't been a reference to Wanda like he originally suspected. He made a mental note to search for the bush the boys had described to him even though the flowers were likely gone seeing how it was October.

"It's off to the side of the house near that old dead cedar tree that looks as if it's going to fall over," Billy said. "The leaves are large and green and the flowers are pale yellow with a black or dark purple center. They smell real bad, too."

"They probably ain't no flowers left on it now," Bobby had chimed in. "We took the only ones left last time we was there."

Weed Jack expected, even understood. After all, he'd been a teenager once. But flowers?

He pulled up next to the office of the motel and cut the engine. The Southern Pines, the Pines to locals, was a one-level structure that formed a square U around a cracked pool that had been dry as long as neighboring Hart County. The white sign out front had glowing green letters that had at one time read The Southern Pines but because some of the letters had burned out, it now read Southern P-I-E-S. Jack could see the E flickering now too. Soon, it would just be Southern P-I-S.

The motel offered rooms nightly and weekly, but everyone knew though not advertised, an hourly rate was also available upon request. He checked the messages on his phone then got out of his truck and walked inside. The bell on the door jingled.

"Hey, Sheriff," the woman behind the counter addressed him, pulling herself away from some kind of soap opera show she was watching on a small television that looked even to Jack, archaic and out of place. The woman's eyes were rimmed in thick black liner drawn to severe points at the outer edges. "What can I do for you? You aren't here for a room, are you?" She smiled and ran a hand through her fuzzy blonde hair. Her nails were long and neon green, a few decorated in sparkly jewels and stickers.

"Not today, Pam. I'm actually looking for Janet. Sorry, I have to interrupt her work schedule, but I need to talk to her. It's important."

"Work schedule? Yeah, not so much. I told her not to be doing that shit here. That's all I need is to have the cops all over this place. No offense. Besides, I barely have enough business to keep the place running. If she doesn't pay by tomorrow, I'm going to have to ask her to leave. I mean I feel bad for her and all, but she's freeloading at this point and using on top of it. It was only a matter of time before the police got involved."

Jack reached for his wallet. "Well, I'm not the police, and I'm not here about that. Is she around?" He quietly slid three fifty-dollar bills across the counter. "Put that toward what she owes you."

"Well bless your heart, Sheriff. That is so sweet of you. You're a lot like your father, you know that?"

"So, I'm told." Jack wasn't sure how to respond to these types of remarks anymore. At one time, they made him proud. He'd always felt so close to Joe. His voice had guided him nearly every day since his death over both trivial and more serious matters, law and other. But that voice had grown quiet after he discovered his father's secret friendship, relationship, whatever it was called, with the Truelove girl. But what Jack wanted to believe most is what everyone else did. That Joe Towns was an honorable man with only the best intentions. That he was the best damn sheriff Rayburn had ever had. And most importantly, that it was this man that he was so much like. But something was stopping him from doing so, and it made him feel horrible inside. Regardless of what kind of man Pearl and the rest of Rayburn believed his father to be, Jack's intuition was telling him that Joe Towns had at least one secret.

"Anyhow, she's in 109," Pam said. "To the left and round the corner. But don't expect her to be coherent. She hasn't been straight for some time, you know, with Kelly and all. Bless her heart. Too messed up to work most days, and I keep finding her passed out in the rooms she's supposed to be cleaning. Hell, I think she's even been turning tricks with passing truckers. The whole damn situation just sucks, but I heard at least you have a suspect now with Kelly's murder."

Jack felt it best not to comment on this. "Thanks, Pam. See you around," he said, stepping out the door. He walked down the walkway in front of the rooms then crossed over toward the pool that was enclosed by a chain link fence and had seen better days. A faded sign on the padlocked gate claimed the pool was closed, but this hadn't discouraged people Jack noticed. He could see empty liquor bottles, crumpled beer cans, a lawn chair, a few scattered toys, and a lone cowboy boot at the bottom of the desiccated pool. Someone had also tagged the inside wall with graffiti, fat black letters that read: THERE IS NO TOMORROW. THERE'S ONLY TODAY. Jack immediately thought of little Simon, Hailey, and Ben. Tomorrow morning the drilling would start, and he wasn't any closer to finding them. If those children were anywhere on the mountain, they only had today.

Room 109 was the second from the end. The curtains were closed, but Jack could see light inside. It flickered and danced like a strobe, and he assumed the TV was on. He rapped lightly on the door and called Janet's name a few times before trying the doorknob.

"Janet? It's Sheriff Towns. You in there?" The knob turned and the door opened but stopped short. The chain stretched across it leaving just enough room for Jack to catch the scent of vomit and stale beer, cigarettes, and hopelessness. No sound came from the TV, but flashes of color bounced around the room and bathed it in eerie shades of blues and greens. He listened for running water thinking she might be in the shower, but he was met with silence so Jack called her name again.

"Janet, I need to talk to you. It's important. Can you open the door?" Jack knew she had to be in there. Maybe passed out as Pam mentioned she would be. He reached his hand inside the door to try and unlatch the chain using his fingers at first then an ink pen. Neither of these ideas worked so he pulled out his phone, held it in the open crack of the door and snapped a picture. When the image filled his screen, he saw Janet lying on her back on the floor, her eyes were wide, her skin as blue and shriveled as a dried violet. Jack slammed his shoulder into the plywood door several times before the chain busted. Once inside, he dropped to his knees next to the unconscious woman.

"Janet!" he said loudly. "Janet!" He patted her cheeks gently. Her skin was balmy and cold, but he checked for a pulse anyway. Nothing. She still had her arm tied off with a rubber strap of some sort, a syringe on the floor next to her bloomed with blood. Jack called for an ambulance then started performing CPR.

"Come on Janet. You can do this," he said between moments of pumping her chest and blowing air into her lungs. "Breathe. Dammit just breathe," but he knew it was useless. She was too cold and blue and heartbroken to stay. There would be no tomorrow for Janet Marsh. She only had today, and it had ended unfavorably. He sat next to her and waited for the EMT's who also tried to revive her but couldn't. While they secured her lifeless body to a gurney, Jack collected a few personal belongings scattered about the room among the empty Pabst cans and vodka bottles. There wasn't much there but he took what he felt was important: her purse and a photo of Kelly in her cheerleading outfit sitting on the dresser.

He watched the ambulance pull out of the motel lot then walked over to comfort Pam. She had been crying so much that her eyeliner had dripped down her face like black oil paint, and Jack hadn't noticed until then how much she resembled Tammy Faye Bakker. Now, she stood in disbelief, shaking her head and dabbing at her eyes with a shredded tissue. She was surrounded by motel guests who stepped out of their rooms to see what the hell was going on but lost interest once the ambulance was out of sight. Jack left too, after he walked Pam back to the office, reassuring her the entire time that this was in no way her fault.

Maggie was on the phone when he made it into work. He could smell fresh coffee brewing so he headed back to grab a cup and begin the task of writing up reports. He had to close the Marsh file or at least update it and open one for Janet and the two bodies found in the lake. And then there was the report he had yet to even start for Kitty. Hopefully, he could get her to come in quietly so he wouldn't have to arrest her with so many sets of Rayburn eyes watching. He wasn't at his desk for very long before Deputy Wayne came by with an evidence box.

"I was in Fannin County earlier today so I went ahead and picked these up from the coroner to save you a trip." He placed a box on the edge of the desk. Jack could see the clear plastic bags inside. "Personal effects from the two from the lake. Belle said she's waiting on prints and dental records, but that you might be able to pull identity from the belongings. Maybe someone will come forward. Belle said she'd give you a call in a bit. Also, Maggie's running the VIN."

"Thanks, Wayne."

"You doing okay?"

"I guess. Janet Marsh is dead. OD'd at the Pines. Found her about an hour ago. She'd been gone for a while."

"Oh man. That's too bad."

"I went there to tell her that Kelly hadn't died at the hands of a stranger. That she was actually amongst friends. I thought it might comfort her in some strange way to know that."

"How'd you find this out?"

"The Thrasher boys. They said she ingested some kind of hallucinogenic flowers over at the Truelove place and went into a seizure as a result of it. The flowers somehow reacted badly with her asthma, I guess. Apparently, this is how kids are getting high these days."

"Are you serious?" Wayne asked. "That's ludicrous. Flowers? What kind of flowers?"

"I don't know. Some type of yellow flowers they call witch bells or something. Never heard of them. Will you do me a favor and have a look around the Truelove property? See if you can spot a plant or shrub with yellow flowers. Billy said they had a purple or black center and that they smelled like a dead animal. Said they were near an old cedar tree near the house. I have to finish these reports or I'd go with you."

"You got it."

"Thanks, Wayne. It's a long shot but give me a shout if you find anything. I don't want any more kids finding those things. They're dangerous. I'll call Belle and let her know about Kelly." Wayne left and Jack pressed the Fannin County Coroner's button on the phone then put it on speaker.

"Belle?"

"Oh hey, Sheriff. I just emailed you some images I thought might be helpful in identifying the Jane and John Doe from the lake."

"Let me get logged in so I can have a look. I'm actually calling about Kelly Marsh. You were right. She was poisoned. By her own hand apparently and not by over-the-counter meds. She was partying with friends and ingested some kind of psychoactive flowers that, from what I can understand, mimic ecstasy. The Thrasher brothers concealed her death. Wrapped her in some old insulation and buried her. Then felt bad and dug her up."

"If the insulation was from an older house that would

explain the formaldehyde. Probably UFFI. Popular in the seventies but loaded with formaldehyde, which is why it's no longer used."

"The boys claim she OD'd on some psychoactive flowers that made them feel like they were flying. Do you happen to know what kind of flowers she might have eaten? I need to make sure the entire plant is destroyed."

"Well, my mother would know for certain, but if I had to guess, it would be something in the Solanaceae family. Datura, henbane, deadly nightshade—otherwise known as yours truly, belladonna. Could be any of these. They all produce a form of hyoscine, hyoscyamine, or atropine. The latter is actually used for heart conditions but also for dilating the eyes before an exam. Small amounts are often beneficial. Large amounts can be deadly."

"One of the boys said it's a dark-centered yellow flower and either the flowers or leaves or maybe both, smell like something rotting. A group of kids from the high school has been getting high on them for a while."

"Sounds like black henbane. Definitely toxic at certain levels. Bane is Old English for death if that gives you an idea. It wouldn't be the first overdose case of this kind, but it has grown increasingly popular among teens these days. It produces a euphoric state that can make those ingesting it feel as if they are flying, which is how it became associated with witches. The high is accompanied by a purple rash. That would explain the marks around the Marsh girl's neck. And we wouldn't know this in her case, but it can affect memory. Both long and short term. The main reason it was given to women delivering children. So that they could forget the pain. As if. Well, I'm going to go ahead and close out the Marsh case then."

Jack's only familiarity with henbane came from Shakespeare where it was supposedly used to murder Hamlet's father. He just never imagined it was an actual plant still killing people today.

"Now," Belle went on. "As far as Jane and John Doe, I'm not sure how long the dental records will take, but fortunately for us, they both have tattoos that were not totally dissolved by the water. Images are in the email I sent. Otherwise, this is what I have so far:

Male, twenty-five to thirty-five years of age, cirrhosis of the liver or what's left of it, partial remains of a viper tattooed on his left shoulder. Two missing molars, some bridgework, and one remaining wisdom tooth. No water in the lungs though, which means he was dead before ever taking a swim in the lake. As was the female. Neither of them drowned."

Jack listened closely as he logged into his email. "Then how did they die?" Just below Belle's email, he saw one from the Zoning and Planning Commission. He'd been waiting on that map to see where if there were any original test drill sites here in the seventies or eighties. He glanced at the image. There were so many red dots around the Truelove property that it looked like it was infected with measles. He downloaded the map and hit PRINT then opened Belle's email.

"Well, after performing both clinical and laboratory tests, I found extreme abnormalities in blood parameters, a dramatic fall in platelet count, and changes in white and red blood cells. I also found the presence of myoglobinuria in the urine. This is a sign of muscle deterioration generally brought on by convulsions associated with atrophy or paralysis of the breathing passages. Though there are a few things that can produce opisthotonus, or the rigid arching of the body during a seizure or spasm, the most common is poison. I thought it might be tetanus, but when I tested the blood, I found extremely high levels of—"

It was the second time in two days that Jack heard the term opisthono—whatever it was. "Let me guess," he interrupted. "Strychnine."

"Very good. I'm impressed. I'm going to have you trained to take my place before you know it. So, that's it. Official cause of death for the unidentified male: Strychnine poisoning that led to seizures and suffocation. It would have been a horrible way to go."

"What about the woman?"

"Same COD. Between the age of forty and fifty, and in near perfect health other than a few broken bones, long healed childhood injuries from what I can tell. No caps, no bridges. Movie star perfect teeth. And though it's faded, there's a tattoo near her wrist. A bird...I think. I don't know. Let me get my other glasses."

Jack had by then opened Belle's email, downloaded

the zipped folder and extricated the images. He started sifting through them but stopped abruptly when he recognized the black butterfly tattoo and the angel birthmark above it.

Now that I look more closely...it could be a—"

"A butterfly," he said not even realizing right away that he'd spoken. "A black butterfly," he said again, the words singeing his tongue, the only place he seemed to have feeling at the moment.

"Yeah, that's what it looks like," Belle said.

"I'm going to need just a minute here, Belle," Jack said, trying to keep his composure. "I'll call you back." He ended the call, got up, pulled down the blind, and pushed his door close. He hit the light then sat in stillness in the silent, dark room. After a few minutes he threw up in the garbage can then put his head down on the desk. He couldn't gauge how long he had disappeared from the world before the sound of Maggie's voice outside the door brought him back.

"Jack, are you okay in there? Wayne told me about Janet Marsh. That poor woman. I'm sorry. Can I come in?"

"Sure, Maggie," Jack said. "I'm all right or I will be at some point."

"Well, for Heaven's sake why are you sitting in here in the dark? Are you ill?"

He could hear her fumbling for the light switch. "Please don't turn that on. It's just where I need to be right now, okay?"

"Okay."

"Listen. I need you to do something for me."

"Anything. I'd do anything for you, Jack. You know that. You're family to me. Like the son I—" her voice caught and she stopped.

"I appreciate that. I really do. And I know you mean it. You're not going to like this, but I need your help in locating Lisa's last known address and any relatives she may have. Can you do that for me, please?"

"Lisa? Harrison? Your Lisa?" Maggie hadn't forgotten that it was she who talked a pregnant Lisa into leaving Rayburn, and she remembered the reason why too. She shouldn't have made those decisions for Jack. It wasn't her place to do so, but she just felt it was the right thing to do. It was true that she didn't feel Lisa was good enough for Jack. But Maggie knew these weren't the real reasons she talked Lisa into moving on. She'd learned something about Lisa that she wished she never had. Mrs. Harrison had told her in confidence that Lisa had been adopted and that her biological mother was dead. But it's what she told Maggie next that made her react the way she had. It was a secret she'd take to the grave. She told her that Lisa was rumored to be Joe's illegitimate daughter. "Oh Jack, why on earth do you insist on causing yourself so much grief? I wish—" Maggie stopped short when she heard the pain shredding Jack's voice.

"She was the Jane Doe we pulled from the lake this morning. No ID on the male yet, but the female is Lisa

Harrison. She's dead, Maggie, and I have to let her family know. You said she had a husband and daughter. Find them for me. Please. I just need to sit here for a minute longer and soak up a little more quiet darkness. Do you mind closing the door behind you?"

"Sweet Jesus. Of course not," Maggie replied. "I'm here if you need me," she said then pulled the door closed leaving only a sliver of light glowing underneath it. And it was still too much for Jack.

Minutes passed and he could still feel her presence, see the dark shape of her shoes, under the door. She probably had her ear to it, ready to run in at any minute. Maggie Sheppard was as solid as they come. When she finally walked away, Jack got up and turned on the light, knocking the evidence box to the floor in the process. He squatted down to pick it up and felt an eerie déjà vu moment when he spotted the silver necklace in one of the clear bags inside the box. It was the necklace he'd tried to extricate from the woman in the submerged vehicle. The woman he now knew was Lisa. His Lisa. The only woman he'd ever loved. The memory of her made his heart ache in a way he didn't know was possible. It was an empty sort of pain, deep but resonating, and he imagined this was what a phantom limb must feel like. Not there yet always there. An absence that would never be pain-free.

He picked up the plastic bag to get a closer look at what he could see now was a half-moon with ST ENDS engraved in it. Had Lisa converted to Catholicism? Didn't seem likely. As far as he remembered, she had never held any respect for organized religions of any kind except for maybe Buddhism. Jack stood and took the bag over to the computer where he searched for Saint Ends on the Internet. After visiting numerous Catholic saint sites he'd come to the conclusion that there was no Saint Ends. He looked carefully at the charm once more. And then he saw it. It wasn't half a moon. It was half a heart, and maybe because he was feeling like he only had half a heart himself right now, he sensed a familiarity with it. He'd seen this same charm before. His mind thought back, trying to recall where.

Jack swiped the plastic bag off the desk and darted out of the office. He whizzed past Maggie at the desk. He could hear her calling to him.

"Where you running off to?" she asked but he was in too much of a hurry to answer. "Okay," she called latently, her words trailing off as he headed out the door. "I'll call you if I find any...thing."

Fifteen minutes later, Jack had managed to work his way through all of his shirt pockets in the laundry bin in his bedroom. Then frantically, he rifled through the pockets of every pair of jeans as well, but other than a few singles, a paperclip or two, and Randolf Wolfe's business card, the pockets were empty. He sat on the bed and tossed the card on his nightstand. *Asshole,* Jack muttered then had a memory surge. He shot up and headed for the closet in the hall that housed his washer and dryer. The jeans he had on the day he encountered Mr. Wolfe were on top of the washer next to the Spray-N-Wash he used to try and remove the red clay stains that still lingered. He rummaged through the pockets and pulled out the silver half-heart he'd tucked away the day he'd gone to Bone Hollow to see Wanda. He rubbed the charm against his pants and could see now that it wasn't BE FREE engraved on it like he originally thought but BE FRI. When he placed the jagged silver piece next to the ST ENDS half heart Lisa had been wearing at the time of her death, the two pieces fit perfectly together forming one complete heart. BEST FRIENDS. It was then that it came to him. A chain of moments that until now might not have meant anything unless they were linked together. The empty chain around Nelle's neck. The pale spot in the dip of her throat. The call to Billy Thrasher about borrowing his bike. She'd been out to the hollow searching for her missing friend. Her best friend. Her mother. How could he be so stupid? No wonder the girl seemed so familiar to him. He'd seen the bird tattoo over her heart peeking out from under the neckline of her sweater. Had to be a Mockingbird. Even her name. Harper Nelle. It would be just like Lisa to name her daughter after her favorite author. How could he be so damn blind? He had to find her. Tell her what had happened.

Jack snatched his keys off the counter on his way out the door. He called the diner from his truck.

"Pearl. It's Jack. Is the new girl around today? Nelle. Is she there?"

"No. I gave her the day off after that episode she had. Thought she might could use some time away from work. What*choo* you need her for?"

"Do you know where she's at?"

"Well, hopefully she's at home gettin' some rest."

"Your house?"

"Well yes, but—"

"Thanks, Pearl," Jack cut her short then ended the call. He made an illegal U-turn and headed back the way he came. Pearl lived two miles up the road from Jack in an area that had yet to try and redeem itself with gentrification. She'd been in the same old white clapboard house with sky blue trim since she moved to Rayburn. Her front yard had so many angel statues and cherub birdbaths, it looked like a cemetery. It was a known fact that she'd never sell the house because her only child was buried behind it. Georgia was a state that allowed people to be buried on their land. What folks didn't know and Jack had recently become privy to was that Pearl's husband, who had *mysteriously* disappeared years before, was also buried on Pearl's property. So, it was more of a cemetery then people realized. And though she wasn't the only one to have them in Rayburn, bottle trees surrounded her house. They were, strategically placed around the windows she had once told Jack to catch evil spirits before they blew inside when the wind stirred. The way things had been going lately, he felt Rayburn might be able to use a few more of the trees.

Jack pulled his truck in the gravel drive next to the

green Focus hatchback he recognized as Nelle's. It was parked off to the side in the grass near a camellia bush with dark red flowers that bled petals on the ground around it. He could see Nelle peeking out the side of the curtain in one of the front windows, and by the time he walked up the stairs, she had opened the door.

"What are you doing here?" she asked, pulling off the knitted cap from her head.

Jack noticed her scarf and puffy down jacket. "You going somewhere?"

"Just got back from a few errands."

"Well, I want to talk to you for a minute. You mind if I come in?"

She didn't answer but pulled the door back wide enough for him to enter, and he followed her inside.

"You want something to drink?" she asked heading back to the kitchen. Coffee or sweet tea? Water?"

"No. Let's sit," he said motioning her toward the oval Formica table.

Nelle sat, unzipped her jacket and removed her scarf, which she placed on the table.

Jack didn't know how to begin this conversation so he took small unsteady steps. "Were you out by the Truelove property a few days ago? Monday?"

"What if I was. Lots of people go out there. I saw a woman out there that same day, poking around the trees and bushes looking for something. Tall redhead. She took off when she spotted me. You going to harass her, too? I mean, what's this about really?"

This was going to be more difficult than he imagined. He didn't know if this was just teenage angst or if the girl had a personal vendetta against him. "So, it was you. On Billy's bike."

She looked away then back. "What's the big deal? Didn't see any No Trespassing signs. Is there a law against exploring?"

Those eyes. That attitude. So familiar. Part of him wanted to laugh. The other part wanted to cry. "Did I do something to piss you off? Because if I did, I'm sorry. I'd like us to be friends."

"*Why* are you here?"

"Because I have something I think belongs to you."

He reached in his pocket and took out the silver half-heart. He set it on the table and slid it toward her.

She instantly reached for her neck.

"You know, when I first found this," Jack continued, "I thought it said BE FREE. Then today I realized it was the other half of this." Jack pulled out the silver half heart that had been around Lisa's neck. He pushed it next to the one in front of Nelle and locked the two pieces together. "Best Friends," he said and Nelle burst into tears.

"I knew it. She's dead." She picked up both pieces of the heart and clutched them in her palm. "It's the only way she would ever be without this." Her tears stopped as quickly as they came and Jack could see something desperate in her eyes then, a look he knew came from lost hope.

"Where is she? I have to see her."

"Oh, Nelle. I'm sorry. You can't see her, honey. Just try and remember her the way she was. I promise it's better that way."

"No! I want to see her. Take me to her. Right now."

"I can't do that, and believe me, you do not want that image as a final memory."

Nelle started wailing again, unable to control her grief. She got up, grabbed a handful of paper towels and wiped her face. "How did she die?" she asked dryly and completely void of tears once again.

Jack stood, walked over to her and wrapped his arms around her. He pulled her close and tight, but she pushed him away. "How. Did. She die? Somebody killed her, didn't they? Tell me the truth. I have a right to know."

"Yes, Nelle. It looks that way." Jack didn't want to explain how, but he didn't even have a chance before she pounded him with another question.

"It has something to do with that box of shit I took from the room where she was staying, doesn't it? All that Truelove and Hixson research. That woman at the nursing home in Rome had her convinced that she was a Truelove. Did you know that? You know that old woman just pretends that she can't remember so she doesn't have to go to trial. Or at least that's what my mother said. Anyhow, this woman, Miss Cave, gave her a photograph of my—your father. She came here to meet with him, and now she's dead! And that diary your girlfriend had at the diner, my mother got that in an antique store. It belongs to her." She started sniffling again. "Belonged to her." Her voice caught. "And I want it back."

"Okay. Okay. We can work all that out. Just try and calm down." Jack took out his wallet and removed the photograph of Joe and the Truelove girl. "Was this the picture the woman gave your mother?"

Nelle leaned in. "Yes," she sniffed. "That's it. She told her that woman was her birth mother."

"Did she say why she thought that?"

"Because she recognized my mother's birthmark or some shit. She told her she was Sarafina Truelove's daughter, and she'd been brought to Dr. Hixson's after Sarafina had perished in a fire. Dr. Hixson adopted her out to a couple who used to live here, the Harrisons who both died when I was a baby."

Jack had no idea that Lisa had even been adopted. Evidently, she hadn't known either.

Nelle took a breath and blew it out. "Miss Cave said that your father might be able to give her more information about Sarafina because they were friends."

Jack wanted to tell her then that he had been incredibly close with her mother at one time. That he still loved her and always would, but he didn't think it was fair. It wasn't the right time to burden her with his grief when she was suffering with her own.

"I know how upset you must be," he said. "But it's

important we inform your father that your mother has... passed." He felt his stomach twist. "Whether or not you are close with him, he has a right to know."

Nelle zipped her coat and swiped her backpack off the kitchen counter. "Inform my father? Are you fucking serious? News flash, Dad. You already know!" she shouted then took off out the back. The screen door slapped behind her, and it was so much like a slap across Jack's face that he took a step backward.

"What? Nelle, please. Wait," Jack called after her, but by the time he made it outside, she had already cranked up Billy's motorbike and was aiming it toward the trees beyond the house, leaving a trail of oily smoke in her wake. *Dammit*, he muttered jogging back to his truck. What the hell was going on here? He jumped in the front seat and dug out his cell phone. He'd missed a call from Maggie; she'd left him a message.

"Jack, listen. I ran the VIN number on the lake car. It's a Hertz rental registered to Lisa Harrison. She's had it about a month. Also, I think I've located her ex-husband. Just thought you'd like to know. Call me."

He was in disbelief trying to digest it all. Could Nelle actually be his daughter? He added up the years but it still made no sense. Why hadn't Lisa ever told him? Why would she leave especially if she knew she was pregnant? He didn't understand any of this. He had to find Nelle, but there was something he needed to do first. He searched his phone log and tapped Angela's name. It only rang once.

"Hey, I was just going to call you," she said before he could speak. "I just got through talking with Ronnie over at the pizza place. Get this. Years ago, she gave up a child and Dr. Hixson handled the adoption. I believe Liam Tate was that child, and he was adopted by the people who lived on my street. Years later, Ronnie received a package the same month and year that unbeknownst to her, Liam Tate was murdered. The package contained a child's finger and a note that had to be written by Knox. She no longer has the finger but she thinks she still has the note. Remembers word for terrifying word what it said. Knox is seeking some type of revenge. It's not about the children, Jack. It's about their biological mothers. I'll fill you in on more when I return. I'm headed to Rome to see Anna Cave, Dr. Hixson's former nurse right now. I think she might have some answers."

"You won't believe this, but that's exactly where I'm going too. Where you at? I'll swing by and pick you up."

thirty

He'd not given the folders a thought in twenty-nine years. But whatever they contained had gotten Sara killed so they had to be relevant in some way. He knew this much. Once he fled the hollow, he'd never looked back until a few weeks ago when he saw the man in the square. Then he recalled the day Sara had been killed as if it happened only yesterday.

Once she had saved the infant from the fire, the woman from the hollow had instructed him to follow the glowing mist through the tunnel, which led to the doctor's secret door. There he left the child in the care of the nurse. Afterward, he wandered around in the dark until he found an opening overgrown with brush and climbed out, not deducting until he saw the Old Mountain Arts Hotel sign that it was the same way the man had brought him into the hollow. Other than a few stray hikers, the place had been abandoned. It took him a few hours to find his way to Rayburn, hiding in the shadows until he found the church. It was a place he no longer considered safe, but it was shelter if nothing else. He pilfered food from the kitchen behind the rectory and slept in the pews for days before the pastor discovered him and took him in as a child of God. When the pastor finally left the church, Pastor Briggs continued to let him stay on. Not that he had any place else to go. He stopped thinking about being reunited with his family. He didn't know how to find them. They might have been dead for all he knew, but even if they weren't, they'd probably forgotten all about him.

Years passed before he saw her again, the Cherokee woman people called the Fire Bride. Walking toward the diner, carrying a basket of apples, she wore a long full-sleeved white dress that looked as if it was made of a table cloth and a veil of lace that partially covered her scarred face. He wasn't sure it was her until he recognized the large turquoise ring on her exposed hand. The angel ring. She never spoke a word to him as he passed, but she nodded and he believed she recognized him too. Other than the day that connected them forever in grief, their pact had remained silent. Her body was covered in burn scars, but Tomb hadn't forgotten that she had healed the burns on Sara's daughter that horrible day with her magic prayer. He wondered what had happened to that child.

He would have never thought for one second that he would ever by choice return to the hollow, but that changed when he saw the man who had killed Sara, the man who had stolen him from his family, weaving through the picketers downtown. He'd come back for those folders;

Tomb was sure of it. Why else would he have returned? He should have tossed them in the fire that day but there was no time. He knew though even then that they were very important in some way. A way he didn't understand. Sara had died for them, and he wouldn't let that be for nothing so he went looking for the shoebox he'd hidden so long ago, thinking it would be a miracle if it was still there.

It took him three tries to find the tunnel that led to the hollow. It was obstructed by years of overgrowth but still identifiable by the faded and splintered Mountain Arts Hotel sign dangling from a post of petrified wood half embedded in the ground. It was the way Knox had taken him to the trailer all those years ago where he left him for days before bringing Sara. He knew that if he followed the tunnel it would dump him out in the hollow, the place of whispers and fog and memories that still burned in his mind.

With the flashlight and shovel he'd borrowed from the church, Tomb walked for what seemed like forever before he found the opening. Pushing the overgrown vines and branches aside, he made his way out onto the rocky edge of a place he'd always wanted to forget but never could. Above the entrance, he eyed the circle with a cross carved into the red rock. He'd forever associate that symbol with freedom but learned after his escape that for the Cherokees, it represented the morning star, which symbolized hope and guidance. And he knew first hand, anyone traversing the tunnels would certainly need those two things.

He marked his pathway with pieces of ribbon left over from a wedding at the church then wandered for a long time before finding the scorched remnants of the trailer. The makeshift shed behind it had collapsed entirely. The only thing left was a rusted piece of aluminum siding that had grown into the ground and the large rock he'd used to mark the spot. He pushed it out of the way and began digging. About a foot down, the shovel hit the metal container, an old green ARMY locker he'd found in the hollow one day. Inside, the shoebox of files he'd wrapped in a piece of plastic tarp and hid all those years ago waited patiently, worn and moldy but still intact. Whatever power they contained in their state of decomposition was still prevalent. Sara had kept these particular records from Knox, and he obviously still wanted them. Tomb studied the names on the folders. At least one of them he recognized as the sheriff's mother, Katherine Towns. Hers was the only legible name listed. The woman had never cared for him. Thought he was ignorant. She'd even accused him of having something to do with the children that had recently started disappearing. The state police had investigated him. They wanted him to take a lie detector test but they couldn't administer it because he couldn't speak. He answered their questions only in writing, and he assumed they hadn't yet figured out a way to detect lies in ink or pencil. For weeks they followed him around, spying on his every move. But this didn't matter. For whatever reason, Sara was trying to protect the sheriff's mother as well as the other two women, and this had gotten her killed.

Paging through the contents of the folders, it was clear that all three women had given up babies for adoption. Margaret S-h-a or S-h-e something or other—the last part had been blacked out, in 1966, and Katherine twenty years before under the last name of Lynch. However, Katherine had also adopted a child in 1976, on the exact same day, he discovered, that the third woman, Wanda D-r-a—he couldn't make out the rest because the paper was so worn, had given one up. None of this meant anything to him. He stuck the folders back in the box when the trees behind him rustled. A low dense mist began to creep slowly toward him. It was the same fog that had once guided him out of the hollow years before, and he was still just as terrified of it. When he heard the whispering like a swarm of winged insects near his ear, Tomb knew it was time to go. To forever leave behind Bone Hollow and the tragic memories it stored in its unexplainable fog and strange whispers. Its fire and death. Its blood and bones. So once again, he looked for the morning star.

It was on his way back through the tunnel that he heard the faint cry for help. A small voice, echoed in fear. The voice of a child that for one terrifying moment, made Tomb believe that the hollow would never let him go. That he might never escape it. But the voice, he realized, was coming from beneath him so he laid the flashlight and shoebox down and did something he had a great deal of familiarity with. He started to dig. Once he had made a sizeable hole, he peered down into it with the flashlight and saw a young girl below. He didn't realize there were other tunnels running beneath the one he'd traveled but apparently not all of them were throughways. This one ended abruptly in blackness. What was she doing down there all by herself? He carefully lowered himself down and lifted the girl up through the fresh hole he'd just made. Before climbing back up himself, he looked over the edge and saw what seemed like endless emptiness. His foot kicked a piece of rock and it went over the edge, but he never heard it hit bottom. He didn't know how long he'd been lost in those depths before he heard the girl call to him.

"Mis...ter, are you ok...ay down there?" Her speech was stuttered. "We have to get...out of here."

Once he managed to crawl out, the girl, covered in dirt and debris asked him his name and he told her. It was the first word he'd said in a very long time.

It felt good. He said again. It was like being released from a spell.

The girl ran her tiny fingers over the scar on his forearm where he had carved it. "Thank you for saving me. I heard some men talking but they didn't hear me calling for help. I'm glad you did." The girl didn't tell him about how she'd escaped. She didn't really know. The power went off just as her captor was setting food inside the door. She slipped out and ran. Then suddenly she found herself in total darkness, but the tiny flickering fairies guided her along. They disappeared when the men's voices echoed around her.

Tomb had heard the men's voices too on his way into the hollow. Thought at first it might be city men working on the water lines or maybe some park rangers from Blood Mountain. Whoever they were, he knew he could never explain to anyone that he just happened across the girl in the tunnel. It was no doubt she was the sheriff's niece. There were fliers posted all over town. He'd once again be tossed into the spotlight of a town that didn't understand him. Most people in Rayburn feared him, disliked him, hated him, and distrusted him. He was already called freak and Frankie by many of the locals, especially the high school teens who passed him while he worked in the cemetery. He'd once found a paperback copy of *Frankenstein* tossed near a tombstone, likely by one of the students to mock him. They probably didn't know that he could read. His silence was often equated to ignorance. But once the pages dried out, he'd read the book in its entirety.

Tomb was tall but not eight feet tall. He was deformed but not hideously ugly. His shoulders were hunched slightly from the physical work he performed daily, and his heart was on the wrong side of his body, but he didn't feel like a monster. However, he understood long before he finished the book how someone who didn't fit into society could be made into one. His silence helped convict him of this.

He and the girl made their way through the tunnel, down the mountain, and back towards the square. Once she began to recognize her surroundings, she reached for him, and he squatted to meet her eyes. He remembered then what his mother used to tell him. That children could see things adults could not, and he wondered what the girl saw in him. She wrapped her small arms around his neck, something no one had done for many years then darted across the street to the diner. She stopped at the door, turned to wave then disappeared inside. He stood, and when he did, he noticed a locket on the ground near his feet. It must have slipped from the girl's neck. He picked up the chain and rubbed his thumb over the small heart to remove some of the dirt then went inside the church to hide the folders and ask God if maybe the girl was the reason he'd escaped death all those years ago.

Now, as he sat awake in the hospital bed, recalling the day he was shot, he heard a commotion in the hallway. Some kind of altercation. He carefully climbed out of the bed and wheeled his IV over to the door where he peeked through the narrow window. Two armed officers were wrestling with a man, trying to secure him with handcuffs, but the man was out of control. Several trays soared through the air, a cart overturned, its contents spilling out onto the floor, and when a nurse ran towards the aggressive man with a needle in her hand, he backhanded her so hard she slammed into the wall. Blood poured from her nose, and one of the guards reached to help her. That's when the man ripped the gun from his holster and began firing shots. It all happened so quickly but not quick enough so that Tomb didn't recognize him. This was the same man who'd stolen his life all those years ago. He'd never forget those cold, empty snake eyes. Even now, the sight of him made Tomb shake in fear as he huddled in the corner until the man fled. It wasn't long after that the hospital swarmed with officers and news people. All searching for Levi Knox. The devil had a name.

When Tomb found his strength, he secured the seeping patch over his chest and gently pulled out the IV wedged into his arm. He pinched a piece of gauze in the fold of his elbow then found some old scrubs in a closet. He changed out of the paper gown, and because of all the commotion was able to walk out of the hospital without anyone noticing.

Back in his room at the church, he readjusted the patch with first-aid tape the pastor kept for emergencies then changed into a pair of jeans, a cable-knit turtleneck sweater that was three sizes too big—someone had donated it, and his favorite black rubber boots he used while tending the graves. He then grabbed the box with the folders, shoved it into his backpack, and walked in the direction of the trailer park on Shadow River. Katherine Towns was the only name he recognized on the folders, which is why he wanted her to have them. He hoped she'd know what to do with them. Whatever Knox wanted the files for was sure to bring about more death. He felt this in his heart, which had always beat on the wrong side of his body.

He laid the ragged, rotting box on Kitty's stairs, knocked loudly and walked away. By the time she answered the door, Tomb was across the lot. He looked over his shoulder only once when she started swearing at him. He could see the anger in her face even at a distance. It wasn't the first time she'd wished him dead. He wondered why she hated him so much. She'd blamed him for the missing children, and now she'd blame him because he had not died after she shot him. Maybe people just needed to someone to hate, someone to blame other than themselves, but he also knew firsthand how easily being voiceless could condemn a man.

"You son of a bitch!" Kitty continuing yelling. "What the hell are you doing here? Get off my property and don't you ever come back! You were supposed to be dead, you pervert! You hear me? DEAD!"

But he already knew this. He *was* supposed to be dead. But whatever poison Knox had given him all those years ago hadn't worked. And he hadn't bled to death either after his finger had been taken. Knox said because of this, he was meant to live. There was a reason he survived, and only God knew that reason. And it was because he desperately wanted to know what it was himself that Tomb had never left the church where he silently searched every day for it. But even if he never discovered it, Sara was buried there and he could watch over her as she did him when she was alive. He wanted to believe that was reason enough.

Heading back to the church in trepidation that the pastor would no doubt make him return to the hospital, he saw the girl from the tunnel sitting on a bench with a woman he assumed to be her mother. They both had ice cream cones. Hastily, he turned and walked in the other direction, hoping she hadn't seen him. No good would come out of her recognizing him. He'd be blamed for taking her and quite possibly the others. Because he was different, people would find a way to make him the monster.

thirty-one

The assisted living facility was nested in a wooded area off Calhoun Road a short distance from downtown Rome and adjacent to the Etowah River. The entrance, flanked on both sides by two brick columns and a white aluminum fence had bright pink and purple flowers at its base. On each column was a gold oval sign engraved with a set of wings with a heart in the center and the black scripted words, Guardian Angels. The sun sparked against the metallic signs, and Jack adjusted his visor as he snaked his way up the asphalt drive. The commute had taken longer than expected, but it gave Angela and him a chance to get caught up, discuss what they needed from Anna Cave, if she was willing and able to speak with them. Jack hoped that she had answers that might lead to Hailey, Simon, and Ben. He was almost out of time to find them. Drilling was planned for the next morning, but according to Deputy Wayne, who had no luck locating the stinky flowers, the drilling team had already started setting up on the Truelove property.

"Are you relatives?" the young woman at the front desk inquired.

"No," Jack answered, fishing out his badge. "But this is official business. It's urgent that we speak with Miss Cave."

"Miss Cave doesn't receive many visitors other than people requesting to talk to her about the Hixson trial. They always leave disappointed. She's in Memory Care. Not sure how much she will be able to help you."

This wasn't a good start Angela thought even though Jack had told her what Nelle had said about the old woman's memory being just fine.

"Just follow this hall toward the double doors, take a right at the bench, then an immediate left. You'll see the signs. We keep that area locked at all times for the safety of the patients. There should be someone at the desk to buzz you in. I'll let them know you're on your way."

The chatty young CNA who walked Jack and Angela down the hall explained that the reason they wore green scrubs in Memory Care was that green had a calming effect on the nervous system.

"The walls and carpet are all color coded as well," she told them. "Greens, yellows, and blues are best. It's easier for patients to find their way back to their room. For some reason, those with memory problems never forget color. One of the nurses here in Memory Care is into color therapy and its effects on psychological functioning. She's one of those save-the-planet people. I mean, God love her and all, but I think it's too late, if you know what I mean."

The girl rambled on and Jack and Angela listened, trying not to be rude.

"I do like the community garden she started for our residents. It's pretty sweet. Anyhow, she's a lot more familiar with Miss Cave, *but* she isn't here today because of her eye."

"Well that's too bad. I hope it's nothing serious." Angela said.

"Nothing contagious, thankfully. Justine has ongoing issues related to some childhood eye injury. It gives her headaches sometimes. She should be back tomorrow though if you have any questions."

"Great," Jack said. "I'll keep that in mind."

With a crocheted blanket draped over her legs while soaking up the sun's vibrant rays, Anna Cave stared out at the yellow and pink roses planted just outside only occasionally glancing at the television mounted to the wall in the corner. The picture was crisp; the volume barely audible.

She didn't seem as frail as Jack expected. Short white curls swirled around her head like frosting, framing her minimally lined face. Her makeup accented her high cheekbones and her eyes, which were the color of weak tea. She had readers around her neck but no other visible glasses. The TV controller was gripped in one hand. The woman looked good, Jack thought, for someone who must be nearing ninety.

"Hi Miss Cave," the CNA addressed her in a sweet, cheery voice, opening up two folding chairs as she spoke. "You have visitors." She positioned the chairs near the old woman who glanced up but never once spoke. She kept her focus on the bumble bees hovering around the flowers. The sky was blue and clear, the room warm. Jack was hot just looking at the old woman all bundled up in blankets and cooking in the afternoon sun. Beads of sweat formed on his brow and his pits grew damp.

"I'm Shannon. Let me know if you need anything," the CNA said before leaving. "She's quiet most of the time, but I assure you, outside of a slight tremor, she's as sound as the rest of us. She can speak, hear, and understand just fine. Isn't that right, Miss Cave?"

The woman continued to ignore her. Jack and Angela took a seat.

"Miss Cave, my name is Jack Towns and I'm the Crow County Sheriff. You know where that's located, right? In Rayburn." He didn't wait for a response. "This is Angela. She's from a missing children's organization. We are working on something incredibly important right now and could really use your help. We understand that you used to be employed as Dr. John Hixson's nurse at the Hixson Women's Clinic."

The woman showed no emotion or acknowledgment when Jack mentioned Hixson's name. She merely adjusted the afghan over her legs then set the controller on the table next to her chair. Her hand shook ever so slightly, and she folded it into a ball to stabilize it.

"Do you know of a woman by the name of Lisa Harrison? She may have been here doing some genealogy research. You led her to believe she was the daughter of Sarafina Truelove. Do you recall any of this?" Nothing. Jack was beginning to wonder if what Nelle and the CNA said about her mind being just fine was true or not. Or maybe she was just afraid.

"Miss Cave, just to clarify, we are not here in regards to the Hixson trial, but information you have may help us find some missing children. He looked over at Angela. "And possibly put a child killer away for life."

The old woman didn't budge. She didn't smile, move, twitch, jerk, or sigh. Even her hands were stilled. Jack wasn't even sure she was breathing at this point.

"What about the name Levi Knox? Ever heard of him?" Angela chimed in, slight frustration in her tone. This garnered a cursory glance from the woman in her direction but nothing else. "Or Rhonda DiCarlo?" Angela added. "Do you remember her from the clinic? Please, Miss Cave. We're desperate here. Can you give us something? Anything?"

Jack stood, stretched his legs and took a deep breath. Something sticking out from under the twin bed caught his attention, and he walked over towards it.

"This is useless," Angela sighed. "A waste of time. I'm not even sure she can hear us." She reached in her pocket and took out a card then stood and placed it gently on the old woman's blanketed lap.

"If you think of anything or feel like talking, please give me a call," Angela said loudly. She grabbed her bag and walked over to where Jack was standing. "Let's go," she said, defeated then stopped short when she saw what he'd been distracted by.

What Jack thought was a magazine ended up being a large print crossword puzzle book. When he bent to pick it up, he saw many more under the bed, stacked in neat piles. He flipped through a couple of them and found that most of them were completed in ink. The letters forming the answers looked like they'd written by someone with shaky hands. An elderly person who, without a doubt, had a very capable mind.

A wave of melancholy took over Angela. She felt her face warm as she grabbed one of the books and sat on the edge of the bed. "My mother loved these things. Any kind of puzzle, really."

Jack and Angela were both shocked when they heard Miss Cave's scratchy southern voice. "Archer? As in Linda Archer?" She stood then and turned to face them, the business card in her hand, the blanket now crumpled on the floor at her feet. She had her readers on now, low on her nose. "You don't look much like her," she said, staring straight at Angela.

"I take after my father," she said curtly. "You knew my mother?" Angela set the puzzle book on the bed and stood.

"Linda Archer is my sister, but we haven't spoken in

years."

"So, you're the long lost aunt. I didn't see that coming. Well, auntie," Angela relayed with detectable bitterness. "You won't get another chance. Mom died in August. Brain tumor."

"This is your aunt?" Jack suddenly feeling confused and out of place. "I'm confused. Do you want me to step into the hall?" he motioned with his thumb.

Angela shook her head. "Not necessary."

A sullen pall took over the old woman's face. "That's too bad," she said. "I was so hoping I'd go first."

"Why's that?"

"Because then I could stop wondering if she was ever going to speak to me again. We had our differences, but I loved her."

"What would make two sisters not speak for so long?" Angela asked.

"Your mother didn't like me working for Dr. Hixson. She thought he was doing the devil's work, and that I was just an enabler. She was angry that she and your father had tried so hard for years to have a child, and women coming to Dr. Hixson were just giving them away. Or aborting them," she added bluntly. Then one day I called her and said I had a gift for her. A baby girl whose mother had died."

"Wait a minute. Are you saying...am I a Hixson baby? This can't be true. It just can't be."

"No, child. Don't get your drawers in a bunch, now.

At first, your mother swore at me then hung up the phone. An hour or so later, she called back to say she wanted the child. Then she changed her mind again. More swearing. More tears. More back and forth phone calls. Two days passed and she called with the news that she was pregnant. So, the Harrisons adopted the baby girl. Named her Lisa. Eight and a half months later, you were born, but your mother had stopped talking to me by then. She was on a mission to find out what happened to that baby girl's mother. She wanted to see the clinic fold and Hixson go to jail. I wouldn't oblige her, and in all honesty, I didn't know until later how Lisa's biological mother had died. But I did suspect that she was a Truelove baby, most likely Sarafina's. I put those things together myself, by the way. Your mother wasn't the only puzzle solver in this family."

"Who *was* the father of the child?" Jack interrupted a little too aggressively. "Any idea?"

"I always had my suspicions. But it wasn't Joe Towns if that's what you're thinking. Not that he was your—" She stopped herself. "There were rumors, but in my heart, I knew it just wasn't possible. Joe Towns was a decent man."

"Well, who do you think it was then?"

The old woman sat down and removed her glasses, let them dangle from the beaded cord around her neck. She motioned to the metal padded folding chairs. "Why don't you both sit. I'll tell you what I can remember. It may answer some of your questions, but I'm praying for the day

I wake up and remember none of it."

Jack and Angela each took a chair and listened as the old woman continued.

"When I first started working for John...Dr. Hixson," she clarified. "I wanted to help women who had few choices in life. Thankfully, I never got into any kind of female trouble, but being raised Catholic, I completely understood what was expected of women in our society. After graduating high school, I went with a friend who had gotten pregnant because her family was also Catholic and never stressed the importance of contraceptives. It was the 1950s you understand. Anyhow, she'd heard about a doctor in Tennessee who could help her. That's where I first met John. I never went back to Pennsylvania. Instead, I took nursing classes at night, while working for him during the day. He wasn't a bad person. I know that sounds crazy because he was after all a baby killer, but he was trying to keep women from attempting it themselves. His initial intentions were good. I don't know why I stayed with him so long, but I think it's because at one time, I may have loved him. Or thought I did. Anyway, no other place would have hired me if they knew I worked for John. He had over the years gained quite a sub-rosa reputation that bled into mine."

Jack pinched his chin. Caught himself doing it and stopped. "So, you worked with Hixson even before he moved his practice to Georgia?"

"Yes. We were all set up in Rayburn by 1957

though."

"When did he start selling babies?" Angela asked.

"That same year, I believe. Or maybe the year following. That's something, in all honesty, I don't recall." She chuckled, uncomfortably then spoke soberly. "In the beginning, he was selling the babies as an alternative to aborting them. But somewhere along the line, something happened to him. Greed got the best of him. Humanity took its toll. I don't know. He changed. Started *making* the babies to sell. But he was getting older and he knew that wouldn't last. So, he worked out some deal with a sperm bank in Savannah, I think, and while doing routine examinations, he would impregnate some of these girls then profit later when he adopted out their babies."

"Jesus Christ," Angela said. "Didn't anyone notice what was going on?"

"Upstairs, he ran a women's clinic. Downstairs, he ran a black-market baby operation. No one but Sarafina and I knew about it. I knew because he required my help delivering the babies." She took a deep breath. "Poor Sarafina knew because she'd become a way for him to make money. A victim. Or at least that's what I believe. She was not going to let him have that baby, though."

So Pearl was right, Jack though. Hixson was the father of Sarafina's baby. Which meant that Lisa had been his daughter and Nelle was his granddaughter. "I never knew the clinic had a basement."

"It does. It's just hidden. Hard to find if you don't

know what you're looking for. There's a delivery room down there, a nursery, and an office where we kept the files and handled the abortions and adoptions. The entire basement had been previously soundproofed probably by the Mob who once owned it. There's even a safe down there."

"Knox had files from the clinic with him when he was arrested," Angela said. "They must have come from the clinic."

"It was Knox who killed Sarafina, you know. There's no way of proving that, I realize, but I knew the minute the boy brought the child to the door, that she was a Truelove. Those eyes couldn't have come from anyone else. Large spooky windows the color of periwinkle. She had this perfect pink angel burned into her arm, and she smelled like smoke, but surprisingly there were no burns on her body."

"What boy?" Jack and Angela asked at the same time.

"I didn't know his name. Never saw him before. He never said a word. Just handed over the child and left. He was missing a finger. I do remember that. When I heard about the fire, and the woman who perished in it. I knew it had to be Sarafina. She'd been missing for months. Joe knew too, but her body was too badly burned to identify. Knox had taken her and hidden in the hollow because he knew nobody would look for her there. And then he killed her. I believe that with all my heart."

"You said the boy was missing a finger?" Angela

questioned. "His ring finger?" Her mind began to spin.

"I believe so."

Jack interrupted. "But even if Knox hid her, why would he want her dead? She was just a hopeless young girl."

"What I believe is that Knox charmed her when he came into the clinic one day. A handsome stranger with a promise. They exist outside of fairy tales, you know. Sarafina worked for Hixson part time because her parents owed money to John for land or something—not my business. Regardless, she was working off their debt and she was there the day Knox came in looking for adoption records from a certain year. I don't recall the year right off the top of my head. I told him we didn't have any such records because we weren't in the adoption business, but he was very persistent. He said that he knew what we were doing there. I remember that day like it was yesterday because a woman from Tennessee who'd adopted a boy from the clinic some years before had called to get information on the boy's biological mother. She wanted to determine whether or not the boy's heart condition was genetic. I told her I could not give her the name of the biological mother, but that I would try and see if there might be anything in the file in regards to the woman's health. I retrieved the record from the basement, and laid it on the counter while I assisted another patient, but the entire folder disappeared. I knew Knox must have taken it. He was lingering around even after I told him we wouldn't be able to help him with the information he wanted and that he should leave. Anyhow, the biological mother of the boy with the heart condition was no longer alive. A young thing, she'd OD'd a few months after giving birth. They found her out behind the bowling alley, you know. This wasn't in the file, of course. I just remembered seeing the girl's photo in the paper. Knox wouldn't have known any of this though because he was gone by the time I returned Mrs. Blake's call. And so was the folder with all her information. That's the only time that had ever happened, which is probably why I remember so well."

"The woman's name was Mrs. Blake?" Angela asked. It had to Thomas Blake's mother. She died without ever finding her son. She knew now Knox had taken him but if so, why was his body never found?

"Yes. She told me she'd named her boy, Thomas. Anyhow, not long after that incident—maybe a week or so, Knox returned. Sarafina must have at some point confided in him that Hixson got her pregnant and planned to sell the baby, but that she wanted to keep it. All true, by the way. Knox offered to hide her if she could obtain *these* records for him. I think she attempted to do this because more than a few boxes of records disappeared from the office."

Jack was puzzled. "Well, how did she get them out of there? I mean, wouldn't you have seen her taking them?"

"Not if she used the basement door. The one that opens to the tunnels. I've never used them, but there's a labyrinth of tunnels running under and around the mountain. They were originally carved by leased prisoners who were forced to mine or so that's the rumor. Later they were used during Prohibition by the Mob. Plenty of hidden rooms full of moonshine down there even now. Surprised they haven't caught on fire in all these years. From what I've been told, one of the tunnels leads straight to the hollow. Not that I'd ever make that trek. It's no secret that the only people able to find their way in and out of the hollow are those born to it."

"Tunnels?" Angela asked. "And what the hell is the hollow?"

"Bone Hollow," Jack clarified. "It's sort of an historical preservation."

"Hardly," the old woman spoke up. "It's a goddamn graveyard for lost souls, and you'd do best to stay out of it. It's haunted. Owned by the dead."

Jack moved in another direction. "What do you think went wrong with Knox and Sarafina? If she gave him what he wanted, why did he kill her?"

"I don't have the answer to that. All I know is when the boy showed up at the tunnel door with Sarafina's child, I knew she was dead. And that rotten bastard had killed her."

"And what about Lisa Harrison? How did she get involved in all of this?" Jack asked.

"Lisa was hired by a woman, a Hixson baby, all grown up and looking for her biological parents. From what I understand, there are tons of them slowly coming forward now. Lisa came to me with questions, most of which I couldn't answer. The first time I saw her, I knew. The eyes were a dead giveaway, but it was purely by chance that I noticed the angel birthmark on her forearm that I was certain. She was a Truelove. Sarafina's daughter. No doubt in my mind. She didn't believe me, of course. She told me it wasn't possible. That her parents were Mike and Sue Harrison. She was skeptical but she kept coming back so I knew she might have suspected I was telling the truth. It was pure kismet that she discovered the journal that belonged to her ancestor at an antique store somewhere between here and Rayburn. There was a photograph inside of it, and the woman was the spitting image of Sarafina. I remembered then that I had a picture of Sarafina and Joe together. I told Lisa that her mother and Joe were good friends, and that she should seek his help in trying to understand. Maybe she would uncover the truth about her true identity."

"Look," Angela said pointing toward the TV screen and Knox's face on it. She reached and hit the volume on the controller.

Before his escape from the hospital, Knox was being held at the Fannin County Jail for possession of drug paraphernalia and desecration of human remains. And though he has not been confirmed as a suspect in Rayburn's missing children, GBI is investigating his possible connection to two bodies found submerged in Ghost Lake earlier today. Knox is considered armed and dangerous. Proceed with caution.

An image of Lisa's car at the impound lot flashed on the screen.

"Christ," Jack said reaching for his vibrating phone. He took the call in the hallway. Two seconds later, he was back.

"Angie," He said with calm sternness. "We have to go. Right now."

"What's going on?"

"Knox. He's escaped. That was my deputy." Jack grabbed her arm and tugged her toward the door. "He just confirmed."

"We'll be in touch, Miss Cave," she called. "You've been very helpful. Thank you."

Walking briskly down the hall, they heard the old woman call to them. "It just came to me. Nineteen sixty-six. Knox. He wanted records specifically from 1966."

Jack whizzed by the desk with a quick plea for the nurse to open the door. She hit the button and he and Angela were out in the parking lot in less than a minute.

"How did this happen?" she asked, frantically.

"Wayne said that he had to be transported to the hospital because his nose wouldn't stop bleeding. He must have pulled some trick and escaped."

"Was anyone injured?"

"No, but apparently, he scared the shit out of the nurse working in the Hematology Department. She's bruised and shaken but okay."

"Hematology? Is that cancer?" Angela questioned.

"Blood. The nurse said he forced her to give him the names of all the women in Rayburn who were listed as hemophiliacs for whatever reason. Specifically, anyone sixty-five and older."

"Why? What's he up to?"

"No idea," Jack confirmed. But as he said this, a thought was taking shape in his mind. Something he'd forgotten about until now. Something he knew was significant. It made his hair like needles on the back of his neck.

"Well, there can't be that many. Hemophilia is rare, isn't it?"

"Yeah," he said, that thought still trying to work itself into something tangible. "I guess originally there were three, but one moved, the other passed. Now, according to the information Deputy Wayne received, there's only one. He's working on getting the name from the nurse now. What year of records did your aunt say Knox was looking for at the clinic?"

"She said 1966. Why?"

Jack grabbed his phone, tapped the main office line, and waited for Maggie to answer. "Just a hunch," he told Angela. "Maggie, it's Jack."

"Hey, Sheriff. I was just about to call you. First, I managed to get in touch with Lisa Harrison's ex. Though divorced he took the news pretty hard. His main concern right now is his daughter. He hasn't heard from her in days. Believes she's in Rayburn. Not her biological father but seems to care for her a great deal regardless."

"Does he know who the biological father might be?"

"No. Lisa never told him, but that's something we need to talk about, Jack. In person. It can wait, but I need to tell you something I should have told you a long time ago. It's been weighing on me for a while, and I hate myself for it. But right now, I do have some other news for you in regards to Knox. I was able to convince the hospital administrator where Knox was admitted for two years, to give me copies of his records. They're being faxed over any minute. Also, I did manage to track down an old neighbor of his parents. Her name is Jill Latham and she and Mrs. Knox were good friends. She was devastated to learn about Levi, but she made clear one thing. Levi was not the Knox's biological son. They adopted him, Jack."

"From where?"

"I don't have that information yet. The woman said she couldn't remember but would try and find out and get back to me as soon as she could."

"Well, can you do me a favor and text me a copy of Knox's license?"

"Right away," Maggie said.

"Thanks. Wayne's calling. I gotta go. Talk soon."

"What's going on?" Angela asked.

"I'll fill you in. Hang on. Wayne, did you get a name from the nurse?"

"I sure did. And you're not going to believe it."

thirty-two

Kitty watched the Cemetery Man make his way across the park and disappear between the trailers. She was full of fire about it. He had no business coming around her place. What the hell did he want with her anyway? He had a lot of nerve, and why hadn't Jack let her know he'd been released from the hospital? Dottie said she read in the paper that the reason he'd managed to live after being shot was that his heart was actually on the other side of his body. This confirmed to Kitty what she suspected all along. The man was a deviant. A circus freak.

She stared at the box at her feet a long minute, gave it a kick to make sure it wasn't full of spiders or snakes, then picked it up and brought it inside. It was soft and damp and split at the seams. A fetid odor escaped it. She set the box on the counter, filled a fat glass tumbler with whiskey, and drained it. The box stared back at her. She filled the glass again.

Idiot, she mumbled, pulled off what was left of the crumbling lid and tossed it aside. A cloud of dust engulfed her. It reeked of campfire smoke and irritated her throat. She coughed and ran her hand across the underside of her nose. Peering inside at the yellow mildewed folders, Kitty watched some type of small winged creature escape from the box. She gave it a shake and watched a few more flutter out then dumped the contents upside down on the counter. The smell of smoke filled the room, and she realized what she thought were insects were actually cinders.

It wasn't until she saw her own name on one of the folders that she started to feel sick to her stomach. It might have been the cancer. She opted not to have treatment so it couldn't have been the effects of the therapy. Not that many people lived with a diseased pancreas for very long even with radiation and chemo so why bother. She opened the file and the nausea worsened when she saw it was from the Hixson Clinic. Instead of vomiting, she reached for the whiskey bottle and lit a cigarette.

Oh, Lord. How in the hell? That was a chapter of her life she'd closed long ago. Of course, she opened another one when she brought Jack home. But staring into her past like that made her feel vulnerable, and she detested weakness. It brought back a rollercoaster of emotion and way too many painful memories. Things she longed to forget and had pushed away in hopes that one day she would. But she never had. The pain shot through her like a bullet, and she clutched her stomach. Why couldn't she have dementia instead of cancer? Then she could forget this whole damn life. But that would mean forgetting Jack, too, and she could never face that. At least not with any sort of valor. Or dignity. No, she'd keep the bad so she could have the good.

Kitty leafed through the papers in the folder, dropped it on the counter and pushed it aside, though she knew it would never be anywhere but right there in front of her. There could never be enough pushing away to erase it entirely. An image of Harland flashed in her mind, and she shut it down as quickly as switching off a light. She refocused and took a look at the other two folders. It didn't take her very long to figure out that one of the women, Margaret, was Maggie Sheppard. Her birth date was a dead giveaway because she and Kitty were both Virgos. Same month, same day, different year. They'd never been close, and all the rumors milling around about Maggie and Joe didn't make it easy to try and establish any kind of friendship with the woman. But Kitty knew that was all just gossip, and she refused to give it any strength by either trying too hard or not trying hard enough. She remained indifferent to the woman, though seeing now that she had gone through something just as agonizing, gave her a new found respect for Maggie Sheppard. Pain had a way of connecting people. Even total strangers could be linked forever by it.

According to the faint typewriter print, Maggie had given up a child to Dr. Hixson in 1966. She couldn't have been but fifteen or sixteen years old, about the same age Kitty was when she first visited Dr. Hixson, pregnant with Harland's child and so incredibly naïve.

The remaining folder was marked with the name, Wanda. Kitty couldn't make out the last name, but she only knew one Wanda in town, and that was Wanda Drake, the Fire Bride. It had to be her. Three completely different women bound together forever by a man who couldn't remember any of it. Seemed so unfair.

She discovered Wanda had given up a boy also. Kitty wondered if she had done this voluntarily or been forced into it as she had. She was just about to close the folder and slide it over with the other two when her eyes caught something that made her reach once again for the whiskey bottle. She'd always known he must have come from someone in town. She just never imagined it was Wanda Drake of all people.

Kitty stared at the year 1973 and at the day and time Wanda had signed over her child to Dr. Hixson. A sharp stab sliced through her back, almost folding her in half and leaving her breathless.

She stubbed out the cigarette and reached in the drawer for paper and a pen. It was time to write the letter. She'd been putting it off, but her moments here were limited now. Jack had a right to know. She snatched the bottle and her cigarettes from the counter, and moved toward the kitchen table, leaving the empty glass behind. After several heavy pulls straight from the bottle and two more cigarettes, she stuck the finished letter in an envelope, sealed it, and wrote Jack's name across the front. She took one last drink from the bottle—the amber liquid almost drained empty, then propped the envelope between the mushroom salt and pepper shakers. Gathering the folders, she walked out the door, not bothering to lock it behind her. She had nothing left to take.

thirty-three

"Are you certain?" Jack asked Deputy Wayne.

"Yes, the nurse confirmed that Margaret Sheppard is the only known person in Rayburn with a record of hemophilia, something to do with Christmas. There were others at one time, but they either moved on or died. They even did some kind of study on her years ago. And she's not an actual bleeder. She's just a carrier, whatever the hell that means."

Christmas? Jack recalled Maggie telling him she couldn't donate blood at the Halloween blood drive because she had a blood disorder, but she said nothing about Christmas. *It comes from Royalty, you know*, she had once mentioned jokingly. *Queen Maggie*, Jack heard his father's words so lucid and loud, he had to glance over his shoulder to make sure he wasn't there in the truck with him. "What else did the nurse say?"

"Well, she said he demanded to know where Miss Sheppard was. Held a damn gun to her head. Then he mumbled something about that he wished he had thought of this before. The nurse said she had no idea what he was talking about. He took her car. I put an APB out on it. Brand new Blue Nissan Sentra. Do you think Maggie's in danger?"

"I do. I'm still about thirty minutes out. The traffic on 76 is historic. Head over there right away and check on her but be careful. Angela's been right all along. Knox is a killer, Wayne. I'll give Maggie a call now and alert her to the situation, but she has the police radio on at all times so I'm sure she already knows he's escaped." Jack didn't know what he was going to warn her about other than the fact that an armed psycho interested in blood disorders might be heading her way. He opened the text she sent and zoomed in on the license. Knox was born in 1966. According to Anna Cave, he'd come to the clinic looking for birth records from that same year. Jack felt a rush of panic take over with his next thought.

He rang the office, got a busy signal then redialed. He remembered then that when receiving faxes, the office phone sometimes became unavailable so he tried Maggie's cell. She didn't answer. He was getting one of those feelings, but this time he couldn't push it away. A memory of Knox's hearing flooded Jack's mind. What was that over-the-counter powdered substance found in Knox's possession at the time of his arrest? Some Asian powder that coagulated the blood and stopped the bleeding. But the finger from his victims had been removed after death. There was no need to stop the dead from bleeding. The powder, Jack determined then must have been for himself. Knox was a bleeder. A hemophiliac. Like Maggie. He'd been shedding his own blood for years, and this is why he must have said that blood was his salvation. He thinks that because he's a bleeder, his sins are automatically forgiven. And yet, he still hates himself. Or more realistically, he hates his origins. The hairs on the back of Jack's neck must have been two inches high and stiff as wire. Knox wasn't looking for any kind of cure with the hematology nurse; he was looking for someone to blame. The one person he could blame. He wanted revenge.

"Here, take this. It's on speaker." Jack handed Angela his cell. "Keep redialing until Maggie answers. And buckle up." He swerved right, narrowly sliding between two cars in the lane next to him.

"What are you doing?" Angela asked, more than a hint of apprehension in her tone.

"Just keep redialing and hang on." Jack hit his siren, yanked the truck all the way to the right onto the shoulder, and hit the gas. Angela jolted, nearly dropping the phone.

"Easy there, Mario Andretti," she said only half-jokingly. "You're scaring me."

"Still no answer?"

"Nope."

"Shit. Try the main number."

"Hello. Jack is that you?" Maggie answered.

"Got her," Angela said, handing Jack the phone.

"Maggie! What's going on? You okay?"

357

"Yeah, fine. I just...I just got off the phone with the woman I told you about. The former neighbor of the Knox's. Her name is Jill Latham. She and Levi's mother were close friends, and she confirmed that Levi was adopted from Rayburn, Georgia. It was all very secretive at the time. Mrs. Knox couldn't have children but didn't want anyone to know that. Levi's a Hixson baby, Jack." Her voice skipped but she continued. "The neighbor said it wasn't until he became sick that he discovered he'd been adopted. Lost his football scholarship and his fiancé on the same day. She had told Jill over drinks one night that she couldn't deal with his health issues or more realistically his inability to *perform*. Then he joined some extremist religious group and sort of fell off the map. Never spoke with his family again though Jill believes she did spot him at his parents' funeral a few years later. He inherited some money, she believes, but she doesn't know how much or if he ever had access to it. Apparently, there are stipulations with the inheritance. One of which is Knox has to be married. With at least one child." Maggie added then blew out a breath. "But this likely would have never happened if he's impotent as the ex suggested."

"Maggie, are you sure you're all right?" Jack heard the beeping of the fax machine and the rustling of paper before she answered.

"Yeah. I'm fine. The hospital records just came through." There was slight hesitation then Maggie began reading. "Says here, Levi Knox was hospitalized for nearly two years because...because of complications due to—" She stopped abruptly. "Christmas disease. He was so sick he almost died." She sniffled. "Christmas disease of all things." She swallowed hard and explained before Jack could ask. "A blood disorder inherited from a birth mother and named after Stephen Christmas, the very first case."

She took a minute and Jack knew she must be processing what he had already determined.

"Dear Lord, this is all my fault. I didn't know. I thought I was doing something good for him, and I ruined his life. Turned him into some kind of deranged sociopath. A child killer."

"Maggie, don't think about that. It's going to be okay, but you are in danger right now. I have reason to believe Knox is headed your way. He—"

"I know. He escaped while at the hospital. I heard. There's an APB out on him." There were tears in her tone, now, and something Jack speculated might be regret.

"Maggie." Kitty's voice cut in. "I need to talk to you. It's important."

"Hang on a sec, Jack," Maggie said. "Your mother's here. She looks upset."

"Take a look at this bullshit," Kitty said, hoisting the folders onto the counter.

"Where did you get these?" Maggie asked, flipping through them.

"The Cemetery Man. That dumb shit dropped them on my porch today. I told you he was no damn good."

"How did he get them? These records are from—"

"I know. From a long time ago. Long before computers and likely the only copies. And I don't know how he got them," Kitty relented. "He probably stole them from Hixson so he could blackmail us. No idea. Part of me wanted to light them on fire the moment I discovered exactly what they were, but I felt you had a right to know. You, Wanda, and I will all be dragged into that damn trial if this gets out. Take them," Kitty said, shoving the worn folders across the counter. "In case something happens to me. It was only a matter of time before Jack found out. I should have told him years ago." Her breath was labored, her skin pale and moist. She clutched her stomach with one hand and held onto the edge of the counter for support with the other.

"Told him what? Kitty, honey? Are you all right?" Maggie hurried around and helped her to one of the chairs in the small waiting area. "Let me get you some water."

Jack listened to the conversation through the receiver, and it was beginning to make sense now. Miss Cave had told him Knox wanted certain records from Hixson's. When he couldn't get them, he made a deal with Sarafina, but she must have kept certain records from him, and this is what got her killed. She might not even have known why Knox wanted them; she was just protecting the privacy of three women she knew and cared for, one of which was Kitty, the wife of someone who'd treated her like a daughter. How the Cemetery Man got a hold of these files was baffling, but Jack felt in the deepest part of his heart that Tomb had been trying to do something good by handing the records over to Kitty, a woman who had tried to kill him just days before.

It came to Jack then. Knox had come back to Rayburn for his birth mother. This was all about her. It couldn't have been any clearer. "Maggie!" Jack hollered into the phone. "Hello? Dammit, Maggie! Answer me."

"Jack, I'm here," she said. The phone screeched. "With your mother. I have you on speaker but I need to call 9-1-1. She's not well. Something's wrong with her. She doesn't look good."

"Maggie, listen to me. "You both need to get out of there, right now. Lock the front door, radio Wayne, and have him meet you around back. He's closer than I am. You are in serious danger. Get out of there! Now."

But it was too late. Jack heard a male voice in the background then. It had a distinctive tone. One he recognized. Sweet and calm and diabolical. Knox.

"Hello Mom," he said. "I've been looking for you for a long time. Have you missed me?"

Maggie cried out and Jack pressed the pedal to the floor. "I'm coming, Maggie. Just hang on."

"Well, if it isn't Sheriff Towns," Knox's voice echoed. "Glad you could join us, but I should warn you that the last Towns to get in my way had a terrible accident."

"Is that what happened to Sarafina Truelove, too?" Jack tried to remain calm.

"We had a deal, and she broke it. She had to die. Besides, the world is full of whores. What's one less? I didn't start the fire though. That must have been God."

"What about her siblings?"

"Never touched them. Never even met them."

"So why Lisa then? Why did you have to kill her?"

"Who the hell is Lisa?"

"The woman you sunk in the lake. Sarafina's daughter."

"Ah, yeah. That one. She was never part of the plan; she just got in the way. I didn't realize she was Sarafina's daughter though. Makes sense now. Same eyes. And she navigated the hollow like she'd been born there. Unknown to me, she had. She even managed to find the tunnel that led to Dr. Hixon's baby manufacturing plant. Now that's a sick fuck who deserves to die. Anyhow, that's how she discovered those kids, the *missing Rayburn children* you've been trying to pin on me. I didn't even know they were down there at the time. She must have heard them but couldn't find them. I told you I didn't take them. I may be many things but a liar isn't one of them. Anyhow, she got your father involved, and the last thing I needed was people foiling the plan I worked so hard on for so many years. So, when she met your old man at the old hotel, I pushed him off the mountain and put that bitch in a choke hold until she passed out. Then I dosed her and some moron from the pawn shop with strychnine, stuck them in her car, and watched it sink in the lake. I wish I could say I didn't enjoy it."

This cold-hearted bastard. Jack was going to end him, law or no law, but first, he needed the children to be safe. "Where are the children? Tell me and I'll make sure the courts go easy on you. You can work out some kind of plea deal."

"No chance in hell. They're not part of my redemption, Jackie boy. They belong to someone else's plan."

"Then tell me who took them."

"Again, not my deal. And I have no idea anyhow. What? You think I'm the only person in this world with a vendetta? After this, you'll have one too. This entire world was created upon vindication."

"I'm going to find them with or without you. Let Maggie and Kitty go, Knox. This is over. You're done." Jack bit down hard on his bottom lip. Tasted blood.

"It's over when I say it's over!" Knox shouted, losing his composure then reigning it back in. "But, if you're nice, I'll let you listen."

Jack tossed his cell to Angela then gripped the steering wheel with both hands. His knuckles whitened.

"Hold on," he said.

Angela hit the speaker button and they both listened, helpless and fearful as they raced toward Rayburn.

thirty-four

"What did you do to my Joe?" Kitty stood, prepared to fight. "You fucking bastard."

"You couldn't be more right," Knox replied. "That's exactly what I am," he chuckled maniacally. He was enjoying this. "Did you know I was a sick baby, and this bitch abandoned me? Isn't that right? *Mom.*"

"That's not true," Maggie said gravely. "I wanted you to have a better life. I didn't know you were sick. I didn't abandon you. I wanted you to have choices. I was just a—"

"A whore?"

"No. A young girl who trusted a stranger for a ride," she illuminated.

"So, I guess I'll never know for sure who fathered me then?"

"That makes two of us," Maggie said, her tone derisive. "Now, what is it that you want? I've got to get this woman to a hospital." Without taking her eyes off Knox, she furtively began moving her hand around the desk for something she could use as a weapon.

"What do I want?" He waved the black 9 mil around in the air as he spoke. "I want to make all of you whores pay. I want to make you feel pain and remorse. I want to give you a reminder of what you do to children bringing them to life, filled with sin, and then abandoning them. Marriage is sacred and blood is the only truth in this world." He moved his ring finger up and down. "I know. It doesn't actually go to the heart. It's what it symbolizes that matters. We're all just God's metaphors. My original goal was to find you and make you pay, but when I couldn't do that, I relied on other resources to satisfy my needs. Unfortunately, some of these whores had already offed themselves, so I didn't get the joy of sending them a little reminder of their sin. In that regard, I kept a few fingers for myself. My mistake. If I hadn't done this, I wouldn't have been caught, but I also wouldn't have had the brilliant idea to check for your name while I was at the hospital. Most hemophiliacs have some kind of hospital record. I have many, thanks to you."

Maggie felt like she was going to throw up everything she'd eaten for the last week. How could she have given birth to such a monster? It was her fault all those children had died and that Lisa was dead, too. She should have never sent her away. How would she ever be able tell Jack?

"Maybe some of us don't want a husband or a marriage," Kitty said sharply. "Love and marriage are two totally different things you whack job. Besides, who appointed you to be God's middle man? He's quite capable of handling his own retribution. You must have skipped over those parts in Bible class."

"Shut up. You sluts think you can just go around *shittin'* out babies you don't want then selling them, abandoning them, killing them. Then you make yourselves feel better by pretending you're saving them. Isn't that right? Giving them some kind of better life. Do you know what it feels like to be given anything and everything you want in life, but to go to bed at night knowing it will never be enough? That it will never change who you are. Who you were born to be." Knox caught sight of the folders on the counter then chuckled deviously under his breath when he recognized what they were.

"Having these would have saved me a lot of time, but the big picture is what's important here. I found you regardless. God guided me to you. He told me that in blood I'd find truth and forgiveness. And I did. Even if it was poisoned blood. Records can be destroyed, hidden, altered, but blood can never be denied." With one hand, he brushed the folders off the counter. Papers scattered everywhere.

"Don't you dare get God involved in your sick little game. He has nothing to do with it," Maggie snapped.

"I gave those children a chance at an afterlife. One free from eternal damnation. I even earned myself a fancy name for it. They had to be sacrificed in order to be exalted. No fault of their own; they were sinners. Just like I am, but I was born a bleeder, and my sins will be washed away. You think a single one of those children were destined for greatness? They didn't have a chance. I saved them from who they were to become. It was only a matter of time before they figured it out."

"Figured what out?"

"What I could already see so clearly. Their fate. Rotten roots don't produce beautiful flowers, *Mother*. Blood always wins. I am who I am because of you. Your tainted blood runs through my veins, and though it's my ticket to Heaven, it disgusts me." He pointed the gun toward Maggie. "You disgust me."

"You're out of your mind," Maggie said. "You killed innocent children, and it had nothing to do with saving them, and you think you are going to Heaven? You just wanted to get back at me. This is all about retribution. Some sort of sick blood redemption. You vested your entire life into a moment that will pass as soon as you pull that trigger. Then how will you go on? You'll have nothing left to fuel your reason for living." Maggie's fingers found a letter opener. She palmed it then slid it up the sleeve of her sweater.

"Oh, I have no intention of killing you. There are worse things than death. I'm living proof of that. I'm just going to do to you exactly what you did to me." Knox moved toward Maggie but the sound of Kitty's voice caused him to turn.

"Get away from her, you sick son of a bitch." Kitty reached down inside her boot, unhitched the knife she kept there and took aim. "Or I'll kill you where you stand."

"Kitty, no!" Maggie shouted!" But the obstinate old woman had already thrown the blade.

Knox moved but not fast enough. He yelped like an injured dog when the knife pierced his skin. He laughed then took a deep breath before using his free hand to pull five inches of steel from the area below his left clavicle. From the box on the counter, he yanked a wad of Popeye's napkins off the counter and pressed it to his wound. "It's going to take more than that to stop me from doing what I came here to do. He smiled then. "I think this belongs to you." He whipped the instrument in her direction.

"Kitty, look out!" Maggie shrieked."

Kitty jerked sideways and the knife stuck into the wall behind her. She turned, grabbed the handle and ripped it out, then lurched toward Knox, her aging compact frame no match for the fire burning inside her. She showed no fear of the gun Knox had trained on her.

"What the hell is going on there?" Jack yelled into his phone. "Maggie? Kitty?" Some kind of scuffle was ensuing. "Somebody answer me!" Jack demanded. A loud thump resonated throughout the cab of the truck and Maggie's scream rattled the windows. The last thing Jack and Angela heard before the line fell dead was the sound of gunfire.

thirty-five

"Still ringing busy," Angela said to Jack as he took the Rayburn exit doing seventy. She had a hold of the cell with one hand, the other was desperately clutching the utility handle between the front and side window. "You might want to slow down."

"Just keep trying. What about Maggie's cell?"

"Going straight to voicemail."

Jack barreled down the access road. He swerved onto Church then made a left on Main barely missing a protester dodging across the street. Deputy Wayne's cruiser was in front of the office, but movement by the ice cream shop two doors down caught Jack's attention. Fairy wings. Skyla. She was running. Camille was chasing her. Jack pulled over and jumped out. Angela followed.

"Skyla, come back," Camille pleaded. "Please."

"What's going on?" Jack asked his sister, catching up to her.

"I don't know. She just saw something and took off."

"Skyla!" Jack yelled. "Where you going, sweetheart?"

But as soon as he asked, he could see that she was heading straight toward the Cemetery Man who was standing at the end of the street, doing his best to avoid her.

"Skyla! No! Wait!" Jack picked up his pace, moving past his sister and looking over his shoulder to find Angela at his heel.

"It's that your niece?" She asked out of breath. "What's she doing?"

"Yes, and I have no idea."

Skyla kept running, dropping her waffle cone on the ground just before she reached the man who had saved her, dug her out from a grave. He turned and she launched herself into his arms, knocking him back a step. She called his name, and it stopped Jack in his tracks. *Tommy.* Angela plowed into him from behind. They both stood still for a moment, trying to grasp the situation as Jack took slow steps forward.

He was still in disbelief when he reached them. "Skyla, what are you doing, honey?" he asked as calmly as he could.

"Uncle Jack. This is Tommy. Re...mem...ber I told you about him?"

The Cemetery Man set Skyla down. A nervous smile slid across his face, but Jack could see it was shadowed by the small gray space that divided panic from fear.

"*This* is Tommy?" he asked.

"Um-hum," Skyla confirmed then twisted Tomb's forearm around and pointed. "See. Tom B. Tommy. I don't know what the B stands for," she added. "He saved me from the dirt and brought me to the diner," Uncle Jack. "You said you wanted to know."

Not Tomb. Tom B. Jack nearly fell over.

Angela looked on in confusion but then she saw it. Or didn't see it. The missing finger on the man's left hand. Could the B stand for Blake? Thomas Blake? Living in Rayburn and no one ever knew it. How long had he'd been here?"

"Sheriff," Deputy Wayne called from the front door of the sheriff's office. He jogged toward Jack and when he reached him, he was out of breath and pale. "Oh Sheriff, I— I. Your—I—Kitty. Oh, God."

"Take a breath Wayne and tell me what's going on." Jack could hear a siren in the distance, panic in Wayne's voice.

"It's your mother. I called for an ambulance but—"

"Stay with Skyla," Jack said and ran toward the office. "Mom," he called rushing through the door. "Mom." He knew when he saw Kitty on the floor, pale and still, a puddle of blood around her that she was already gone. He checked her pulse anyway, hoping for a miracle. His phone buzzed then. Unknown number. He let it go to voicemail. Two seconds after the ambulance arrived, it bleeped with a text.

It's Nelle. I followed the man who took that lady who works for you. I know he's the one who killed my mother. It's all over the news. We're at the old Hixson Clinic. You better come. I'm going in. My battery is dying. I hope you get this message.

"Shit," Jack cursed. He jumped up and headed out the door, nearly smashing into Angela in an effort to reach his truck.

"What's going on? Can I help?" she offered.

"Knox took Maggie. Nelle followed. No time to explain."

"Your mother?"

Jack shook his head.

"God, I'm so sorry, Jack."

"Wayne!" he yelled. "Knox has Maggie. Took her to the old Hixson Clinic. Call Fannin County PD. Have them meet me there. And make sure Camille and Skyla get home okay." He eyed the Cemetery Man, still uncertain with his role in all this and yet relieved that this man, this outcast that Rayburn avoided at all costs—didn't even know his name, had rescued Skyla. The town monster saves a little girl then gets shot. Jack could understand why the story of *Frankenstein* must have resonated with him so much.

"Got it," Wayne said. "I'll meet you there ASAP." He quickly guided Camille and Skyla to his cruiser, opened the door, and helped them inside.

Jack hopped in his truck and Angela was suddenly at his window, her deep brown eyes pinning him to the seat.

"Be careful. Jack," she said. She didn't bother telling him that she'd be right behind him. That she wanted to be the one to end Knox. That she wasn't much different from him in the fact that she had lived her life waiting for the moment she could avenge herself. Avenge Liam.

Jack nodded then sped off, Angela growing smaller by seconds in his rearview mirror.

When he was out of sight, Angela ran back over to where the man she believed to be Thomas Blake.

"Do you know where Hixson's Clinic is located?" There was desperation in her voice. She could hear it herself, and it scared her.

thirty-six

The Hixson Women's Clinic had been closed for almost two years, but this hadn't kept people away. The HCC sign above the door had been tagged with a giant X and someone had hung a rusty wire coat hanger from it. Most of the windows were busted out, and shards of glass clung stubbornly to the frames like jagged teeth.

Knox pulled Maggie out of the car then yanked her toward the front door of the old converted house where a broken padlock dangled from the latch. Around his shoulder, he'd secured a rag, but the wound Kitty had inflicted was bleeding so heavily, the cloth was soaked with blood. He kicked the door open and pushed Maggie inside, the gun still firmly gripped in his hand. Garbage was strewn on the floor, and the walls were lined with graffiti. Furniture had been overturned and Maggie caught the faint scent of something medicinal mixed with a scent relegated to hopelessness.

"Where are you taking me?" she demanded.

"You'll see. It's a surprise."

"I don't much care for surprises."

"We have that in common then. I remember my surprise when I found out I was cursed with your tainted blood. I lost everything because of it. Because of you. And not a thing in the world I could have done to change it."

"I don't understand why you're doing this. You have a choice."

"So did you." He forced her down a small hall in the direction of the back of the house and to a pantry door off what must have once been a kitchen.

Inside and to the right was what looked like an empty row of storage shelves. Knox yanked on the frame, and Maggie could see that it was actually a door. A cold, damp darkness hit her in the face as it opened. Her vision adjusted, and she saw stairs leading downward.

"Go on," he said grasping the back of her blouse in his fist. "And don't do anything stupid. Anything *else* stupid," he clarified.

Maggie used the wall for support with one hand. With the other, she did her best to keep the letter opener from slipping out, considering now was probably not the best time to use it since she couldn't see shit.

She felt for the first step with her right foot and proceeded with caution. When she reached a small landing, she saw more stairs to the left. A sporadic yellow light danced under the door at the bottom of the stairwell. She didn't realize the clinic had a basement, but she'd never actually been inside. Knox had been born in the hollow. For each step Maggie took, she remembered another painful moment from that time.

She had been making her way back from Devil's Backbone that day—a fifteen-year-old desperate girl who had trusted a stranger for a ride and ended up pregnant. Was it rape if you didn't say, STOP, because you were too frightened to utter a sound? Too ashamed to tell anyone.

Her parents had kicked her out once they found out she was pregnant. She'd been staying with the family of a friend from high school. Kind people but dirt poor. They were a week away from being evicted. They planned on moving out of state to stay with relatives and Maggie knew she couldn't go with them. She was already a burden to them though they never once brought that to her attention. So, she stood there looking down at the rocks of Devil's Backbone wishing she had enough of one to actually jump like she'd planned. Instead, she thought of the only person in Rayburn who might be able to help her. Dr. Hixson. She had to get to the clinic. But her water broke near the orchard and she never made it. Wanda heard her cries and helped her to her feet and to the hollow where she delivered the baby. Then they took the infant to Dr. Hixson's. Maggie and Wanda never spoke again. Desperation had a way of creating inexplicable and often silent bonds.

"Keep moving," Knox told her. "Through there."

The door led to a room that was cast in a golden glow from the fluorescent lights above. It looked like a waiting room for Hell. One of the bulbs had burned out and the two left flickered. "What is this place?"

"The good doctor's baby-making facility and adoption headquarters. Don't tell me you don't remember."

"I've never been here before."

"Liar. What you probably don't know is that this building was once used by the Mob to distribute alcohol during Prohibition. They used the tunnels to transport spirits to the old hotel. Just one of the many things I discovered along the way."

"I'm not lying. It's the truth. You were born in the hollow. I swear to God." Maggie could see Knox thinking about this, trying to digest it. Not believing it but considering it.

"You're a damn liar. Sarafina Truelove had your records. She just hid them from me. Must have thought you were special. Being connected to the sheriff and all. I was born here and you let them sell me off to a wealthy couple who couldn't have children like some kind of puppy in a pet store window. Sadly, they may have honestly cared for me. I don't know for certain. It doesn't matter. They didn't understand. Once I found out that I wasn't their biological child, they made me promise I wouldn't tell anyone. They didn't want anyone to know that they paid for a child. They were embarrassed of me. My trust fund was based on a secret. I'd get a million dollars if I just kept pretending. If I never said a word to any of their friends or mine. All I had to do was keep quiet, get married, and have children. Who knew silence could have such power? But redemption is not a quiet feat. And neither is retribution." He pressed on the rag against his shoulder and moaned.

"You're going to bleed to death if you don't get to a hospital."

"Like I said, there are worse things than dying. Besides, it's a little late for mothering, don't you think? That way," he nudged her along. The lights went out then flashed back on. "Faulty generator, but you'll get used to the dark." He reached in a cabinet and pulled out a flashlight. "There," he directed, shining the light toward the back corner to an oversized safe.

"Clearly, I'm not quite as welcoming with darkness as you are," Maggie retorted. Next to the safe was a door with a padlock on it. She heard movement behind it, followed by a cough. "What was that?"

"Well, what I believe it to be is a room that contains Rayburn's beloved missing children. It's the old operating room according to the blueprints I discovered. But as I said before, that's a part of someone else's plan. Mine is in here. With you." Knox motioned the gun toward the walk-in safe. The thick vault door was open wide enough to see inside.

"I don't understand," Maggie said, confused by the shelves of canned goods lining the walls inside. It looked like a makeshift bomb shelter.

"It used to be the safe the Mob used during Prohibition. More secure than any bank. At one time it was filled with money. Now, I've stocked it with food and toiletries that should last you for...I don't know...a little while. When the safe door is closed, a piece of the wall slides over it like a pocket door, making the vault behind it undetectable. And soundproof. No one but God will hear your cries for help. I know how that feels though. The only issue I have is that in all the research I did, I could never find the combination. Tragic, right? So, once the safe door is closed, it can never be opened. At least not without explosives. That's the beauty of it. For what's left of your existence, you will know how I've felt my entire life. Alone and ready to explode."

"So, you're just going to lock me up in here and leave me?" She laughed nervously trying to hide her abject fear of being closed up down here with no one ever finding her.

"Leave you? Don't be ridiculous. No, Mother. I'm going to abandon you. Like you did me." He shoved her into the safe, pointed the gun on her when she resisted. Then he aimed the light for the shelf where it glinted off the tarnished silver pruning shears. He picked them up and Maggie took a step back. "However, I would like to leave you with a little reminder of your sin. Something to help ensure my place in the afterlife and yours in Hell."

"What are you doing?" Maggie looked on with confusion as she watched Knox set the flashlight down and without any hesitation, snip off his ring finger as easily as if he was trimming back rose vines. Blood spurted onto Maggie's face, and Knox laughed ominously as his severed finger landed near her feet. He howled in pain but kept laughing.

"Being forgiven."

Maggie, horrified, reached to wipe the blood from her face then instinct kicked in. She used both hands to thrust Knox backward before jamming the letter opener directly into the blood-soaked rag over his clavicle. She twisted the weapon and he dropped to his knees. Then, she swiped the flashlight off the shelf and darted out of the safe. The lights went out again, and she clambered in the dark, smashing into something sharp that pierced her thigh. She yelped but kept moving, reaching out her hand in front of her until she found a doorknob. She fumbled with the lock, flung the door open, and darted into the dark tunnel where she flicked on the flashlight.

"You bitch," Knox called after her. "Did you forget that I have the floor plans for this entire place? I know every nook and cranny under this mountain. I'll find you."

He was only a few steps behind her, but Maggie was the one with the flashlight. He'd be running in the dark and losing blood while doing it. But she was also losing blood. She could feel her thigh wet with it. Her only chance was to outrun him. As horrible as it sounded, he'd bleed out soon and collapse. But maybe she would, too. Neither of them had blood that coagulated, but at least a carrier had a better chance. There was some kind of sick irony in it all, but she was too frightened to try and define it. She had to keep moving.

Strange noises filtered throughout the tunnel. In the faint distance, she could hear footsteps pounding behind her, but they were silenced by the sudden grinding din of a drill and what sounded like a large hammer beating against metal. But it was the sound of running water that terrified her. Dear God, she remembered. The fracking project. They must have started early. If water flooded the tunnel, the children locked in that room would all drown. Everything would be wiped out down here. Her included. She had to try and stop them. "Stop!" she yelled. "Stop it. There are children down here. I need help."

The tunnel branched off, but she kept running straight. The noise grew louder and the flashlight flickered. She prayed to the gods of Duracell that it would remain on long enough for her find help. The blood seeping from her puncture was cold as it soaked into her jeans, and she could smell the tinny scent of her own approaching death drifting up to her face. She'd heard the rumors that these tunnels led under the mountain. There had to be a way out. The clanking noise was deafening now, and she could no longer hear Knox behind her. Weak but determined, Maggie kept moving.

thirty-seven

Jack slid his truck in next to the blue Sentra parked in front of the clinic. He recognized the motorbike with the alien skull, the Thrasher boy's bike, propped up against the side of the house. The front door of the building was cracked open and Jack whispered Nelle's name as he approached.

"Nelle. Where are you? Nelle?" She didn't answer and Jack knew his daughter had gone on inside. She had definitely inherited her mother's courage. The thought of something happening to her made him crazy. He didn't even know her yet felt he had known her for years. He pushed those thoughts aside, drew his weapon and proceeded inside, his heart pounding with every step.

He wasn't familiar with the clinic—never had reason to be, so he moved with caution as he made his way from room to room, checking behind doors and in closets. Squatters had made a mess of the place, but it looked as if they had moved on. From what Hixson's former nurse had told him, there was a basement under the building, and once he made a full inspection of the house, he looked for a door that would lead him downstairs. It was in the pantry that he saw the empty shelf cocked open. There was a smear of blood on one of the shelves. Jack unhooked his flashlight and headed down the stairs. A loud crash behind him made him jolt forward, and he turned and ran back up the stairs. He suddenly felt like he was in one of those zombie movies that had taken over the world or at least Georgia. With his back to the wall, he glided from the kitchen to the area that from the looks of it had once been the main room for the clinic. The only light came from the busted windows and cracked door.

"Who's there?" Jack asked. "I'd advise you to come out now or risk being shot. I'm not fucking around here." Jack heard the creak of a door in one of the exam rooms off the waiting area, and he moved in that direction.

"Nelle," he whispered again. "Is that you?" He advanced into the room, scanning it for movement with his flashlight. It reeked of garbage and something he couldn't quite place. Cat piss. Ammonia? Then he saw the scattered bottles and the hotplate. The burn marks on the counter. Somebody had used this place as a meth lab but because the stench often penetrated the paint, Jack had no way of knowing whether or not the lab had been abandoned. He noticed then that the closet door was slightly ajar. "Last chance. Anyone in here?" He held his breath and listened, the rapid beat of his heart drumming in his ear. He turned to leave but then caught it. Sniffling from the closet. He flicked off the flashlight, crept over to the door, yanked it open and blasted the light inside. He pointed his gun on the emaciated figure huddled in the corner.

"I'm sorry, I'm sorry, I'm sorry," the man cried, trying to block the bright light from his face. There was black eyeliner smeared around his sunken eyes, and he was naked except for a pair of soiled men's briefs that may have once been white. "Don't hurt me," he pleaded. He looked like one of those skeletons people hang on their door at Halloween.

"What the hell? You could have been shot. "Who are you and what are you doing here?"

"I'm sorry, I'm sorry. I'm soorrrrry," he kept saying over and over.

This guy was high as hell, Jack decided. "Get up and get out of here, right now," he demanded quietly. "Move it."

The man crawled out of the closet and stood cowering, all sharp angles and bones. "She's coming back," he said scratching at his face.

Jack smelled fresh shit. "Who's coming back?' he asked, confused.

"The woman who lives downstairs," he said softly. "The one with the apples. She's a pirate. *Shh,*...she'll hear us. Ahoy, Matey," he slurred then laughed maniacally before he began to cry. "She steals children. And eats them." A stream of shit streaked down his leg.

The poor soul was obviously impaired. In some kind of delusional drug haze. It hadn't taken long for this place to fall victim to urban legend. Dr. Jekyll and his baby-killing nurse. He wondered how long before one of those reality crime shows would run this story. "Okay, buddy. I don't have time to deal with your..." Jack almost said, shit. "I don't have time to deal with you right now so consider today your lucky day." Jack shoved him toward the front door. "Get out of here and don't come back. If I catch you here again, I'm going to arrest you."

The man starting crying hysterically. "Noooo. She's inside," he whispered. His pupils were so dilated that Jack couldn't tell what color his eyes were. "Don't go back in there. She's waiting," he warned.

"There's no pirate here, buddy," Jack said trying to comfort him before pushing him gently but firmly out the door. He watched him stumble over to a patch of green grass and curl up on a stone bench in his shit-soaked drawers.

He couldn't waste time calling it in. It would have to wait. Jack hurried back to the pantry and followed the stairs down into the basement. Miss Cave hadn't been lying, and her memory was spot on. Jack decided this would be the Dr. Hyde part of the urban legend. The space was eerily lit but more so it was the smell of desperation and despair that had infiltrated the entire place that made Jack sick with nausea. He scanned the room with the flashlight, noticed the open safe and the padlocked door next to it. Toward the back of the room another door, half open, darkness beyond it. It had to be the access to the tunnel that Miss Cave mentioned. He was just about to head that way when the beam from his flashlight caught a bright spot on the gray cement tiled floor. A folded white paper bird. Jack bent and picked it up. He unfurled the wings and read Skyla's words written in red crayon.

SAVE US UNCLE JACK

This was the place. Sklya had told him she shoved a note under the door for him. This was the cold dark place. Jack jiggled the knob and did the same thing with the padlock. He slapped his palm against the metal door.

"Is anyone in there?" he called but was met with silence. "Hello?" He heard a faint cough. "Simon," is that you? It's Sheriff Towns. "Ben? Hailey? You in there."

"Help. Please." A girl's voice, tiny and frail.

Hailey. "Hang on. I'm going to get you out of there, honey. "I'll be right back."

"No," he heard one of the boys yell. "Don't leave us," he pleaded. "I *wanna* go home."

"I promise. I'll be back. Just hang on, okay?"

"Please hurry," Hailey said. "Simon won't wake up. He's real sick."

Jack frantically started searching for something to cut the lock on the door. The safe was oddly full of canned goods, but he couldn't find so much as a can opener until he spotted the bloody garden snips. He reached for them. The blood was fresh. He tried them on the lock but it was useless. They weren't strong enough. Jack tossed them then picked up an old Steelcase chair and hit it hard against the lock. The vinyl seat broke off the chair and went flying across the room. The metal legs scattered.

Shit. "Okay kids, listen carefully. "I want you to stand as far away from the door as you can, okay? Get in a corner and cover your head. Drag Simon with you and do your best to curl up in a ball. Get behind a table or cover yourself with something. Can you do that for me?"

"Okay," he heard Hailey whine.

"Good girl." Jack waited a minute then aimed his gun on the lock but something cracked against his skull. It rang out like a church bell then everything went black.

When he came to, Jack was sitting in a chair with his head cocked forward, his hands secured behind his back. He had the worst headache, and he felt like he was going to puke. His neck had a crick in it, and when he raised his head and opened his eyes, everything was blurry. He had no idea how long he'd been out.

"Sorry about that," he heard a female say. "You left me no choice. Kind of an odd thing to say in an abortion clinic, right?"

He tried to focus on the sound of the woman's voice. A blurred figure in green sat across from him. She rolled closer in the chair but her features became even fuzzier. He squinted. She seemed to have a big black eye in the center of her forward.

"Don't worry. It's just eye drops. They'll wear off but probably not in time."

"In time for what?" Jack slurred feeling a little like the addict he discovered upstairs.

"The unfortunate explosion. You know," she said, "when I first had the idea to take the children, I believed that by doing so, I could stop Starpoint from drilling. If they suspected children might be involved, they would stop fracking. Stop destroying land, causing earthquakes, and poisoning water. It worked for my father when they initially began laying their lines on the Truelove property in 1985. The fire he started destroyed much of what they hoped to be a future fracking site. But he didn't have the heart to kill the Truelove children so he took them with him. All his efforts were for nothing though. Starpoint came back. That's when I realized something my father never had. In order for people to care, someone has to die. Preferably someone innocent. Even better if it's children. It's the only way people take notice. It's the only chance we have to save this god-forsaken planet."

As she spoke, Jack worked conspicuously at loosening the rope holding his hands behind the chair. But the knot wasn't budging. His fingers felt fat and stiff, and his mind was as foggy as his vision. Was she saying her father had taken the Truelove children?

"You know, killing in Georgia still warrants the death penalty," he said in an effort to rationalize with her. "And if the victims include children, you won't stand a chance for an appeal. Even as a woman."

She stood and the chair rolled slowly backward until

it hit the wall.

Jack still couldn't make out many details, but it was obvious she was tall, broad shouldered for a woman. And it looked like she had on a red hat.

"The explosion will be blamed on Starpoint. Unfortunately, the men drilling will probably not be alive to deny it or stand trial. So sad. With all the flammable alcohol hidden in these tunnels, there won't be any way to determine that the fire actually started in the meth lab upstairs. The flames will move through the tunnels like water and, well, you can figure out the rest."

"Let the children go," Jack pleaded as the woman moved, a green smear in the glowing light toward the stairwell. "Isn't one dead person enough for your *cause*?"

"Oh, you will definitely help," she said. "But you're hardly innocent," she added. "My father may have resorted to unscrupulous tactics for the environment, but your ancestors hung a woman from a tree on the mountain. A Truelove woman they believed was a witch. I read about it in my research. They shoved rotten apples down her throat to keep her quiet. There's so much blood on this mountain it's no wonder how it earned its name. Regardless, I do appreciate your unexpected assistance," she said then disappeared behind the door that led upstairs.

Once she was out of sight, Jack began frantically rocking the chair until it tipped, and he crashed onto his side. He heard something snap, and he hoped it was the chair and not his shoulder. But sharp pain radiated down his arm and he stopped being optimistic. She must have been a girl scout because he was having a tough time with the rope. He struggled for quite some time before he heard a voice he recognized.

"Need some help?" Angela didn't wait for an answer. She began working the rope until it was loose enough for Jack to free one hand then the other. Tommy stood next to her holding a flashlight as the yellow overhead flickered and cracked above.

"Angie?" Everything was a blur. He felt around, his fingers finding something small and plastic like a tiny toy. He latched on to it, cupping it in his hand. "Is that you?"

"Yes," she said. "I'm here." She reached to help him up. "Tommy showed me the way. What the hell happened? Are you okay?"

"I think so but I can't see clearly. She put something in my eyes. It's like everything around me is wrapped in thick plastic."

"What are you talking about? Who put something in your eyes? You know there's an emaciated dead guy out front, right? Looks like he OD'd. He's in his underwear. What the hell is going on? Where's Knox?"

"I don't have time to explain. We have to move fast. The children are locked in that room over there and the woman who took them—" But before he could finish, he smelled the smoke. "...is going to burn the place down." He looked around for his gun one last time, but the floor was moving. It felt like being underwater. He couldn't make out any sort of detail. He stumbled but caught himself on the wall. "Come on, we have to get the children out of there."

Tommy began moving the flashlight around the room, and it caught on a fire extinguisher attached to the side of a cabinet.

"There," Angela said. She grabbed it and handed it to Jack. He began knocking against the padlock, missing it entirely on some swings. His shoulder throbbed. Flames began to lick under the door that led to the stairs, and Jack aimed the extinguisher in that direction and tried to pull the ring, but it was rusted and nonfunctioning. "Dammit!" He tossed the worthless piece of shit aside and turned to see Angela digging in the bag she had over her shoulder. She pulled out something black and shiny. A gun?

"Get back," she said, aiming the weapon on the padlock. "Both of you." The first shot missed the lock entirely. The second snapped it open. She wanted to think that practicing at the gun range in Philly had sharpened her skills, but she knew it was pure luck.

Jack couldn't focus. He was disoriented, and the room seemed to be spinning. He yanked on the door until it opened, braced himself on the threshold then called to the children.

"Is everyone okay?" The stench of rotten fruit and bodily fluids hit Jack in the face and he held onto his breath so he could hold onto his stomach.

Hailey and Ben came running out but Simon wasn't with them. The overhead surgical light, the one Sklya had mentioned was like a spaceship, had completely burned out and the room was lit by one small floor lamp in the corner. Jack fumbled around, steadying himself by grabbing onto the operating table. He slammed into a cabinet, banged his knee hard on the door before spotting a small motionless ball in the corner. Simon. He picked the boy up, lost his balance but regained it, and carried the child out, the fire breathing heavily just beyond the stairwell door. Whatever that woman had given him not only affected his vision, it made his heart race. It beat like a drum in his ears. He steadied himself and did his best to stay upright.

A wooden beam, engulfed in flames, dropped from the ceiling, taking the last remaining fluorescent bulb with it. The bulb dangled on a wire, flickered then snapped out entirely. The room was pitched in total darkness. Hailey screamed and Angela felt for her hand then reached for Ben.

"It's okay. We're going to be okay," she comforted them, but she wasn't sure of this. Which way?" she asked, and Tommy shone the light on the door in the back of the room.

"The tunnel," Jack said. "It's our only chance, but someone is going to have to take him. My legs feel like spaghetti. I'm not steady."

Tommy reached blindly for the small boy, secured one arm around him and led the way out into the tunnel. Angela pulled the two other children closer, tightened her grip on their hands and followed. She hesitated, listening for Jack's steps.

"Go on," Jack told her. "I'm right behind you."

The unlikely group fled through the door and made their way into blackness, flames licking furiously at their feet.

thirty-eight

Maggie felt like she'd been running for days when she finally saw the light at the end of the tunnel. She couldn't decide if it was her time to go or if there actually was a white glow leading her out of the darkness. It sounded both biblical and cliché at the same time. But she didn't care. She just wanted out of the underground hell hole she'd been trapped in and away from Knox.

The drilling had stopped again and she listened carefully for the sound of approaching footsteps behind her but heard nothing. Dead silence. It was too quiet. A man seeking revenge for so many years wouldn't give up. Unless of course, he passed out from blood loss. Something she would soon be facing if she didn't get help. Some kind of furry creature scurried over her foot and Maggie tried not to scream. She took a deep breath which coincided perfectly with the flashlight crapping out leaving her enveloped in darkness. Terrified, Maggie let out the breath she'd been holding, dropped the flashlight, and moved as fast as she could in the direction of the opening at the end of the tunnel. Her first thought was the children, but she was going to have to find something to tie around her leg to limit the bleeding or she wouldn't be alive to see them saved.

Exiting the tunnel, Maggie was blinded by daylight. She stepped out onto the slippery rock slabs, covered her eyes and faltered, her hand inadvertently finding the knobby trunk of a bare spindly tree. When her eyes adjusted to the brightness, she leaned against the tree, tore off a piece of her shirt and tied it around her thigh. It was going to be okay. She'd made it out. Now, all she had to do was find help. Her victory was short-lived, however, when she noticed the dense fog moving slowly toward her. It hissed like a box full of snakes, and she knew then that she was in Bone Hollow. She felt her face gray.

"Glad you made it," Knox said apathetically. "I was beginning to worry that you wouldn't find your way out."

Maggie cursed, cupped her hand over her eyes and looked around. She was sure he could hear her heart beating frantically in her chest.

"Tenacity. Yet another thing we have in common. Must run in the bloodline." A bloody mess, he was leaning against a large rock jutting out from the side of the mountain. His left hand was wrapped in what looked like a hand towel, soaked in blood. In the other hand, he held the gun.

"We don't share anything. There is none of me in you," she said, wondering if because he was so weak, she might have a chance of overtaking him. Joe had taught her how to protect herself.

"You couldn't be more wrong. We share blood. Toxic blood. Sadly though, it doesn't look like my plan is going to work out after all. But don't let that give you hope. I'm going to give you a choice. You know about those, right? Choices." He held the gun out to her.

Maggie stepped back. This had to be a trick.

"Take it," Knox said. "You can kill yourself. Or. You can kill me." He chuckled deviously. "You could have killed me once before but you didn't. I'm just curious to see if you can do it now." He pushed the gun toward her once again. "I'm giving you something I never had. A choice. Go on, Mom."

Maggie smacked the gun, knocking it out his hand and into a thicket of rhododendrons that lined the entrance to the tunnel. Darting to the left, she realized, too late, her mistake. She stopped short at an overhang, the drop beyond it masked by the encroaching fog and whispers that sounded like a waterfall. Knox limped toward her, and she carefully backpedaled away from him until her heel dangled precariously off the edge of the craggy rock. When Maggie looked over her shoulder and down, she saw sharp rocks jutting out the side of the mountain but no discernible bottom.

"Looks like you have another choice to make now."

"Don't take another step," Angela commanded. She had come out of the tunnel, set Hailey down and corralled both children behind her with one hand. With the other, she held her gun on Knox.

He turned. "Well, well, well, counselor. I didn't know you had it in you. I thought your killing days were over." He moved toward her. "Poor Denny Sherman."

"I wouldn't," she said. "You don't know what I'm capable of."

He stopped. Put his hands up. He was covered in blood. "Sure, I do. You're my attorney. Now, how's that gonna look, you shooting me? An unarmed man? Not the best defense." He laughed. It was deep and somber and layered with evil. "Sounds like false representation to me. Could do jail time."

"Well, I agreed to represent you on drug charges and desecration of human remains. Not murder. But I didn't come here to set you free; I came to set me free." Besides, she wanted to tell him; none of it was legal. Boone had only weeks to live, which is why he agreed to help her. That and the money she gave him. All of her savings. He wouldn't face any repercussions. The dead don't care about reputations. And she was willing to risk incarceration and even disbarment if that's what it came down to. Liam was worth all of it. She mentally began to count the seconds that passed, wondering if she'd make it to a hundred and three before she pulled the trigger on this son of a bitch.

"Well, I've got nothing to lose here. Whether you shoot me or I bleed out, I'm going to die. I've been shedding blood since birth. I'm already forgiven in God's eyes. My curse is also my salvation. My ticket to eternity. I'm not afraid to die, counselor. Are you?" He stepped toward her.

Angela focused her attention on Maggie who was pale and pasty. One of her pant legs was saturated in blood. She looked like she was going to go down any minute. This was not going to end well. "You're deranged. Don't come any closer. I'm warning you."

A loud grinding noise rattled the air. The ground shook, dragging the scent of fire from the tunnel. Angela was concerned about Jack. What was taking him so long? But just then, he stumbled out of the smoke. Tommy had one arm holding him up, and in the other, he clutched Simon, who had somewhere along the way opened his eyes and was now starting to cough.

Jack leaned against a large flat rock jutting from the mountain, put his hands on his thighs. Nothing around him had defining edges. It was all a great big blur. He swayed then puked.

"Jack!" Maggie yelled, forgetting everything and running straight for him. She barreled into Knox, but he grabbed her by the arm, and a tug of war ensued.

Tommy carefully set the boy down next to the other children. He watched the patch of opaque fog crawl toward them, and over the sounds of the machines drilling into the earth, he could still hear the whispers. It was like a wall of water rushing toward him.

The mountain suddenly jolted. It threw both Maggie and Knox to the ground where she managed to break free from him. She crawled over toward Jack and clung to his leg. He pulled her close.

Knox stood and Angela dug blindly in her bag for her cell phone, tossed it toward Maggie then tightened her grip on the gun. She closed her free hand over it to try and steady the shaking then focused on his heart. "Call for help."

"There's no service in the hollow," Maggie said with resignation in her face. "They installed cell towers on the mountain after a woman hiker was killed. But the Bone Hollow is and always has been a haunted black void. We're on our own."

"Just as well," Angela said. I don't want anyone coming to his rescue." She glared at Knox.

"Angela," There was reserve in Jack's tone. "Don't do it." He stood, fell back then stood again, his outstretched arm reaching for her, for the gun. "Give me the gun. Killing him won't help you to forget or lessen your guilt. It will only cause you more guilt. Let it go so it can let go of you."

Tears ran down her face but she held her position. "I can't." She took a few steps back, out of Jack's reach. The earth jarred again. The movement knocked her sideways and thrust Knox backward over the edge of the mountain. "No," Angela yelled. "You do not get to escape that easy." She'd waited so long. This couldn't be happening. "No," she screamed again.

Tommy hurried past her toward the ledge. Part curiosity. Part confirmation. He looked down at Knox who was barely clinging to a buckled pine root breaking through a crevice in the rock. This man had terrified him at one time. Took him away from all he knew. Stole his voice. Maimed him then killed his only friend. And now, this man didn't even recognize him. Had no idea who he was. He raised his foot to stomp on Knox's fingers and loosen his grip on the root. It wouldn't take much. But the whispers were there then by his ear and in them he heard Knox's words from all those years ago. *There's a reason you lived, boy.* Tommy didn't know what the reason was but he knew what it wasn't. He hadn't lived so he could let a man die or worse, kill him. Even one as evil as Knox.

He wouldn't let this be the reason. He lowered his foot, dropped to his knees, and grabbed Knox's hand. It took all his strength and in the process of pulling him up, Tommy felt his own wound reopen. Out of breath and bleeding, he collapsed on the ground.

Knox wasted no time getting to his feet. Angela still had the gun pointed at him. Her hand was shaking so badly even if she would have fired, there is no way the bullet would have hit him.

"Oh, come on, counselor. You're not going to shoot me. It just isn't in your blood. You're more of a third-party killer." He laughed and rushed toward her. He knocked her to the ground and wrestled the gun from her hand but never stopped laughing. He raised it, but before he could take aim, a bullet pierced his eye. The force knocked him back, and he disappeared over the ledge into the strange fog.

Maggie screamed, averted her eyes and Angela turned to block the children's view. That's when she saw Nelle standing at the tunnel entrance, her arm stiff, the gun still in her hand.

"That was for my mother, you evil fucker," she said. "She was my best friend. I hope you rot in hell."

"Nelle!" Jack called out. His vision was still cloudy but he recognized her voice. And he knew what she'd just done. "No, Nelle. No." He stumbled over to her, but before he could reach her, fire shot out of the tunnel and covered her in flames. Angela threw herself over the children. The explosion knocked everyone including Jack backward. They were all coated in black soot. Maggie had been thrown against a rock. She lie unconscious, her head bleeding profusely.

"We're all right," Angela confirmed. "Help Nelle. I'll get Maggie."

Jack crawled toward his daughter. Flames engulfed her entire body. He watched in horror as layers of Nelle's skin melted, words of scripture dissolving into the air that fueled the fire. It was like watching the delicate pages of a Bible burn; the girl's screams buried by the sound of crackling skin. Jack did his best to reach his daughter, but he couldn't get anywhere near her.

The mist of the hollow was closing in on them, the sound of hundreds of wings flapping in the air. It was so loud Jack closed his eyes and willed it to stop. When he opened them, Wanda Drake stood near Tommy. The fog had begun to recede and the only audible whispers were those being made by the old woman's prayer. Jack caught bits and pieces of it when she moved on to Maggie.

"... passed by thee...thine own blood, I said unto thee...Live. You will live."

Maggie's head wound healed before Jack's eyes, and her leg stopped oozing blood. "How are you doing that?" Jack asked, but the old woman didn't respond.

"You silenced the fog, didn't you?" He asked, perplexed.

The old woman moved quickly toward Nelle. "No. That was you." She dropped to her knees next to the burning body and began running her hands over the flames. She worked fast, gathering them in a ball and tossing them aside as she contained them. The girl was motionless. Her burned skin smoldered like a piece of charred wood doused with water.

Angela stood watching, slack-jawed and in complete disbelief as to what she was witnessing.

Wanda's eyes rolled back into her head. She looked possessed. She began to rock. Then she leaned and whispered near the girl's ear. She did this two more times. The last time, it was loud enough for Jack to hear.

"Come three angels from the North. Hear me now. Take this fire. Leave the salt. Hear this prayer and take the fire now. Fire. Salt. Fire. Salt. Heal this child. I beg you, Father, Son, and Holy Ghost." She blew out a breath so frosted the air took on a chill. Then she sucked it all back in, the fire, the flames, the leaves, and the red earth.

They all watched as Nelle's skin began to mend, layer by layer, letter by letter, word by word. It was as if time was moving backward, the scripture being once again recorded on her skin from left to right by some spectral tattoo artist or one of God's scriveners. They were all so mesmerized by it that they didn't notice Wanda until it was too late. She now laid still and quiet beside the girl.

"Wanda," Jack called. His vision had improved. Details were coming into focus. He stood and made his way over to her. She was barely breathing, the scarred skin singeing and pulling away from her bones as if it was burning from the inside out. He pulled a leaf from her face, wiped the dirt from her mouth. Her one good eye was open. She showed no signs of fear in it though it was clear she was in great pain. He heard a helicopter in the distance. Looked up and scanned the sky.

"I'm sorry I scared you that day in the hollow," she whispered.

"What?" Jack asked. "What are you talking about?"

"You were just a boy, and I a naive woman, thinking I could fool the hollow by giving you up. Like every mother, I wanted only the best for you. But you were born to this place. It will always be a part of you, and you, a part of it." Her voice was raspy and weak. She wasn't being rational.

"You're not making any sense, Wanda. Hold on. I'm going to get you some help." Jack stood and started waving to attract the attention of the helicopter pilot who was now circling, but the light was fading and they'd soon be in the dark of the hollow.

"Here, let me try." Angela started jumping and moving her hands over her head.

Wanda motioned for Jack and he knelt beside her again. "It's okay. My time is here," she said and grabbed firmly onto his wrist. She pulled him close to her dry cracked lips. Her voice quivered. "I have something to give you," she said and whispered the two healing prayers her father had taught her into son's ear. "One for blood. One for fire," she said. "You must keep them secret until it's your time. And even then, they can only be passed to a blood relative." She reached for his face, cupped it with her hand then drew in a quick, tight breath that would be her last. Jack wondered if he was the only one who heard the owl screech in the distance. He reached to close Wanda's eye, trying to grasp what had just happened.

He looked over at Nelle, finding her recovery a complete mystery. She was still out, but there didn't seem to be a mark on her. It was inexplicable. Both Maggie and Tommy had also seemed to make a full recovery and were now conscious and getting to their feet.

The helicopter had spotted them but couldn't make landing in because of the trees. Deputy Wayne lowered a basket, and Jack loaded the children and Nelle safely into it. Then he picked up the gun she'd used on Knox, recognizing it immediately as Kitty's. Nelle must have taken from his desk somehow. He tucked the weapon under his belt and tried to make sense of it all.

What did Wanda mean by him being a part of the hollow as much as it was a part of him? He thought about how comfortable he'd always felt in this place. He'd never once been lost in the hollow even as a boy. In fact, he'd been pulled there almost magnetically. But the question that haunted him most right now was what Wanda had said about giving him up in an effort to fool it.

The darkness made it more difficult, but Jack was able to lead Maggie, Angela, and Tommy safely out of Bone Hollow, through the orchard, and onto the Truelove property, which was swarming with police cars, ambulances, and news people. The explosion had killed most of Starpoint's men, and the operation would be brought to a halt for certain now. The few men left were badly burned and disfigured. Jack watched the EMTs load Randolf Wolfe into the back of an ambulance. He was barely conscious but breathing. An early start had almost cost him his life. Jack had this sneaky suspicion that it wouldn't matter though and that he'd be back at fracking as soon as there was a full moon. But he wouldn't be doing it on this property. Or the Hixson property. Nelle legally had rights to both now because the blood running through her veins was a mixture of Truelove and Hixson. It would be up to her what happened to the land now, especially since Jack got word that Hixson had passed a few hours earlier.

thirty-nine

Early the next morning, Jack led a rescue team into the hollow to look for Knox's remains and retrieve Wanda's body. His first thought was to bury her in the Rayburn Cemetery, but she belonged in the hollow. There was no doubt about that. He'd have her buried there. It's what she would have wanted. He knew this in his heart.

After searching for hours, Knox's body couldn't be recovered. The river that ran beneath the ledge where he'd fallen funneled into Shadow River, which fed into the Chattahoochee River and meant Knox might be in Florida by now. Not the vacation he may have planned. Jack had informed the GBI that he had simply lost his balance while wrestling with Maggie, never bothering to mention this was because he took a bullet to the eye. It was out of Jack's character to do this, and it had a strong possibility of coming back to haunt him, but he'd deal with it when and if it did. He didn't have any idea who he was right now. Some of what made him the man he was had been, if not compromised, shifted in a way he couldn't explain. And

Lisa's death just made it worse. He had lost her all over again. But this time it was much more permanent.

And he shouldn't have been surprised but he was. When he returned to the area just outside the tunnel where Wanda had died, he found only traces of ash and a few pieces of blackened turquoise jewelry, which he shoved in his pocket. He was still trying to piece together what she had shared with him. Because he couldn't ask Kitty or Joe, he worried he may never know the truth.

Jack found the letter while cleaning out Kitty's trailer later that week. Bullet, the old gray tomcat that had once been a stray was sitting outside the door when Jack showed up. Stray Bullet was the full name Kitty had burdened him with, and Jack was reminded just how straight forward this woman had always been. There was something admirable in it though he hadn't appreciated much when she was alive. The cat climbed in Jack's lap as he sat at the table and opened the envelope Kitty had left for him.

Dear Jack,

I don't have to tell you that I've always been an established keeper of secrets, some belonging to others but many my own. It's no excuse for my behavior, I know, but as an only child, I didn't have anyone else to confide in so I learned to trust only myself. Besides, I learned quickly that secrets, once divulged, never cause anything but grief. This one will be no exception, but I feel taking it with me will only cause even more pain.

My parents devoted their lives to God, and though I do believe they loved me, they often put their devout Baptist faith before me not distinguishing the difference between God and religion. We spent a great deal of time at church, and I was okay with this until I turned fifteen and met Harland, Pastor Winter's son. You see, you already know that I gave up a child, a decision that has kept me from any kind of peace whatsoever, but I never shared with you or your sister exactly what happened.

Harland and I fell in love as young first-time lovers often do. Don't get me wrong. I loved your father deeply but not like I loved Harland. We had a special connection. Before long, I became pregnant and we made plans to marry. That's what you did back then even at such a young age. Only, before this could happen, we were separated by our parents who believed us to be lustful sinners. The Winters moved their family to North Carolina before the rumors started to spread. A few months later they sent a letter to my parents saying that Harland had hanged himself in their barn. His little sister had found him dangling from the hay rafter. His parents enclosed a photograph of a newly-covered grave in a remote part of the cemetery in the town where they lived. Because Harland was a suicide, he couldn't be buried on consecrated ground even by his pastor father who was mocked and scorned. His congregation dispersed, and the family lost everything. His parents blamed me and I, them. I never stepped inside a church again afterward. It was my first understanding of the difference between God and religion. From that day on, I never felt the need for a middle man or a place to worship. My relationship with God was between Him and me even though I know we have both pissed each other off over the years. But this happens in any relationship worth a grain of salt, I suppose.

I was foolish to think that when my mother took me to Dr. Hixson's that I'd be able to keep my baby. I never even got to see him. They figured if they told me he'd been stillborn I'd never search for him and they were right. But deep in my heart, my maternal instinct told me that my boy was alive. I learned later that they had given him away to a couple from Canada. I would never see him again.

Life doesn't stop for the wounded and broken though. Eventually, I met your father, but I never got over the anguish of losing a child. Some years after Joe and I were married, I went back to Hixson's to make it right. In truth, I wanted to make *me* right, but I'd soon learn that I'd been irretrievably broken. Granite on the outside, glass on the inside.

At the time, no one knew that the good doctor had been running a black-market baby ring, though hypocritically most were aware that he was the man to see if you were a girl in trouble. Regardless, with his help, I adopted a child. This will undoubtedly come out in the rumor mill at some point. People will assume it was Camille. With her blonde hair and brown eyes, she looks nothing like either your father or me. But she isn't the child I adopted from Hixson. You are, Jack. We chose you specifically because, with your features, especially your eyes, you resembled Joe so much that no one would ever guess you weren't his. We lived so far out of town then that the pregnancy was easy to pull off. Sure, there were people afterward who were skeptical, but when they looked at you and saw your father's eyes, they refrained from even inquiring. I don't give a damn about what the rest of Rayburn thinks, but I regret that I let both you and Camille live in the shadows of my mistake. I know how close you were with your father. Honestly and somewhat cowardly, I didn't know how you'd handle the idea of not being blood-related to him. As terrible as it sounds, I was just going to let it go. Let people assume what they wanted, but this is my last chance to right something made wrong so long ago even if I have to do it from the grave.

I'm not asking for forgiveness. I just want you to try and understand the reason I was always so damn tough on you. I hid my sorrow under a false layer of courage, which made me seem a whole lot stronger than I really was. Or maybe stubborn is a better word. However you choose to look at it, misleading you was never part of my plan.

Though until a few hours ago, when the Cemetery Man left the folders on my doorstep, I had no idea that Wanda Drake was your biological mother any more than I know where Camille got her brown eyes, freckles, and button nose but I know this. My love for both of you is equal and has never faltered. Whatever you take from this letter, I hope you walk away with that much. You may have scars from how I raised you, but I rarely let go of anything I love fiercely without digging into it with everything I have. So, cherish those scars. They're proof that you were loved.

I know I've put you in a terrible position with this knowledge. Being the sheriff requires a legitimate birth certificate as you know.

Something you've never had. The people of Rayburn elected you because they believed you to be Joe's son. They don't have to know anything else. The one good thing is that you are the only other person aware of this, right now, so it's up to you whether or not you want to disclose it. That forged birth certificate of yours has always worked. I will warn you that the business of keeping secrets is exhausting and unrewarding. Unloading them is often worse. I may not have always shown it, but you make me proud, Jack Towns.

If you can, bury my Bible and gun with me. I may still need one or the other. Or both. Not exactly sure where I'm headed. And don't even think about shedding a tear. I taught you better than that.

—Kitty

Jack dug out a pack of matches from one of the kitchen drawers, held the letter over the sink, and watched it turn to ash. If Wanda Drake was his mother, then who was his father? The only thing certain in his life right now was that he had a daughter, one with a special gift. One who had murdered a man. If Knox's body was ever recovered, GBI would have a chance of tracing the gun—unless of course, it really was buried with Kitty. It was doubtful that they'd spend the money to exhume her even if they did suspect a murder weapon was in the coffin.

He wondered if Nelle would stay on in Rayburn. Wherever she lived, she wasn't going to be able to escape the news. Once people discovered she was a Truelove she'd never again have a quiet moment. She'd be the spotlight in every headline out there. Sarafina had been located but her four missing siblings had never been found. But Jack knew something he hadn't shared with anyone. Something other than the empty bottle of atropine eye drops he'd managed to find on the floor in Hixson's basement the day of the explosion. The woman who'd kidnapped Skyla and her friends and started the fire at the clinic had told him that her father was the one responsible for burning the Truelove's house to the ground in 1985 when Starpoint had first started to map their drill sites. She also insinuated that he was the one who took the Truelove children to keep them from perishing in the fire. It was quite possibly the only solid lead out there. Now all Jack had to do was find this woman. Easier said than done. He had very little to go on. For one, he couldn't identify her, and two, any viable evidence had been destroyed when the tunnels exploded. The children had never actually seen their abductor so the only witness was an addict who even if he hadn't OD'd might not be able to provide a credible statement.

Buddy would publish the Redeemer story soon, and there was a chance someone might come forward with a lead, but this wasn't likely. It would scare off the perpetrator if anything. Though Jack had given Buddy his blessing to move forward with the piece, he had conveniently omitted a few things that would probably surface when he started digging. He could easily win a Pulitzer for it without any of that information, and well, Buddy deserved that. His father would have been so proud.

Angela had given Jack the journal that once belonged to Grace Truelove for him to pass on to Nelle. But Jack kept that information from Buddy, too. It would be up to Nelle if she wanted to disclose it. She was still recovering and had some healing to do both on the inside and out, though miraculously, she carried no physical scars. One day she would be curious about her bloodline. She would find a great deal of interest, Jack believed, learning that her great-great-grandmother Grace Truelove had once been a woman by the name of Emily Capeheart who escaped from an asylum with money that was never found. A mystery if there ever was one. And that seeing *things* others didn't was a part of their lineage on his side. Perhaps then Nelle wouldn't feel so much like an outcast. Maybe she might learn to embrace her gift.

When the GBI finished their investigation, Jack would be able to bury Lisa just as Joe had done for her mother. But not on Strangers' Row, he decided. It would be impossible to relocate Sarafina Truelove's bones, but the one thing he could do was give her a headstone with her name on it. She was, after all, no longer a stranger. She'd become over the last week, a relative.

Jack put Bullet in the carrier he'd brought, and locked up the trailer. On the way to his truck, his phone buzzed.

"Dr. Tash. What's going on?"

"Hey, Sheriff. Just calling to let you know that the labs I resent in for Skyla showed the same results. High levels of lorazepam. And even more disturbing is that I just got back Ben, and Simon, and Hailey's labs, and they show the exact same thing. The person who took these children was sedating them with lorazepam it seems. We couldn't locate injection sights on any of them, so the doses must have been given orally. With food or drink."

Apples, Jack thought. Isn't that what the addict who'd OD's at Dr. Hixson's that day said? Something about a pirate with apples? Skyla had mentioned before that all they did in that place was eat apples and sleep. That had to be it. "What exactly is lorazepam described for anyway, Dr. Tash?"

"Well, a variety of things but mostly it's used to sedate or calm people with anxiety. Patients who struggle with mental illness or Alzheimer's are the most common recipients. It has several different trade names. I believe Ativan is the most recognized, but they come out with something new it seems every day."

"Interesting," Jack voiced, his mind pulling in a sudden and unexpected direction, the hairs on the back of his neck bristling. This time, he didn't fight it. He got the cat situated at the office then hopped in his truck and headed for Rome, driven purely by the intuition he'd always managed to drive away.

He tried to piece it all together on the way by recalling his first trip to the Guardian Angels Assisted Living Facility. It was ridiculous to think that a ninety-something-year-old woman had been the one to take the children and poison them with laced apples so she could use them and him as pawns in her environmental *cause.* And yet Jack knew someone from this facility had. Besides, after what he'd been through over the last week, nothing was too shocking or implausible.

Anna Cave wasn't in her room.

"She must be in the garden area. She likes to sit out there when the weather is nice," the woman changing the sheets told him.

"Are you her nurse?"

"Not anyone's nurse yet," she sang with an island accent. "Still in school. If you're looking for Nurse Dunn, she's making her rounds."

"Petite blonde?" Jack asked, fishing.

"Hardly," she chuckled. "Justine is more the Viking type. Tall and sharp-boned with long red hair she coils behind her head like a snake. Kind but hot-tempered. You don't want to get on her bad side if you know what I'm saying. You aren't a smoker, are you? If so, you're going to get an unwarranted lecture. She can smell it a mile away. Consider yourself warned."

"Not a smoker but thanks for the warning. Which

way to the garden?"

On the way down the hall, Jack texted Wayne to run a background check on Justine Dunn. He had a feeling that she didn't have a record, otherwise the prints he'd pulled from the atropine eye drop bottle would have registered in the database. Whoever had peeled off the label did so in order to remove their name from the prescription but inadvertently left behind latents and the number to the pharmacy. But getting a name from the pharmacist would involve a warrant, which would mean Jack would have to catalog the bottle as evidence. He didn't want to do this because if it got out, his chances of catching this woman would be very slim.

Jack sat down on the bench next to Miss Cave who was soaking up the sun in front of the roses. He was about to ask her if she remembered him, but she spoke first.

"Hello, Sheriff. I saw on the news that you caught that Knox fellow. I had no idea that he was a serial killer. Damn dirty bastard. To think that the clinic inspired such a monster. I hope he truly is dead."

Me too, Jack thought but didn't voice this aloud. "I wanted to come by and let you know that Dr. Hixson—"

"Yes, I know. He's gone. That was also on the news. No disrespect but I find it hard to believe that you drove all the way out here to tell me that."

This woman would have made a good detective. She reminded him of Kitty in a way. "I do have some other things on my mind, yes."

"Well, go on. The day's not getting any longer, and I'm not getting any younger."

Jack became aware then of a tall red-haired woman in green scrubs, pushing a patient in a wheelchair out to the courtyard. She had to be at least six feet if not taller, but it wasn't her height or her hair that drew his attention. It was the patch on her eye. He pulled out his phone and furtively snapped a picture, remembering only then that Nelle mentioned seeing a tall redhead out by the Truelove place the day she borrowed the Thrasher boy's bike. He shot her a text with the image.

Nelle. It's Sheriff Towns. He deleted this. *It's Jack.* He deleted this too. *It's your father. Hope you're feeling better. I need your help with something. It's kind of important. Is this the person you saw out by the Truelove property the day you followed me?*

Jack continued watching the nurse while he waited for Nelle to hit him back, which she did almost immediately.

I'm doing okay, I guess. Doc says I can home tomorrow only I don't know where that is at the moment. Yeah, that looks like her. Same bright red hair. Not sure about the patch. Is she tall? The woman I saw was like an Amazon. Why?

Thanks, he texted back. *I'll be by later on to see you. We'll talk then.*

"Sheriff?" Miss Cave spoke up. "You going to keep ogling the pretty nurse or do you have something to say?"

"That's your nurse, isn't it? Nurse Dunn."

"Yes. Nosy little parker. I've never much cared for her. Always eavesdropping on the conversations Lisa and I shared. She once even had the audacity to ask me about the journal Lisa had brought in. You know, the one I told you about. She was particularly interested in that part about the devil and the dead. I can't remember exactly what it said. Obviously the woman who wrote it was mentally ill. Regardless, I don't trust Nurse Dunn and you shouldn't either."

Both Jack and Angela had googled the section of the diary Anna was talking about and came up with nothing. He had no idea what it meant. But hearing that Nurse Dunn was so interested in it made something inside him uneasy.

"Will you excuse me for just a minute?" he asked then got up and walked toward the Viking. But at that very moment, he was thinking of her as more of a pirate. A nurse pirate with apples.

She locked the wheelchair into place and quickly headed for the door. Jack called to her.

"Hey there," he said. "You got a minute?"

There was no way she hadn't made him. She picked up her pace and headed inside through the double glass doors that connected the corridor to the courtyard. She punched a code into the keypad on the wall and Jack heard the lock click into place. He yanked on the handle anyway, and the two of them stood face-to-face. The eye without the patch was as green as her scrubs and gravitated slightly toward her nose. It was like looking into the eye of a storm. A calmness that signaled an impending and volatile fury. The two remained in that position until she turned abruptly and walked away as if she had nothing to do with setting a fire that was responsible for the death of seventeen men and threatening the lives of many others including three children and himself. Without so much as a cursory glance over her shoulder, she tucked a loose strand of rope-like hair into the nest on the back of her head and casually rounded the corner. Jack glanced around the tall white aluminum fence that enclosed the area and saw Miss Cave waving her hand to get his attention. She pointed to another set of doors on the other side of the courtyard, and he made a mad dash toward them.

"Nurse Dunn?" Jack asked a guy in scrubs passing him in the hall. The man motioned behind him to the double doors that led to the main entrance and Jack ran toward them, hitting them hard before remembering to ask the nurse at the desk to disengage the automatic lock. It jammed his already injured shoulder, but he sucked it up and kept going. He got to the parking lot just in time to see a mint green Prius speeding down the drive toward the exit. It had to be her. He ran to his truck and zipped out after it. When he reached the access road that ran in front of the river there was no sign of the car. He started to turn right but something told him to go left instead, away from downtown Rome. He sped along the two-lane asphalt road winding along the water until he spotted a green blur making the curve ahead. The car was traveling so fast, the rear passenger wheel lifted off the ground. Jack punched the accelerator and when he rounded the curve, he saw the Prius smashed into a cluster of trees at the edge of the river. He slid in next to it. The driver door was open, the front end of the car slowing disappearing into the brown murky water. Just beyond, he saw movement on a footbridge that led into a wooded area across the river. He jumped out of the truck and headed after her.

"Dunn!" he yelled. "Stop." But she didn't stop. She kept on running. If she made it into the woods, he'd have a tough time finding her. Jack drew his weapon though he had no intention of using it unless he absolutely had to. He wanted her alive. He needed her alive not only because she was a murderer, but because she was the only link to the missing Truelove children.

She was halfway across the bridge before he reached it. That's when she turned and fired at him.

"I'll kill you if I have to," she screamed.

"Not shooting like that you won't. And if that's my gun, I want it back." He ran toward her and she fired another shot over her shoulder and kept running. When she hit the end of the bridge, she turned and faced him, aimed the gun in his direction.

"You can't prove anything. Nothing can tie me to the explosion. The junkie's dead. I made sure of that. And you can't place me there either. Your compromised vision would never hold up in court."

"That may be true, but I'd be willing to bet your prints are all over the empty eye-drop bottle I found at the scene. And there's also a witness who saw you on the Truelove property. Those two things alone should help convict you. The courts find extremists quite unfavorable. On a personal level, I respect your views on the fracking business. However, I have this feeling that your environmental motives weren't as pure as you led me to believe. I think there was another kind of green involved in your *cause*. Wasn't there? You were looking for the money Grace Truelove hid on the property all those years ago, weren't you? Was that your real intent all along?" Or was it just an opportunity that presented itself to you along the way?"

Jack was close enough to see her expression change. He'd hit a nerve. He had stopped running and now stood less than twenty feet from her.

"You don't know what you're talking about," she said.

"Oh, I think I do." He raised his gun and pointed at her. "And I'd also be willing to bet that I'm a much better shot than you." He wanted to add that his mother had taught him to shoot, and he'd never miss, but Kitty wasn't his mother. Not really. A part of him would always think of her that way though. "Look, I don't want to have to hurt you. But I will. Put the weapon down."

"Fuck you!" she said and jammed the barrel of the gun in her mouth. "Don't forget. This is your gun. How's that going to look?"

Jack remembered then that he hadn't reported his gun missing after the explosion. But he also hadn't realized, right away, that she'd taken it. Regardless, he needed her alive.

"Wait," he held his hand up, lowered his gun. "Let's talk about this." He set the weapon he was holding down on the bridge next to his feet.

"Like I said. Fuck. You." The nurse pulled the trigger and Jack braced himself, but they were both met with an empty click.

That was definitely his gun. "I didn't have a chance to warn you about that," he said.

Before she had a chance to try again, Jack tackled her, and they both fell hard. She fought back, thrusting the heel of her palm into his throat and taking his breath. He rolled off of her, and she cracked him in the head with the gun. She raised her hand to do it again, but he grabbed her wrist, flipped her onto her back, and pinned her. He dislodged the gun from her grip and turned her over as she thrashed about like a gator caught in a net. Then he cuffed her.

forty

Angela shoved her suitcase in the back of the car. She'd stayed in Rayburn to attend Kitty Lynch's funeral out of respect but also because she wanted to be there for Jack. Whatever happened on that mountain had changed him in some way. He seemed lost and distant. But it had also changed her. She closed the hatchback then spotted Ronnie outside the pizza place. She was leaning against the bricks, lost in thought, smoking a cigarette.

"Ronnie," she called heading over to her. "Got a minute?"

The women had exchanged their stories about Liam, shared their heartbreak with one another, and it would connect them forever whether or not they ever spoke again. Angela dug in her bag and pulled out her wallet. "I have something for you."

Ronnie looked surprised, a little uneasy. She'd learned a long time ago to distrust gifts.

Angela handed her the photograph of Liam. "I think you should have this. It's Liam's school photo. The last one ever taken," she added wistfully.

Ronnie reached for the picture. Her hand was shaking, the quick of her nail, raw and bloody. She stared at the boy staring back at her and tried to decide if those were her eyes. Then she pulled the photo to her heart and held it there. Minutes passed before she spoke.

"Thank you," she said, taking another drag from her cigarette, stubbing it out under her shoe, and going back inside.

Angela took her time walking back to her car. She had finally let Liam go so that he might let her go, too.

"Miss Archer?" she heard a woman's voice behind her. She turned to find Thomas Blake's sister, Carolyn. "I just want to thank you for everything you've done for Thomas and me. For our family. My mother, God rest her soul, always had faith that we'd find him. I just knew it was our Tommy when I read the article in the paper about a man whose heart was on the other side of his body, surviving a gunshot. I can't help but think this is the same reason he survived that serial killer. I mean, I know the ring finger doesn't really go to the heart, but it sure is something to think about isn't it? That someone's defect might have actually saved their life."

Angela had learned from Jack that one of the finger bones in Knox's possession belonged to Tommy Blake. Knox obviously couldn't mail it to the boy's real mother because she was dead. "Yes, I guess it is," she responded. "Will Tommy be going back to Tennessee with you?"

"Not right away," she resigned. "He's decided he isn't ready to leave Rayburn just yet. It's too much for him. He's very close to the pastor, you see. Also, he likes to make sure Sarafina Truelove's grave is cared for. But he is going to come visit us. He has nieces and nephews that are very excited to meet him after seeing his picture in the paper. People have started treating him more like the hero he is rather than the monster they assumed him to be."

"Well, you both have my contact information if you ever need anything. I'm heading back to Pennsylvania today. Good luck to you." Angela reached to shake Carolyn's hand, but the short round woman grabbed her in a bear hug and embraced her. The woman had tears in her eyes.

Angela would need luck considering what she was facing. Disbarment was one thing. Incarceration was another. Jack had asked her if she had plans to return. "Not sure," she'd told him. Then out of nowhere, he kissed her. Not what she was expecting, but it was because of this tiny seed of hope he planted on her lips that she could suddenly see herself having some kind of life.

On her way out of Crow County, Angela passed the faded billboard with the five Truelove children staring at her with those haunted eyes. She tried to imagine what it would be like not to be consumed by loss and pain and guilt. These emotions had ruled her existence for so long that a relationship of any kind never had a chance. It was time to let others in her life. People who weren't missing or dead or part of some personal quest for vindication. Maybe she'd even be able to forgive herself one day, stop counting her steps.

forty-one

Two days after her arrest, Justine Dunn was still not talking. Her public defender had told her to keep quiet even though she'd been offered a plea deal if she could provide information that would lead authorities to her father and brother, who had both been on the FBI's most wanted list for years.

Back at the office, Deputy Wayne sat across from Jack reading from his cell phone what he'd pulled up about Justine Dunn. "Father: Carl Douglas Dunn. A farmer who agreed to have his Colorado land fracked by Starpoint because he owed the bank so much money. They took over mineral rights, but the drilling poisoned his animals and left his wife with cancer. She died in '83, leaving behind a son, Cole and a daughter, Justine. Carl began living off the grid after that, but his name became well known in the drilling business. He's like the Ted Kaczynski of the fracking world. To date, he has no known address." He sneezed and this was followed by three more sneezes.

Jack had forgotten about his deputy's cat allergies.

"Meanwhile," Wayne continued, no longer reading from his phone and reaching for a tissue from the box on the desk, "Justine has never even had so much as a parking ticket. Her apartment is as empty as a prison cell. Just a bed and some clothes. No personal items. I found out from coworkers that she graduated from Georgia State University's nursing program a few years back, then moved to Rome to campaign against Starpoint when she discovered they had been approaching landowners, farmers mainly, about selling their mineral rights. They said she's a big proponent of House Bill 205 set to pass next year. Not hard to believe. Is that a litter box?" He pointed to the corner near the filing cabinet.

"All that bill will do is regulate the fracking. It won't stop it," Jack said as he typed ATROPINE into the Google search bar using only one hand because of the sling on his other. "And with the state of Georgia earning a percentage of the revenue for each barrel extracted...well, let's just say there will be room for oversight. I'm sure that's what Miss Dunn must have realized when she came up with her crusade. Just between you and me, I'm more on her side than theirs. I just would have gone about it a little differently. And yes, that's a litter box. We have a cat now."

"Oh great," Wayne sniffled. "What are you doing over there, anyway?"

"Just a little research." Jack had been right about Justine's prints being all over the atropine bottle he'd found at the clinic. He had learned from Belle after the death of

Kelly Marsh that atropine was a derivative of plants in the deadly nightshade family and was used medicinally for a variety of issues including amblyopia or lazy eye and certain heart conditions such as arrhythmia. The drops were an alternative to the patch. They blurred the vision of the good eye so the lazy one would work harder.

Hundreds of hits came up for atropine. Jack visited several sites before clicking on a black henbane link. It opened to a Wikipedia page and an image of a yellowish flower with a black center, just as Billy had described, appeared on the right. Beneath it, a brief description: *Hyoscyamus niger commonly known as Henbane, Black Henbane, Stinking Nightshade, Hogbean, and the Devil's Eye is a poisonous plant in the family Solanaceae. The plants grow up to thirty-six inches tall and have hairy leaves that are sticky to touch and emit a foul odor reminiscent of decay.*

Jack scrolled through the information, acknowledging Wiki wasn't the most credible source, but it gave him what he needed. He stopped on the Folklore heading and read about henbane's connection to witches, Vikings, and Shakespeare. Just below this, his eyes caught on the topic regarding Greek Mythology.

According to legend, the dead who wandered the banks of the River Styx wore wreaths of henbane to keep them from remembering their previous lives.

Jack scrolled back up to the photo and the description under it.

"Devil's eye," he said aloud not realizing he'd done

so. He opened his desk drawer and pulled out the Capeheart journal. Flipping through the pages, he found what he was looking for near the middle of the book where the same words were written over and over again. "Where the Devil watches, the dead forget," he said softly.

"What was that?" Deputy Wayne asked as he fiddled with his cell phone he'd picked up once again. He reached for another tissue. "Can we talk about this cat thing?"

But Jack wasn't paying any attention to him. He was too focused on what he'd just put together. "Come on, Wayne," he said. "I'm going to need your assistance." Jack stood and motioned to his injured shoulder. "We're going to be doing some digging."

forty-two

It was the scent of death that led them to it. The plant had lost its flowers, but when Jack compared the leaves and stems to the image of the one he'd saved on his phone, he knew they'd found Kelly Marsh's killer. And he remembered enough about being a teenager to know that even though the henbane was deadly, it wouldn't be long before the fear of dying was outweighed by the thrill of getting high.

The recent rain had no doubt helped the henbane to flourish, and since Jack read the leaves of the plant were just as potent as the flowers, if not more, he wanted it all dug up and disposed of.

"God, this thing stinks," Wayne moaned.

"I have to agree with you on that. Once you start digging, get as much of the roots as possible, but be cautious," he said, handing Wayne the shovel.

"Okay, Boss," he told him. "Do you think the money is really under here somewhere?" He took the shovel, and prepared to start digging but Jack held up his hand.

"Hold up, Wayne," he instructed then squatted near the base of the stinky and sticky plant. He moved the lower stems to the side, and that's when he saw the hole. It was about a foot deep and just as wide. "Well, I think it's where the money used to be." Had Justine decoded Emily Capeheart's message and found the money? No, that wasn't it. Jack thought back to the moments of a story hitched together by what would seem like insignificant images. One of those images eclipsed the rest. So many things had happened over the last few weeks, and until now he had forgotten about it because at the time it didn't mean anything. It was just a jar on a teenage boy's dresser. "But I have an idea of where it might be now."

The sun was slipping from the sky when Jack pulled into the Thrasher's dirt drive. He and Wayne had spent the afternoon searching for the black henbane plant on the Truelove property. They were both covered in mosquito bites, and though Wayne had stopped sneezing, his stomach was growling so loud it sounded like he'd swallowed a hive of bees.

"Are you sure about this?" Wayne asked as they stood on Clint's porch.

"Never been surer." Jack rapped on the door.

"Door's open," Clint called.

Jack and Wayne both wiped their feet and went on in. Clint was sitting in the same reclining chair with his leg propped up. He was drinking a beer and reading the paper.

"Hey boys. What do I owe the honor?" He set the

paper aside.

"Clint, how you doing? You still laid up I see," Jack said.

"Two more weeks of this shit if you can believe that. Billy," he called. "Come out here and get these boys something to drink, son."

"I thought I was on restriction," the boy said snidely as he walked into the living room. His face whitened when he saw Jack and Wayne.

"Don't be a smartass. Get these fine gentlemen some water or coffee or pop. Whatever they want."

"No need, Jack said. "We won't be staying."

"You didn't change your mind about filing charges?" Clint asked nervously. "I haven't been able to get a lawyer just yet. Money's a little tight."

"No, nothing like that. The state will likely pick up the case, but as I said before, I don't think you have to worry about them pressing charges against Billy or Bobby. They will probably get some community service and be placed on some type of diversion program. The state can provide you with a public defender if you can't afford an attorney. But I'm actually here for another reason. It won't take long. I just need to ask the boys if either of them happened to find a jar of old money on the Truelove property while they were out there."

"Billy?" Clint looked toward his son. "Please tell me that on top of everything that's happened that you did not also steal money."

"No," the boy whined. "I'm not a thief. I mean, we found a jar of money months ago, but it's not real. It's Monopoly money or something. Somebody buried it out there. Probably some kids playing a game. It's not worth a shit. A bunch of fake fives."

"Boy, watch your mouth. Don't think I won't get up on this bad knee and bust your ass. I've warned you about that sharp tongue. Now go and get the jar. Bring it out here," Clint demanded. "Right now."

"Fine," Billy stomped down the hall. Two seconds later he was back with the jar. He handed it to Jack. It was the same jar he'd noticed sitting on the dresser when he came out to talk to the boys about Kelly Marsh that day.

The jar still had traces of clay on it and the lid was rusty. Jack could see the bills folded up inside, and he had to admit, they did resemble Monopoly money. "Thanks, son," he said unscrewing the lid.

He pulled out the bills. They were thin and slightly dank but in good condition otherwise. He counted fifty 1923 Lincoln Silver Certificate five-dollar bills. Jack was no Civil War money expert, but he figured they were easily worth anywhere from five to ten thousand dollars each. The Trueloves had been sitting on a fortune and they never knew it. They died penniless. But Nelle wouldn't. Even after taxes, she'd be set for a while.

Jack didn't have the heart to mention to Clint that there'd been between a quarter and half-million dollars right under his nose for some time. Enough money to pay for a few attorneys and his knee surgery, too. Not that Clint would have accepted it. He was the kind of man who upheld that "no legacy is as rich as honesty," even if he didn't know who the hell had said it.

AFTER

It was a month later that Jack made his way into the hollow once again. He hadn't been back since he and the others had searched for Knox's body and discovered that Wanda's was also gone. Busy wrapping things up, this was the first chance he had to honor the woman he knew now to be his mother.

He'd been to see Justine Dunn a few times while she awaited trial, but she was keeping quiet about her father. Jack remembered what Kitty had said about harboring secrets. At some point they become a burden. Dunn was facing a long sentence. Prison had a way of making people divulge things. If her father had set the Truelove fire and taken the four children, what happened to them? Where were they now and providing they were still alive, why had they never returned as adults?

Through the whispers and fog, Jack carried a white wooden cross and a silver and black plaque engraved with Wanda Drake's name and the date she left for the Darkening, as she had referred to it. He stuck both the cross and the plaque in the ground where she had taken her last breath then listened for the sound of her voice in the encroaching mist. It settled around him, and Jack found comfort in it just as he had as a child.

He'd be lying if he didn't admit he felt lost. Not in the hollow but in himself, the person he'd become over the last five weeks. His identity had been completely restructured, and yet there was a small part of him that felt the same. That he was still Jack Towns, son of Joe and Katherine, even though he wasn't. Not by blood, anyway. Instead, the blood running through his veins had pulled him to this place even as a child. As insane as Knox was, he was right about one thing. Blood doesn't lie. It was trying all along to lead Jack to the truth about who he was. His ancestors who died on the mountain had helped it earn its name. Their blood had spilled down into hollow, darkening the soil and filling the air with sorrow but not peace. Even in death, they would not be silenced. He didn't care what Starpoint believed about owning the mountain. That was just a piece of paper. A bloodline was stronger than a paper trail.

As he wound his way back down the mountain and toward the orchard, Jack sensed the feeling of being watched. He stopped in front of Wanda's old place and the fog dispersed enough to reveal a white dog in the distance. It sat so still and quiet Jack thought it was a statue at first. Then it moved and he recognized his mistake. It wasn't a dog. It was a wolf. *Entre chien et loup*, he recalled Wanda's words, finally grasping how things could appear to be something they weren't. The animal turned and just before it fled, Jack noticed that one of its eyes was covered in thick white scar tissue.

ABOUT THE AUTHOR

Nova Breedlove Cash was raised on Grimms' Fairy Tales and Appalachian folklore. Currently, she lives near Athens, Georgia in a 170-year-old Antebellum home, haunted by faulty plumbing, dated wiring, and dust. Lots of dust.

www.ingramcontent.com/pod-product-compliance
Lightning Source LLC
Chambersburg PA
CBHW020500260626
47156CB00006B/1796